PRIMEVAL ORIGINS® 1

PATHS
OF
ANGUISH

B. A. VONSIK
AWARD-WINNING AUTHOR

CELESTIAL FURY
PUBLISHING

Primeval Origins® 1
Paths of Anguish
All Rights Reserved.
Copyright © 2014 B.A. Vonsik
v3.0 r3.0 (2nd Edition)

Cover Illustration by Marcel Mercado
Design and art direction by Asha Hossain Design, LLC

Celestial Fury Publishing

Paperback ISBN: 978-0-578-13860-2
Hardback ISBN: 978-0-578-13861-9

Primeval Origins® News and Lexicon at: www.primevalorigins.com

PRINTED IN THE UNITED STATES OF AMERICA

SHURUPPAK +
NORTH TURIL

NORTH UR
UR
SOUTH UR
MADRAKH HADD
RED CLIFFS

SHURUPPAK
BARUDI
SANCRIS
SPADUSAN

SEA OF MISTS

VALKUNTARS
(CITY OF THE DEAD)

BLOOD BAY

GIRIN

WILDS

WASTES

TURIL

Awards and Praise for Primeval Origins

Destruction echoes once again as this cycle approaches its end; another civilization achieves greatness only to descend into the abyss -- corrupted by the depraved, the self-proclaimed elite, the immoral...all of whom, in their undeserved arrogance and folly, offer only a fouling of the Light.

Light...the most precious of all Creation; the everlasting essence, bright in its majesty, strong in its endurance, indestructible to all that is known; the Light...incorruptible except for the choosings of the mortal shell encompassing it.

Purity of Light is consequence of decisions made in the moments of each existence; choosing between Creation's absence and Creation's embrace, between selfishness and selflessness, evil and good; each mortal shell filled with Light is graced with the freedom to choose their path without Creation's compulsion...'tis this essence of the struggle that stands in Judgment.

Only in the mortal struggle may the purity of Light be confirmed: in the pain of existence, the darkest of moments, in the clash between evil's expedience and good's sacrifice can the nature of Light be revealed; only in the raging inferno of turmoil stripping away all but the core can the true nature of Light be confirmed through Final Judgment.

When the Light is weighed, measured, and tried for breaking, only then can it be confirmed in Judgment to receive Creation's Offering; or if found wanting, the Light must be returned to the mortal dust to be remade and tested once more.

Only the most pure may share presence with Creation's Glory; only the most honorable, the incorruptible, and meek may wield a shadow of Creation's authority; for the strength of the Light is not in the mortal but in the immortal, the everlasting: that unconquerable spirit of moral purity and honor, that bright inextinguishable Light containing all that is good in the cosmos must be found and confirmed.

It is my burden, my everlasting duty, and my honor to serve the usherings of Creation's Judgments; to seek the most pure Lights of each civilization and confirm them for Herald service. In the smoldering dust and ash of all remaining, I shall sentinel the remaking of the next, to try in Judgment Humanity's Light once again.

The Harbinger of Judgments

Fossils and Finds

S wirls of lazy white mist floated on a chilly breeze, like frost ser-
pents of lore intently slithering their way toward prey, passing
over the tops and around the flaccid sides of the three olive twenty-
man canvas tents where the dig team kept their equipment and fossil
finds. Old and having seen better days, the tents were all the American
Embassy in Bolivia could find in the area around Sucre. They were
functional, though barely able to keep out much of the rain the team
recently suffered. The rains left the tents damp overall and wet in
spots–unfortunately they were where the fossils had been, forcing
the dig team to repackage many of the already plaster-encased fossils.
The repackaging was the job of several of the less-popular graduate
students on the dig, overseen by a rather excitable professor.

Nikki Ricks slid her way across the slick packed dirt road running
through the camp after having been woken out of fitful sleep by a call
on her wrist-worn PDA. She had been up late reworking the plaster
casts on the last of the large fossils, and was hoping to get a few more
hours of sleep before returning to the tent to prepare the smaller fossils and fragments for travel. The dig's leader, Dr. Anders, had made
the call, demanding her immediate presence at the excavation site
then went silent and would not respond to her numerous attempts to
return his call over her PDA. How she disliked technology and how it
connected everyone to everyone else all the time, except out here it
seemed. Despite her frustration of not knowing what Anders wanted
of her, she welcomed the opportunity to get away from the constant
monitoring of hers and everyone's activities as the "Man" did back
home.

Nikki thought Anders sounded anxious, but she wasn't about to be his lap dog and go running when he barked. He was only a few years older than she, and a fellow graduate student before she took her needed time off. It just wasn't right for her to now be his "go do this" and "go do that" girl. So she rolled out of her dry one-person tent, her home of the last five weeks, intending to make her way to the fossil preparation tent for a cup of the horrid-tasting black coffee she would pour herself before seeing what the "Great Leader" wanted. The coffee was her morning ritual to kick-start the day…it was her "Nikki time."

While carefully traversing the slick ground, the deep blue sky and dusky mountain ridges were suddenly swallowed in a brilliant yellow glow that broke over the mountain ridges high to the east. Dawn. Nikki stopped when her eyes involuntarily closed to allow her sight time to adjust to the sun's powerful rays. She welcomed the warmth bathing her face, hands, and body while she stood waiting for her sight to return. Nikki found herself thinking and wishing she had completed her dual-doctoral degree in geoarchaeology and paleontology from Carnegie Mellon and Pitt Universities instead of taking time off to get her head right on the Florida beaches. Her self-proclaimed "sabbatical" had left her now a graduate assistant performing menial tasks on this dig, instead of being one of the principals making and taking credit for the discoveries.

A strong burst of anger swept through Nikki, still harboring anger at her parents for withdrawing their financial and more important political support after she took time off from school, telling her she wasn't taking her education seriously. When she decided to return to her studies, she had to beg her way back into the PhD program…a political favor granted by the head of the department, and only after a painful search for a private scholarship to cover much of her costs. Since then, she had worked any and all jobs she could find to pay for the rest, as she didn't qualify for the government's student loan any longer. She cursed at everyone for her pain, starting with her parents for making her beg others for permissions and money, and at the chaos called the US government that had complete control of student loans and determined which degrees warranted eligibility for government financing, and which degrees did not. And it seemed to change with the wind as to which degrees qualified. Her degrees were not high on the government's list, as she discovered when she returned to school. Then there was that favoritism thing and being told she wasn't the "right race" or a "foreign student" to make her eligible for reconsideration for a student loan. The almost bored-looking government representative working her student loan application told her she just wasn't "loan-worthy." *What the hell was that?*

Nikki recalled leaving the applications office feeling as if she was the lowest form of life on the planet. Then, luck found her when she applied to one of the few surviving education scholarship programs and received money to continue her education. *Why were things so difficult, now?* With eyes still closed, Nikki saw her Bubba Jules and heard her wisdom, usually given to her at times when Nikki felt the world was against her. "Always look for the bright spot in everything." Nikki's smile came and went with thoughts of her grandmother. Accepting her death was still difficult, even after more than a year. Feeling the sadness of her loss darkened her mood. She sought a distraction and tried to focus on why she was amidst the camp's tents instead of snuggled in her sleeping bag…another thing darkening her mood. *He probably wants me to wipe somebody's butt. Though, Anders does have a nice one to look at,* Nikki thought with a snicker.

Nikki pulled her yellow jacket close to fend off the chill air as she slid her way toward the center tent's wood steps. The smell of diesel from the camp generator made her scrunch her nose in protest. Diesel made her stomach turn. Why they didn't have a micro-fusion power supply for the camp baffled her. Looking to the fossil preparation tent, she recalled the tedious and boring job she made of cataloging and packing the re-plastered fossils into crates. Most of the remaining fossils were small or fragments, the larger pieces having been repacked into crates. All were destined for the Carnegie Museum back in the United States. She dreaded returning to yesterday's tasks, as she had more fossil fragments to catalog and pack away, but that would have to wait until later. She was summoned, after all, but her summoning would wait for coffee.

Beyond camp, the pinging sounds of chisels, hammers, and unintelligible voices at the dig site were washed out by the low rumble of the generators powering the equipment in the tents. She heard their voices, a number of them excited, but they would need to wait. Coffee first. As Nikki approached the wood steps, the flap entry to the center olive colored tent pulled back revealing two men standing in the entryway. Nikki heard them speaking in the regional highlands dialect of Spanish, but they spoke much too fast for her to follow the conversation. Their conversation went abruptly silent when they realized she was near. One of the men dressed in bright clothing and a round-brimmed hat quickly departed, without uttering a word. He walked briskly toward the sounds of muffled metal chisels and hammers before Nikki could see who he was. The other man, unmoving as if made of stone, waited as she climbed the wooden steps to the platform that served the purpose of a porch to the prep tent and doubled as the evening gathering place for the team to discuss the day's activities and speculate about their discoveries. Nikki strained a little to see the man's face as she climbed. It was the camp's handyman, but she held her tongue at greeting him, fearful of embarrassing herself if she were to be wrong about his name. After all these weeks, she still was unsure of his name.

"Buenos dias, Señorita Ricks," Luis Sebastian Fernandez said in his thick ascent and rough English. "Is that you sneaking?"

"Yes…Luis," Nikki answered carefully, hoping she had his name right. Ashamed she didn't care to learn his name after all these weeks, she pressed on, hoping to slip by him and avoid further conversation. Her coffee and the dig site were already on the schedule.

Luis eyed Nikki as if he were measuring her. It made Nikki uncomfortable and caused her to break stride before the tent opening. The unremarkable handyman and camp scrounge spoke "Señorita, what do you think of the new find?"

"What new find?" Nikki asked.

"Up there with the big head bones." Luis pointed in the direction to the dig site beyond the tents. "They found blue bones."

"What...?" Nikki gave Luis an "Are you stupid?" stare before stepping into the tent, seeking to put distance between her and the confused scrounger. He unsettled her. She couldn't put her finger on why, but the almost-nightly occasions she found him lingering around the showers did nothing to endear him to her. A shiver rippled down her back and a soiled feeling swept over her.

The inner tent was nothing like she had left it last night. Standing in stunned silence with mouth slung open, Nikki stared at chaos. Boxes and crates everywhere had been hastily opened and the meticulously packed contents were in disarray around the tent. Plaster, burlap, and foil wraps once encasing the large chest sections were everywhere except where they should have been. Small fossil fragments were scattered about, with Doctor Hugo Ramirez Costa sitting on the floor cross-legged in the center of the chaos, wearing the same khaki pants and shirt Nikki left him in last night when she went to her tent. Spine, rib, gastrile, and upper arm bones of the big theropod, along with the rock encasing the fossilized bones, lay arranged on the floor in front of Ramirez. He preferred being called Ramirez instead of Costa for some reason he wouldn't share with her. He was so intent on studying a set of rib bones that he didn't notice Nikki enter.

"What the hell is this?" Recovered from her initial shock and with anger boiling at her work being undone then tossed all about the tent, Nikki wanted answers. Ramirez sat up stiff-backed, eyes wild with excitement. She and Ramirez had become friends over the past few weeks, but this…this tested her sensibilities.

"Nikki!" Ramirez acknowledged her presence. His short, dark hair was disheveled, eyes bloodshot, and his usually clean-shaven appearance lost to a day's heavy growth. It looked as if he had not slept at all.

"You must see this." Ramirez announced with a sparkle in his eye and a broad smile, pointing to the fossils in front of him. Nikki would have sworn she was watching a child opening gifts on Holiday Season morning, with his excitement. "You not believe what I have found. Look!"

The large rock he pointed to show the exposed rib bones of their extinct carnivore. Some of the rock had been chipped away by Ramirez, exposing sections of the largest two bones. Nikki approached, unsure of what she was to look for. Ramirez -- his excitement high since the team realized they had found a massive meat eater, potentially larger than anything previously known, possibly a tyrannosaur or a hybrid, the first of its kind in South America -- was nearly overcome with his new find. Ramirez leapt to his feet and crossed half the tent in a couple of bounds to take hold of Nikki's arm to hasten her along. He pointed to one of the large ribs -- the bones showed obvious signs of stress fractures. Nothing unusual. Ramirez spoke, almost out of breath. "Rub your fingers over this separation."

Giving Ramirez a skeptical smile, Nikki crouched to examine the ribs. The fossilized bones, as thick as her arm, looked as if they had been placed under tremendous pressure, from their flattened shape. Nikki discerned the fine details of the dark bone from the dark, but lighter-colored surrounding sandstone; all she saw were the stress fractures before noticing what she believed he was so excited about. Running her fingers across a smooth, straight break in the bone, Nikki looked at Ramirez quizzically. He could barely contain his excitement, "It's a clean edge: straight…completely linear and with no irregular structures associated with a break."

"The bones are well-preserved," Nikki stated. The team had not been able to stop talking about the excellent condition of the find since the day they uncovered the first bones, the left foot. The speculation was that the animal must have been buried completely in hardening sediments at its death or soon afterward, to have been so well-preserved. The fossilized remains didn't have the typical backwards articulation of the spine, neck and tail caused by the dehydration of the spinal ligaments retracting them prior to burial of such a complete specimen.

"That's not a natural break," Ramirez stated with conviction. Pointing at another rib bone with a break, but one with ragged edges and numerous stress fractures surrounding the break, Ramirez continued, "See, this break is unclean, not a clean shear as first one. And neither has signs of healing. Both injuries had to occur just before or at death, but unlike the break with uneven edges and stress fractures…a wound from a blunt trauma, the separation in the ribs I showed you must be from a cut of some kind."

"Cut!" Nikki challenged. "By what?"

"Unknown," Ramirez replied with a calm voice.

"It's an aberration." Nikki stated, half challenging, half dismissing.

"See the next two ribs," Ramirez continued. "Identical and follow same line as if all three ribs were cut at once. What type of animal could have made these wounds?"

"Wait a minute, Hugo," Nikki protested. She was a bit surprised that Ramirez was jumping to conclusions without a detailed study. "We can't conclude this injury came from another animal. For all we know, this carnivore fell or ran into something with a sharp edge…if it is a cut."

"I thought so too, at first," Ramirez stated. "But the cut is clean. Each rib cut is identical. Something inflicted these wounds…maybe it was its death, but with no signs of predation or being eaten. Its killer might also be buried out here. That would be a find. Think of it…a creature that could kill the largest carnivore that ever lived."

Nikki wanted to argue with Ramirez over the facts and stop his speculation, but he made a case...something made the cuts, and it didn't look as if they had been caused by geologic stresses after the bones fossilized. She had to be careful with such positions as a student, as her professors might find her lacking in her pursuit of her PhD, being undisciplined and all. As a student, she was constantly challenged by her fellow students and professors. They forced her to gather facts, form conclusions from evidence instead of speculation, and then articulate those conclusions in a logical structure to effectively communicate her ideas. Looking at the rock-encased bones, enticing as they were for wild speculation, and recalling discussions held by the team over the past week, Nikki thought of another possibility.

"Dr. Ramirez...Hugo," Nikki spoke carefully, not wanting to offend or upstage Dr. Ramirez. He had over ten years of experience in the fields of South America, from Argentina to Brazil, and now Bolivia. He was every bit the paleontologist, and Nikki was only a post-graduate doctorial want-to-be. She questioned presenting her postulations to him. He might think her ideas dumb, but she considered her logic solid. After a few moments of waffling, she decided to continue. "The dark coloration of the rock surrounding the fossil points to heavy vegetation at the burial site; the iridium-rich clay, shocked quartz, and tektites surrounding the fossils leads me to think this animal died at the very end of the Cretaceous, at the mass extinction event, possibly. If so, objects of all kinds hurdling at high velocities could have struck this animal, making these cuts."

Ramirez was silent for a long moment as he appeared to be thinking on Nikki's words. Wearing a repressed smile, he spoke in a kind tone. "Who's speculating now? What about investigation and analysis before conclusions?"

Nikki felt the temperature of her cheeks rise, and suddenly her jacket seemed too warm. Looking around the tent at the mess Ramirez spent half the night making, Nikki made a pout with her face and placed her hands on her hips before sighing at having to redo her work for the past few days. "Well, I think we need to get this tent cleaned up before Dr. Anders discovers this mess. He wanted everything ready for shipment this morning so we can concentrate on preparing the skull tonight."

"Forgive me my excitement," Ramirez apologized after a thoughtful pause, still wearing a smile. "I wish the skeleton was to remain in country for me to study instead of going to the United States."

"You'll be able to study it in Pittsburgh," Nikki replied.

"Yes, I assume I will, for the time I will be there." Ramirez spoke with clear disappointment. "But Bolivia is such a poor country and deserves to have its treasures. I know we will get casts for study and displays as soon as they are made, and that the skeleton will be returned, as all agreed, but I am not pleased with the arrangements now that we know this to be a very significant discovery."

"Well…" Nikki wished to avoid this subject. "I understand how you must feel, Dr. Ramirez, about the…'arrangements,' but I can't do anything about them. Our embassy made them all. And besides, Bolivia is getting paid well for the fossil by the International Paleontological Fund…on behalf of the United States."

"Don't remind me," Ramirez spat as he waved his hands. "The arrangements are almost as bad as those fossil pirates stealing bones from us to sell to collectors. Mother Earth is not to be sold. Treasures gone and without the opportunity to study them." Ramirez paused, appearing to mull over thoughts, then spoke in a softer tone. "At least these fossils will be studied properly. But first…we must repack them."

Relieved that the discussion was over, Nikki picked up several fossils closest to her and began the labor of making order out of chaos… starting with rewrapping the fossils in tinfoil and plaster.

Remembering she hadn't had coffee yet, Nikki looked to the coffee pot. "Damn. Empty."

Suddenly, Luis burst through the flaps, out of breath.

"Señorita Ricks!" Luis gasped with a wheeze. "Señorita Ricks... come quick." Luis gasped again, then sucked in a breath before wheezing out words Nikki could understand. "Dr. Anders is hurt. He needs help and calls for you to bring the medical kits."

"What happened?" Nikki asked as she stared at Luis. "How did he get hurt?"

"I do not know, señorita," Luis gasped, his thick accent filled with urgency. "But there is much blood."

Alarmed, Nikki looked around the tent for and quickly found the emergency medical kit near the front entrance, grabbed it then dashed out of the tent without saying a word anyone could understand. Cursing and angry that the day was just all wrong, with one surprise after another, and she hadn't been awake yet an hour, Nikki recklessly ran to the quarry, slipping, sliding, trying to keep her balance as she went. She envisioned Dr. Anders lying in a pool of blood, dying or dead. Fifty yards away and uphill from the tents, Nikki had to slow to a trot from the pain in her chest and side. The air pressure at near 10,000 feet made it hard to breathe, even after weeks in the mountains. Ahead, the morning had not yet burned off the low-hanging mountain clouds, obscuring most things more than ten yards away. Walking into the mist, she heard muffled voices, barely audible over the pounding of blood in her ears. The voices grew louder and clearer as she approached the cloud-obscured quarry. She could see a ghostly outline of her own feet and vague shapes she took for rocks and bushes as she went. The mist was heavy today. She formed a mental image of the quarry as she had last remembered it, hoping to navigate the obstacles and hazards without tripping or hurting herself, but the image of a seriously injured Anders kept popping into her thoughts causing her to lose focus. Voices...yes, voices...ahead. Nikki shifted her focus to them then followed.

She walked another thirty yards or more -- she wasn't sure, with the voices getting louder with each step before seeing moving silhouettes, ghosts that soon took the form of her colleagues and the dig team's workers. Most hovered and danced around a large rock, while several others were tending to Dr. Anders, sitting not far away on a smaller rock of his own. One of those looking after Anders, Jimmy Zahand, a wiry-built, dark-haired new graduate student, spotted Nikki and ran to her, snatching the medical kit from her hands without the slightest acknowledgment of her before returning to his patient.

Anders yelped and growled at the peroxide Jimmy poured on his hand. Nikki was curious about his wound, and maneuvered so she could see. The entire front of Anders' button-down light-blue shirt was soaked in blood from being used as a bandage. *A lot of blood loss for a cut*, Nikki thought. The front of his pants was soaked in crimson as well. Nikki started to feel guilty for not hurrying more than she had to get the medical kit there. Her stomach felt unsettled at the sight of so much blood, and she turned away, hoping to regain control of herself. She felt warm all over and feared fainting. She tried to focus on other things, anything and everything not red, so she would not topple. The morning mist was thinning rapidly, almost too fast, as it was penetrated by the rays of the morning sun. The mist usually took until mid-morning to burn off at this altitude, and she was surprised at the time when she looked at her watch...before 9:00 a.m. Nikki found herself really wanting her morning coffee.

The scent of acetone was faint in the air. Nikki disliked the odor; it made her a bit nauseous when she got a good whiff of it, and it was making her condition worse now, but it helped preserve the fossil bones by hardening them before removal from the earth. She sought anything else to get her focus on...something that would make her feel better, instead of sending her to the dirt. She shifted her thoughts to the surrounding area and what it was so long ago.

In the waning days of the dinosaurs, this area had been part of a vast inland lake system that connected to the sea and was dotted with rising terrain not much taller than several hundred feet, but now the skeleton of their monster of a creature lay on a rising slope tilted from the Andes mountain uplift over the last sixty million years. The rocky slope rose to the west at nearly a thirty-degree incline, extending almost 800 feet high, making the dig team's work difficult and dangerous, not only from the many opportunities afforded each person to trip and fall, but also from falling rocks above the work area shaken loose by their activities or the occasional earthquake. Most of the team had injuries of some sort from the natural hazards, but they continued, excited about their discovery and the potential of being part of a historic find.

The massive carnivore was buried facing the northeast. Its tail had been oriented higher on the slope than the skull, though they excavated the tail first...it was the first part of the skeleton found by a local group of workers, from the cement facility not far from here, while they hiked the area. They contacted Dr. Ramirez, one of only a handful of paleontologists working in Bolivia at the time. Dr. Anders had been visiting Ramirez also at that time, while on his way to the Valley of the Moon in Argentina. Doctors Ramirez and Anders both examined the find and determined it significant, though at that time they didn't know just how significant. Dr. Anders convinced Carnegie University to make arrangements with the Bolivian government to be allowed to remove the skeleton and take it back to the United States for preparation, study, and display for a number of years.

Nikki was uncertain of Dr. Anders' long friendship with Ramirez, starting back before Anders' graduate studies at Pitt University. As Nikki understood, it played a significant role in the negotiations, but in the end dollars sealed the deal. Just how many, given the devaluation of the US dollar, she didn't know. Nikki was uncertain how she felt about paying for fossils. She considered it bad precedent, but this find was significant and the trustees wanted badly to rejuvenate the museum after it had been raided in the riots years earlier. They had, evidently, significant funds available to them -- from where, she didn't know -- and used those funds to convince those needed to first conduct this dig, and then to bring the fossil finds back to the United States for study and display. The more they dug, the more everyone realized it was a monster find of great significance: the first tyrannosaur or tyrannosaur-hybrid found in South America, estimated some fifty feet long, as best they could tell so far, and the largest land predator to ever terrorize the Americas.

Dr. Anders appeared at Nikki's side with a grimace under his dark goatee. His dark hair was in disarray, with a blood streak where it looked like he had touched his head with his wounded hand. He was in pain, and held his bandaged hand gingerly. Nikki looked at the blood seeping through the bandage and asked, "Are you going to be okay?"

"I'll live," Anders replied with an effort. "Damned thing is as sharp as a razor."

"What?" Nikki asked.

"What I asked you out here to take a look at," Anders grumbled. He grimaced when he forgot his injury and tried to point at Nikki. "You have the archeology background. Not me. And you took your time getting here. Had to have your crappy coffee?"

"No!" Nikki was torn between embarrassment and anger being caught taking her time responding to Anders' call.

Anders wore a light veil of contempt when his gaze turned to her. "Come see this. I hope you actually studied archeology."

Angered at his accusation, Nikki opened her mouth to protest, but Anders had already turned away to climb the rocky slope rising almost ninety feet to where they were digging out the large skull, the last of the beast to be recovered. She started up the steep slope, wondering what she was to see. A new cranial configuration? Enlarged teeth? No, Anders was interested in her knowledge of archeology, not paleontology. *What could it be?* Nikki quickly felt her heart pounding hard in her ears and a side stitch growing painfully. She disliked this high altitude and longed for denser air. She slowed her ascent; her side stitch, pounding heart, and labored breathing grew worse as she negotiated the thirty-degree slope. Jimmy caught up with her halfway to the skull pit then climbed with her. He appeared to be sucking in air as badly as Nikki.

With great relief, Nikki made it to the pit: a twenty-foot round oblong donut hole with the rock-encased skull in the middle, sitting on a rock pedestal. Piled up dirt and rock rimmed the pit, highest on the lower side. Several of the local porters working for Luis stood chest deep in the pit with shovel and pick in hand talking to Anders in their broken English. With her ears pounding with pumping blood, Nikki tried to suck air into her burning lungs as if she just ran a long sprint. She stood doubled over with hands on knees fighting off dizziness. She heard voices, but couldn't make out the individual words or who spoke them for some time until the pounding lessened and her breathing became less labored.

"Nikki!" Anders yelled. Startled, she jumped and almost slipped off her small perch allowing her feet an almost level place to support herself. "You aren't going to die on me are you?"

"I'll be fine." Nikki replied wheezing. "What is it...you want me... to see?"

"Come over here to get a better look." Anders more directed than asked. Nikki slowly and carefully made her way to where Anders stood in the pit, trying not to lose her footing and go tumbling down the hillside. While working her way across the slope on feet, knees, and hands, she felt a moist spot on the rocks where her left hand pressed. She ignored it until she felt secure in the pit. Her hand slick, she looked at it and found find her hand stained in blood. She gasped, "Yuck!"

"Sorry about that." Anders offered an apology. "I forgot to mention that I bled all over the place, so be careful where you step."

"Thanks," Nikki replied sarcastically as she wiped her hand on a barren rock, removing much of the crimson, then her pants to finish up. "Okay. What is it that you want to show me?"

"Look." Anders pointed to the lower jaw region of the skull underneath near the rock pedestal the large mass of stone sat on.

Crimson stains first caught Nikki's attention. They were everywhere on the fossil and ground. Anders had bled more than she thought. Now, she wondered how he hadn't passed out from blood loss. The head of the animal was huge. She didn't understand just how massive it was until she was standing next to it. Somewhere between six and seven feet, as best Nikki could guess, and robust. It was and wasn't like other tyrannosaur skulls. This head was robust, sturdy, and just massive, but longer and taller than any skull she knew. Thick brow and cranial ridges gave it a sinister look. The teeth looked every bit the size of her forearm, but with pointed...not blunt tips and serrated edges.

"It looks to be a more robust form of tyrannosaur, from what I can tell, and it is in absolutely wonderful condition. Except, of course, for the blood stains."

"Yes, the skull confirms that we have a monster of a T.Rex-like animal, though 'wonderful' was not the word I would use to describe it," Anders replied wryly. "More like...astonishing! I know we have one for the record books. Preliminary measurements show the skull at just a bit over six and half feet long, and more robust than any carnivore ever to walk the earth. Not even a spinosaur or a gig tops this one. And look at the teeth." Anders ran the fingers of his uninjured hand over the surrounding rock and the teeth in the upper maxillary, which were proportionally huge. "More than a foot long, root and all, is my estimate. I can't wait to get this treasure in the lab to examine."

Nikki looked at the teeth buried deeply in rock, and became puzzled. Nothing sharp enough to slice Anders' hand was in sight. "How did you cut your hand? Those teeth aren't sharp enough to cut you like this."

"Aaahhh, Hugo." Anders greeted Hugo Ramirez with a tone of professional and personal respect. Ramirez had followed Nikki, and just completed his climb to their location. "I see you came for the unveiling of history."

"No, Shawn," Ramirez replied between wheezes. Despite living at these altitudes most of his life, he too was winded by the climb. "I came to check on you, my friend. I see you aren't injured so badly since you are standing and yapping away, as usual."

"Don't worry about me, old friend," Anders replied with a wide smile. "I'll be getting stitches...lots of them, but it was worth it."

"Want to explain?" Ramirez replied with raised eyebrows.

"Jimmy, would you please remove the rock cover?" Anders asked quietly without breaking his eye contact with his friend. Nikki swore Anders' smile couldn't get any bigger.

"Yes, professor." Jimmy obediently responded as if he had been Dr. Anders' assistant forever. Jimmy positioned himself above the skull then carefully reached down to remove two rock fragments a little larger than his outstretched hand. When he removed the second piece of rock, a bright bluish reflection from the sun's peeking rays set on the skull, momentarily blinding Nikki. She shielded her eyes until they adjusted to the glint. She then saw it. Blue metal. In the form of a blade buried at a perpendicular angle in the lower maxillary of the skull. The blade ended with a handle, and what looked to be fossilized remains of a grip wrapping. A sword?

"What the hell is that?" Nikki asked, astonished.

"That's what I asked you here to tell me, since you have the archeology background," Anders replied in a quivering boyish tone. His childlike excitement threatened to overwhelm him. "A new era in history and understanding of our past, I expect? While we were clearing the earth around the skull, this section of rock broke away when Jimmy and I tried to shift the skull. My hand brushed the edge of the blade -- just touched it, really -- and it sliced me open pretty badly.

The blade looks of incredible quality, and appears unaffected after sixty-five million years encased in rock."

Anders fell silent looking at the skull with the blue metal blade embedded in it. His gaze then shifted from Ramirez to Nikki to Jimmy, as if wanting to hear each of them congratulate him on the find. Nobody spoke, nor even noticed him -- except for Nikki, who opened her mouth several times as if to speak, then closed it without speaking. Anders' excitement threatened to burst from his usual calm demeanor. "Do you know what this could indicate?" he asked.

"I don't understand," Nikki finally said, confused. Anders looked disappointed at Nikki's response. "How did that... sword...get there? Humans didn't live while dinosaurs existed, and dinosaurs didn't live past the KT boundary." Nikki looked at Anders, then Jimmy, then Anders again. She then smiled and placed her fists on her hips. "Okay...great practical joke, guys. You almost had me fooled. Almost. But you overdid it with the blood. Really, did you have to kill one of those stinky llamas to get enough blood to spread around just to make it look good? Everyone knows I'm not fond of the stinking animals, but really, how cruel can you be?"

"Nikki!" Anders was taken aback. His nose scrunched up above tightened lips and his eyes became horizontal slits. Nikki just stared back at him waiting for an answer. "We...did no such thing, and I'm offended you could think me capable of such a thing. This is real...as real as it gets. Come over here and look for yourself."

Ramirez was quicker to position himself near the blade and immediately began examining it as if he were the only person on the entire planet able to do the examination justice. Nikki perched herself slightly below the skull, on the lip of the donut hole, such that she could dig the toes of her boots into secure footholds. Once she felt safe, she leaned over the skull to get a good look at the blue blade. It was almost an inch wide, with intricately inscribed symbols, none of which she recognized, though they bore a vague resemblance to some Sumerian symbols she had studied. The blade was buried into the maxilla such that the plain oval hand guard was about eight inches from the fossilized bone. The hilt was large enough for Nikki to hold the weapon with both of her hands. The wrappings of the grip were almost completely gone, and what remained around the mounting were small pieces of fossilized material that Nikki was unable to identify. Ramirez touched the flat of the blade cautiously with his fingers, as if afraid it would do him harm. Nothing happened. With more confidence, he then ran his fingers up and down the metal several times.

"Be careful, Hugo." Anders warned.

"It's warm to the touch." Ramirez almost sounded giddy. He then held his right hand in the air, palm up, without looking anywhere except the blade. "Someone give me something of metal."

Several long moments later, Jimmy placed a small pick in Ramirez's hand. Ramirez never took his eyes off the blade as he positioned the metallic part of the pick head against the blade edge. A surface cut mark was left on the pick's metal after Ramirez tapped the unknown metal blade edge. No one spoke. No one breathed. Ramirez gently applied pressure on the pick against the blue blade's edge then slid the pick head down the blade. The metal pick head was cut deep, almost completely through. Ramirez jumped back from the blade and the pick lodged on it. "Damn!"

"Damn, isn't the half of it," Jimmy finally said. "Dr. Anders, shouldn't metal break down and decompose, or fossilize, if it is in the ground as long as we say this was?"

"Yes!" both Anders and Ramirez replied simultaneously.

"Then the sword couldn't have been in the ground since the Cretaceous," Nikki stated as if her conclusion was final and everyone should agree with her. She slid closer to the blade and pick as if they were a deadly snake poised to strike. Gently, she took hold of the pick and attempted to pull it from the blade. The head of the pick came away in two pieces. Surprised, Nikki lost her balance and fell against the fossil skull with a thud and gasp.

"Easy...Nikki." Anders cautioned. "I don't want you injured by that thing, too." Anders scurried across the rock next to Dr. Ramirez. He knelt lower to examine the base of the hilt. "Look here. It looks like a gemstone -- or something like a gemstone -- mounted in the base of the hilt. It's strange. Hugo, look at this."

Dr. Ramirez squatted low to get a view allowing him to closely examine the gemstone. His head tilted this way, then that, up and down, then this way and that again. "That is no gemstone. The untrained eye it will fool, but...I am sure it is not. It doesn't refract or reflect light like any gemstone I have ever seen."

"Touch it," Jimmy blurted. Everyone turned their gazes in his direction and looked at him if he had just asked Ramirez to stick his hand into a pot of vipers.

"Not me," Ramirez replied with a sort of chuckle. He rose to a sitting position then looked at Anders. "Shawn, we should leave it alone until we can examine it under better conditions. Maybe get some other expert advice, too."

"You're right," Anders admitted reluctantly. "Guys, let's wrap this skull up so we can get it out of the ground. And for Pete's sake, please take care near the blade. I don't want anyone else getting cut -- or worse, slicing a finger or hand off."

"We can mount a pair of wooden brackets on either side of the blade and tie them to place enough tension against the flat of the blade to hold them in place," Nikki suggested. Everyone now turned their attention to her, looking at her as if to ask a question. "The burlap and plaster should hold the wood brackets in place and keep the blade safe for transport."

No one spoke immediately. They all appeared to be thinking. After a short period of everyone looking at each other, Anders made several hand motions to the group of locals milling around the base of the slope with his cut hand, before pain gripped him and forced him to cuddle it again. "Damn, this hurts. Hugo, would you please ask our support crew to bring the wrapping kit and water up here?"

"I'll take care of it, Doc," Jimmy volunteered. He was a third of the way down the slope before anyone could say a word.

Jimmy soon returned with three Bolivians, one of which was Luis, carrying bundles of tinfoil and burlap, several bags of plaster, buckets half filled with water, and two wooden blocks. Ramirez applied more acetone to the skull in the places not yet treated, giving the exposed bone a brownish sheen as Nikki cleared the area of tools and anything that might prove a hazard. Anders sat quietly, out of the way, holding his hand while wearing a grim expression. The team prepared the top side of the fossil with layers of tinfoil, then plaster-saturated burlap, before they could finish digging it out and turn it over to do the same on the other side. They placed wooden blocks on either side of the flat of the blade and secured them with twine. The tension of the two wooden blocks held it in place as tinfoil and then plaster-covered burlap were carefully applied around the entire blade and hilt. Just before noon, they were ready to start working the underside. After a quick break, they eagerly went back at it, digging out the remaining side rock, and undercut the rock beneath the skull until only a small pedestal of stone remained. By late afternoon, the temperature had risen to an uncomfortable level; most had lost their jackets, and worked in light shirts soaked with sweat. They were ready to turn over the skull. Nikki, excited that she had the opportunity to participate in the dig, hummed several different melodies the entire time she worked. Anders helped where he was able, but the pain of his injured hand seemed to grow as the afternoon wore on.

"Okay, we're ready," Jimmy announced as he crawled from underneath the slab of rock. "A good push, and the pedestal should separate. Nikki, you and Miguel help me on this side near the nose. Dr.

Ramirez, if you and Luis and his guys would guide the back of the skull so that it rolls where we want it, I think we will be in good shape."

Everyone readied themselves to roll the skull slab, some thousands of pounds of fossil, rock, and plaster. Jimmy positioned himself alongside Nikki and Miguel. Miguel was the largest of the Bolivian helpers, standing nearly six feet tall, and with a heavy, muscular build. Nikki assumed Jimmy had chosen Miguel for his size and strength, but still she wasn't certain that even the three of them were going to be enough to topple this slab. Jimmy raised his hand with three fingers held high to signal to Ramirez that they were ready then set it on the slab, ready to push. Ramirez and his team had set a series of wood poles to act as fulcrums they would use to guide the slab to where they wanted it. "On three, everybody. One, two, threeeeeee!"

The slab didn't budge. They tried again and heard a cracking of the rock pedestal, but only after considerable effort. The three of them took several gulps of air, then readied themselves again as Jimmy counted to three, again. They heaved on the slab once more with groans and growls. The pedestal broke and the massive slab started to tilt in the direction of Ramirez and Luis. Someone yelled, but Nikki couldn't make out about what, over the pounding of the blood in her ears. She tried to guide the slab as it tilted, then rolled, but found herself useless against the weight and inertia of the slab. Nikki stood watching as the slab rolled toward Ramirez, threatening to crush him, then veered down the slope of the hill and into the spot they had hoped it would go. On the slab's impact with the hillside, the ground vibrated with a pronounced low-frequency thud, then shuddered. Everyone remained silent for a moment exchanging nervous looks. When nothing happened, laughter broke.

"I thought the mountainside was about to come down," Nikki laughed jokingly. Then she felt it...rock and stone cracking under her feet -- then she was falling.

Nikki fell for only a second or so before impacting something solid, the force collapsing her legs then sending her tumbling down a slope with the dim world spinning out of control. She slammed into and rebounded off rocks as she tumbled. Pain engulfed her body. She squeezed her eyes shut, hoping the nightmare would stop and that she would not be hurt too badly. With a teeth-jarring thud, Nikki landed face down on an almost level surface covered in a powdery layer of something, softening her impact…a little. Rocks rained down on her for what seemed forever. Some small and some not-so-small rocks struck Nikki, causing her pain, but reminding her that she was alive.

Nikki felt dazed from the fall and pummeling. She heard distant voices echoing from everywhere. With a groan, she prepared to push herself up by taking a deep breath of air, but only found herself gagging and coughing. Stale, rank air, thick with dust, unexpectedly plunged into her lungs. Her body convulsed, racked with pain, as she coughed uncontrollably. Nikki's nose, throat, and lungs burned. She had to get it out. Had to make the burning stop. Panic gripped her, but all she could do was cough and gag. After what seemed an eternity of disconnected pains, Nikki heard distant voices echoing unintelligibly all around her. She seized upon the voices, trying to pull herself to safety. Her numerous, intensely-sharp pains gradually gave way to painful aches as the moments passed.

Nikki opened her eyes to a dusky gloom with a circle of bright light high above trying to penetrate the cloud of dust she looked through. Her eyes started to burn, and tears ran freely down the sides of her face. With an effort, she rolled onto her side with a groan then pushed herself up into a sitting position. Her body ached and her head hurt. The smell of sulfur was thick with every breath. She looked around through tear-blurred vision, but saw little except vague shapes and shadows. Blinking, Nikki's vision cleared a little. She had fallen some fifteen feet from the roof of this cavern, then bounced down a sloping wall another twenty feet farther, as best she could make out. She shuddered uncontrollably for a moment with the realization that she could have been seriously injured or worse. Pain from bruises and lacerations covered much of her body despite her thick clothing.

After a quick flex test of her fingers and toes, her panic and fear lessened, as nothing seemed to be broken. She ran her hands over her body to check for injuries not announcing themselves with pain. Blood, mixed with dirt and dust, stained her fingers after she passed them over exposed skin on her arms, neck, face, and head. It wasn't much blood, and she was relieved. All in all, she survived the fall fairly well, she concluded.

"Nikki! Can you hear me?" Anders' voice echoed throughout the cavern. "Nikki! Nikki! Are you all right? Jimmy! Are you okay?"

"I think I'm okay," Nikki replied, tilting her face up to the circle of light above, her shaky voice echoing off the cavern walls. "I don't know how, but I don't think I broke anything."

"Is Jimmy okay?" Anders asked with thick concern, again his voiced echoed.

"I...I don't know." Nikki looked about. "I don't see him."

"I can't see down there," Anders anxiously stated.

"Let me look around." Nikki painfully rose to her feet. Her whole body hurt, and her legs were unsteady. Worse, she had a blinding headache. After a few moments and steps, Nikki spotted Miguel, dazed and sitting on a large rock just a bit higher up the slope from her. He looked to be in fairly good condition despite a nasty cut on his right shoulder that bled freely. She asked Miguel if he was all right several times, but the disoriented man only looked at her with unfocused eyes. She feared he had a concussion. He would have to wait until she found Jimmy. Nikki called out to Jimmy. No response. She called out again. A low, almost inaudible, groan a bit farther up the slope caught Nikki's ear.

"Nikki? Is that you?" Jimmy spoke with a weak and shaky voice.

"Don't move, Jimmy," Nikki told him. She reached Miguel and gave him a quick look-over to make sure he didn't have a life threatening injury; then she started to climb to Jimmy after she was satisfied she could do nothing more for the strongman. "Hold on. I'll be right there."

Nikki climbed to where she thought Jimmy lay. He was somewhere near the point of impact where he fell through the cavern roof. She looked around for him once she was at the top of the slope. Another low groan drew her attention to a dark area off to the side near the cavern wall. She squinted hard before making out Jimmy's outline. He lay just out of the direct rays of sunlight, and was difficult to see. She knelt next to him to get a better look at his condition. Blood covered much of his face from a gash over his left eye, and the little finger on his right hand was bent in an unnatural position. Jimmy held that hand gingerly, protecting it. She could not tell if anything else was wrong with her colleague and friend. Nikki winced at the sight of him, but managed to put on what she thought was a comforting smile when Jimmy looked up at her.

"How bad is it?" Jimmy asked bluntly, in a voice stronger than Nikki expected.

"Well, ah…you have a pretty nasty cut on your head, and I think your finger is broken." Nikki could not see any other obvious injuries.

"Then, I'll consider myself lucky," Jimmy joked. Nikki didn't see the humor in it. "My mother always said it's better to be lucky than good."

"How is everyone?" Anders' voice echoed through the cavern, again. The light above Nikki and in the surrounding cavern dimmed slightly.

"Jimmy has a good-sized cut on his head, and a broken finger," Nikki spoke loudly for everyone to hear. Then she looked up to see the dark silhouette of Anders at the edge of the gaping hole. "I think Miguel has a concussion, but I can't be sure."

"I be all right." Miguel's strained voice rose out of the darkness below, his Bolivian accent thick. His speech seemed a little lazy to Nikki. "I have bump on head. I be okay."

Luis' voice echoed from above. He spoke in his native language and with sharpness Nikki was unaccustomed to hearing from him. She couldn't follow exactly what he was saying, but she heard Miguel's name spoken and words referencing "big" and "idiot," she thought. Miguel responded to Luis' words and tone in the manner he usually did, harsh and loud. They argued without being able to see each other; it had been obvious from the first day Nikki was in camp that Miguel and Luis did not like each other very much.

"Gentlemen!" Ramirez broke in. "Let's get them out of there before they rot."

Ramirez said something in his native tongue; Luis hurried off and Miguel fell silent. "Ricks! We're getting rope to get you out of there. Just don't do anything until we're ready."

"Easy for you to say," Nikki replied then spoke under her breath. "What would I do, anyway?"

"Don't worry about me, Doc." Jimmy's voice was strong and sarcastic. "I'm okay. It's the first break I've had all day."

"Don't start thinking you'll get paid for laying down on the job," Anders joked.

"That supposes the premise that you pay me at all, Doc," Jimmy replied with a smile on his face that Nikki caught in a glint of sunlight.

"Good thing we're almost done with this field trip," Jimmy laughed, but cut it short with a curse as he clutched his injured hand to his chest. "Between the doc and me, we won't have many fingers left at the rate we're going."

Jimmy sat up with a groan and mumbled a curse. "Nikki, the sulfur smell is pretty thick down here. The geology of this place doesn't make it likely that it's naturally occurring. Where do you think it's coming from? I mean, the area isn't rich in the stuff, and this cavern smells loaded with it."

"I haven't a clue," Nikki replied absently. At first she dismissed his words, but then thought about the sulfur. "I suppose the dirt could be contaminated from a pocket of sulfur concentrated in the strata, but for all I know it could be leftover debris from the same event that killed off big ugly up there. Highly unlikely, huh? It probably seeped into the cavern from the surrounding rocks."

"Doesn't make sense," Jimmy replied with a grunt. He was coming out of shock, and feeling the pain of his injuries. "What if it's the left over pulverized sulfur-rich rock from the Yucatan region? If it…."

"Señior Jimmy and Señorita Ricks," Miguel's echoing words broke into their conversation. "Come to see what I found. Hurry. Come see."

"What is it, Miguel?" Jimmy asked skeptically.

"I found more blue metal," Miguel replied.

Nikki and Jimmy stared at each other without speaking for what seemed a very long time. A blue metal sword embedded in the jaw of the carnivore was strange enough. The scientific world was to be turned upside down if it proved to be sixty-five million years old. The significance of the blade alone would be felt around the world… after it held up to intense scientific scrutiny. But more material in the same location? Nikki's thoughts raced. *What happened here? What was this metal and how did it involve dinosaurs? Especially a carnivore at that, and a whopper of a big one?* Jimmy scrambled to his feet in a flash of movement, startling Nikki.

"Let's go!" Jimmy urged without waiting for Nikki to respond. "Doc, you better get down here. Miguel thinks he found more of that blue metal."

"What?" Anders questioned in disbelief, his word echoing in the dim light of the cavern. "What did you say…more blue metal? What the hell is going on down there? No. Wait. I'll be down as soon as Luis gets that damned rope up here. Luis! Get a move on it. Hurry, man, hurry! And bring lights. Lots of them. And my tools. Hurry!"

Jimmy snickered as he used his shirt sleeve to wipe the blood from his eye. He had some trouble performing the task without the full use of both hands, so Nikki helped him by pulling the sleeve down. Jimmy wiped his eye again with better success. He still bled pretty good. "What are we waiting for? After you, Nikki."

"What about Dr. Anders?" Nikki asked.

"He'll catch up," Jimmy declared. "Besides, it sounds like the doc will still beat us down into the cavern, no matter how much of a head start we have."

They carefully made their way into the bowels of the cavern, descending the steep slope into the dimly lit depths. Nikki led and helped Jimmy traverse uneven rocks and large stony outcrops as they went. The going grew increasingly difficult the deeper they ventured. Nikki wondered how Miguel could have seen anything this deep into the cavern. She heard rocks falling down the slope behind them and saw Anders all but running down the incline, with Ramirez right on his heels. At least they carried flashlights. Nikki was amazed by Anders' agility. She never thought of him as athletic, and her impression of him was confirmed when he and Ramirez caught up with them. Anders gasped while choking on the dust they kicked up. In another time and place, Nikki would have found the scene funny, but not today.

"Lead…on." Anders managed to force out his words in between gasps. Neither Anders nor Ramirez appeared concerned for either Nikki's or Jimmy's condition. They excitedly peered into the darkness beyond Nikki as if she wasn't there, and appeared impatient enough to run her over if she didn't get moving. Nikki took the flashlight from Anders then turned to lead the group. She stopped abruptly after only five steps. In the lit circle of her flashlight, Miguel stood looking at them with his hands over his eyes. Nikki thought she caught a glimpse of blue behind him, but dismissed it as seeing what she wanted to see. She continued to lead the group to Miguel. The big man stepped to the side without speaking a word, to reveal two blue-tinted metallic obelisks about a foot wide on each of what looked to be four sides at one end, and flaring out to a greater width at their other ends. Each of the blue metal pillars was about eight feet in length and lay almost horizontal to the eyes staring at them. They were separated some eight to ten feet, as best Nikki could determine, and both obelisks were partially buried in rock, though a blue metal brace spanned the space between the two where the obelisks were widest. Nikki surmised the structure was on its side. She was immediately drawn to symbols and inscriptions on the obelisks, and reached out to touch one of the pillars to run her fingers over them.

"Be careful!" Anders warned forcefully. He, Ramirez, and Jimmy moved to within several feet of one of the obelisks. "Look at the symbols. They look similar to those on the sword."

"Yes, Shawn," Ramirez agreed after examining the closest obelisk with his light only inches from the thing. His gaze was fixed on the obelisks and Nikki believed a herd of bulls would not be able pull him away from this extraordinary find. "No. They are not identical to the sword, but the similarities are not to be ignored."

The symbols covered the visible sides of each obelisk in a straight-line pattern along their lengths, starting about two feet from the smaller of the two ends. The blue metal appeared to have been placed here yesterday. It showed no signs of rust or decay. Ramirez touched the metal surface of the closest obelisk. "It's warm."

"How can that be?" Anders sounded incredulous. "I can make the case that the sun heated the sword blade and that the blue metal has superior thermal absorption qualities, but how can that be, down here in the darkness?"

"Maybe the metal generates heat internally?" Ramirez speculated without removing his gaze from the obelisk. "Ricks, would you please come here and hold the light above this spot so I can examine this?"

Nikki tried to hold her flashlight high enough over Ramirez so it cast sufficient light where he had directed. No matter how Nikki attempted to angle the flashlight, it would not satisfy Ramirez. He appeared to be getting annoyed with Nikki. "Ricks, stand over here and shine the light down without reaching over me."

Angry at his tone, Nikki reluctantly climbed on the rocks between the obelisks and positioned herself opposite Ramirez. She held the light on the spot he directed, bathing the area with enough light for him to examine the symbols in detail. Anders and Jimmy were on either side of Ramirez, with their heads so closely together that Nikki thought the three of them might kiss.

"Look at this symbol," Anders directed. "It's the same symbol as that on the sword blade. And this one. And this one. It's got to be an alphabet."

"Careful, Shawn," Ramirez cautioned. "I've never seen you so excited. I agree the symbols look alike, but I can't say they're an alphabet. At least not yet."

"Look here!" Jimmy's voice was filled with excitement. He was examining a part of the obelisk closest to the small end, approximately a foot from the end. When Nikki looked at the spot Jimmy's flashlight was illuminating, she blinked several times to make sure she wasn't seeing things. A triangular shape glowed from within the obelisk. The glowing triangle was about an inch long on each side, emitting a pale blue light. "It's perfectly flush with the metal, but inside. There's a circular structure all the way around the triangle. The structure is almost imperceptible. The engineering required to create this is fantastic."

"The glowing shape looks similar to the gem in the sword," Ramirez commented. He held his hand close to the triangle, but was careful not to touch it. "The temperature is colder the nearer I place my hand to it."

"Say what?" Anders blurted in surprise. "If it wasn't glowing, I'd swear I was looking at a gem shaped into a triangle." Anders pointed to the center of the glowing triangle then looked at his friend, who was wearing a smile as wide as his face. He positioned his finger just above the surface of the triangle. "See the internal facets and the... aaagggghhhh!"

Anders' finger brushed against the glowing surface, causing it to brightly flare. Then it settled back to a dull blue glow, but brighter than before. Nikki felt a vibration under her feet and looked down to see the rock she was standing on disintegrating before her eyes. Before she could react and jump from her perch, the space between the two obelisks was filled with a brilliant bright blue sheet of light that rippled where her boots touched it. Nikki felt herself falling, again.

Nikki's fall stopped an instant later. She felt suspended in a cool pool of water, weightless and adrift and shivering. A wave of nausea swept over her, then went away. She opened her eyes...slowly, afraid of what she would see. Blackness. She blinked her eyes several times to make sure she had opened them. Blackness, still. *Where am I?* Her heart pounded fast, threatening to burst from her chest, and her head felt about to explode. She darted glances everywhere in the darkness. Nothing. She was alone in a sea of nothing. She felt abandoned, small, alone. She screamed, but could not hear her own voice. It was as if the blackness consumed her desperate pleas for help without a bit of mercy. She screamed again and again. Nothing. A sense of doom and despair washed over her.

A faint whisper teased Nikki's sense of hearing. No, not her hearing...somewhere in her head. "It's just my imagination," Nikki said to herself. Again, the whisper teased her. Desperate, Nikki called out. Nothing. A second whisper joined the first, both teasing her. She wasn't able to make out what the voices said. It frustrated her, but hope surged within her. She was not alone. A third voice added to the chorus, also teasing her. Nikki called out repeatedly to the voices. Nothing. No response. Only the black void. She felt panic within swell up again, but fought to keep it under control. She struggled to win the battle raging within, somewhere between panic and insanity. The voices grew louder. Nikki could make out individual sounds, then syllables, then what she took for words. She didn't understand the meaning of the words. It was a language she was unfamiliar with. Louder the voices grew. They became normal volume, then started to boom in her head…hurting her. *So painful. Pain.* The voices she so desperately wanted to hear a moment ago now made her want silence. *Too painful.* She didn't understand what they were saying to her. Then….

"How long…?" asked one of the voices in soft, melodic tones.

"Who are you? Nikki asked, hopeful the voice would be friendly.

"Me," the soft voice answered, then asked sharply, "Who are you?"

A long silence fell. Nikki feared speaking. Nothing. The silence continued for a time until Nikki could not stand it, and she spoke. "I'm Nikki. Who are you?"

Silence. No response.

"Please, where am I?" Nikki pleaded, desperately afraid to ask the question. "Am I…am I dead?"

"No," replied a deep voice.

"Who are you?" Nikki asked of the new voice.

"Answer! How long?" The soft voice asked again, less sharp than before.

"How long for what?" Nikki asked. She felt tears welling up. "I don't understand. How long for what?"

"How many *Rodenars* have passed?" the soft voice asked, controlled, measured.

"Rodenars? What's that?" Nikki replied, her voiced filled with fear, frustration, and confusion.

"Enough!" a sneering voice demanded. "A waste of my time."

"No!" The deep voice growled defiantly. "She is innocent."

"Do not harm her." The soft voice spoke defiantly, with a tone so threatening it caused shivers to rack Nikki's spine. "She is not part of it."

"She is now," the sneering voice replied flatly.

An intense tingling enveloped Nikki, then pain. The hairs all over her body stood on end as her skin crawled as if the entire kingdom of insects covered her, biting her. She withered and contorted as wave after wave of pain racked her. Then an intense sharp pain struck her, threatening to split her head open as a rush of images and sounds bombarded her mind: images of fantastic landscapes, high-walled grand stone cities, and glowing gems used for many sorts of things by people not quite human, all filled her head. Many kinds of animals crawled, swam, walked, ran, and flew -- mostly in the wilderness, though some in the great cities. Swimming death…crocodiles…*snapjaws*, turtles… *sheller*, lizards…*runners*, frogs…*hoppers*, rodents…*growlers*, and insects…*biters*, *bloodsuckers* and *crawlers*, everywhere. Birds…*featherwings* of all kinds in enormous flocks flew above the lands. Other creatures soared high above the birds, creatures not unlike a bat with translucent wings, but sleeker, larger, much larger, flying reptiles…pterosaurs… *leatherwings*. These were not just images. Nikki felt the breeze on her face and the smell of life in her nose.

"No." Nikki realized with a shock she was looking at pterosaurs, but she didn't want to believe. And not just a few, but hundreds of them, flying in flocks. Then she saw grand beasts emerging from primeval forests, with spiky defenses and the size of elephants, though more brightly colored than she expected. *This can't be. Nodosaurs?* Then there were others, equally brilliant in color and of all shapes: armor-plated sauropods, strangely crested hadrosaurs and a ceratopsian, feathered-covered dromaeosaurs ranging from the tiny to the terrifyingly massive, and then there were carnosaurs, large of claw and tooth and devastatingly vicious in their merciless pursuit of prey. She saw those people riding some of the beasts and others in battle with sword, axe, bow, and with strange devices of horrific power -- people of races she did not recognize as human, all strangely dressed, together fighting for their very existence against creatures of nightmares, man-like and armed with weapons and tails tipped in venom. How she saw all of this, she didn't know, but she knew it all as if she lived it. These were her experiences. *No! How could this be?* Other strange and gruesome creatures armored with glistening scales walked the world, commanding armies before them. And then there were more creatures, still more frightening. Then their images were gone.

Nikki felt relieved for a moment. In another instant, she was in a place of darkness. Shivers of fear shot down her spine and racked her very core. An immense black tower of rock appeared before her, carved from mountains, and the foreboding lands surrounding it spanning as far as the eye could see. A brilliant rainbow-colored light filled the sky and blinded her momentarily. She was now in yet another place. She became dizzy with the swirl. Metallic walls and waist-high angled tables glowed with symbols she did not recognize...yet they seemed familiar. One of the walls was filled with a large rectangular window of the constellations. It dominated the room. In the bottom left corner of the window she saw a portion of a sphere she recognized as earth, but the continents were wrong. North America's central region was flooded partially; Central America appeared as a broken island chain; South America was smaller than she thought it should be, with a long, wide bay stretching from the northern coast southward along the western edge of the continent and east of a diminutive mountain range; and a smaller hook-shaped continent she did not recognize sat off the western shores of what she thought was South America of the past.

Images swirled again. Now she viewed faces of beings wielding great power. She instinctively feared them and their powers. A gemstone of vibrant colors filled her thoughts. No, not a gem...something else...something of enormous potential and wondrous terrors. Something very dangerous in the hands of the unkind, and just a little less dangerous in those some might consider the right hands. More faces and names to those faces filled her mind. So many...she feared she couldn't suffer their memories. Nikki closed her eyes, wishing for this torment to stop. Still more images and sounds came: enslavement, revolt, battles, carnage, death...so much death, intense friendships, principled alliances, tragic betrayal, lost loves, and a shattered civilization. Terrible pain she felt for the lost ones. Their voices... somehow she knew their names. Nikki didn't know how, but she knew them, their lives, their fears, their desires as well as she knew her own. Many were steadfast in their defiance of tyranny; others grew exhausted in their war of eternity. All wanted to be free of their masters. Nikki's mind swirled and tumbled. She felt as if she flew, again, then fell. She smashed painfully with a teeth-jarring thud on a dirt and rock surface. She sucked in a gulp of air, and her lungs burned; the smell of sulfur filled her nose.

Voices echoed in Nikki's ears. She recognized the voices: Jimmy and Anders and Ramirez. They were cursing excitedly about something. Nikki was unsure what they spoke of, and she didn't care. She was free of the hell, and she hurt all over. She was alive, even if her throat and lungs burned. Nikki coughed and coughed more, trying to catch her breath, but it eluded her as she rolled over and opened her eyes, frantically looking around, hoping for help. All three of her colleagues crouched over her with shocked and concerned looks on their faces. The cavern spun and became dim and colorless as Nikki lost some of her peripheral vision. She wanted to retch.

"Nikki! Don't move," Anders instructed. *Was that compassion in his voice?* "You look like crap. Where in the hell did you go?" *No compassion.* "You were swallowed into that bluish...something...and were completely gone, then came hurling back out an instant later."

A piercing sound echoed throughout the cavern. The three men whirled around toward the obelisk as Jimmy's voice cracked with fear. "What's happening?"

Nikki's blurred vision allowed her only a hazy view of things. She felt herself slipping into darkness, but fought to remain conscious. She knew she was losing the battle. Through blurred vision, Nikki saw three strangely dressed people tossed from what appeared to be a blue field of energy between the two obelisks. They landed hard near her feet, one on top of the other. She couldn't focus her eyes to see the details of their faces or their clothes, just their general forms and some colors. The three lethargically moved, trying to untangle themselves as they bitched at each other like children. Nikki thought even the others should be able to tell they weren't friends by the way they poked and jabbed at one another, especially the one dressed in red. He was particularly vicious with his strikes. Everyone stared in stunned silence, except Miguel, who was closest and tried to help the stranger in red stand. Nikki had a vague recognition of the red-dressed man. Her blood nearly froze at the sight of him. She opened her mouth to warn Miguel away from the danger he was about to aid. She knew, somehow, that his kindness would be repaid with death.

She was too late. In a flash of blue metal, Nikki heard the thwop of a blade cutting through flesh and bone, and she realized Miguel's body no longer had a head. A dull, hollow thud echoed throughout the cavern as his head hit the ground and rolled. Yelling and panic filled the cavern. The other two that were spat from the void -- one average in height and lean, and one tall yet stocky -- tried to get up, but both collapsed and remained unmoving. Jimmy no longer kneeled motionless near Nikki. He launched himself with a growl at the red-garbed man, driving them both toward the far wall, but they fell short in a heap on the debris-cluttered cavern floor. Nikki's vision dimmed further; darkness was taking her. She struggled to stay conscious…she was losing. A flash of bluish-green light filled the cavern and Jimmy tumbled through the air, landing awkwardly on the rocks.

Nikki struggled on the cliff between reality and darkness. The man in red slowly rose from the place where Jimmy had knocked him down. Nikki instinctively knew the dangers of the man. She knew he was not bound by any moral code she approved. Nikki hoped the two lying on the cavern floor would rise and do battle with this danger, as they had done so in another time. Anders and Ramirez stood motionless with gawking gazes. Nikki feared for them. She tried to scream for them all to run, but she couldn't summon the strength. A reddish glow grew in the red-garbed man's hands, lighting up the cavern. Nikki lost all hope, and waited for the inevitable. The man hurled the light at them as he collapsed. She didn't have to see the bright flash of crimson…she knew what it would do to her friends before it struck. Then darkness took her.

Chapter 1

Wants and Wishes

Rogaan brooded hotly over his father's stubbornness, denying
him what was his. Frustrated and angry, he sat staring across
the morning meal table at dim wavering shadows on the wall. Yellow
light cast by several mirrored floor lamps illuminated the moder-
ately sized room well enough, driving back the pre-dawn gloom and
filling the air with a light scent of wild flowers -- his mother's favorite. Rogaan's long-awaited day was upon him and his father's decree
unwanted, though not unexpected. He had worked hard for his father in the smithy this year to earn the right to use his *shunir'ra*...
today. Yet, he was denied for reasons unknown except for the ridicu-
lous "tradition" of the *Coming of Age* given to him. Sitting in a sulk,
with his short-bearded chin shoved into his palms, Rogaan looked
at the half-empty bowl of mill in front of him. Strangely, he did not
remember eating. Only his desperate search for words and argument
that would change his father's decree mattered to him, though in
truth, Rogaan thought it might be easier to reason with a rock than
with his father.

Glancing up, Rogaan saw his mother quietly sitting at one side of
the table, watching them both with an intensity she was famous for. A
shiver rippled down Rogaan's back. Her stare unnerved him, especially when it was on him, always seeming to know his thoughts. And she
made sure he knew she did know. In recent days, he found her stare
on him more often than he liked, if he liked it at all. This morning her
stare carried more than knowing his mind, it told him to stop pursu-
ing this argument...and to accept his father's decision... "with the respect and graciousness due father," as she often scolded. Her unspoken

warnings guided him well most times, when he heeded them, but this was different. He deserved to use his *shunir'ra*.

"Father," Rogaan started with a determined voice, after straightening his back and doing his best not to sound as if he were asking for permission. "My *shunir'ra* will best anything given me. I am of age and have *right* to use it…as I see things. I wish your blessing." Rogaan avoided looking at his mother, but felt another shiver rippling down his back, and his neck hairs rose, too. Her words rang like a large bell in his head: "respect and grace."

"Rogaan." Mithraam spoke calmly and firmly in his deep rumbling voice, while lightly stroking his long braided beard of black touched by gray. "Of age you are, but the *Zagdu-i-Kuzu* has not yet passed, making your *shunir'ra* forbidden."

"Father!" Rogaan angrily started to press his point then stopped when he caught in the corner of his vision his mother deliberately shifting in her chair. "Less argument." His mother's words rang loudly in his head. He began again, this time in a calm, almost even tone. "Why must I follow *Tellen* tradition when we do not dwell in *Tellen* lands, and I am not fully of the blood? I am half *Baraan*, as well." Rogaan did his best to meekly smile at his mother. She just held him with that stare. Shivers and chills ran down his back. This was not going the way Rogaan had hoped.

"In time you will come to understand, my son, and pass on to your blood the tradition's birthright." Mithraam spoke solemnly and with unshakable conviction. "We do not dwell in the land of my fathers. Events beyond me and my hand will see me here at the end of my days. Regret…is not in my heart for sharing life and happiness with your mother…or you. Though, I intend you understand your heritage."

Frustration filled Rogaan. His arguments had little impact on his father. He wasn't surprised, in truth. "Stubborn" was an understatement where the man was concerned, and Rogaan had a lifetime of dealing with his father's ways. Few could hope to win an argument with him, and fewer succeeded. And there was his father's masterful maneuvering of others to his purposes, when he so desired. Rogaan didn't understand how his father managed it, but he seemed to have a way with people regardless of their station. This morning, Rogaan simply felt outdone by his father and grew more frustrated at the thought. Nearing desperation, Rogaan thought hard on how to convince his father he was taking his *shunir'ra*. Awkwardly Rogaan worked his mouth to speak, but no words came forth. How to convince him? Lost in his thoughts, Rogaan embarrassingly jumped at the touch of his mother's fingers on his cheek. She had somehow managed to reach across the table without his noticing.

"Rogaan." Sarafi spoke in a soft voice that hit him with the force of a hammer striking an anvil. "Isn't it enough your father granted you permission to join the Hunt? You have asked for years for this *privilege*, and now that you have it, you still ask more of your father." His mother's soft touch and penetrating green eyes held Rogaan completely, despite his best efforts to demonstrate to her that he was no longer affected by her strong will. After several attempts to look away, Rogaan admitted to himself that she was worse than father to argue with. Where his father would use impeccable logic and reasoning to win his arguments, his mother struck with subtle combinations of words, unspoken gestures, and emotions to get her way. Her yellow shoulder-length hair swayed about as she tilted her head in an almost planned way as she held him with that penetrating stare. Shivers. How was he ever to win an argument in this house?

"Though I am not *Tellen*," Sarafi continued in a soft, now motherly tone, "I respect the traditions your father holds true, and see importance in your learning and living by them. The *Zagdu-i-Kuzu* is the defining tradition for *Tellens*, and you must embrace it, as it's your ascension from child-apprentice to craftsman. Your *shunir'ra* defines you in the ceremony, and using it before will lessen you in the *Tellen* World."

"Yes, Mother," Rogaan replied with a frustrated scowl. He wanted badly to use his *shunir'ra* so the other younglings joining the Hunt would see his skill in working the finest metals -- and to impress them, maybe even awe them at the power of his blue steel bow. Maybe then they would stop their taunting and quarreling. More importantly, he wanted the *Kiuri'Ner* to see his bow and his skill with it, so he might be favored in the upcoming selection for this year's *Kiuri'Ner* apprentices. All his efforts would be lost if he wasn't picked. He *needed* to be selected. Not knowing the words or how to say them that would change their minds, Rogaan ineptly replied to his parents, "But...I...I wish.... Neither of you understands."

"Yes, we do...understand." For a moment, sorrow filled his mother's eyes.

"My son." Mithraam's voice was calm and soft...soft for him, that is. His words sounded more like a long horn blowing deeply its warning than like a person, even when he whispered. "Saddened we are for your troubles of youth. Our eyes were not blind to Brigum's unkindness. Your desire to demonstrate your worth and have all see you with better eyes will be lost on them."

"That is but half my desire, Father." Rogaan was calm, with only a hint of frustration in his voice now, and with eyes focused again on the empty bowl before him. He and his father argued many times about his desire to not follow the ways of metal-making, and to become a *Kiuri'Ner*. Rogaan's reasons were simple. The entire town revered the *Kiuri'Ner* and the protection they provided the people. They were looked upon as noble and good -- not even the son of Brigum's magistrate, Kantus, would dare speak badly of them. In becoming a *Kiuri'Ner*, Rogaan would have the town's respect -- or at least its silence. Either would do to satisfy him. "I seek favor and to become an apprentice of the *Kiuri'Ner*...and they regard the bow well."

"Rogaan." Mithraam's tone became almost exasperated. "We spoke of this...I thought no more. The *Kiuri'Ner* are but blades in the struggles of Shuruppak. You will be called to brandish that blade and made to fight against your blood. This cannot pass."

"The *Kiuri'Ner* spoke," Rogaan replied quickly. "Those of Brigum are simple protectors of the people and the mines...no more."

"If you are found in the ranks of the *Kiuri'Ner*..." Mithraam explained, but with great hesitation, which Rogaan thought odd for his father. "They will make use of you...and the force of unseen hands will maneuver family."

"Your beliefs about the *Kiuri'Ner* are unfounded," Rogaan replied hotly, though as respectful as he could muster. "They are of honor and without masters." Rogaan was certain his father was wrong where the *Kiuri'Ner* were concerned. They patrolled the woodlands and the perimeter of Brigum, protecting its people and caravans traveling the roads. They were not soldiers of Farratum, or even Shuruppak. They were the protectors of Brigum. Rogaan grew excited in the moment; his heart beat faster. His arguments might finally reach his father -- though his father's words puzzled him. Rogaan paused to think on them. He realized his father spoke not of the *Kiuri'Ner* being used by faces unknown, but the both of them *Me? Father?* Alarmed and curious, Rogaan asked. "Why would *we* be used?"

"This talk has carried on too long," Sarafi broke in. Put off balance by her declaration, Rogaan wasn't ready for the "discussion" to end. He had not gotten what he wanted, and opened his mouth to speak, but was cut off by that stare. Shivers. "Respect your father's wishes, my son, and go without your *shunir'ra*. Now, ready yourself, or you will miss what you sought and be left behind. Besides, your friend must be waiting for you."

"But..." Rogaan protested.

"Enough!" Sarafi snapped in a stern tone that made it clear nothing more was to be said. "Rogaan. Ready yourself for your...adventure." Sarafi then shooed him on his way with a brisk wave of her hands and that penetrating stare that followed him as he reluctantly retreated from the table and under the archway leading to the resting rooms.

Taking leave of his parents without further protest, Rogaan walked slowly in the hope that he might overhear bits of the conversation they would likely strike up. Silence. Only his booted footfalls on the hallway's rust-red stone tiles echoed. A mirrored wall lamp bathed the hallway with enough light for Rogaan to make out the mortar-less, tight-fitting wall stones. The precision stonework was of his father's hand before Rogaan's birth. The skill had been taught to Rogaan, along with metalsmithing, throughout his youth. While he found smithing enjoyable, Rogaan just never found "stoning" interesting, though he admired his father's skill at it.

Disappointed that his parents would not speak of any secrets, Rogaan quickened his pace, hurrying to his room so he could ready himself and not miss the Hunt Talk…without his *shunir'ra*. A few steps down the hall, Rogaan found himself in front of a brass-bound, heavy oak door ornately engraved with a mountain surrounded by a forest. The door was stained dark, and lacquered such that to the average eye it appeared to be a mirror, the first of three in the hallway. Everything of this father's hand spoke magnificence and quality. And his father was insistent that they keep with the *Tellen* tradition of parents passing on to their children their knowledge and skills. For Rogaan, that meant learning woodworking, stoneworking, and metalsmithing. And Rogaan held his crafting skills superior to most found on the streets of Brigum and equal to those exchanged between private hands. Still, Rogaan conceded his father's hand far surpassed his own, as evident in the door before him and everything else about the house.

Opening the door, Rogaan was struck by the heavy scent of flowers, blended with the faint odor of animal dung and blood, the latter two drifting in from the meat house pens to the north through his open window, and the flowers from his mother's garden just outside. A lit oil stand lamp with reflecting mirrors illuminated his neatly arranged room. It was in the only condition his mother would allow. "Clean and kept is the way of this house, or hungry you will go," she had scolded him, more often than he could honestly remember. The few times he had tested her, he found himself hungry until he put everything in order. He did not know who was the tougher, his father in the smithy or his mother elsewhere around the house.

His room was comfortably large, almost six strides square, with a pair of shuttered windows on the far wall and a cooling vent in the exposed pitched roof above. A cool breeze flowing from the open windows and door, rising to the vent, prickled his skin, making his hair stand on end. The vent was not necessary this time of year, but in the hot, dry season it was worth its weight in gems. In his windows, Rogaan caught the beginning hint of blue in the morning sky, with golden highlights on a few wispy clouds touching the nearby mountain peaks. Hastily, he gathered his clothing from under his neatly made bed. The bed, desk, chair, and a clothing cabinet were all made of heavy wood, ornately carved with symbols telling epic stories, in the *Tellen* fashion, and lacquered to a glossy finish. All had been by his father's hand when he was just a knee-high, but they looked just recently made.

Rogaan collected his things from around the room then shoved them into a green-and-tan striped hide carry pack, with traveling clothes and camp equipment filling up most of the space. Hard brick soap, just in case he had a need to bathe, and salt scrub for his teeth he tucked into a side pocket. "I'm forgetting something," he told himself. He looked around the room in search of the something, not wanting to leave anything behind that he might need. A sparkle from the shelf nearest the door caught his eye. The first rays of the dawn sun reflecting off the polished metal wind vane in the back yard bathed the shelf and brightened the room. Scintillating colors radiating from a crystal figurine mesmerized Rogaan for a moment, drawing him to it and inspect it. The hand-tall figurine was of a female *Tellen* dressed in *eur* battle armor and holding a sword-like weapon high in victory...or defiance? Rogaan was unclear about that point of the ancient tale, though he preferred victory.

The figurine was bathed in a sparkling of soft rainbows as he moved it about, inspecting it, the colors reminding him of his unsettled dreams last night and the fitful sleep that came with them. Normally he slept soundly and did not remember his dreams as he had when he awoke this morning, with their vividness leaving him wondering if they were somehow real. Though now, he found the details fading. The figurine was a gift from an old clan friend of his father from many years ago when a small group of *Tellens* traveled from Kilan, the capital of Turil and the *Tellen* Nation, to visit his father here in Brigum. Rogaan never understood their purpose, nor could he remember the name of the clan friend, but the lack of kinship between the "friend" and his father remained etched in his memory. They were more adversarial than friendly.

Scintillating colors drew Rogaan's attention deep into the crystal figurine. It was said to be a statue of the *Tellen* Lahamu, *Our Lady of Battles* and a legendary Sentii of the Third Age. Rogaan recalled the tale of *Ursane-Ursa* ...first warrior of warriors in the war against the *One Whose Name Was Unmade*. The tale was a favorite of his father's, and told to Rogaan since he could remember. She was the great symbol of courage and bravery in *Tellen* clans and thought of as almost god-like, to judge by the way his father described her exploits. As the legend was told, Lahamu, under command of the Ancients, led a clan of Sentii against the Unmade One's forces in the end days of the Third Age. She led the Sentii in epic battles and was said to have died in the last battle of the *Shiarush* War, but only after defeating the Unmade One's Shunned warriors. A powerful and nasty lot desiring all that was Ancient...and Agni.

"Good dawn." A quick-paced voice announced itself from one of the open windows. Surprised...startled, Rogaan snapped a look at the window where he found his friend, Pax, lazily hanging on the windowsill with a broad, toothy grin of slightly yellow teeth.

"So," Pax continued with an air of anticipation. "Talk him into lettin' ya carry it on da Hunt?"

"No," Rogaan grumbled. He deliberately avoided looking at Pax's frown while walking to his desk before shoving a few remaining items into his carry pack. "He is as stubborn as expected, and gave my words little consideration."

"Ya takin' it anyway?" Pax asked, with a slight hint of hope in his up-to-no-good smile. Rogaan looked at Pax, who was still lazily hanging on the windowsill with both arms, elbows out and shoulder-high. Pax's short-cropped black hair was as usual uncombed and a little oily. Rogaan suspected Pax wore his hair in that manner to spite everyone, especially his parents, since he often played with it, straightening it out. This morning Pax wore blue face paint that contrasted sharply with his light-brown skin. A crude blue shape of a great wyrmm, possibly one of legend, stretched from his forehead to right cheek. He always seemed to want to draw attention to himself in public, possibly to make up for lacking it at home...or so he hinted occasionally. Rogaan suddenly felt comfort in his parents' wanting to know every aspect of his life and always knowing, somehow, when to pull him back from making a big mistake. Pax was one of those mistakes, so his mother told him. She disapproved of Pax's friendship and his' rebellious nature, fearing Rogaan would follow him in style and attitude. Not that he would. Not able to get Rogaan to end the friendship, she chastised Pax, severely, at almost every opportunity, and would certainly do so today if she saw him.

"Only a fool would act against my father," Rogaan said, defeated and a little angry. "He is as thick as stone...unbending. And Mother silenced talk of it." Rogaan finished his grumbling by sealing his carry pack with a firm tug on its drawstrings. Swinging his pack over his shoulder, he started for the door then stopped, looking back at Pax. "Best you stand where Mother cannot see. Her disapproval of you... your face paint will be firm, even if it washes off with rock soap and a good scrub."

"That not be all she disapproves of." Sarcasm was thick in Pax's words. "No more tongue-lashin' like she gave me. I be waitin' out front."

In a blink, Pax disappeared. *How did he do that?* Rogaan wondered? There one moment and gone the next. With a shake of his head in wonder, he pushed Pax and his nimble ways to the back of his thoughts then trudged from his room for the front door. A little sunlight reflecting from polished brass mirrors mounted in the ceiling precisely every four strides pushed back the gloom of the pre-dawn hallway. Rogaan felt uneasy in darkness, despite possessing some of the famed *Tellen* dark sight. He had always felt uneasy in the darkness. It had a way of putting him on edge and making him irritable, or so his mother said. The warmth of the light had the opposite effect. It made him feel at ease, even as a knee-high, and because of that his father made great efforts to brighten the house as much as possible, day and night. Oil lamps with silver mounted reflecting mirrors just above Rogaan's eye level were on every wall. They burned smokeless oil with a scent of meadow lily at night, illuminating every room and hall. The pleasant scent of the burning oil lingered in the cool dawn air. Ceiling mirrors would fully replace the oil lamps once the sun rose high enough to light the house well through them. Despite the brightening hallway, Rogaan remained glum, and wasn't looking forward to another needed talk with his father about his *shunir'ra*.

Rogaan re-entered the meal room cautiously. He expected his parents still to be sitting there, but to his surprise, they were nowhere to be seen. They usually sat every morning talking, sometimes for considerable lengths of time, discussing the day to come and things he did not understand. Three empty bowls sat on the ornate wooden table, surrounded by six matching wooden chairs, all at the center of the room. Several drinking pitchers with beads of sweat trickling down their polished silver sides sat on an ornately crafted serving table to his right. A heavy wooden door with bands of polished bronze stood to his left. It led to the cooking room. Opposite him stood the archway to the common area of the house and the front doors. Curious…it was unusual for his parents not to be here, talking. They had been acting strangely the past few days, arguing instead of just giving each other their typical looks when they did not approve of what the other was saying or doing. Rogaan hoped today would bring a return to the normal happenings about the house despite things not starting well.

Rogaan now stood silently, listening for footfalls or voices that would give away his parents' location and maybe more. Whispers from beyond the archway from the grand room told him what he wanted. He could not make out what they were saying, with their voices soft, but their words seemed edgy. Rogaan's heart sank. They were arguing again. Normally, when they weren't giving each other their looks, they discussed matters of disagreement in a debating manner, never raising their voices or speaking with disrespect. This was different. Though quiet, they spoke to each other with sharp words, disagreeing over something—what, he knew not. Despite his growing concern, Rogaan could not resist the intrigue. He needed to find out what they were arguing over, and silently crept across the tiled floor to the wall separating the rooms. Listening intently, with his breath held tight, Rogaan peered around the corner, hoping to overhear their words and to understand.

"These tasks you ask of me make me uncertain, My One." Sarafi spoke in a sharp whisper. "What you ask is…difficult."

"My One," Mithraam spoke calmly, also in a whisper that was more like gravel being poured into a bucket. "Obey my words. Your family name will shield you."

"No, Mithraam!" Sarafi protested.

"Honor my wishes, My One," Mithraam cut her off, still in a gravelly whisper. "Time is short. I must tend to matters and will return soon."

Bewildered, Rogaan stood silently, uncertain what to do. Disagreeing like this profoundly was unlike them. Rogaan did not want them knowing he was spying on them, and thought to leave or make a loud entrance, but he found himself not able to resist listening further, especially since his *shunir'ra* might be a subject. Their arguing continued for a short while before he heard mention of his *shunir'ra*, though he could not make out exactly what they said about it, but it sounded favorable. Excited that his father might have changed his stance concerning his use of it, he hurriedly thought of words to speak. Try as he might, he was not able to think of a new argument his father had not already rejected. He hastily worked new points of argument that might favor his use of his *shunir'ra* on the Hunt. Silence filled the room and Rogaan grew alarmed. Fearing he would miss his last opportunity to use his *shunir'ra*, Rogaan stepped into the grand room before knowing what he was going to say.

The grand room and main entrance loomed large, almost sixteen strides square, with the ceiling more than five strides high at its peak, supported by dark, heavy wooden beams rising from the outer walls to its apex. A massive wooden beam ran the length of the house above the inner walls, supporting a tiled wood roof. His mother's crystal figurines hung rotating from wooden crossbeams, sparkling in the morning sunlight radiating down from two circular sun-mirrors set in the roof. From the crystals, colors danced across the room, painting walls, tapestries, furniture, rugs, and the tiled floor in a blend of soft hues. Where uncovered, half-stride sized square-cut gray stones gave the walls an impregnable look, with the stones fitted so precisely that no mortar could be seen. His father's hand, Rogaan thought with pride. Gleaming brass hourglass plates anchored the stones together, strengthening the house as if it were a fortress. Several large shuttered windows, head-high on the left and right walls, framed the center wall and its large inset stone fireplace, where a warm orange-yellow fire burned with an occasional crackle. The flames took the chill out of the air, while giving everything a pleasant scent of mountainwoods. Books of all subjects filled hand-sculpted wood shelves framing the windows of both walls.

Schooled by his parents in a number of subjects, Rogaan both grimaced and smiled at memories of his parents reading every word on those shelves to him. His favorites were of history, legends of the Ancients, and great battles of ages long past. Stories from the end of the Third Age, before the Cleansing and Great Leaving, were among his most favorite of those.

Several rust-colored long-chairs with ample padding, and two bare wooden chairs, each ornately carved and matching a wooden table between them, sat in the middle of the room. A roomy padded lounging chair of blue sat off to the right side of the fireplace -- Rogaan's favorite, where he did most of his reading. Small stone and crystal statues of creatures and objects of legend and myth decorated tabletops and shelves. Most were his father's, though his mother took claim of the statues of creatures both common to these lands and of legend. Three suits of burnished armor in the *eur* design, each ornately runed, guarded the corners of the room, along with gleaming swords and maces. All were stunning to the eye, and of his father's hand. To Rogaan's right, heavy wooden double doors almost three strides high dominated the house's entry. His parents stood in its shadow, appearing small in the grand entranceway, his father a few fingers shorter than his mother in height. They both wore startled expressions directed at Rogaan as they nervously separated from an embrace.

"Rogaan?" Sarafi spoke first, in a surprised tone. "Are...are you readied for your travels?" Recovering quickly – not to Rogaan's surprise – her tone changed to that of a steady flow of water as she moved her words away from what she did not want him to sense or see. She tilted her head and held him with her green-eyed stare, then gently swayed her yellow hair with a deftness years of practice brought in what Rogaan assumed was an attempt to break his thoughts. Rogaan had learned her act was a reflex she resorted to out of habit when caught off guard. Her light-green morning dress -- made by her own hand -- gracefully flowed over her light-brown slender body. She was well past forty years, wife to his father for more than twenty-five of those, but appeared as a woman much younger, with only a few lines at the corners of her eyes.

Rogaan's father was very different physically with a powerful, stocky build, though not fat. His father had a broad chest, and muscular arms and legs chiseled from years at the forge. Rogaan attributed his father's physique to a lifetime of working stone and metal, since other *Tellens* appeared to carry a similar build, though not as sturdy in Rogaan's opinion. His face was beginning to show wrinkles hinting at middle age, with lines that also seemed to come from the serious look he usually wore. The *Tellen* very rarely smiled. Rogaan often caught his mother chiding him as being too dour for the town and the family. Rogaan just thought of his father as being ever serious and without humor. His father's straight black beard, touched at the edges with gray, was simply braided, but not so neatly arranged as Rogaan was used to seeing, especially when he was going to be on the town. Shoulder-length top-hairs matched his beard in color, with gray at the temples, and also not as neat as Rogaan expected. He seemed in a hurry. Rogaan was uncertain how old his father was, but knew he had lived in Brigum many years before taking his mother as wife. Though, he did not have the look of a person who some in town claimed to be the oldest person in Brigum, and maybe the entire borderlands. Rogaan dismissed such talk, since there were many elders in town with plenty of gray and wrinkles to spare. They must be older than father. Seeing his father attach his dark-blue cloak as if to travel sparked Rogaan's concern that he would not get another chance to seek permission to use his *shunir'ra*.

With a sense of urgency, and without thinking, Rogaan opened his mouth, trying to work words that would not take shape. He looked from his mother to his father several times while thinking what to say, though nothing came to him that he had not already said. With a glum expression, Mithraam stood stiff-backed, making his less than two-stride height seem taller than usual, with his dark-blue cloak hanging smoothly from shoulders to his black hide boots. The cloak concealed much of his father's charcoal-colored shirt, black pants, and reddish-brown hide belt. His braided beard just touched a silver belt buckle that bore a symbol of three overlapping circles. Rogaan was unfamiliar with the symbol. He had not seen his father wear it before today. Held in his father's left hand was that weathered short-brimmed black hat he favored since Rogaan could remember. With a surprise, Rogaan realized his father appeared prepared for travel beyond Brigum's walls -- something he did rarely.

Rogaan's eyes darted from his father to his mother and back as he considered his words. Not knowing what to say that had not already been said, he held his tongue. He hoped one of them would say something to break the awkward silence, but all they did was stare back at him. Rogan felt uncomfortable. His father's expression changed from glum to one Rogaan was more familiar with: a stolid stone-faced stare that gave you the impression he knew something you did not.

"My son." Mithraam spoke in his calm, authoritative tone typical when he was to give an announcement, a proclamation, or lecture. "Be watchful. Mind the *Kiuri'Ner* and guard against anxiousness and carelessness when seeking to impress."

"I will mind your words, Father," Rogaan answered honestly, a bit off balance from his father's unexpected concern. "But success will be more certain and safer...."

"Rogaan!" Mithraam scorned with a raised hand. "No! We will not speak of it again. I must go and can delay no longer." Mithraam glanced to his wife, who softened his stern expression and mood. "My Son, be watchful and mindful of those near, and take no chances when hunting prey. The Wilds are dangerous."

"I will," Rogaan replied, frustrated and disappointed. "Where do you travel?" Rogaan was curious and wanted to know what drew his father away and, in truth, he hoped to walk with him, even if for a short distance, so that he might speak of his *shunir'ra*, again.

"That is my affair," Mithraam answered dispassionately. "I must go. I will return by Hunt's end." Mithraam hurried out the doors without ceremony or speaking further words, letting in a burst of chilled air hinted with dung, causing Mother to wrap herself tightly in her arms and wrinkle her nose. Rogaan hurried to follow, almost leaping to his mother's side before bending slightly to give her a quick kiss on the cheek. When he turned to bound after his father, a tug on his sleeve held him as if a large weight. He could have easily broken his mother's hold, but her firm yet gentle grasp held him fast for reasons more of love, trust, and respect than of physical strength.

"Rogaan." She spoke softly. "Do not follow. Repeatedly you've asked, and each time his answer is unchanged. More strife will be your only answer if you pursue."

"Mother," Rogaan huffed. "I do not understand Father. We are not in *Tellen* lands. I respect his wishes for me to learn the ways, but I am of age."

"You are too stubborn," Sarafi stated flatly. "As is your father. He is to blame for this. You both will be my darkening with this unrelenting head-butting. Now, heed your father's wishes, as will I. When you return, the *Zagdu-i-Kuzu* will be done and this matter will be no more. Then you both will be free to invent a new concern to argue over."

Sarafi gently straightened Rogaan's collar. "Do well. Remain on guard to keep from injury. Follow your heart."

"I will," Rogaan promised with curiosity, then slumped, glum and defeated. Rogaan grumbled a sigh before giving his mother a kiss on the cheek then stepping from the house. Rogaan stopped on the porch to wrinkle his nose at the heavy odor of animal dung and blood. His father had masterfully built their home to keep a gentle flow of air moving through the structure cooling and warming as needed. The home's design also, thankfully, kept much of the rank odor from the town's slaughter yard at bay with a burning fireplace and scented oil lamps. Rogaan glanced about the budding shrubs surrounding the porch, his hand raised to shield his eyes from the bright morning sun beginning to crest the mountain ridges to the northeast. He looked to the paved stone street, seeking his father, but nowhere was he to be found. Rogaan still hoped to ask his father just one more time, despite his mother's wishes. Unfortunately, she had delayed him long enough for his father to disappear.

Resigned that he would not get his wish, Rogaan looked for Pax and soon caught a shadow at the corner of the covered porch off to his right. *So typical of Pax*, Rogaan mused, *hiding from eyes until he wants to be noticed.* Rogaan looked back at his mother, who wore a forced smile, then bounded down the porch steps onto the lightly traveled street of the early hour.

Chapter 2
Hunt Talk

Rogaan met Pax on the street in front of his house with an exchange of wordless glances before they started north to the meat house. Rogaan noticed Pax purposely looking everywhere except toward Mother. In truth, Rogaan did not wish to spy his mother's face, nor her disapproving eyes. She just did not like Pax. Rogaan was frustrated at that, but said nothing, since it would do no good in changing her mind. The sky was dotted with wispy clouds sliding away on a gentle breeze. Left behind was dew glistening in the rays of the rising sun on everything, including the street's weather-worn paving stones, making footfalls slick and a little treacherous. Rogaan's boots slid a bit with each step, forcing him to walk slower than he wanted. Pax did not seem to suffer from the slick stones, and walked as casually as ever. Warmth struck Rogaan's right cheek as the sun broke almost fully on the high ridges to the northeast, making him squint from the sudden brilliance.

A mix of pitched and flat-roofed houses, many with open-air walkways splitting them, lined the street to the right. Most were of mortared stone construction, with a few newer houses made of modestly colored bricks. All were meager in size, and Rogaan knew from a life living nearby that they sheltered several families each, all of modest means, huddling together to afford the roof over their heads. On his left, carefully kept cedar trees and shrubs just beginning to show new growth surrounded his home's gray stone walls, a dark-stained wooden porch, and a pitched red-clay tiled roof. His home was larger than any near, and appeared fit more for an *ensi* governing over the town, or a coiner, or maybe even a law-maker, instead of a well-to-do stone- and metal-crafter.

"Bow?" Pax asked with a wry smirk.

"Salting the wound, huh?" Rogaan grumbled back.

"No worry," Pax tried to sound apologetic, but failed. "Kantus not give ya respect anyways, even if ya had it."

"His is not the respect I seek." Rogaan spit back, with more anger than he intended. "To prove myself before the Hunt Master and *Kiuri'Ner* is what I need if I am to gain their favor." Pax gave Rogaan a knowing smile that left Rogaan feeling guilty. He quibbled, "Well, a little respect from Kantus and his Band would do, too."

"Would no count on it," Pax stated flatly, then chuckled quietly with that wry smile. Rogaan envied Pax. He never appeared bothered by anything, including things said poorly of him. There were many in the town who did not care for Pax or his family, with them being new to Brigum as of only a handful of years ago. Just as many town folk found it difficult to trust Pax because of the mystery surrounding him and his family. They were not an open lot, and keeping them a mystery was something Pax worked hard at fostering. So Pax went on without a bother, keeping on with whatever he was about. He even kept on when pretty young lasses turned down his bold advances, or the less-frequent polite request to share a dance or a kiss. Rogaan found himself often wishing to be more like his friend in such things, instead of being mired in his own concerns of what others thought of him.

They stopped at the corner of his family's property, where a side street from the left merged with the main. It too was paved with well-fitted cobblestones, though worn smooth with years of traffic. A small tremor shook the tree and vibrated the stones beneath his feet, a normal event these days that he almost did not notice anymore. Next to his house, an old cedar tree vaulted twenty strides up. It marked the edge of family land, with the meat house and its surrounding pens just to the north of the intersection. A ruckus of chirps, clicks, and high-pitched shrieks filled the dawn from pens packed with small, feathered, two-footed *tanniyn* of different colors, some fighting for territory and breeding rights, while most just pecked at the ground searching for food. The odor of dung and blood hung heavy in the air, making Rogaan's nose wrinkle more than before...if that was possible. The coming day's warmth would worsen the smell, Rogaan predicted, and he thanked the Ancients for the east wind that usually carried the pungent odors away from his home. Unfortunately that same wind laid thick the stench of rotting flesh and blood into the west reaches of Brigum, where Pax and many other families less with coin lived.

The *tanniyn* kept for slaughter served as food for many in Brigum. Most numerous were two-legged, a stride long and half as tall, animals of dark green body feathers with long slender emerald tail feathers, and a thin red stripes of feathers running the length of their backs, head to tail. *Red stripeis* were easy to keep, with their unfinicky appetites for plants and crunchy *biters* -- so Rogaan was told by the meat house workers. Rogaan considered *reds* good eating, and the town folk seemed to agree with him. The other *tanniyns* kept by the meat house were held in cages next to the building. They were tough and powerful two-legged animals, two strides long, *leapers*, touting sharp teeth, powerful three-fingered foreclaws and a nasty sickle claw on each foot. These green and red-brown, feathered *leapers* were a handful, and dangerous -- always agitated, so it seemed, with a nasty disposition and seemingly unquenchable thirst to spill their handler's blood. Rogaan shivered at that thought, and from his memories watching them from the safety of the town walls looking over the town's dump on the far north side of Brigum. *Leapers* killed other animals and sometimes each other, with great speed and viciousness, and almost always in packs. As dangerous as they were to keep, many in town considered a serving of *leaper* a delicacy and as such they brought a good price, making them profitable. Rogaan smiled as he recalled mornings and sometimes late afternoons spent with the town guard on the wall killing *leapers* with bow, some at distances more than one hundred fifty strides. Not an easy thing to do against such-sized targets, which moved like the wind.

Rogaan gained a reputation as an excellent shot among many in the town's guard, and he hoped it would gain him favor with the *Kiuri'Ner*.

"Rogaan..." Pax's tone carried a sardonic ring. "Remember me... and what we be doin'?" Rogaan blinked -- twice -- before realizing Pax stood before him with arms crossed. Rogaan suddenly felt warm, even hot in the face. Pax's smile broadened. "Thinkin' of me sister, again, ya be? Ya be seein' her soon enough."

"What?" Rogaan looked at Pax with a slung-open mouth as his entire body suddenly felt uncomfortably warm, and a shiver ran down his spine.

"Suhd be seein' us off," Pax smiled a toothy grin.

Panic seized Rogaan and his throat tightened, threatening to keep the breath from him. He was conflicted of his desire to see her beautiful eyes and smile, and in dreadful fear of talking to her in the company of others and likely making a fool of himself.

"Hurry before she shows!" he managed to cough out to Pax, in his desperation to avoid Suhd. He set off in a run—slipping and sliding on the damp paving stones as he went.

"What be wrong?" Pax asked innocently, after catching Rogaan and easily keeping pace with him at a run. "Ya like Suhd."

Rogaan briefly considered lying to Pax, telling him he thought of him as a brother and Suhd a sister, and no more, but he could not bring himself to it. It would be such an obvious lie. Instead, with a gasping voice, he answered honestly. "Pax...I speak stupid when Suhd is about. I cannot do this...not with others...not today."

"Then, fast we run," Pax urged with a thoughtful smile. "She was to leave soon after me."

With a surge of worry, Rogaan broke into a sprint, with Pax keeping pace at his side. Rogaan hoped Suhd had taken care of errands before heading for the meat house. He did not need or want this, not today. Not today. The distance to the place of the Talk was less than two hundred strides from his house, but for some reason it felt much farther to Rogaan now that he raced Suhd. Not a particularly fast runner, Rogaan cursed his *Tellen* heritage in between gasps for air for his slow sprinting abilities.

They ran onto the road at the north side of town, Perimeter Road. It surrounded all of Brigum's houses and markets, except for the upper and lower farming fields and Coiners Quarter, with their large houses and expensive ways, across the bridges on the east of town. Rogaan lost his feet when turning left toward the meat house, now some fifty strides away. Sliding and stumbling and almost falling, Rogaan righted himself before making a fool of himself in a tumble. Ahead, hunters gathered in front of a two-story, pitched-slate-roofed stone building that was his destination. Hunters, old and young, in various dress of browns, tans, and charcoal garb, mingled in small groups and with family and friends. Many were dressed in worn or tattered work clothes, while some wore their festival best, though all milled about with their sons or husbands before sending them off into the Wilds. On the far side of the crowd, several *Baraans* towered over all others. They were dressed in the traditional red-brown *eur* armor of the *Kiuri'Ner* and arrogantly pushed their way through the people on their way to the meat house. Rogaan's hopes rose...no Suhd. Just as Rogaan started to slow his pace with a sense of relief, Suhd caught his eyes. She stood near the entrance of the building with her waist-length black hair and yellow knee-length dress flowing gently in the gentle morning breeze. Rogaan's heart started to race, both at the pleasing sight of her and at the terror welling up within him. Her almost matching wide-brimmed sun hat blocked enough of the rising sun to allow her to catch sight of Rogaan and Pax's coming. He wanted to see her, even talk to her, touch her gentle hands -- but how was he going to do so without being seen as a fool by everyone around?

"What be wrong?" Pax asked sincerely, now standing ahead of Rogaan.

Rogaan realized with surprise that his feet were barely moving, less than a leisurely walk, and he was a bit short of breath -- not so much from running as he was able to run long distances without tiring…much, though not as fast as he wished. Rather, the tightness in his chest and the uncomfortable prickling welling up in his gut was from fear of the anticipated talk with Suhd in front of so many people, some of which did not think of him or his family kindly.

"Nothin' ta worry," Pax spoke playfully. "Suhd has eyes for ya. Stop thinkin' words, and talk ta her."

"You do not understand," Rogaan managed to choke out. "She is so beautiful…and has wits…and is kind." Rogaan's eyes remained fixed on Suhd. He did not want to look anywhere else. She was all he wanted…all he needed. Her beauty held him firm, from the thin strap sandals on her slender feet and legs to her slender, yet curvy body that her yellow dress embraced, to her slender face and that perky nose and those deep blue eyes, and her long black hair. Rogaan was awestruck. She was perfect. "What could she wish to say to me? What do I say?"

"Ya not be sayin' much." Pax jerked his head to the crowd beyond Suhd. "Ol' puffy chest be makin' way through da crowd."

Rogaan scanned the crowd and quickly found Kantus, with his three-member Band, arrogantly pushing their way through the crowd. The knots in Rogaan's guts immediately started aching. The one person he wanted most to avoid was making his way toward Suhd. Rogaan did not fear that Kantus had true feelings for Suhd, but his attempts at courting her tormented him. Kantus seemed to enjoy giving him that torment, or at least Rogaan's reaction to it.

"What wrong have I done to him?"

Pax shrugged and grunted. "Nothin', but for him nothin' is all be needed."

"Well," Rogaan reluctantly forced his words out with a long exhale. "Let us be done with this." Jaw set, Rogaan quickened his pace to get to Suhd before Kantus did. Kantus too quickened his pace, and snuck up behind Suhd, placing his hands over her eyes with a whisper in her ear, before Rogaan or Pax could reach her. Rogaan held his breath as his gut-ache twisted while an unpleasant feeling welled up in him…anger…jealousy. He did not know which was more powerful, maybe both, but he pushed on to rescue Suhd from Kantus' advances. At Rogaan's approach, Suhd smiled simply before gracefully twirling out of Kantus' grasp. Rogaan came to a halt less than four paces away.

"Ya know I not be one of those youngling lasses," Suhd said playfully, but edged with a serious tone. "And that ya hold little interest to me, Kantus." Suhd shot a quick glance at Rogaan, then at Pax.

"Maybe you are and don't wish to admit it," Kantus countered gruffly and sarcastically as he tossed Rogaan an arrogant and overconfident look.

"Kantus!" Pax spoke boldly and with more forcefulness than Rogaan expected. "Leave me sister alone. Ya be no wanted here."

"I'm *wanted* everywhere, Pax," Kantus boasted with arms outstretched. "Who can resist me? Not your sister." Kantus' eyes shot quickly from Pax to Rogaan then back to Pax. A deeper smile, no…a smirk…grew on his face.

Rogaan took in everything: from Suhd's disapproving scowl directed at Kantus, to her light scent of wildflowers, likely from scented oil; to Pax standing tall with chest out, hoping to make his slender build more intimidating than it really was; to Kantus' casual disregard of Pax, and Kantus' three bandsmen spreading out to surround them. This was already not going well. Almost as tall as the average *Baraan*, Kantus stood just short of even with Rogaan, but was leaner, though not by much, despite the bulk of the new brown hunter's suit he wore. Pax stood taller than both, by half a hand, but his slim frame made him less impressive to the eye, especially with his tattered and heavily patched dark pants and well-worn gray tunic. Kantus' three strong-arms wore less impressive attire than their "master." Jantaa, dark-haired and the smallest of them, wore simple work clothes" shirt, breeches, and ankle-high sandals. Urhug was as round in face as he was in body, with oily brown hair that seemed to stick to his head. He wore a green tunic, likely because he tended to rip out the seams of any pants he put on, and low brown boots. Harrod, the biggest of them–as tall as Pax, and wider–with his light-brown hair and struggling beard, wore greenish hide-padded armor over his tunic and breeches. His dark hide boots came up almost to his knees and looked new. All of them wore shoulder packs in various states of repair.

By themselves, Rogaan suspected that only Harrod could show himself well enough in a scuffle, maybe even challenge Kantus for the top spot. But together, they presented a problem for Pax and Rogaan. Past scuffles with Kantus and his Band told Rogaan that Pax was no match for "ol' puffy chest" without help, though he admired his friend's boldness in defending his sister's honor. After his bandsmen flanked them, Kantus quickly closed on Pax while holding him with an intense, intimidating stare from his mean green eyes, just daring Pax to swing. Kantus' round, close-bearded face with its wide nose looked dark and angry as he eyed Pax. Pax's thin hairless face and sharp features, stood in contrast with Kantus', wore a hint of fear.

"What do you think you're doing here?" Kantus snidely demanded of Pax, while using every bit of his straining body and stitch of his hunter's suit to appear large and intimidating. His suit looked somewhat like the protective *Kiuri'Ner eur* armor, with shoulder pads, a chest pad, layered hip and thigh guards, a wide black belt without the *Kiuri'Ner* rank sash, and calf-high strapped sandals, all of *tanniyn* hide. It matched the brown color of his combed shoulder-length hair, and appeared never worn before today. Likely another benefit of being the son of Brigum's Council Leader, the *Dubsa'Sauru'Saar*. Favored with both coin and associations through his father, Kantus got much of anything he desired. Rogaan struggled with holding back his deep disgust at Kantus' selfishness and use of his station, while envying his fortune. Pax stood in complete contrast to Kantus. He had on those tattered and patched clothes, a small bottom pack to hold his traveling items, and a wide-brimmed hat of dark gray that had seen better days long ago, hanging on his back and secured by a string about his neck. Kantus clearly was the more confident of the two, and for good reason…he had the backing of his Band against Rogaan and Pax.

Despite the numbers, Rogaan felt strangely calm, except for his growing urge to pound Kantus into the dirt. His promise to his father that he would not scuffle, again, after that messy incident with Kantus at the town's Harvest Festival not a year ago, was all that held him back…mostly. It did not matter that Kantus started the brawl -- or more accurately, had one of his Band start it. That fight quickly got out of control and a mess made, with the whole town watching as the six of them were hauled off before the town's Keeper of the Me for judgment and punishment. Kantus received only chores in the lower fields for a short season as punishment for his part. Kantus' Band, Pax, and Rogaan all received the cane in addition to those same chores. Justice was not equally handed out, and that sat badly with Rogaan. Scars on his back long since had healed. Rogaan always was a fast healer, but Pax wore the marks still and his anger never lessened from it and at the injustice handed out. Rogaan's father tried his best to explain to him why Kantus was treated differently, regardless of how unfair it appeared to him. No matter how his father explained it, Rogaan still felt the injustice, as Pax did. A bitter tasting drink to swallow every day.

So started the feud, with Rogaan and Pax mostly on the receiving end of things. Even their families became entangled in the feud, with the *Dubsa'Sauru'Saar* making town business dealings more difficult for his father. Rogaan never once heard his father complain of it. He just made Rogaan promise not to scuffle again with Kantus. Rogaan did not understand it all then, and still did not now…why the favoritism to certain citizens? But he did his best to honor his father's wishes, despite Kantus pushing at him in every way thinkable since. So, things were as they had been for almost a year: Kantus acting as if he could do anything he wanted and get away with it, and Rogaan struggling against his urges. At least Pax seemed to feel unrestrained, but Rogaan feared that his friend would prove no match for Kantus, little alone the entire Band. As things unfolded before him, a growing fear welled up within that he would not have a choice in breaking his promise to his father to keep his friend from harm.

When it looked as if Pax was not going to succumb to Kantus' intimidations, Kantus whispered something at Pax too softly for Rogaan to hear, all the while glancing at Suhd. Pax fumed as anger stiffened his posture.

"Kantus!" Rogaan fought his welling anger, and he feared he was losing. Insults at him or Pax could be tolerable, but spoiling Suhd's honor was too much. Too much! "Did not your family teach you to behave properly? Or have you bought favors so long that you have forgotten manners?" Kantus' Band stood impatient, waiting for their leader to give them the signal to attack. Rogaan smiled while deliberately staring each of them down in turn. Rogaan had held his tongue and his anger. He was…pleased with himself. "Courage, too, seems lost on you."

Kantus' face darkened with anger as his gloved fists balled tightly. Kantus glanced at his Band, then back at Rogaan. He appeared confident, for those not knowing him well, but Rogaan saw something in Kantus' eyes he did not expect…uncertainty. Confidence grew and rippled through Rogaan. Two against four. Outnumbered. Nothing had changed. Rogaan did not care about the odds as he readied himself for their assault. It was time for this fight…for her honor.

"Younglins," Suhd scolded as she wedged herself between Pax and Kantus then pushed them apart with an effort. She shot Rogaan a glance that could have chilled a wyrmm. "No fightin'. Not here. Not today." She turned her determined blue gaze on her brother, holding his eyes for several moments before Pax backed down, reluctantly.

"Saved by *little* one," Kantus taunted Pax over Suhd's hat. It almost came to his chin. A flash of relief showed on Kantus' face before regaining its usual smugness.

"And you...son of *Dubsa'Sauru'Saar*," Suhd said slowly, pronouncing her words carefully. Being the youngest among everyone, her scolding was out of place yet accentuated as she craned her neck to stare up defiantly at Kantus. "What a good example you be for *little* ones?"

Kantus took pause at Suhd's words then looked with thoughts to strike her as contempt contorted his face. A surge of prickles racked Rogaan's body, giving him the shakes. He suddenly felt deeply unsettled, atop his bristling concern for Suhd and anger at Kantus. His vision blurred then sharpened so finely that he thought he could see the whiskers and sweat on Kantus' face. Rogaan felt light-headed, his stomach near sicking-up, and the hairs on his nape bristled until they became painful. Everything around him stood out vibrantly while seeming to move slower than expected. Staring at Suhd and Kantus, Rogaan felt confused and disoriented and did not know why. He shook his head trying to clear the feeling of being distant and somehow separated from his surroundings. His head shaking helped a little. He tried again, but could not rid himself of the feeling that he was watching a dream. Slowly, unnaturally so, Kantus stepped closer to Suhd, his intent unknown. Rogaan resolved himself to protect Suhd no matter the consequences or his condition. *Surely, Father will understand.*

"Well," Lady Eriskla's flirtatious voice chimed, drawing everyone's attention. She wore a fine dress of blue that clung to her slim figure as she approached. Lace trimmed her high neckline, elbows, and hem, complementing the pearl buttons gracing the front of her dress. The younglings of the Band stood staring at her with stunned, even dumb looks, not knowing how to respond. With a few graceful steps around several of the Band, she settled herself into the middle of them, next to Suhd. "What a lovely dress you are wearing, Suhd. And you Kantus, you look so dashing in that hunter's outfit. Did your father have it made for you for this season's hunts?" Lady Eriskla, daughter to House Isin, stood no taller than Suhd, yet her presence overwhelmed everyone and seamed somehow to compel all eyes to pay her attention. Her blue ankle-high, tanned hide sandals danced over the paving stones as she wove her way around the four of them lightly touching each on their chins or shoulders while gazing directly at their faces with unblinking green eyes outlined in black. A trail of flower scent followed her, filling their senses as she glided about. Lady Eriskla's yellow mid-back hair swayed gracefully under a blue sunhat decorated with red and yellow flower petals. Jewels of blue, red, and yellow sparkled from her necklace and several rings on each hand. Attractive lines betraying her age creased her brown face at the edges. She looked every bit a sister to Rogaan's own mother, though a little older.

All things returned to normal for Rogaan. Everyone moved normally, his dizziness faded, and his stomach grumbled, but he no longer felt sick or slow of wit or confused. He certainly disliked how he had felt a few moments ago, and wished never to feel that way again.

Rogaan returned his attention to those before him, noticing Kantus stood taken aback, his mouth slung open. He seemed unprepared for someone interfering with his enjoyment of a good taunt. He gathered himself and composed his face in a mask of sternness before he spoke. "Ah...well...yes...Lady Eriskla." Kantus fumbled his words, causing his cheeks to darken and his eyes to grow angrier. "He commissioned its making from a famed armor-maker in Farratum. It's of the finest *tanniyn* and will wear well."

"I am certain it will," Lady Eriskla agreed with a suppressed smile. "If I may, I have some matters to talk over with your friends. You won't mind, will you, if I impose upon them a moment?" Her request, though polite, was more a demand, it seemed to Rogaan, but Kantus nodded his approval, despite the challenge she had made to him, and then he agreed only after a moment of hesitation. "I did not think you would. Good dawn, young Kantus."

She looked to his companions, the Band, with a practiced smile that could win over a king or send you scared for what was to come. "And...good day to all of you, younglings. Suhd, Pax, Rogaan, please accompany me. I have questions."

Suhd hopped at Lady Eriskla's words, with a relieved expression. Pax looked at Kantus with narrowed eyes before following Suhd. Rogaan stepped cautiously by Kantus, half-expecting him to take a coward's punch. Nothing happened, to Rogaan's disappointment and relief. Rogaan joined the three a short distance from a brooding Kantus. As custom was in this region, younglings did not address a lady before she spoke to them first. Eriskla remained silent for a short while as she inspected the three of them head to sandal, then looked back at Kantus and his Band now scuffing their way to the meat house, mumbling and complaining to each other. Within blade distance, Lady Eriskla's armed escort stood, an almost big, black-haired man wearing a well-made tunic and breeches of dark-brown hide. The man kept his hand on the hilt of his long-knife buckled to his belt, and he looked to be watching everything with the intensity of a *leaper* spying prey.

"That was...*interesting*." Lady Eriskla spoke plainly, almost too plainly for her station. Her eyes focused on Suhd, and her tone turned to a scolding. "And what did you think to accomplish, lass, by getting in the middle of those young bulls?"

"I...I..." Suhd stuttered with darkening cheeks, and her eyes seeking her feet. "I did no want Pax or Rogaan ta be hurt. Kantus be a brute, especially with da Band of his." She looked at Pax with watery eyes. "He hurt ya bad da last time ya scuffled."

"I do not think it would have been Pax or Rogaan that would have gotten the worst of it," Lady Eriskla stated while glancing at Rogaan. "Your intentions were admirable, lass, but misplaced. Stay out of the way of the young horns when they are about to knock their wits out, otherwise you may also get hurt." Lady Eriskla then turned her attention and stern gaze on Pax.

"And you," Lady Eriskla scolded while fixing her gaze on Pax. "You are Rogaan's friend, or at least pretend to be. Protecting your sister's honor was something I had not expected of you, but then you always seem to be full of surprises. Regardless, you know of Rogaan's promise to his father. You should have found spine enough and the wits to avoid a *scuffle*." She held up her right hand to silence Pax, who had a protest on his lips. He stood with opened mouth a few moments before biting back the words he planned to speak.

Lady Eriskla then turned her full attention on Rogaan, with stern eyes that made him shiver. "Rogaan. Breaking your promise to your father holds consequences you are not aware of. Up till now you have shown yourself worthy of your father's *Zagdu-i-Kuzu*." Rogaan's jaw slacked open at her boldness and knowledge. "Do not be so surprised. Your mother speaks much to me, despite hard feelings within the *House*. Maybe I should speak to Mithraam to postpone the ceremony until you prove yourself more worthy of it."

"That won't be necessary," Rogaan replied with a grumble while finding his mid-calf *tanniyn*-hide boots to stare at. "I will honor my promise and avoid dishonor for the family. I just wish someone would put Kantus in his box. He...."

"Kantus," Lady Eriskla interrupted, "...is not your greatest concern. He is a pebble in your boot to be emptied and discarded when you understand this." Rogaan regarded Lady Eriskla with confusion. She continued, "Stop minding Kantus, Rogaan. What I want to discuss with you, I must do in private."

Pax and Suhd retreated several steps at Lady Eriskla's expectant gaze. She turned to talk with Rogaan so nobody would be able to hear her words. "Do you know of where your father travels?"

"No," Rogaan replied, shaking his head. Had she been waiting here to talk to him about his father? It was not usual for persons of station to be about this early, leaving Rogaan to conclude that more was happening than he knew. Rogaan decided to answer honestly. After all, Lady Eriskla had always treated him well and fairly, despite the circumstances over the family spat…which he still did not understand as well as he wished. Maybe she could enlighten him if he worked his words just right? "He said nothing of his destination, though he looked to be dressed to travel beyond Brigum. Why? What is …?"

"I am uncertain." Lady Eriskla cut him off, though with a calm casualness. She paused, considering her words before continuing. "Many rumors fill the streets and halls. Rumors of war with the *Tellens*, of war parties in the Borderlands, of the Farratum *Anubda'Ner* march for Brigum, and farther…."

"The *Anubda'Ner*," Rogaan repeated excitedly, and a little too loud at that, by the way Lady Eriskla speared him with her blazing green eyes. Rogaan suffered a strong shiver before clamping his mouth shut in a brood, wondering at her harsh reaction. Why would she not want him to speak too loudly of the region's protectors? He recalled his readings of Shuruppak's rebuilding and its new laws that came about from the long *War of the Houses* some thirty years ago. Most of his reading was from his father's library and included the titles *Shuruppak's Proclamation of the Govern* and *Reconstruction* and *Commoner Revolt of 2612, The Challenge of Houses,* and *Shuruppak by Sword and Spear.* Now only a distant memory for many on the streets, Shuruppak's civil war reshaped the ruling houses, lessening their hold on the *People*, and brought rise to Shuruppak's force of arms as protectors of the *People* instead of as hands of the Emperor and some of the more powerful Houses' whimsical desires. Words of such times in the streets and pubs in Brigum were few. Rogaan suspected, though was uncertain, that so little talk was due to the town having been largely untouched in the struggle.

The *Anubda'Ner*, in the remade nation, were given charge as guardians of Shuruppak's city-states, defending each region's capital city, towns, and villages from Turil to the west and all other invaders. The *Anubda'Ner* were remade to serve the will of the *Anubda'Zas*, the

Houses of Laws…the *Me*, those chosen by the *People* of each region to represent them instead of being beholden to the Emperor or the Houses. The *Tusaa'Ner*, local guardians of towns and villages, and the *Kiuri'Ner*, protectors of the outer walls and roadways, all answered to their regional *Anubda'Ner* and local Councils. Now, the *Anubda'Ner* on the march for Brigum was a sign not of a matter of laws, but of invasion from…Turil, Rogaan feared with a growing lump in his throat.

"Hold your tongue, young Rogaan," Lady Eriskla scolded. She glanced about, looking for something, but seemed not to find it, which allowed her to relax, slightly. Pax and Suhd only stared at Rogaan, as if he had just grown horns. They must have heard him. The crowd about the Meat House was thinning, as hunters left their families and friends and started to assemble inside the building for the Hunt Talk. "It's only rumor, but I fear, if true to be, their arrival in Brigum would hold greater meaning for this land and possibly peril for your father. I came to give my sister warning, and learned of your father's plans for secretive travels."

Stiffening her back, she continued in a casual, almost resigned manner. "It will be what it will be, regardless. You need to take leave of me to avoid being denied what you have wanted for so long. Say nothing of what we have discussed, and remember your promise. Dishonor upon your father's name also brings dishonor upon House Isin. That…would be unwise."

Lady Eriskla whirled away without ceremony, her skirt rising like a sun-shade, then settling before she glided off in the direction of Rogaan's home, with her escort a pace behind. Always a gossiper, often meddlesome, his mother's older sister usually had an ear for the tiniest rumors, and a gift for making herself involved, even where others did not wish her to be.

"The *Anubda'Ner*," Rogaan mused with a smile, before turning for the Meat House, collecting Pax and Suhd on his way. Pax immediately started questioning Rogaan, pressing him to reveal what he and

Lady Eriskla talked of, with Rogaan revealing nothing of importance. Suhd kept silent, but Rogaan felt her eyes on him, making him uncomfortable, especially since he could only guess at her thoughts and hoped they favored him. Fortunately for Rogaan, the walk was short to their joining with the last of the hunters shuffling through the main door of the plain stone building. Suhd quickly said her goodbyes and well-wishes to Pax, with a hug and a sisterly kiss on the cheek. She then awkwardly offered Rogaan a bashful smile and unsettled glances that brought a tinge of heat to Rogaan's cheeks, and knots to his innards. She retreated from them, walking westward, toward her home. Rogaan stood, mouth a little agape, lost in watching the sway of her backside until a sharp nudge in the side drew his attention to a grinning Pax, who was motioning him toward the door.

As they entered the Meat House, the stench of blood struck Rogaan powerfully, repelling him backward, almost driving him back outside before he staggered to a stopped on unsteady feet. His head spinning as his legs went weak, Rogaan struggled to keep his feet. A distant voice called to him, an echo -- from where, he could not tell. The words were too garbled to understand. Rogaan felt the urge to sick-up as he fought to keep his feet. With hands now on knees to steady himself, and head low, Rogaan sucked in short then deep breaths to clear his head, and with it the swirling dizziness.

"What be illin' ya?" Pax asked concern thick in his voice.

"Do not know," Rogaan replied. "I just went wobbly." With an effort, Rogaan willed himself upright struggling to take calm, deep breaths. His head started to clear and his roiling guts settled despite the pungent stench that still wafted around him. Determined to join the Hunt, Rogaan pushed on with a wrinkled nose and short, shallow breaths.

The Meat House's main work area had paving stones like those of the streets outside, only much larger, nearly all stained dark with the blood of countless animals. The powerful stench made it difficult for

Rogaan to think of anything more than to take short, shallow, controlled gasps, though he managed a quick glance around in between breaths. To his relief, nobody looked his way. Common folk dressed in everything from plain tunics to hide armor that had seen better days were either talking to those closest or silently standing, many covering their faces with hand or sleeve trying to keep the pungent odor away and maybe not sick-up. The room smelled of blood from slaughter that filled the town's cook pots and spits. Even Pax's face, half covered by his hands, was a shade off its usual brown.

By Rogaan's count, a bit more than fifty hunters and helpers filled the room, many just waiting for something to happen, but some talking, boasting, telling tales, or looking about seeming to measure others. Whether silent or not, most in the crowd looked to the raised area at the far end of the high-roofed, stone-walled room with varying degrees of anticipation. With forced concentration, Rogaan looked for and felt relief that Kantus and his Band were nowhere to be seen.

"It always smells as bad," Pax informed Rogaan. "I come here sometimes when we be good on coin. Ma no like spoiled meat from da street if she not have ta."

"Mother gets our meat from this place," Rogaan confessed, while trying to keep from gagging. Despite his battle with the stench, he felt his cheeks heat a bit and he cast his eyes down from long held guilt for not helping her more. "I have not been inside here for some time, and do not care if I ever come again."

The din of the crowd quieted suddenly, drawing Rogaan's attention up from the floor. He swiveled his head left and right, seeking what the crowd was reacting to, but became dizzy, forcing him to cast his eyes down, again, in the hope that it would make the world stop spinning. After a few controlled breaths he felt strong enough to look up, slowly. Rogaan's stomach growled at him. The crowd was looking at three *Baraans* on the raised platform, all standing like statues. Each wore red-brown *tanniyn* hide *eur* armor with layered shoulder, outer thigh and chest plates, and stout rib straps securing the armor in place. Under their armor, dark charcoal tunics were secured at their waists by wide olive belts visible between chest and hip armor, each with red and yellow front tails, signifying Brigum's colors. Attached to their belts were triple-layered *tanniyn*-hide hip guards, protecting their upper thighs. The big *Baraan* wore *tanniyn*-hide wrist guards and thin headbands holding down their hair, each decorated with feathers. Their powerful arms and lower legs were bare, except for markings Rogaan could not make out in any detail. Short bows, quivers filled with feather-fletched arrows, and sword pommels stood high on their backs. Long spears, held in left hands, stood firmly planted to the platform with blades pointed high. Clean-shaven, unflinching faces bore expressions Rogaan could describe only as brewing storms, with hawking eyes sweeping the crowd, taking in everything and everyone. The Wing and Eye markings on the right sides of their faces were plainly visible with the hair of all three *Baraan*, two dark and one sandy-colored, pulled back into tails. Two of the three were no taller than Rogaan -- he sized them up as best he could -- and lean, though the sandy-haired man in the center stood more than a head taller than the others, and was broader in chest and shoulders, and much more heavily muscled. They were the *Kiuri'Ner*: three of five master protectors of Brigum and the surrounding lands. Despite his best attempts over the years, Rogaan never was able to get closer to these three before today. An unexpected shiver of awe rattled Rogaan as he looked upon what he wished to be.

The crowd fell silent at the raised hand of the largest *Kiuri'Ner*. Firik Umsadaa, best known and most successful of Brigum's *sharur*, the beast hunters, dressed in stout brown and black hide armor that fit him perfectly, climbed the steps before taking a place in front of the *Kiuri'Ner*. Firik stood silent for a long moment as he surveyed the crowd with an intense, scrutinizing gaze. A tall, lean man, almost as tall as the *Kiuri'Ner* standing behind him, Firik wore a short beard and tightly knotted top hair of black, each touched with gray. Long knives with simple hide handles hung from his wide black belt, which looked worn of use. Dangling around his neck hung a necklace of claws and teeth. Rogaan assumed them trophies of hunts past. The *sharur* had the look and attitude of what Rogaan imagined a commander of a guardsmen troupe, a *sakal*, would be, addressing his warriors before a desperate and important battle.

"What a wretched and ragged bunch of wish-to-be hunters," Firik insulted as he swept his disgusted gaze across the crowd. A murmur rose. Rogaan made out some of it, grumbles and curses of those closest, and it was obvious many did not like Firik. "Dubsa Jir again chose me Master of Hunt. For all that last hunted for me and failed, you're to leave…now."

The room fell silent, with most nervously looking at others to see who would leave. A murmur rose, quickly turning to a clamor, with several *Baraan* shouting curses at Firik with fists raised. Firik stood like a stone, watching them as they accused him of things in past hunts that Rogaan did not understand. Firik remained unmoved, with only his blazing stare a response. The disgruntled folk, shouting and accusing done with only Firik's gaze showing any recognition of them, now faced the blazing stares of the *Kiuri'Ner* as well. With a few final curses they reluctantly made their way through the crowd and retreated out the door, all the while grumbling.

"For the rest of you," Firik arrogantly addressed the crowd. "Listen and obey. No charity will be given to those who fail the Hunt, and especially for those who bring harm to the Hunt Party. Darkness hungers for us in the lands to the east. Only those with courage and obedience to command will survive. Those disobeying my commands or cowering in the face of our prey will not survive me…if they survive tooth and claw. Heed my commands and that of the *Kiuri'Ner* and your success is assured." Firik surveyed the crowd, again, with his intense gaze of judgment. When Firik's eyes looked upon Rogaan, he felt the *sharur's* stare bore through him, personally weighing and measuring him. It was unnerving. From the murmur and scuffling of feet in the room, it seemed to Rogaan that everyone shared his discomfort, except for the long moment when those eyes rested on him and only him. Firik stepped to the side of the platform as he gestured to the largest of the *Kiuri'Ner*.

"Kardul," Firik announced, "will assign and arm each of you as he sees fit. He is a master of the Wilds and leader of Brigum's *Kiuri'Ner*. You will pay him the respect he well commands."

Kardul stepped forward and stood large and in charge. "You'll sleep and hunt with only that which you carry. No room will be spared in the wagons for anything more than supplies of camp and our kills. I'll set you to hunting groups after arming at the wagons outside Hunter's Gate. We'll head east for a day to the Valley of the Claw, where we'll be several days hunting large prey. We'll return on the fourth day, successful in our hunt. Those felling the largest beast will win the favor of the Master of the Hunt, the *Kiuri'Ner*, and all in Brigum. Those failing a kill won't be welcomed in the next hunt. Now, make way to the wagons. We leave immediately."

Firik and the three *Kiuri'Ner* stepped from the platform and disappeared from Rogaan's sight as the crowd shuffled their way to the door, pushing, shoving, and cursing. Rogaan sought Pax and found him several persons ahead, being pushed along with the throng. Rogaan fought the crowd at first, receiving curses from those closest, before resigning himself to move with it. He was almost to the door when someone grabbed from behind, pulling him off balance before he could catch his feet. Rogaan pulled free with an angry grunt then whirled, looking for who had grabbed him. Kantus stood before him, smiling and obviously pleased with himself.

"Fight and you'll *fall* in favor, Rogaan." Kantus smirked and wagged his finger.

"A fight started by your hand, Kantus," Rogaan growled in cold anger. Frustrated and angry at Kantus' ever-present nits and jabs, Rogaan wanted badly to strike out, but instead resisted the powerful urge, convincing himself that he had more important things to tend – mostly not failing in the hunt and losing his chance with the *Kiuri'Ner*...and not dishonoring his family name. Kantus had made a life of irritating Rogaan with petty insults and pranks. It seemed at times that was all he and his Band had a taste and want for. Now, he and Kantus stood nose-to-nose, staring unblinkingly and sparing little hatred between them as the crowd pressed and pushed them toward the door, despite their best attempts to hold their ground.

"Get on!" Kantus provoked while struggling to keep his feet. "Swing your best, Rogaan. You're a coward and unwanted half-breed in town. My town. Go back to that rock of a place where you and your father crawled from."

Anger grew in Rogaan until it became almost blinding. His fists reflexively balled tight as his arms and chest shook with the lust to strike smug Kantus where he stood, to smash his teeth. Unexpectedly, the crisp and pungent odors of the slaughterhouse filled his nose, staggering him momentarily, while all about him colors and details sharpened and everyone around seemed to slow. Rogaan's heart beat loudly in his ears...strong and paced, not racing. Swirling air currents prickled his neck almost painfully as his blood ran hot – hotter than he ever remembered -- and he grew deeply aware of everyone and everything around him. Again he suffered a growing confusion, dizziness, and the need to sick-up. Wanting to pounce, but feeling not in the condition to do so, Rogaan weighed the scales, balancing satisfying his blood lust, his long desire for revenge for everything Kantus had ever done to him against losing consideration by the *Kiuri'Ner* and bringing dishonor to his father's name and his mother's family. Satisfaction...oh, Rogaan wanted it so. He battled his rage and repressed lust for a fight through his dulled wits and dizziness. Struggling within himself, he regained his reason and considered...duty...duty to his family. Reluctantly, he forced himself calm, cooling his emotions.

Almost immediately, the world became less…less vibrant, less alive, less familiar than a moment before. The dizziness and sick feeling were gone, replaced by hunger. Oh, Rogaan hated this *thing* that was gripping him. It frightened him that he did not know what was happening or why it was happening. He wanted it never to return. A distant voice caught Rogaan's attention and he looked up, finding Kantus with a set jaw staring him down. Dismissing all else, he focused on his nemesis, Kantus. The insufferable Kantus…was… "a pebble." *Only a pebble,* he told himself. "I will not scuffle, Kantus. Not here. Not now."

"Coward!" Kantus pushed back at the crowd until only Rogaan could hear his words. "Soon enough you will be nothing but a memory."

"What?" Rogaan asked, confused. He grabbed Kantus' chest plate at the sides to ensure he could not get away. He wanted answers. *A memory?* A powerful hand grabbed Rogaan's left arm, pulling him from Kantus more easily than he thought possible. Rogaan fought being dragged, stalemating mostly, but lost his footing and found himself outside the Meat House doorway before he was able to find his feet. Digging in hard with his boots, he slowed to a halt. Frustrated and angered at the boldness, Rogaan twisted to see who dared to handle him. He found the deeply gouged chest plates of red-brown *tanniyn* hide *eur* armor staring back at him. The strong odor of sweat and old blood filled his nose, causing it to wrinkle. Looking up, Rogaan found the brown, clean-shaven, stony face of Kardul.

"What trouble are you making?" Kardul demanded in a deep, mocking voice, hinted with anger.

The *Kiuri'Ner's* grip held him firm as Rogaan attempted to stammer a response, with few words intelligent or recognizable rolling off his tongue. This was not how Rogaan imagined his first meeting with the leader of the group he so much aspired to join. In fact, this could not have been further from any of Rogaan's expectations. Realizing everything he hoped for was unraveling in the moment, Rogaan stopped struggling against the giant's iron grip and looked squarely into the man's hazel eyes, which were filled with what Rogaan could describe only as deadly intent. Rogaan thought of speaking truthfully, telling the *Kiuri'Ner* that Kantus was a spoiled and privileged youngling, arrogant, full of himself, and more than a trouble, but he reconsidered when the *Kiuri'Ner's* stony face changed to a building thunderhead. Thinking fast and hoping not to deepen his troubles, Rogaan spoke. "I am not making trouble, *Kiuri'Ner*. Kantus and I were...making a wager."

"A wager?" Kardul repeated skeptically while eyeing both Rogaan and Kantus. "A wager on *my* Hunt better not cause trouble, or you two will be striped and worse."

"No trouble, Master *Kiuri'Ner*," Kantus broke in with a smile that made the hairs on Rogaan's neck bristle. Kantus was up to something. Rogaan saw it in his eyes and heard it in his voice. "We...were wagering who will take down the largest and most dangerous beast."

The *Kiuri'Ner* kept silent while continuing to scrutinize them with his intense gaze. Rogaan felt the man's grip lessen, then fall away from his arm. The *Kiuri'Ner* looked back at Rogaan with an amused smile of slightly yellow teeth. "Then a wager it is. You're that half-*Tellen* youngling the Wall Guards have spoken of? I look forward to seeing your 'famed' skills with the bow. You'll be with me on the Hunt. Don't show late to the wagons."

Without further discussion, Kardul turned in the direction of Hunter's Gate. Rogaan stood stunned. *He knew of me.* This was the opportunity he had been hoping for. Rogaan's thoughts raced as he struggled to keep his emotions under control. He needed success.

"What about me?" Kantus asked after the *Kiuri'Ner*.

"What about you?" Kardul replied flatly, without looking back or breaking stride.

Rogaan looked to Kantus, who stood next to him with mouth agape and an inner fire blazing. Rogaan smiled. A pebble. Kantus narrowed his eyes and set his jaw full of clenched teeth.

"Remember my words, Rogaan," Kantus grumbled coldly while watching the *Kiuri'Ner* walk away. "You'll be a memory soon enough." Without allowing Rogaan to get a word out, Kantus bolted in the direction of his Band.

"What be happenin'?" Pax asked, joining Rogaan as quickly as Kantus left. "I thought ya goin' ta put Kantus in da stones. Wished ya had. Then da master giant grabbed ya and now we have ta hunt with da brute. Ya know how ta make a day bad."

"No, Pax," Rogaan answered, hopeful. "Not bad. A change of fortune…finally. I will meet you at the wagons. First, I need to get something."

Chapter 3

Shunir'ra

F illed with hope and excitement, Rogaan bounded to take what he believed his best chance at gaining acceptance of the *Kiuri'Ner*. His father's words nagged at him for reason, responsibility, caution, obedience...they went unheeded. This was his chance. With hope springing in each stride, Rogaan sprinted past the old cedar guardian at the north side of his house and bounded through the flower-filled courtyard at the back, not stopping until he stood before the smithy's steel-bound heavy wooden door at the south side of the building. He produced a key he carried around his neck and quickly opened the door, then slipped into darkness. He sighed heavily with relief that his mother did not spy his passing then suffered a terrible shudder...darkness.

The scent of old burnt charcoal mixed with sulfur struck his wrinkling nose as he trembled. He closed his eyes for a long moment to regain himself, but the smell of the darkness invoked images in his head. Fond memories of him working with his father were replaced with images of his burning arm and shirt and hands reaching for him from the shadows. Rogaan's heart raced and his skin prickled. Fearing unseen things, he snapped open his eyes to deep shadows...no longer total darkness. He fought to get control of his breathing. His heart would follow. The urge to sneeze built quickly and he fought it back, as it always happened when he entered the smithy, giving him a sense of comfort at the regular rhythm of things. A few more moments passed, allowing his eyes to better adjust to the darkness. Rogaan's heart slowed. He was mastering himself. His father's voice then rang in his head, again, demanding his obedience and to leave without it. Rogaan fought with himself for a long moment with an overwhelming feeling of guilt. *What to do? This might be my only chance!* No, he would not leave without it.

Putting his weight on the door at his back saw a sliver of light come from the doorway allowing Rogaan to make out the familiar interior of the smithy. Some seven strides wide and seventeen long, the neatly organized smithy was as he remembered, with an oven and forge set against the right wall, and tools along both. His father demanded order, and he *always* got what he wanted where the smithy was concerned. Hammers, tongs, files, and other tools hung on the wall closest to the forge, with a fan bellows attached to the oven, all in place to serve their purposes. A long wood cooling trough filled with water, stacks of wood, and several large barrels of black rock used to fire raw iron and other metals sat on the floor to Rogaan's right. The left wall was lined with shelves full of copper and iron ores, and worked ingots of metal. The shelves on the right wall beyond the forge were sparsely populated with finished works of cooking pots and tools of different kinds, and several weapons, including a short sword and long spear that Rogaan had a hand in making. Pride swelled within him at the thought of having made the blades of both weapons. His father had insisted he make them despite Rogaan's insistence that the buyer would refuse the workmanship because it was not of his father. After some of his father's usual rough talk, and some arguing that seemed to come more easily as Rogaan got older, he made the blades. His father seemed satisfied enough with his work, despite it taking him longer to finish than his father had expected.

Rogaan shook off the past and tried to focus on the present. This was his chance. The *Kiuri'Ner*. "Do not fail," he told himself. He looked to the shelf of finished items beyond the forge, where he left what he had come for. His cased *shunir'ra* was gone. "Where…?" Panic seized him, surged through him. Then after a few moments of wild-eyed searching in the unnerving shadows and finding things as they should be…all except his *shunir'ra*, he regained control of himself well enough to start thinking. Almost frantic in his search, and forgetting stealth, Rogaan searched the shelves, crates, boxes, corners...nothing. The search left him frustrated and the smithy in disorder. Rogaan wondered if his father had taken his *shunir'ra* on his travels or had secreted it away to remove any temptation on his part.

Determined, Rogaan pressed on, looking to the floor next to the forge where his father sometimes stored valuable items and works. He hastily lifted the heavy flagstone and peered inside. Darkness. The unknown. Uneasy of it, he groped deep into the storage area, hoping to find it. He grabbed on to something, but disappointingly, it did not feel like his *shunir'ra*. He pulled out a cloth-wrapped bundle...too small to be it. Curious, Rogaan unwrapped the object, finding his father's rod-shaped *Tellen* talisman, the *imur'gisa*. The talisman had been in the family, his father claimed, since the dawn of the Fourth Age, and had a history that Rogaan could not recall. In the gloom, the gold and platinum rod shone almost as if by its own light, and the encrusted gems sparkled as if light came from within them. It was beautiful and mesmerizing, more so the longer Rogaan looked upon it.

Rogaan had caught a glimpse of the talisman once, many years before, when those of his father's Turil Clan visited. It was a strange gathering with talk and ceremonies Rogaan failed to understand then or since, and his father never offered more about it all. They left the rod in his father's care. Since then, the talisman had been forgotten and never spoken of in the house. The *imur'gisa* was of the finest craftsmanship, superior to his father's own, if that was possible, with metal that seemed to flow around the encrusted gems with the largest and most impressive gem, a black one, at the top of the talisman. Inscriptions and symbols covered its surface, all unfamiliar to Rogaan. With a start, Rogaan cursed himself for wasting valuable time. The wagons.... "Cannot be late." He had to find his *shunir'ra* and get to the wagons before they left for the Wilds. He quickly rewrapped the talisman and stuffed it back in its hiding place with a hollow clunk when it struck the bottom stone. Curious, Rogaan lifted the bottom stone, revealing a second hiding place he never knew existed. In it he found an elongated black and tan hide case he was familiar with. Retrieving the half-stride-long object, he sighed loudly in relief...his *shunir'ra*. Rogaan quickly checked to make sure everything was as he had left it in the case. All was as he remembered. Replacing the stones, *imur'gisa*, and hastily returning most of everything he ransacked back in its place, he ran for Hunter's Gate.

Rogaan took the quickest path to the gathering he knew. He ran south past the Hall of Council with its column-shaped trees fencing in a groomed courtyard and winding flowerbeds of reds, yellows, and more colors surrounding a central fountain. Low, flat roofed buildings made of cut stone dominated the center of the courtyard. The Town Council decided the affairs of Brigum within those walls.

Rogaan turned sharply left onto well-worn paving stones of the East Road now thick with the morning's cart traffic of traders and merchants preparing for their daily ritual of selling and buying and town caretakers cleaning the streets. Two and three-story buildings of mortared stone and brick lined both sides of the street, with some plastered over in tans. Merchant stands stood in front of many, with goods being readied for anyone with coin. A few heavily burdened canvas-covered wagons were pulled by squat, four-legged, *tanniyn niisku,* beasts sporting stubbed horns and frills of blue and yellow, and with bony-plated backs and stubby plated tails. They made their way toward the town's center market, south of the Hall of Council. Running in the opposite direction, Rogaan weaved through patches of people dressed in all manner of styles and colors, hurrying this way and that and around beasts, wagons, carts, and stands of foods and wares, most topped with awnings of reds, greens, and browns to shade away the coming day's sun.

"Cannot be late." The crush of people and beasts slowed him. He grew frustrated. Pushing and shoving, Rogaan broke free of throng after throng, finally able to launch into a full sprint toward the stables nearest Hunter's Gate. "Cannot be late." The pungent odor of dung grew stronger with each step as he came to fenced yards. Animal handlers within the timber fences worked stout two-horned *niisku* and leaner, longer-legged one-horn *sarigs*, and more stout *kydas*. *Sarigs* were the favored steeds of the *Kiuri'Ner*. *Kydas*, stouter forms of *sarigs*, were the steeds of choice for those with coin, and troupe commanders. They were sturdy animals, bred for endurance more than the speed *sarigs* were known for. The handlers somehow seemed unaffected by the stench, as Rogaan did his best not to breathe. Despite his best efforts, his guts turned as he passed the stables lining both sides of the road and several heavily laden carts of animal dung that were being prepared for travel by several unhappy workers. Rogaan hurried on.

At the east end of the stables, Rogaan entered the courtyard of Hunter's Gate. He did so with a sense of hope and relief, as he slowed to a brisk walk while looking for Pax. The courtyard was some thirty strides square, framed by an eight-stride-high stone and mortar wall of gray on his left, and a line of evenly spaced cedar trees to his right, separating the south-running Waterside Road from the cliff and river beyond. In between, a stone gatehouse stood with twin watchtowers topped by red-tiled coned roofs. The watchtowers stood some ten strides apart with massive cut-timber gate-doors, bound together by thick iron bands and stout bolts. The gate stood open allowing the last of the hunting party through to the stone bridge separating the main town of Brigum from Coiner Quarter, the well-to-do side of town.

A sense of foreboding taunted Rogaan. He dismissed it as his leeriness of the deep shadows hiding the mountain foothills ahead, beyond the safety of Brigum's walls. Looking for Pax, Rogaan quickly made his way across the stone courtyard with a sharp eye on the *Tusaa'Ner*, Watchers of Brigum, standing the walls and watchtowers dressed in their soft hide uniforms dyed sky-blue, and belt sashes of red with yellow stripes. All held spears grounded with shining blades pointing skyward. They watched all who passed, and made Rogaan feel uneasy when they turned their stares on him.

Rogaan sighed with relief when wagons and milling hunters came into view beyond the bridge ahead. He was not too late. Now, all he needed was Pax. Scanning the crowd, he found his friend shuffling slowly through the gate at the rear of a line of hunters, looking over this shoulder. Rogaan gave a quick wave then broke into a run to him. The *Tusaa'Ner* gave Rogaan only the slightest glance as he ran through the stone pillars of the gate. Rogaan came to a stop next to a grinning Pax in the middle of the gray stone bridge of Hunter's Gate.

Pax's grin widened as he bobbed his head about, looking at the hide case slung over Rogaan's pack. Without saying a word, Pax returned to his shuffling in line toward a rabble of hunters at the other end of the bridge, all awaiting the issue of weapons and equipment from *Baraan* standing in an open-top wagon. Rogaan followed Pax. He was eager to get on with the Hunt, and he *now* had all he needed. As he shuffled to the wagon he lost himself in visions of success and glory on the Hunt, with a massive beast felled by his bow…and the *Kiuri'Ner*, cheering and exalting him as the greatest *sharur* ever, and Kantus cast out of the Hunt in disgrace.

"Ouch!" Rogaan barked through gritted teeth at the sharp pain in his side. He snapped a look to find what or who hit him. He found Pax stepping back wide-eyed, not expecting Rogaan's reaction to an attention-getting jab. Surprising to Rogaan, they now stood much closer to the wagon than he expected. Rogaan opened his mouth to snarl unkind words at his friend, but was abruptly cut off.

"Well…." Kardul spoke while standing next to the wagon holding a wood bow, a quiver of arrows, and a curved long knife. He looked agitated. A dark-haired youngling in the wagon above continued to hand weapons to the other *Kiuri'Ners* who, in turn, issued them to the last of the Hunters. "Are you going to hunt or aren't you, stoner?"

"If I catch you dazing, again," Kardul threatened as he pointed a sheathed long knife at Rogaan's chest, "especially while hunting, I'll skin you alive and leave you to the Wilds." With agitation, Kardul tossed the bow, quiver, and long knife at Rogaan. Fumbling to catch all three, Rogaan twisted and turned and juggled, finally meeting success, but less gracefully than he had wanted. Another *Kiuri'Ner*, standing next to Kardul, tossed a long spear and another sheathed long knife at Pax, who managed to drop both. Rogaan felt badly for his friend as some of the hunters chuckled, though the *Kiuri'Ners* remained stone-faced.

Firik Umsadaa and the *Kiuri'Ner* began to bark orders for everyone to form up in loose columns at the sides of the wagons. Rogaan was relieved when Kantus and his Band stationed themselves in the column on the other side of the wagon...out of sight, and unable to do their usual taunting. Six wagons made up the caravan, stretching almost one hundred strides in all, each pulled by a single stout *ni-isku*. The lead wagon was open-topped and filled with supplies and folk to tend camp. Non-hunters sat on crates and sacks. Rogaan could only guess what filled them. Second in line was a high-topped hide canvas-covered wagon filled with cooking tools and supplies, followed by three low-sided wagons filled with sacks of what Rogaan believed to be salt from the smell of them -- and cutters, folk experienced in carving away the meat from *tanniyn* bones. The trailing wagon carried more folk: carriers, those with fewer smarts than muscle, to haul the meat the cutters stripped from the kills. Four *Baraan*; Firik Umsadaa and the three *Kiuri'Ner*, now sitting atop leanly built *sarigs*, briskly approached the front of the line. In their saddles, they appeared supremely confident, no...arrogant, Rogaan realized. At the command of Firik Umsadaa, the line of wagons lurched forward and the columns of armed hunters started their march, guarding the caravan's flanks.

The march to the Valley of the Claw started orderly, with the hunters keeping loose columns despite the grueling pace set by Firik and the *Kiuri'Ner*. The wagons snaked along a heavily rutted packed-dirt road, winding their way through low mountain passes and red-rock cliffs peppered with long-needled pines rising as high as thirty strides, wide broadleaf trees even taller, and cedars half their heights. Ferns, shrubs, and flowers abounded. The *niisku* seemed untouched by their burdens, keeping a steady pace in flats and hills alike. It was a sight to see, impressing Rogaan with their power and stamina. Small *feather-wings* flew about, but kept low to the trees, while the larger *leatherwings* patrolled the bright blue, cloudless sky of the morning and mid-day. Small green-feathered *tanniyn* darted about in the underbrush while keeping their distance from the caravan, occasionally chirping as wagons and people passed.

Rogaan caught glimpses of larger *tanniyn*, *leapers* he thought, during the morning, but they swiftly disappeared into the shadows of the forest like *daimons* before he could get a good look at them. In the late morning, Rogaan stepped into a hole at the side of the road, causing him to stumble, almost falling as fatigue started to make his footsteps a little less certain. When he looked back at the hole, he realized it was a rounded footprint almost a stride across and more than a hand deep. He spotted more footprints among the knee-high ferns leading into a large grove of tall broadleaf trees towering over shorter cedars and ferns, all had nearly half their limbs stripped of leaves or trampled flat to the ground. Rogaan felt a surge of fear and excitement as he looked for the animals that had left the tracks. His excitement soon faded as the march continued without the fortune of spotting one of these giants. His fear of the unknown Wilds stayed with him, at the edge of his thoughts.

The march continued without break into the late afternoon. Most of the hunters were wearily trudging, struggling to keep up with the wagons and those relentless *niisku* that somehow continued on at the same steady pace they had started with in the morning. Several of the hunters had recently collapsed. They were unceremoniously tossed into the back of the last wagon by other bone-weary hunters at the orders of Firik. The caravan did not slow in the least for those fallen, nor for those with the task of gathering them up. Still, some of the hunters, those at the front, showed little or no sign of fatigue from the day-long march. Rogaan had long since stopped looking at the countryside, instead concentrating on Pax's back almost three strides in front of him. Pax appeared to be struggling to keep pace with the wagons, shuffling his feet at times and sometimes tripping, but still able to keep his feet. Pax was stubborn and Rogaan doubted he would give Kantus the pleasure of seeing him lying on the ground, gasping for breath. Rumbles from Rogaan's innards reminded him that he had not eaten since the morning meal. He began to wonder how much longer they would march. *Dusk? Through the night? No. Surely they would not force a march through the night?* Rogaan feared asking, since he already felt certain of the answer. Despite wanting to join the Hunt since as long as he could remember, Rogaan found himself starting to reconsider his wants.

They marched on, right past Rogaan's evening meal time, causing his stomach to protest, loudly, almost with each step, but he stopped caring about it some time ago, and now focused only on wiping sweat from his eyes and placing one foot in front of the other. Dripping sweat and looking every bit exhausted, with a darkened, slung face, Pax starting falling off pace. Trudging, Pax pushed on, refusing to give up. Rogaan felt for his friend and admired his stubbornness, but occasionally needed to help him to keep up with the wagons and the other hunters. Tired, Rogaan surprisingly felt well enough to march on -- indefinitely, he thought -- while most about him appeared more like Pax. They marched on with their burdens getting heavier. Pax had been using his spear to keep upright since mid-afternoon; now it was all he could do just to drag it behind him.

They marched on. Rogaan found his thoughts wandering, with visions of Suhd popping into his head. He felt a smile grow at the vision of her sweet face, and especially of her walking away with her swaying backside, glancing over her shoulder at him from time to time. Rogaan bumped into something, causing him to stumble before catching his feet as Pax slipped from his supporting hand and collapsed to the ground with a thud. Rogaan looked about to see what he had struck. Another hunter, a grizzled, gray-bearded man in his middle years who had been walking ahead of him, was bent over with hands braced on knees, doing his best to not fall over.

A wave of panic washed over Rogaan, fear of being left behind. Looking around, Rogaan found the entire column halted, with most of the hunters bent over or sprawled on the ground. A sense of relief filled him as he exhaled strongly. Quickly, Rogaan stiffened his back, trying to look unaffected by the march. He wanted the *Kiuri'Ner* to see him undefeated and strong, but his body betrayed him when a stitch of pain racked his left side, forcing his hands to his knees.

"Not a poor showing, youngling," Kardul complimented from atop his *sarig*. Rogaan struggled to straighten himself and turned to face the *Kiuri'Ner*. He wanted to say something to impress Kardul, but nothing except for the desire to breathe came to him. Kardul smirked before urging his *sarig* up the column while shouting insults and orders. Rogaan frowned at Kardul's back. All he wanted was rest -- sleep, really, but he knew camp set-up would come first.

Chapter 4

Valley of the Claw

R ogaan woke with a sharp pain in his side. Grimacing, he rolled to stretch his ribs and rid himself of the cramping muscles, but managed only to toss off his blanket. Shivering against the chill air, and confused, Rogaan opened his eyes to see where he was. A lightless abyss engulfed him. Panic gripped his chest, jolting him upright, and his body shook visibly if anyone were to look. Darkness! Alone? Rogaan fought to regain his self-control, push away his panic by seeking something -- anything -- to focus his eyes on. Slowly a moonless valley came into poor focus in the gloomy pre-dawn. *I'm lost?* He caught sight of a dark figure approaching from out of deep shadows. *I must get hold of myself before anyone sees me!* Rogaan stared at the figure, trying to focus on the form as his heart wildly beat. *Focus. Breath.* Rogaan sucked in deep breaths and exhaled. His heart slowed. With his wits returning, he squinted at the person nearing, making out vague features... Kardul. Rogaan found himself exhaling so strongly with relief that it hurt.

"Rise time, youngling," Kardul ordered, too enthusiastically. "Day is wasting. Get yourself ready and be at the lead wagon before I get there. And wake that friend of yours. Get moving." Kardul slipped into the shadows and out of sight, without a sound. *How does such a big man manage that?* Rogaan wondered. Rogaan realized the pain in his side was gone, though the glee of being free of it was cut short by the darkness pressing in on him, again. At least distant cook fires were visible to push back the gloom, some. A small help, at least, for Rogaan in his battle. Using the breathing trick taught to him by his mother, he gained a little relief at first, but as he persevered he slowly started winning the struggle with himself. Rogaan further sought to distract himself by trying to remember anything of last night. Vague images of the camp flashed in his mind, but it all seemed a dream to him, now. Hoping Pax was awake and ready to talk, Rogaan looked for his friend and found him curled up under a blanket nearby, sound asleep, and snoring lightly, though his snoring was quiet compared to several others in camp.

"Wake up!" Rogaan shook Pax lightly. Pax responded by rolling onto his side with a few snorts. The darkness pressed in on Rogaan again. Forcing himself to ignore the lack of light and the a few buzzing *bloodsuckers*, Rogaan rose with a deliberate stretch, then rubbed his face, trying to fully wake up while pretending the darkness lifted. A small smile came to Rogaan before he kicked Pax's backside. "Wake up!"

Pax rolled and bounced up to his knees with a short knife in each hand. He glanced left, then right, looking for trouble, but only found Rogaan smiling back. "Why ya kickin' me?"

"Kardul ordered us to the lead wagon, with haste," Rogaan eagerly replied, eager to be with others in the dark and to get his first hunt started. Excited, he gathered his equipment, shoving things hastily into his carry pack, all the while trying to ignore the darkness that still pressed at him. Rogaan's muscles protested with every move, and with a stiffness he seldom experienced. The march yesterday really taxed him, as he was not used to it. Rogaan looked to see if Pax was up and moving. His friend was gathering equipment, but slower than Rogaan wished. "Hurry, Pax. I do not think Kardul will be understanding if he is made to wait."

"I be hungry," Pax complained. "Rogaan, do ya have any of da dried meat we made?"

"Yes," Rogaan replied in a questioning tone. "Why? Where is yours?"

Pax sat unmoving for a moment. He looked to be thinking -- about what, Rogaan could only guess. Days earlier they had dried enough meat strips to last each of them five days and then some. Rogaan had other rations packed too, mill bread and nuts, but little else. Pax looked to be struggling with words to speak. Unusual. "I have me a day of meat left."

"How?" Rogaan asked, not certain he had heard right.

"I had some before da Hunt," Pax sheepishly answered while returning his attention back to his equipment. "And...I had me some more yesterday. And...I gave some ta Suhd. Ya can no blame me for givin' me sister some?"

Rogaan groaned and rolled his eyes. No surprise at Pax's lack of preparation. Pax had a poor head when it came to planning and then sticking to the plan. With a slight chuckle, Rogaan tossed a day's ration of dried meat to his friend. "Try not to eat it all before mid-day -- and hope we kill us an eater, or we will both go hungry."

They quickly collected their things then made way to the wagon and Kardul. Rogaan walked nervously, the darkness continued pressing in on him with him fighting it back in his head, while vigorously scanning the path ahead for things, though he was not certain what. Not surprisingly, Pax was chewing a piece of dried meat as they walked. Rogaan felt his stomach rumble. The smell of wild herbs and meat on cook fires made Rogaan's stomach protest loudly several more times at his lack of eating, though he was more focused on seeing what was ahead. The fires they passed pushed back the darkness enough for Rogaan to make out forms of folk, beasts, and stacked equipment -- not perfectly focused, but enough to know where folks and things were and what folks were doing. All were quietly going about their morning rituals and chores, with the constant song of *hoppers* and buzzing *biters* drowning out conversations. Pax acted as if he saw everything just as well, but Rogaan knew better of his friend, who followed closely on his heels for reasons other than getting to Kardul.

The camp was laid out in an orderly way with the wagons forming a semi-circle on the far side. Bedrolls tucked under the wagon where the helpers slept were all now empty. *Niiskus* and *sarigs* were tethered at the far end of the wagon line, opposite the camp and cook fires -- downwind, mostly -- and Rogaan was thankful for it. The smell of the fires and cooking became more intense as they went, but did not completely cover up the odor of the tethered beasts. Ahead, a fire burned between the last two wagons closest to the animals, with a dozen or so hunters milling around it. All were talking and eating. Beyond, more folks surrounded another fire near the last wagon. Rogaan guessed Kardul was at the closer of the two. As they drew near, the smell of cooked meats and spiced drink made Rogaan's stomach ache and grumble all the more. No longer able to put his hunger out of his head, he pulled several strips of dried meat from his pocket and gobbled them down.

"You two didn't return to your tender dreams…good," Kardul, standing among the hunters, sardonically taunted. An attendant took a large wooden bowl from him then retired into the darkness between the wagons. Kardul wiped his mouth with the back of his hand then rubbed his hand on his armored thigh while eyeing Rogaan and Pax as they approached. "What have you hunted before today?"

Rogaan hesitated in answering. He felt his face heat in embarrassment that he had little in the way of real experience. Hesitantly, he opened his mouth to answer…honestly, but was cut off.

"I thought as much," Kardul flatly stated. Grabbing his spear and bow, he started off into the surreal dark landscape of the waking dawn. "Come along, you three. Maybe you'll learn something of the Wilds. Then again, maybe you won't live to see the sun at high."

Rogaan looked to Pax, who stood with a blank stare back at him. He then looked to find who this third was that Kardul spoke of. Nobody stood out except a middle-aged, grizzled gray-bearded hunter, whom Rogaan recalled seeing doubled over last night, and who stood quietly at the edge of the campfire light. The leanly built man had neatly combed black hair streaked with gray, and his face was that of stone, betraying nothing of his thoughts. He stood tall, almost as tall as Rogaan, with dark hide armor of a design unfamiliar to Rogaan, high-laced sandals, a short tan cloak, and a small carry-pack about his waist. A spear in his hand and a long knife secured to his wide belt were the only weapons Rogaan could see. The man stood quietly, studying Rogaan as if he were prey.

"What be he lookin' at?" Pax asked.

"Me, I think," Rogaan replied. He stared back at the hunter for long moments, hoping to learn something of him. The grizzled man just returned the stare without flinching, causing Rogaan to feel uneasy. "Gray-beard can do as he wishes. I want a kill to prove my worth to the *Kiuri'Ner*. Let's get traveling, Pax."

They set off after Kardul, who now was lost to their sight somewhere ahead -- Rogaan hoped he was ahead -- and for this darkness to be burnt away by the daylight. Not long after they set off at a trot to the northeast, Rogaan thought, the darkness did start giving way to the rays of the morning sun rising ahead. Pink wispy clouds became visible against a gray-blue sky above, as the songs of *featherwings* started overtaking those of the *hoppers*. Dark silhouettes of what Rogaan knew to be otherwise colorfully plumed *featherwings* sat in the top reaches of trees ranging from cone-shaped broadleafs ten strides tall to sporadic oval giants three times that. Dawn was about to break, and Rogaan felt great relief for it. They slowed to a walk as they passed through a grove of tall oaks and squat ferns, arriving on the other side at a cliff overlooking a deep dark expanse. Nothing of detail could be seen below. It was a void of blackness...the Pit of Kur. Rogaan's stomach turned and he feared for a moment he would be sick. A stick cracked somewhere behind, close. Rogaan spun around with his heart racing wildly and vision blurred, distorted. He almost lost his balance and fell over before he widened his stance a bit to steady himself. Out of the gloom strode gray-beard, confident and bold-stepping. The man watched Rogaan intently as he approached, stopping at the edge of the cliff as boldly as he walked. He kept silent.

"Who are you?" Rogaan asked cautiously.

"Of no concern to you," he replied flatly while scanning the darkness below, then the forest about them. The man seemed to look in all directions at once, and showed an awareness Rogaan had missed earlier. The hairs on the back of Rogaan's neck bristled when the nameless hunter glanced at him. An almost sneering glance from gray-beard, which Rogaan caught in the briefest of moments, just gave him the shivers.

"Ya no look like someone of no concern ta me," Pax spat, almost challengingly. The hunter showed no reaction to Pax's words, nor gave any indication that he even cared Pax existed.

Rogaan decided he wanted nothing of this intrigue. He wanted only to hunt and prove his worth to the *Kiuri'Ner*, and he was not going to make that happen if he and Pax were fighting with one of their hunting party. Resolved to not cause strife, Rogaan lightly grasped Pax's arm, then spoke. "What my friend is saying is that you look to be with much experience, and he wondered if you hunted before?"

"I did?" Pax asked Rogaan quizzically.

The hunter only tossed Rogaan a smirk then scanned the area around them again. Gray-beard then placed his hands on his hips -- more relaxed, but only slightly. Rogaan tried, but was not able to shake his uneasy feeling about the *Baraan*. Mystery and intrigue seemed to fill the air about him of late, and he found himself worrying about nearly everything. Another shiver passed as quickly as it came, as a slight breeze blew from the deep gloom below, carrying the heavy scent of fetid animal dung and rotting flesh. It caused Rogaan to wrinkle his nose at the strong stench. Pax placed his hand over his mouth and nose, while making a prolonged gag. Gray-beard only wrinkled his nose and blinked hard several times.

"That...younglings," Kardul's words came from just behind them.

"And, Akaal, is the scent of what we seek." Startled, Rogaan and Pax spun around to find Kardul and almost fell from the cliff. Rogaan's heart raced, though his head remained clear. Akaal remained calm, casually looking over his shoulder to acknowledge Kardul's presence.

Kardul stepped out of the shadows without making a sound. If Rogaan had not been looking, he would never have known the *Baraan* approached. The *Kiuri'Ner*'s sandaled footfalls passed over sticks and more, without a sound. He walked with a silence Rogaan continued to wonder at, and envied.

"I like your footfalls, youngling," Kardul complimented Pax with a stare, as if measuring him. "Slow and uneven, but you have some promise." Kardul passed by Rogaan, stopping at the cliff's edge. He stood silent, looking into the gloom far below. "We make camp on this plateau overlooking the Valley of the Claw to keep ourselves from everything but *leapers*, though they only sometimes climb the cliffs when their hunger drives them to it. Eight of the less-promising hunters are to be placed on the wagon trail and the several footpaths from down there as outlooks to alarm the camp if danger approaches. They'll sound their horns at any trouble and protect the wagons when they come to cut and carry our kills." Kardul looked at Rogaan, Pax, and Akaal in turn as if considering something, before continuing. "The valley is a day's walk across and three long, and is filled with nesting beasts of all kinds now. That means danger. The other *Kiuri'Ner* and Firik are leading hunters to different places in the valley, but all will stay near these cliffs. We enter the valley here by way of a footpath. So, take care where you put your feet. In the valley we'll work north and east then come back down the center of it. Danger will be all about us. The beasts own this land and are very protective of it. They're unforgiving, and roam about while there is light. Night is more dangerous. Don't seek glory. It'll make you careless...and one with the darkness. Now, follow and don't make a ruckus."

Silently they descended the narrow and uneven path to the valley below. With fingers clinging to rocks, branches, shrubs, and exposed roots of all kinds, Rogaan followed Kardul, Pax in turn followed Rogaan, and Akaal trailed the whole lot. Their descent was fast -- too fast for Rogaan at times. After his second slip and fall on slick or loose footing, Rogaan wanted to ask Kardul to slow, but feared it would make him look weak in the *Kiuri'Ner*'s eyes. Several of the times Pax lost his footing, Rogaan managed to catch him before he went tumbling off the cliff. Akaal was surprisingly agile and sure-footed, not slipping or falling even once that Rogaan knew. Rogaan had thought the old man to be a towner with little skill for the Wilds. He was unsure why he thought of Akaal that way, but it felt *right*, though what he observed betrayed his feelings. Not long down the cliff, Rogaan found himself focusing almost solely on his foot placement and what he could grab while holding his breath, often. Before he realized it, they had descended almost to the valley floor, just as the sun's golden rays broke over the mountains to the northeast. Kardul acted as if he were unaware of the breaking dawn, continuing his descent into the shadows below at a relentless pace. The scent of decay and animal dung grew stronger as they descended, causing Rogaan to wrinkle his nose at the wafting and sometimes overpowering odors carried on a light swirling wind. The gloomy blanket covering most of the valley gave way to the morning sun as they set foot on level ground. Deep shadows still hid much under the broken canopy of twenty strides tall trees and the whole valley seemed to come alive with their arrival. Deep reverberating bellows from *tanniyns*, squawks and chirps from *featherwings*, croaks and song from *hoppers*, and the steady buzz of *biters* and *bloodsuckers* filled the air. The ruckus helped mask their movements, the din drowning out many of their footfalls, and the occasional misstep.

Kardul quickly led them to a ravine, a stone's toss from the cliffs. The ravine spanned almost twenty strides wide, and from the gloom far below, the sound of flowing water could be heard. Not a large flow -- maybe a stream. Kardul motioned for them to follow then approached a massive fallen tree, over a stride and some wide that had fallen and bridged the two sides of the ravine. Kardul climbed the trunk and crossed to the other side without hesitating or faltering. Pax paused before climbing on the tree. He peered over the edge of the ravine, looking down to see how far he would fall, if he slipped. Cautiously, Rogaan joined his friend, looking into the gloomy depths with him. The darkness unsettled him, though the heights had little effect on him.

Trying to look all the part of confident, Rogaan shrugged at Pax after a few moments. Pax looked at Rogaan as if he did not believe the heights held not a bother for him, then slowly and carefully made his way across the ravine without slipping too often. With his heart pounding loudly in his ears, Rogaan paused, thinking of walking above so much empty air, the gloom below. He found himself unable to move at the image of falling into darkness, then being alone and in-jured within it deep below. Akaal cleared his throat impatiently, draw-ing Rogaan's attention and thoughts away from the replaying image in his mind. Rogaan gave Akaal a quizzical look, as if asking him why he was making the strange noise, and hoped it was enough to cover the true reason for his hesitation. All Akaal did was stare back at him with slightly raised eyebrows. Not wanting to be accused of being afraid, Rogaan swallowed hard then climbed the tree trunk. A flat walking path large enough for his feet seemed too narrow to his liking, but passable. Not wanting to look fearful to the *Kiuri'Ner*, Rogaan sucked in a deep breath, then took a step, then another, and then another -- all the time focusing on the tree beneath him until he found himself on solid ground on the opposite side of the dark expanse. Akaal quickly followed, appearing not to be bothered by the heights or the narrow tree bridge. Once they were together, Kardul hastily led them into the edge of the forest where they stopped for Kardul to listen to the wind or something else Rogaan did not hear.

Kardul stood motionless with chin held high, and eyes slits. He tilted his head several times then held still. Pax eventually threw up his hands in exasperation then sat on a large rock with less grace than it appeared he wanted. Akaal leaned casually against a pine tree as thick as himself. He seemed amused as he watched everyone. The man just unsettled Rogaan, and he did not know why.

"Don't rest," Kardul said quietly, but sharply enough that Rogaan's skin prickled with concern. "We must move quickly...quietly." Kardul was off, silently stepping into a large grove of thirty-stride-tall cone-shaped cedars and shorter, waist-high razor ferns. He moved like a shade through the ferns, subtly turning and twisting to pass without disturbing all that surrounded him. It looked a difficult thing to do, but it seemed natural for Kardul.

A rumbling roar reverberated throughout the forest -- then all went quiet, except for the buzzing *biters*. More than startled, frightened half out of his wits, Rogaan closed his eyes tightly, wishing away what he felt more than heard. After a few moments, Rogaan opened his eyes and quickly looked about to see what made the terrible bellow, but found Kardul staring at him with anger-filled eyes from a semi-concealed spot in the grove of trees ahead. Kardul motioned discreetly but urgently with his hand for Rogaan to follow.

Alarmed at Kardul's demeanor, Rogaan's heart began pounding hard, his hair stood on end, and his skin prickled. Everything came alive, vibrant and slow-moving. He suddenly became aware of the living things about him: plants and animals, brilliant details of all and overpowering to his nose. Rogaan's throat and chest tightened such that he could not breathe. Rogaan did not understand what was happening to him, and it frightened him almost to panic. Quickly, confusion and dizziness gripped him and his stomach felt as if he would sick-up. Rogaan was besieged...completely overwhelmed and defenseless at the barrage to his senses causing his legs to go wobbly and weak, shaking with the strain of holding himself up. Through his suffering, Rogaan heard

Pax on the move, drawing closer with footfalls so heavy that he may as well have been riding a *niisku*. And Pax's heart -- its beating, he could hear it, and Pax's breathing clearly rapid and shallow as he passed by. Without seeing him, Rogaan knew Akaal remained still, but not far off. Rogaan thought he heard the *Baraan's* heart beating at a quick pace and his breath, not loud, but steady. Rogaan's urge to sick-up started to overpower him as pain boomed in his head, forcing him to close his eyes tight, hoping for all the sounds and smells to go away. Rogaan wanted his head to stop hurting. He feared he would pass out at any moment. He suffered for what felt a long time. Then his head cleared, as quickly as it had started. The pain lessened...almost disappeared and the forest noise *felt*...normal...and his stomach settled with only a grumble. Rogaan suddenly felt hungry. He looked up and found the concerned eyes of his friend who held him firmly with both hands on his shoulders. *What is happening to me? Stay away! Never come again.*

"What be wrong?" Pax whispered with fear-filled eyes.

"What is happening to me?" Rogaan asked, blank-faced and con-fused. He looked around and found that they were alone. Kardul and Akaal were nowhere to be seen. Something struck him in the chest then thumped at his feet. He looked down to see what it was, finding a small rock next to his knee. *I am on my knees...how...when?* Rogaan felt as confused as ever. He looked up, searching for where the rock had come from. In the broken shadows at the edge of the grove, a crouched Kardul sharply motioned with his hand for them to follow.

"Let's be goin', Rogaan," Pax whispered with a trembling voice, while urgently tugging at Rogaan's shoulders. Pax pulled him toward the empty shadows, where Kardul had stood a moment ago. They entered the grove running, and immediately found themselves plow-ing through razor ferns and around long-needle pines in their search for Kardul. They made more noise than wanted, with fronds cutting at them as they passed. A tremor shook the ground. Uncertain what it was or what to do, Rogaan stopped to look about the forest, seeking

its source. Another tremor came, and another, regularly timed, growing stronger.

"What ya waitin' for?" Pax whispered with hushed frustration.

"Something is coming." Rogaan whispered. "Something big."

Pax rolled his eyes. "Of course, somethin' big be coming.
Everything out here be big."

Tremors came, one after another, and another. Rogaan got a sense
of where *it* was coming from–to his left. He heard a deep breath and
froze...froze in the shadow of a large pine tree, his back to the tree
trunk. The tremors had stopped. All that remained was deep rhythmic
breathing, so deep he felt it. Rogaan dared not look, dared not move to
see what *it* was for fear of being found. A foul stench of putrid decay
struck him in a powerful wind from behind. It filled his nose, assault-
ing his senses, and made him sick. He fought to keep down his innards,
several times, before stalemating rising bile in his throat. The shadows
about him deepened. The danger was close, on top of him. Another foul
wind washed over him, this time from behind and above, forcing him to
renew his battle to keep his stomach down. Prickles painfully rippled
over his body as lights flashed in his vision, even when he closed his eyes.
The forest around him plunged deep into shadows and the sickening
odor burned at his nose and throat, yet the forest was so vibrant to him
in every way. His ears filled with a reverberating pounding and his head
hurt so badly he feared it would burst. Rogaan's lungs burned with each
breath. The foul air was too much, forcing him to breathe shallow. He
silently gagged. Then the stench retreated as the tremors started, again,
growing weaker with each new one. With uncertain courage, he peeked
around his tree shielding him and caught a glimpse of a reddish fin, its
height some five strides above him, and a reddish tail, passing beyond
the trees. Everything moved too slowly to be real, Rogaan thought. He
must be living a waking nightmare. He wondered at it then everything
seemed faster than a moment before, more as normal, and all his ills
started to fade as hunger pains rippled through him.

"Fool!" Kardul chastised in a harsh whisper. Rogaan found the *Kiuri'Ner* crouched near in deep shadows with spear at the ready and his face in a fume. Despite his size, Kardul was almost invisible to Rogaan. Relieved he no longer felt sick or dizzy, he worried about what was happening to him and what *it* was doing to his body. Rogaan swallowed hard, not only for the fear of illness, but also for fear of being dismissed from the Hunt. He waited…silently. And waited some more. "You're too slow. Thank the Ancients *redfins* have poor sight. If he had found you, you'd be off to the darkness and the rest of us trouble. Enough. Let's travel."

Kardul disappeared into the foliage in a blink. *How does he do that?* Rogaan asked himself. He breathed a sigh of relief then started after Kardul, moving as fast as he could without making a ruckus…which was not as fast as he wanted. Rogaan felt unusually hungry, with his middle grumbling and growling as he ran. He chose to ignore it, mostly because he figured they were not going to eat any time soon. The grumbling and growling kept on with his steps. Rogaan was relieved that Kardul had not dismissed him outright. Rogaan then started worrying over his wounded chances to gain favor with the *Kiuri'Ner*. He tried to put his mistakes out of his head, but it was not possible. *How am I going to make things right?* Rogaan asked himself over and over again, while trying to keep up. After a time it seemed to matter little, and Rogaan settled into a hard trot needed to keep pace with Kardul. Pax easily bounded just ahead, while following the *Kiuri'Ner*, but Akaal was nowhere to be found. Rogaan feared they had lost him, and considered speaking up before deciding not to, mostly out of fear of appearing less competent than he already felt. *Maybe he is ahead of us?* Rogaan asked himself -- hoping, actually. Sure as hoped, Kardul soon passed gray-beard who then settled in line between Pax and Kardul.

Kardul set a hard pace that he kept for several marches before slowing. Rogaan struggled to keep up, though he managed, with a determined effort, and was relieved when the pace slowed to a walk.

Their fast traveling left him drenched in sweat, with more pouring out of him everywhere, further soaking his clothes and stinging his eyes. The forest had grown oppressively hot for this early hour, the decay-filled air making it difficult for Rogaan to catch his breath. Pax, too, seemed winded, but a determined look on his face told Rogaan that his friend remained focused, steady – unusual for him.

"Hold!" Kardul's voice was low and stern. He stood like a statue, with his gaze set on the forest ahead. "Listen. We avoided a *redfin*. They're the bigtooth of the valley, but not the worst. They hunt the day, and in open spaces. Not what we travel, now. *Leapers* hunt the whole valley, even this heavy stuff. And they're a mean bunch, with kicking claws to split you open in a blink. *Fern runners* are just as dangerous. The ground-running *featherwings* are as tall as a *Baraan* and then some, and attack all that come near. They like *tanniyn* to eat and are just as dangerous. Stay away from their nests, especially. *Two-horns* can get to more than three thousand stones, move like thunder, and can run you down. They're mean and more likely to charge than retreat. *Longwalkers* are easier going, and that's what we hunt today. But don't be fooled; they'll crush you to the ground, given half a chance, especially if you're near their nests. And take care crawling around. Down low has many things that bite and sting, especially where there is lots of water, which is everywhere in the Wet here. A shallow river runs the valley, making this place alive with poisonous things. And don't forget the *snapjaws*. They're in all waters no matter how small, and the big ones can get near as big as *redfins*." Kardul fell silent, looking at them as if asking if they understood.

Rogaan caught a glimpse of Akaal watching him before shifting his eyes away. The man unnerved him for reasons he still could not put a finger on. *What does he want?* Rogaan wondered. Rogaan found Pax looking at Kardul, absorbing all of his teaching. Rogaan was a bit surprised at that. Pax usually took poorly to those trying to teach him... anything. Maybe the *redfin* shook up Pax? Recalling his own actions with the *redfin*, Rogaan grew uneasy and a little shamed about the way he reacted. He almost got himself and the others killed, and he wondered why he had not been dismissed for it. And to further confuse Rogaan, the *Kiuri'Ner* now acted as if these things were just as normal as taking a breath.

"Our hunt plan," Kardul continued in a low, serious tone. "Is to get a youngling *longwalker* away from the nesting area and drive him toward the cliffs where the cutters and carrier won't have far to go to do their work, after we make the kill. Killing the animal too far from the cliffs, and *leapers* and *redfins* will be on us before we can take our cut of meat...and that'll end someone's light." Kardul grabbed a handful of purple flowers and pulled them free of the soil. He placed the lot between his hands and started working his palms in a crushing rub. When he was satisfied the petals and upper parts of the stalks were nothing resembling what they once were, Kardul rubbed the remains on his exposed skin. "Do the same. It'll keep us from the flying *biters* and *bloodsuckers*."

With a growing buzz of a swarm about him, Rogaan eagerly did as Kardul. The flowers carried a pungent odor once crushed and mixed with his sweat, and he found the swarm instantly repelled by it. He wished someone had shown him this long ago, and eagerly rubbed more on himself, and just for good measure, rubbed some more in, then pocketed as much as he could stuff into his pockets; Pax and Akaal did the same.

"Why not take da big ones?" Pax asked, as he applied a fourth coating of the purple flower rub.

"The younglings," Kardul replied, shaking his head. "They don't protect nests, and have a streak of rowdiness that makes them easier to get apart from the rest. Besides, a youngling can be two thousand stones or more...the right size for the Hunt." Kardul fell silent, again, this time with his eyes closed. "Listen. It's the *longwalker* song."

Rogaan heard only the wind and distant water, and *featherwings* and swarms of flying *biters*, which now kept their distance. Skeptical, he closed his eyes. The wind, water, and animal sounds became louder to his ear, but no "song" came to him. The light breeze cooled him, drying his sweat. It felt good, but was futile to getting dry. More sweat poured from him just as quickly, keeping him wet from head to toe. He listened, yet heard nothing except his own heartbeat...slowing. Unconvinced, Rogaan took the moment just to rest with his eyes closed. He relaxed into the moment. He then heard something more: a vibration more than a sound. It had an awkward rhythm, but it was a "song." A low, reverberating melody, almost inaudible, tickled his senses. *The animals were singing.*

"I hear nothin'," Pax complained. His eyes were closed and he appeared to be straining to hear the song. He scowled. "Nothin'. Except da *biters* and da wind."

"It's there, youngling," Akaal chastised with closed eyes. "You've spent too much time inside walls. You don't belong here."

Pax's eyes snapped open and glared at Akaal. "Meanin' what?"

A smile -- more a smirk, really -- came to Akaal's face. Akaal seemed pleased with himself. Pax's scowl grew deeper yet; his eyes narrowed as his body tensed. Just when Rogaan thought Pax was going to jump at Akaal, the haft of Kardul's short spear struck the ground between them.

"Enough!" Kardul growled.

"*Kiuri'Ner*, forgive me my bluntness." Akaal spoke seriously. "These younglings aren't fit for hunting, and you know it. They're going to bring the Wilds down on us."

"We be just as ready as ya!" Pax growled.

"They will learn." Kardul spoke flatly at Akaal. He gave Pax and Rogaan each a hard look. "If they live to sunset."

"They'll have to prove that," Akaal declared dismissively.

Rogaan felt his guts sink to his knees at Akaal's words. There it was, out in the open for everyone to agree with. Rogaan started to feel unworthy as a forest warrior. *Maybe Father was right?*

"Enough!" Kardul growled. "Rise and get ready to travel...hard. We have ground to cover to get in place to pick our prey and drive it to the cliffs." Kardul impatiently flicked his hand at the three of them, motioning them to move then started off at a hard pace, without waiting to see if they followed.

Pax looked at Rogaan and offered him the favored position, with the wave of his arm and a half smile. Rogaan only shook his head, letting Pax know he did not intend to follow Kardul so closely. Pax then looked at Akaal, who shrugged his shoulders while he kept his place. With a frustrated snort, Pax started off, but only after giving Rogaan a disappointed glance. Rogaan looked at Akaal, expecting...no, hoping...that he would follow Pax. The man remained still, though he cocked his head a bit while returning Rogaan's stare. Rogaan shrugged and hoped Akaal would see it as indifference, then followed after Pax. The *Baraan* waited from Rogaan to move out. Akaal fell in behind Rogaan, all sprinting to catch up with the *Kiuri'Ner*.

They traveled fast through the valley forest, with Kardul keeping a hard pace until the sun had risen past halfway, to its mid-day height. A strong tremor in the valley struck in the late morning sending all the *featherwings* and *leatherwings* flying. Traveling was difficult with the humid forest overgrown and dense. In places so much growth impeded their travel that Kardul needed to hack a path to pass. Open spaces between stands of gum, cedar, and pine groves protected by low razor-frond ferns were common when they were not in a thicket. Rogaan welcomed open spaces, despite having to all but sprint to keep up with Kardul's trot. Stinging and bleeding cuts on his arms and legs made him curse the Ancients for creating the plants. Kardul avoided most open areas, except when crossing them seemed his only choice, and he plunged them all back into thicker foliage as quickly as possible. They stopped twice for water, and once to allow a pack of two-stride-long *leapers* to pass. That was an unnerving experience for Rogaan. Rogaan welcomed the short rests and was thankful to

Kardul that the green and rust-colored *leapers* did not notice them. They pressed on with sweat pouring, Rogaan suffering stinging eyes and soaked clothes, making him uncomfortable from chafing in several choice places. Pax, just as soaked with sweat, fought with his spear as they worked their way through the forest. He was struggling now to keep pace, and looked close to exhaustion. Kardul kept at the hard pace, and Akaal proved able to keep up without much struggle. They both somehow seemed immune to the heat and the grueling run.

Just short of mid-day, when Rogaan started to think the dense forest would go on forever, they came to the edge of a large clearing dotted with broken stands of twisted oaks, pines, and patches of ferns, all completely stripped of their greenery except the very tops, though the area was anything but empty. The pungent odor of dung hung heavy in the air, making Rogaan's nose wrinkle. *Longwalker*s, two-footed plant eaters that sometimes walked on all fours, with blunt noses and large sweeping tails, moved off the clearing at a browsing pace, honking and bellowing deeply as they went. They were spectacular to Rogaan, with rust-colored heads and irregular white and blue vertical stripes from shoulders to the tail tips. Rogaan started wondering how these *longwalker*s could be taken down as prey. They were so big -- too big. Many raised ground-nests made of dirt, plant branches, and leaves dotted a nearby clearing. At most raised circles, large adult *longwalker*s tended their eggs. Rogaan stood in awe at the sheer number of beasts, ranging in size from about three strides long to more than twice that. The largest moved in pairs when running off creatures considered a threat to their unhatched eggs. Green and red-colored *stripeis* and other small, fleet-footed *tanniyn* scampered among the giants, seeking any opportunity to get at a meal just as the myriad of *featherwings*, flying above, circling, swooping, and diving for a meal when the *longwalker*s left nests undefended. Several different sized and colored *leatherwings*, moderate in numbers, circled high overhead, occasionally squawking while looking for opportunities to feed on eggs and small prey, but they were not as aggressive as the annoying low-flying *featherwings*. Low to the ground, thick clouds of *biters* and *bloodsuckers* buzzed amongst the *tanniyn* just about everywhere.

"There must be hundreds of them," Rogaan mumbled in amazement.

"A thousand," Akaal added. "Maybe more."

"All!" Kardul spoke calmly, but in a serious tone as he pointed to the opposite side of the clearing, more than three hundred paces distant. "Look to the far side of the herd…there. *Leapers*. And more over there." Rogaan found both packs by following Kardul's pointed arm. Without the *Kiuri'Ner*, Rogaan would have likely missed both packs, until it was much too late. *Leapers*, green and black in color, lingered in the shadows of large patches of trees and underbrush at the far edge of the clearing. They were almost invisible against the forest; only their movement gave them away.

"I no see 'em," Pax complained, while squinting.

"Big surprise," Akaal chided sardonically. "No experience -- and blind. A wonder they're not in the darkness already, *Kiuri'Ner*." Akaal exchanged unfriendly glances with Kardul then lazily leaned on his long spear, continuing to speak as if talking to air. "Which one?"

"We'll take one with a few years of growing done," Kardul answered in a less than friendly tone.

"Why not an adult?" Rogaan asked, disappointed. "They are bigger and will feed more."

"Too much animal," Kardul replied simply. "We must kill close to the ravine over there, where another felled tree will allow the others passage to this side. We'll have to drive it there, or we'll be in the open and vulnerable to *leapers* or *redfins*. That means we take one not guarding a nest."

"Too much animal?" Pax repeated sarcastically. "Da cutters be done with da big one faster than me blinkin'." Kardul shot Pax a hard look, making it clear this wasn't a discussion. Not able to let the moment go,

Pax puffed his chest, readying a response, but was cut off by a bone-aching grip from Rogaan on his forearm.

"*Leapers* stalk the edges, looking for easy kills," Kardul continued with his teachings. "Keep eyes sharp and listen for their talk. They attack in numbers and are fearless, merciless, and quick. When we get closer to the ravine, we'll pick our prey, make our kill, then defend it until the cutters and carriers get to us and are done." Without looking back, Kardul started off in the direction of the ravine. Pax, Rogaan, and Akaal obediently followed, though with more noise than Kardul wanted, by his looks back at the cracking sticks or brushed ferns. Kardul followed the edge of the clearing just inside the tree line, not unlike how the *leapers* traveled.

A reverberating bellow sounded close, startling the hunters and bringing them all to a halt. Only Kardul did not swivel his head back and forth, searching its source. Instead, Kardul held his hand high, signaling for the group to keep silent and unmoving. At first, Rogaan thought the sound was a *longwalker* bellowing, but a second and third sounding convinced him otherwise. It was a horn.

"Trouble has one of the groups," Kardul spat, then launched himself in the direction of the horn. "Follow!"

Chapter 5

Fern Runners

Pax and Rogaan plowed through branches and cutting fronds, trying to keep pace with Kardul. Snapping sticks and branches and the shuddering ring of brushed fronds close behind told Rogaan that Akaal was on his heels. They covered nearly half a march of hard going when another blast of the horn sounded, this time closer. Adjusting their path towards the horn, in less than fifty strides they found themselves falling out of the thickets next to Kardul and looking upon chaos. Ahead, in a small gully next to a rise, Kantus and his Band scampered about, defending themselves against the attacks of an angry pair of *fern runners*, heavily built ground *featherwings* with big powerful beaks. Standing three strides tall, *featherwings* fiercely squawked as they repeatedly struck out with their bone-breaking beaks. The *fern runners* danced about a pile of leaves and forest debris two strides across and a stride tall; sitting atop that rise was a nest. The *fern runners* aggressively defended against…attacked the Band one at a time, alternating between targets with each charge. Kantus and his Band were unable to coordinate themselves, disorganized by the *fern runner*'s ferocity. All of them were bloodied, and two wounded badly enough that they cowered behind an outcrop of rocks close by.

"Dumb enough to steal eggs," Rogaan grumbled between breaths. Rogaan expected no less from Kantus and his followers.

"And be dumb enough not ta run," Pax finished after gasping a deep gulp of air.

"Too arrogant to run," Rogaan corrected Pax, after gulping a chestful of air himself. "May the Ancients protect them."

"Ya be serious?" Pax asked incredulously. Kantus dodged several lunges from one of the *fern runners*, the one with a red body and yellow chest, its massive beak catching and slicing off a piece of his new armor. "Where be da *Kiuri'Ner*? Look! Kantus be stuck by da runner and gonna get his knees cut off. Dat ta size him down just right."

Kantus scrambled, wedging himself between several pine trees and a boulder with just enough space between him and the *fern runner* to make its strikes uncertain of hitting. After another several failed bites at Kantus, the *fern runner* stomped its powerful clawed feet, then looked for another position to attack from. The other *fern runner*, a brown and black-feathered monster, held tight one of the Band by his backpack. Rogaan thought it was round-faced and -chested Urhug, the *fern runner* dragging him flailing and bloodied across broken ground. Rogaan stepped toward the two with the intent to help then caught sight of Kardul running toward Urhug and his attacker. Rogaan held fast still needing to catch his wind.

Kantus frantically waved his long knife to fend off his *fern runner*'s vicious attacks. Rogaan smiled with a sense of satisfaction at Kantus' predicament then felt a wave of guilt wash over him for it. "We must help Kantus."

"Ya hit ya head?" Pax asked with his eyes nearly popping out of his head. "Let him be. He be deserving this."

Rogaan paused, considering what to do, weighing Kantus gone from his life against how he thought he would feel about himself for not trying to keep Kantus from harm. It was only a moment, but Rogaan felt as if he spent much longer making up his mind. In a single smooth motion, Rogaan nocked an arrow and raised his bow, the one given him for the Hunt. He had to act, even if he only distracted the *fern runner*.

"Rogaan," Pax protested. "Kantus would no help ya and ya know it."

"I know," Rogaan answered flatly. He took a deep breath and exhaled, calming himself, while focusing on the *fern runner*'s yellow chest, where he thought the heart should be, then drew the bow half-way. Rogaan focused on the spot he wanted to strike. He saw only his target. He took another breath and exhaled. His heart slowed. All else disappeared from his vision. *Focus on target. Forty strides. Breath. Exhale. Forty-two strides. Focus on the target where red feathers touched yellow. Breath. Exhale. Follow target...anticipate.* Rogaan drew fully the bow. Crack! *Ignore the distraction.* His concentration lapsed, almost ruining his focus. *Focus. Follow target...only the target exists. Breathe. Exhale. Where red meets yellow.* Rogaan loosed the arrow. The bow felt and sounded... wrong...weak, as the arrow flew slow, falling far short of Rogaan's intended target.

"That not be like ya," Pax sounded surprised. "Did ya eat somethin' ta keep up ya strength? Maybe ya be seein' da sign from da Old Ones ta let Kantus get his come-uppin'."

The red and yellow *fern runner* drew blood when it nipped Kantus' left leg. Kantus cried out in pain then started whimpering as he frantically flailed his long knife at the *fern runner*. The animal's size and speed proved too much to fend off, and it struck Kantus several more times in the legs, drawing more blood. Rogaan felt helpless, and Kardul was occupied with the other *fern runner*. Akaal just chuckled at it all as he casually leaned on his spear a few paces to Rogaan's right. The man seemed to be enjoying the spectacle. A cold man, Rogaan concluded. Dismissing his thoughts of Akaal, Rogaan nocked another arrow and focused again on the *fern runner*. *Bow to half draw. Deep breath. Exhale. Calm yourself. Focus. Forty-two strides. Red feathers meet yellow. Follow target. Full draw.* Crack!

The bow broke. "What?" Its splintered remains lay in a tangled mess in his hands. Pax looked at the bow, then at Rogaan with a quizzical expression, while Akaal's chuckle deepened. Frustrated, and with a growing anger, Rogaan tossed the bow away and reached for his hide case, then paused. "Useless. Pax...your spear. No time for my *shunir'ra*."

"Rogaan," Pax said heatedly. "Kantus deserves da pain. Let him get outta his mess himself."

Rogaan's anger swelled. Anger at Akaal for his callousness, at Pax for not wanting to help, and at himself for thinking Pax was right. Rogaan snatched the spear out of Pax's hands then leaped into the gully leading to the chaos.

"Kantus would no help ya!" Pax yelled after his friend.

"I know." Rogaan answered and kept running, vaulting knee-high rocks, side-stepping fallen logs, and plowing through ferns. *Thirty strides.* Rogaan scanned the ground to the *fern runner* and picked a path to the beast. *Twenty strides.* He readied his spear in both hands while continuing his charge, bracing it against his right side and securing it under his arm. *Ten. Focus. Red to yellow. Follow target.* Rogaan slammed the spear into the side of the beast, striking close to where he aimed. A hideous squawk bellowing from the animal surprised Rogaan, causing him to freeze where he stood. The *fern runner* twisted, trying to pull itself from the spear then snapped at Rogaan when it realized it was impaled. Through the spear, Rogaan felt the *fern runner* shifting its weight, and anticipating its moves, drove the spear deeper. The *fern runner* bellowed again then angrily lunged at him with snapping beak, missing his nose by a hand's width before collapsing to the ground with a thud. The beast came to rest an arm's length from a shaking Kantus. Rogaan held the spear deep in the beast, expecting it to rise and renew its attacks. Nothing. No movement. No rising and falling of the chest. *No breathing. Maybe its light is gone? Hopefully, gone.* When satisfied that it was indeed lifeless, Rogaan pulled the spear from it, but kept the spear pointed at the *fern runner* for a few moments just in case. In a ruckus, Kantus recklessly jumped on the lifeless body, plunging his long knife into it as if he meant to kill the already lightless creature, with both his blade and taunts.

Rogaan looked upon the scene of blood and chaos: the *fern runner* red and newly colored in crimson with Kantus atop it, wailing away at its lifeless body. A mix of surprise and disgust filled Rogaan as he watched Kantus. Pax and Akaal were where he left them, some forty strides away, Akaal leaning casually on his spear without a hint of concern about anything as far as Rogaan could figure. *No...*Rogaan decided he did not like the *Baraan*. Not one bit. Kardul stood over the other *fern runner* carcass a short distance away, wiping his short sword clean on its feathered body. The Bandsman, blood thick on his head, chest, and left arm, slowly crawled away from his now-stilled attacker. The other two Bandsmen still hid behind the large rock they had found some twenty strides beyond, peeking over it with eyes wide. After a few more loud moments, Kantus finished his assault on the lifeless body, and rested with his weight on the hilt of his long knife, his head down, and the blade deep in the *fern runner*. Calm returned to the forest. Rogaan realized with surprise that he had not gotten sick or dizzy. A sense of relief washed over him.

"Guard the area!" Kardul commanded, looking straight at Pax and Akaal. They both jumped at Kardul's words. Kardul then turned to Rogaan. "Make sure its light has been taken."

"It is," Rogaan replied, then jabbed it with his spear to prove the point.

"I see everything here is in hand," Firik Umsadaa announced with hands on hips at the edge of the clearing opposite Pax and Akaal. Firik projected a calm and strength of confidence that made Rogaan feel safer, somehow.

"What happened here?" Kardul demanded of Firik.

Firik stood in place, surveying the scene for long moments, as if he were considering his words. He walked casually toward Rogaan, speaking simply. "Kantus and his companions disobeyed me. They were to keep concealed until my return from a quick scout, though it looks they felt it better to do things in their manner." Firik looked at the *fern runner* lying between Rogaan and a now-standing, blood-splattered

Kantus. "Kantus has a good kill there, in spite of his arrogance and poor judgment."

"Kantus?" Rogaan protested, shocked and indignant. "Kantus could not save himself. The kill is mine."

"Doesn't appear so," Firik disagreed. Firik looked at Kardul, who only shrugged. "Doesn't look that way at all."

"Kantus did no kill da *fern runner*," Pax joined Rogaan in protest before a satisfied smirk came to his face. "But, he almost got pecked ta da darkness."

"Not by my eyes," Firik replied sardonically.

Pax took up a place next to Rogaan, dark-faced and with anger building to boil, again. He snatched his spear back from Rogaan, raised it in the air, and sucked in a deep breath, readying himself to hurl words at Firik. Fearful of what his friend might say and do, complicating things for him and harming his opportunities with the *Kiuri'Ner*, Rogaan squeezed Pax's arm enough to give warning. Pax shot him a look with eyes ready to pop out of his head.

"No point arguing," Rogaan grumbled low, as he fought to maintain command over his own anger. He wanted the satisfaction of seeing Kantus revealed for what he was: a coward, a bully, a manipulator, and a spoiled youngling. But that was not likely to happen here...not now. Firik seemed to clearly favor Kantus.

"No," Firik coolly stated. "There won't be arguments. Only obedience, or you'll make your own way back to Brigum." Firik waved for the Band to emerge from their hiding place and join him. They came limping and grimacing, and surprisingly silent. Firik looked them and Kantus over, then spoke. "Looks to be no one got hurt badly. Tend your wounds. Make sure you're cleaned to keep the blood scent from carrying, and you don't get the burning." Firik scanned the area, then the distant cliffs barely visible through a section of twenty-stride tall cedars.

"Kardul, we're too distant from the cliffs to strip these animals and not be meals ourselves," Firik stated matter-of-factly. "Take your...

hunters…and go on. I'll meet up with you after the younglings here are cleaned to my approval." Firik leveled an intense gaze on Kantus, staring him down for a long moment. Kantus at first stared back defiantly; then his posture and face softened, then he seemed to cower a bit as the unspoken tension between them grew thick. When Firik looked to be satisfied, he continued. "Kantus, collect eggs…that is what you were after when you disobeyed me, wasn't it?"

Kantus glanced around to see if anyone was watching him. When he looked at Pax, his face grew dark -- Rogaan suspected from embarrassment. Pax returned a large, toothy grin and was obviously enjoying the moment. Kantus' face grew darker, if that were possible, when he realized Rogaan shared his friend's grin.

"What are you two fools grinning at?" Firik demanded, with his harsh gaze fixed on Pax and Rogaan. "Kardul, get these two away from here before they find what regret means."

Kardul motioned with his head toward the cliffs to the west then waited with his stolid stare set on Rogaan until the two moved. He watched Rogaan and Pax intently until they passed by him. Quizzically, Kardul looked at Rogaan then spoke. "Youngling, where's your bow?"

Rogaan felt his cheeks warm and prickles dance up his back. Embarrassed that he had broken the bow, Rogaan searched for a response that would not require further explanation. Search as he did, nothing came to him. After a few moments, Rogaan decided the truth was best. "It broke."

"Broke?" Kardul sounded as if did not believe Rogaan.

"Broke," Rogaan said again, pointing to where he threw it to the ground. "It is over there."

"Bring it," Kardul demanded. "I must see for myself."

Rogaan stopped -- hesitated, really, wondering why Kardul "must" see the bow. It was broken, and that was all. Kardul maintained his uncompromising stare until Rogaan flinched and recovered the broken tool. Once it was in his hands, Kardul inspected it with scrutinizing eyes, running his fingers over the tattered bow across the break point. The *Kiuri'Ner*'s expression changed every-so-slightly as he inspected the weapon. Kardul looked at Rogaan while he stripped the bow sting from the broken wood.

"Broke it on the draw?" Kardul asked matter-of-factly.

"Yes," Rogaan replied. "Second draw."

Kardul grunted then threw the ruined wood to the ground. He looked at Pax, and then at Akaal. His eyes fixed on Akaal longest. The two *Baraan* exchanged hard looks, with neither of them blinking. "Get moving, all of you with me. We have a *longwalker* to hunt before the day grows late."

Chapter 6

The Hunted

K ardul set the pace harder than before, leaving Rogaan struggling to keep up. The four traveled single file north through the valley for more than a march before Kardul led them west then south to an elevated outcrop of gray and black rock some forty strides long and nine high, overlooking another large break in the forest. Deep, reverberating honks and bellows filled the air, along with the pungent odor of dung heavy on a hot breeze. Rogaan wrinkled his nose at the air, and it looked as if Pax could not keep from doing the same. Kardul climbed the rocks and set himself crouched near the top, where he could survey a large open plain with little chance of being seen. Rogaan, Pax, and Akaal joined Kardul at the crest of the rock formation near where they all took in a magnificent scene of *longwalkers*, in the hundreds, spread across the open ground in between dense stands of trees. *Biters* and *bloodsuckers* swarmed about them, trying to get at their blood. Fortunately, most were unable to get past the purple flower's invisible protection they had put on earlier.

Longwalker nests abounded, spaced apart to allow adults passage between them. Pairs of mature *longwalkers* tended most nests, as yearlings weaved between both adults and nests, frolicking or looking for anything green to eat. Some of the larger young, almost mature by the looks of the size and coloring, were busy in contests of domination that seemed more about pushing and making noise than anything else. Kardul had approached the herd from the north with the warm, light wind in his face, and the strong smell of dung carried on it. The animals seemed oblivious to their presence, or just did not consider them a concern, making it difficult for Rogaan to discern what senses the animals used to bring them to alarm of dangers. Here, close to the western cliffs of the valley, the number of young seemed greatest, diminishing in numbers the farther east he looked. All stayed close to their mothers, though the large females showed little tolerance for them and shooed them away when they got too close to incubating eggs. Swirling flocks of fast-moving *featherwings* and soaring *leatherwings* high above, swooped down from time to time at things unseen on the nesting grounds. A ravine to their right ran the edge of the plain north and south near the red, rocky cliffs. A little more than twenty strides beyond the ravine, a rugged path, maybe three strides wide, twisted its way up from the valley floor to the height of the thirty strides, where it led off to their camp. Halfway up the path were two carts slowly pulled down by *niisku*, cutters and carriers following the last cart while armed hunters led. They were to keep their place on the path, waiting for a sign before descending to the valley below, where they were to make quick work of anything the hunters killed.

"Why run about the valley instead of taking that path there?" Rogaan quizzically asked Kardul, while pointing to the cliffs. Kardul offered no answer, keeping his attention on the *longwalkers*. Rogaan thought on his question in Kardul's silence, coming to the conclusion that they could simply have come to this place without need of traveling about the valley all morning. Frustration and anger swelled within Rogaan at having been played with by Kardul. Rogaan's tone turned demanding. "Why?"

Kardul returned Rogaan a satisfied smile. "I wished to see if you three are ready for what we're about to do. A simple walk down the cliff path wouldn't have told me what I needed, youngling. Besides, look over there...and there...and there. We needed to stay upwind and unseen."

Rogaan's eyes followed where Kardul pointed. He looked at each place, seeing nothing at first then barely making out...*leapers*, packs of them -- and large animals, if he judged right. Most rested almost motionless in the deep shadows of tall pines on the other side of the herd, almost four hundred strides away. They were well hidden, disappearing so well into the background that he had to peer intensely to make out their forms. Even then only the occasional movements of the *leapers* betrayed their positions.

"I no see what ya pointin' ta," Pax complained. "What be it, Rogaan?"

"Trouble, Pax," Rogaan answered solemnly. "*Leaper* trouble."

"Not so, with some good fortune," Kardul corrected with another knowing smile and a matter-of-fact tone, confident in his knowledge and experience, Rogaan assumed. "*Leapers* hate heat. It tires them. *Longwalker*s tolerate the heat by keeping slow, unless in danger. Even when pushed, big males and most females won't travel far. Those tending nests will almost never leave them, defending their eggs till their lights are darkened."

"Sooo?" Pax questioned.

"Think, youngling," Kardul demanded. When Pax didn't answer, Kardul continued his teaching, though with a slightly exasperated look. "Our path has kept us upwind and from *leaper* and *longwalker* notice, allowing us to pick when and from where we strike. If the *leapers* move at all in the heat, it'll likely not be far or for long. Taking down and carving a *longwalker* will be easier, not having to worry about them, much."

"What's next?" Akaal asked impatiently.

Kardul made an effort not to look at Akaal as he flexed his jaw muscles a few times. "We wait for a *longwalker* to leave the nest area -- hopefully a young one with only a few seasons on him, and that he wanders near the ravine. We attack, driving the animal into the ravine, where it'll fall to darkness."

"What about *leapers*?" Rogaan asked.

"If done soon," Kardul said, looking into the cloud-peppered blue sky. "The heat will keep them from us and the ravine. We'll be where their eyes and noses won't notice us. But we must kill quick before it can bellow, or the three *leaper* packs might all come on us."

"Are we waiting for Firik and his younglings?" Akaal spoke with a disdainful tone, and seemed a bit anxious.

"We attack when an animal makes itself vulnerable," Kardul replied flatly, his eyes fixed on the herd, watching for…opportunities.

They watched and they waited and watched and waited and watched and waited and watched. Kardul had long since readied his bow and slid his quiver forward on his belt to allow easy access its arrows. He told all of them to ready themselves and to remain so.

Rogaan tormented over using his *shunir'ra*. Taking it against his father's wishes bothered him much more than he expected, and more so the closer it came to his actually needing to use it. At first, he put off deciding to use it and did not think of it for a time, but after the other bow broke, needing it was almost certain, and that made the afternoon painful for Rogaan, his decision swinging back and forth between his father's wishes and his need to gain the favor of the *Kiuri'Ner*. Kardul never gave him a second look. Rogaan feared that the *Kiuri'Ner* assumed he was not going to be much help in taking a *longwalker*. That ate at Rogaan -- his hopes, his dreams. Slowly, tormented, Rogaan decided. He hesitantly pulled his *shunir'ra* from its hide case and assembled it. Kardul and Akaal stared while he worked, Kardul with a curious look and Akaal wide-eyed. Pax wore a grin wider than Rogaan ever remembered. Rogaan fit together the metal-blue *nisi'barzil* limb mounts and handle, the grip wrapped in the best animal hide he could afford. The recurved limbs snugly attached to the mounts where Rogaan locked them in place with a set of clamps, top and bottom… a design of his father. He strung the metal-blue string to the bottom notch, then wrapped his leg around the lower limb and grunted to bend the bow enough to set the string in the upper notch. Sweat dripped from his forehead at that last effort. Try as he might to come up with a way to make the stringing easier, this was the best he could figure, though his father, watching much of his bow crafting, always looked to have a better answer, but never shared it.

Once it was assembled, Rogaan inspected his *shunir'ra*, his masterpiece of *Tellen* tradition, signifying his transition from young to the wisdom and expertise of an adult able to contribute to the *Tellen* Clan ...though only after his *Zagdu-i-Kuzu* ceremony. In the centerpiece above the grip, five gems each the size of Rogaan's thumbnail were mounted. Four sparkled in the spotty sunlight where he sat: red, blue, yellow, and green. The center gem, black, was slightly larger than the rest, and it seemed to absorb the light, appearing as dark as dark could be even when the sun's rays touched it directly. Rogaan could not help himself and wore a prideful smile while holding his *shunir'ra* for the *Kiuri'Ner* to see. Even his pangs of guilt washing over him in waves started to wane. Rogaan sneaked a look at Kardul to glimpse his reaction. The *Kiuri'Ner* wore an approving look and was unconsciously nodding his head just enough for Rogaan to notice. Relief filled Rogaan. With his smile threatening to become permanent on his face, Rogaan tested his bow with a single draw that demanded every bit of his strength and left his muscles trembling at the strain.

"Impressive," Kardul stated with a bit of admiration in his tone. "*Nisi'barzil.* I've heard stories of Mithraam working such metal."

"Mithraam no make it," Pax broke in, his voice full of pride for his friend. "It be Rogaan that worked da blue steel. It be his *shunir'ra.*"

"Him?" Akaal spat, with a raised chin and a disbelieving wave of his hand.

Pax pressed. "He did. He did. I saw him make it."

Kardul gave Rogaan another approving nod then returned his attention to the herd, some animals now walking by not more than sixty strides to their south. With no discerning expression or tone of voice, Kardul spoke with his eyes following a *longwalker* about half the size of the full-grown adults. "Can you shoot that thing straight?"

Rogaan opened his mouth to assure the *Kiuri'Ner* his aim was always straight, but held his tongue from concern that Kardul might think him a braggart. Instead, he answered with a simple nod. They all followed Kardul's lead, falling silent and watching the herd. The larger animals remained close to their nests, sometimes grooming the mounds of leaves and sticks with their snouts or foreclaws, or adding more plant stuff they returned with. A fight erupted when a *longwalker* not of the parenting pair wandered too closely to a nest. Such intruders were driven away most of the time with a mock charge or warning bellow, but some retreated bruised and bloodied when a mock charge was not enough. Others moved about slowly in the building heat of the afternoon, weaving their way between nests, seeking things Rogaan did not understand.

As they watched the herd, Rogaan assembled his arrows from the eight fletched wooden shafts and two-bladed arrowheads made of blue steel that he kept in his case and blue steel based quiver. He took great care in handling the arrowheads, as they were sharper than anything he knew, and he had experienced cutting himself when making them. The wound bled and bled, then took many days to heal well enough for him to use hand again. The dangerous arrow assembly left Rogaan's shirt clinging to him with sweat pouring from him in the hot and muggy air. Pax looked worse, fidgeting and pulling at his tunic and breeches frequently, and constantly rearranging his tan hat, now dark with sweat along much of the brim, his face paint long since washed from his sweating face. Akaal appeared comfortable despite his shirt dark with sweat where it stuck out from under his hide armor. Kardul seemed impervious to the heat, as he kept an intense watch of the *longwalkers* and *leapers*, studying them.

Several times, Rogaan thought Kardul might order them to attack when *longwalkers*, maybe four strides long, broke from the herd, but they veered away from the ravine before the *Kiuri'Ner* was ready to declare them their prey. Unconsciously, Rogaan fingered the heavy wood shafts now in his waist quiver where the blades of the blue steel arrowheads where kept safe from cutting fingers and everything else. When he caught himself and realized what he was doing, Rogaan sheepishly pulled his hand away from the blades. The arrows issued him for the Hunt was stowed in his *shunir'ra* case and out of the way, as Rogaan considered them inferior by far to his arrows. He fingered his quiver as much out of habit as nervousness, but wanting to put forward his best showing for the *Kiuri'Ner*, Rogaan wanted to look all the part of a seasoned *sharur*. The afternoon wore on and on and on and he fought against feeling discouraged and falling into dazed lulls caused as much from the heat as boredom. After a while, *biters* ignored his purple flower protection and painfully kept him alert, until Rogaan applied more of the flowery protection.

"Ready yourselves." Kardul's command surprised Rogaan, making him jump. Rogaan hoped his "jump" had not been noticed by Kardul or Akaal. *Unimportant at this time*, Rogaan chided himself. Finally, a chance at a proper hunt caused his heart to start racing and his ears feeling as if they would explode from the pounding noise of his blood. Rogaan's palms quickly became slick with sweat, making holding his bow difficult and frustrating him. Following Kardul's gaze, Rogaan spotted a *longwalker*, their prey he guessed, maybe six strides in length, nearing the ravine. Rogaan glimpsed Kardul's body tensing, as if the man were his bow string on the draw. Rogaan mimicked the *Kiuri'Ner* by setting himself ready to spring forward when commanded. "Ready. Ready your weapons. Ready. NOW!"

Kardul exploded from his rocky perch with bow and nocked arrow in hand, and spear somehow slung to his back. The big man's speed stunned Rogaan, mesmerizing him for a moment before he realized he was the only one left on the rocks; Pax and Akaal were already ahead of him, sprinting. A wave of embarrassment passed through him as quickly as it struck. Shaking off the unwanted feeling, he jumped from the rocks and ran after the three, losing ground to them with every stride, in spite of his best sprinting. Rogaan pushed himself even harder, trying just to keep up with the others as they covered nearly two hundred strides to their quarry. Kardul slid to a halt some twenty strides from the animal and immediately fired two arrows, both striking the massive beast's chest just behind its left shoulder. The arrows penetrated to the fletchings.

The *longwalker* bellowed and shook at the arrow impacts. The *longwalker* turned to escape then stopped after a few steps at the edge of the ravine. Confused, it turned about several times before finally staring down Kardul, who now stood ready with spear in hand and the spear-carrying Pax and Akaal at his sides. The *longwalker* bellowed and bluff charged several steps. Kardul and Akaal reversed direction then held their ground. Pax looked unsure of what he was doing and backed away even farther before realizing he was no help to the others where he stood; he looked for a place to move in as they shifted about, countering the beast's moves.

Rogaan slid to a stop less than thirty strides from the wounded *longwalker* and drew his *shunir'ra*. With muscles straining at the tension, he looked for a spot to strike—the chest, low behind the front legs, where his arrow would pass through the heart, killing by bleeding it. Kardul and Akaal danced to avoid being trampled as the beast became more agitated and both of them kept getting in its line of step. Trying to time his shot with their movements, Rogaan let loose his arrow in a rush. He knew it to be a bad shot the moment he released it, and prayed to the Ancients that the arrow would not hit any of his companions. It whistled between Kardul and Akaal, very close to Akaal, missing the *longwalker* altogether. Both *Baraan* snapped hard looks back at Rogaan. With a strained toothy smile, Rogaan gave them an apologetic shrug before they returned their attention to the *longwalker*. Embarrassment flushed Rogaan's face hot, and his body shivered; then anger at himself replaced it all as he saw the inept shot again in his mind.

Fighting to control his anger and a growing fear of making another embarrassing shot, Rogaan closed his eyes and forced himself to refocus as he had many times before on the town wall. Pushing aside the blunder of his first shot, Rogaan sucked in a deep breath then exhaled, calming himself. Then, with his eyes on the *longwalker*'s chest, on the spot where he expected the heart to be, Rogaan drew his bow. *Focus on target. Twenty-six strides. Breathe. No...twenty- nine strides. Breathe.* The rib cage, where rust-shaded hide extended from the neck met with irregular blue-white vertical stripes of the body became Rogaan's world. *Follow target and anticipate. Breathe. Draw full. Breathe. Target. Where rust meets blue. Rust meets blue. Release.* The arrow struck the *longwalker* close to where he aimed, punching through its thick hide and completely disappearing into the chest. Rogaan let another arrow fly. Then another. And another. All four arrows sank deep, disappearing from sight, leaving wounds a hand apart with blood pouring out of them in spurts. The beast let out a sorrow-filled bellow and staggered. Immense pride surged through Rogaan and he looked to see the *Kiuri'Ner*'s reaction. Kardul simply gave Rogaan a quick nod before returning his attention to the dying animal.

Akaal's expression was of wide-eyed surprise, and Rogaan smiled broadly at that. Pride beamed from Rogaan. Pax just wore that dumb grin of his. Kardul yelled something that Rogaan did not make out, but Akaal and Pax heard and they both snapped their attention back to the *longwalker*. Together, all three drove their spears into the animal, though Pax was a little slower than the others. The *longwalker* bellowed again, and stumbled, caught its balance, and pivoted on its hind legs, swinging its massive tail at Pax. Pax went down hard from the tail slap then lay motionless. Kardul ducked under the tail easily, as if anticipating it. Akaal also ducked it, but just barely then danced to keep his feet. Without hesitation, Kardul jumped, positioning himself over Pax, and drove his spear into the wounded beast's right side as it swung around. Rogaan realized he was watching the battle instead of joining it, and with heated cheeks and a strong curse, he let loose

two more arrows that found their mark in the animal's neck, passing through completely. Blood immediately spewed from the wounds.
Rogaan caught a glimpse of one of the arrows shattering on the cliff
beyond. A moment flashed in his head, with Rogaan realizing the cost
of the *nisi'barzil*-headed arrows, in both his time and coin. The moment passed. Becoming a *Kiuri'Ner* was more important to him. The
animal staggered, awkwardly this time, its bellow weaker, more sor-
rowful. Kardul shouted something at Akaal, and they both drove their
spears deep into the *longwalker*'s chest and side. It teetered at the edge
of the ravine, fighting to keep its balance, but the ground gave way under its weight, sending it into the chasm with a final bellow cut short
followed by a slight tremor under Rogaan's feet.

Kardul turned and scanned the open plain behind Rogaan. Rogaan
realized he was looking for dangers that might be stalking them, and
suddenly felt vulnerable with his back to the *longwalker* herd and the
leapers. He spun and snapped a look in the same direction, half expecting the world to be jumping at him with bared claws and teeth. He was
relieved when all he saw were the *longwalker*s going about their lives,
seeming not to care that they had lost one of their herd -- and there
was no sign of the *leapers*. Not in immediate danger, Rogaan's thoughts
turned to his friend. He rushed to Pax where he had fallen and still
lay, praying to the Ancients for him to be alive. *Please not in the darkness.*
Not in the darkness. Kardul was on bent knee tending to Pax by the time
Rogaan reach them.

"Is he...?" Rogaan choked, afraid of the answer.

"He's not on the road to Esharra." Kardul's voice was steady. He
looked to Rogaan with a slight grin. "At least, not yet. He's only dazed,
no more. Should be singing praises of you, again, when his head clears."

Rogaan let out a sigh of relief. *Praising me...?* A flush of embarrassment washed through him, driving him into denials. "Pax does not
praise my deeds!"

"Of course...," Sarcasm was thick on Kardul's tongue. "A good friend to you. He speaks of your skills with that thing." Kardul nodded approvingly at Rogaan then lifted Pax to his feet with one hand. He made it look as if it were no effort at all. Pax wobbled at first and did not seem to have his feet, so Kardul held him standing. Kardul then gave Rogaan a look that made him take his friend from the *Kiuri'Ner*, holding him up with a left arm slung over Rogaan's shoulders and Rogaan solidly grasping his friend. Kardul scanned the open plain, again, and put on a concerned expression. "Let's be gone from here, before *leapers* or *redfin* find us."

Rogaan followed Kardul at a brisk pace. As he trotted, it dawned on Rogaan that he did not suffer the sickening attack when hunting the *longwalker*. He smiled to himself. His confidence grew and he started to feel like his old self. They trotted a short distance to a steep and treacherous foot trail, if one could call it that, leading down some nine strides into the ravine. Pax got back on his feet, though still shaky, by the time Kardul took his first step down. Pax pushed away from Rogaan, muttering some indignities under his breath. It was obvious he was in pain, though able enough to walk without aid. Rogaan sought to give his friend time to regain his strength and head before descending into the ravine, motioning for Akaal to go ahead of them. Akaal put on a skeptical look as he stepped to the trail head. After an awkward moment eyeing the two, Akaal grunted and followed Kardul. The man unsettled Rogaan. He seemed somehow suited for the Wilds, yet not. Rogaan could not put together the words to describe what or why he felt so about the *Baraan*. It seemed Akaal was eager for something, and it was not hunting. Looking at Pax, Rogaan dismissed thinking on it further, and shrugged off his suspicions as foolish before starting down the trail, clinging to vines and roots as he went, while helping Pax as best he could, when Pax would allow it.

At a bit more than fifteen strides across, the ravine was large enough to keep *leapers* from jumping it. It offered some degree of protection from the packs for the wagon train of cutters, skinners, and carriers making their way to the opposite side. A shallow four- stride-wide stream ran down the middle of the ravine and was now partially blocked with water pooling at the back of the *longwalker*'s lifeless body lying on its right side. Kardul had already started preparing the carcass, his long knife out, making a cut in the hide under the neck and chest and around the left shoulder. Akaal was on the other side of the ravine, climbing the cliff with skill and grace he would not have thought the *Baraan* capable of. *Odd...why is he not helping Kardul?* Rogaan stood wondering at what he was up to when Kardul barked for them to get moving and help him with the *longwalker*. Pax moved gingerly, but without hesitating. Rogaan quickened his pace. They approached the felled *longwalker* carefully, Pax patting the animal's tail as he walked around it.

"That be a lesson," Pax said, more to himself than for Rogaan or Kardul.

"Duck when *longwalker*s dance," Kardul instructed while his eyes kept focus on his blade as it sliced hide as easily as water. "You two get over here and prepare this hide for the cutters. We must move fast before the *leapers* smell the kill and come to claim it."

Kardul instructed them where and how to cut. In no time the neck, shoulder, hip, upper legs, and tail of the carcass had deep cuts exposing muscle meat, as the hide was pulled back. A glance up by Rogaan found Akaal standing at the ravine's edge, with spear in hand, looking about. Was he their watcher... alerting them of danger be- fore it would catch them off guard, or at least before it reached knife length? On Akaal's right, four ropes dangled down the cliff with tunic- garbed figures climbing down. *Cutters and skinners*, thought Rogaan. Each wore a long knife and carried a handsaw on their rope belts. Once their bare feet touched the ravine floor, they quickly swarmed the carcass, forcing Kardul, Rogaan, and Pax back as their knives flashed in confident strokes that appeared more a performance than the messy work they replaced. More tunic-clad folk followed. *Carriers.* Each had sacks and spools of hide cord used to pack meat and vital innards, such as liver and heart. They did so as quickly as the cutters stripped hide and meat from the carcass. More carriers, and some of those assigned to guard the wagons, stood at the top of the ravine near Akaal. All were hauling up bounded bundles on yet more ropes tossed down the cliff. Rogaan stood amazed at their speed and coordination as the carcass was stripped by half in short order. Everyone knew what they were to do, and did it well.

"Danger north," Akaal yelled. "It's in the chasm and coming fast. It's big."

"Everyone, up the ropes," Kardul commanded with a steady voice, speaking as if he had been expecting this. "Rogaan and Pax, stay with me to guard after them." Kardul quickly positioned them between those climbing and the approaching danger, the carcass slightly to their left. Kardul and Pax readied spears, while Rogaan nocked his last blue-tipped arrow. Ten more common arrows in a quiver handed to him by Kardul were all he had to fight with. Beyond that, his long knife was all he had to defend himself and the others.

Gripped with dread, Rogaan's chest pounded hard anticipating the worst. It felt as if it would burst any moment. On his left, Kardul wore a determined scowl, his spear at the ready as the *Kiuri'Ner* stood like stone, staring into the depths of the ravine, waiting for danger to find them. To his right, Pax looked panicked and about to scream. Rogaan wondered if his friend would run. Beneath his booted feet, rhythmic shaking, tremors, almost imperceptible at first, regular and growing stronger, told Rogaan that what approached was big. Looking down, he watched a small water-filled puddle ripple inward from its edges with each tremor as small bits of dirt and rock started falling from the rocky walls with each impact tremor. Deep shadows of the late afternoon seemed to swallow the ravine, making what was coming all the more terrifying…death coming out of the Pits of Kur. Whatever it was, it was big, and Rogaan feared he was to fade away this day. It started happening, again. The urge to sick-up at the thick smell of blood hit Rogaan and the foul stench of the *longwalker*'s remains burned his lungs. His skin prickled painfully, his vision blurring and head throbbing, and that unwanted dizziness gripped him. Rogaan's heart sank -- *the sickness is back*. He blinked several times to clear his vision. Looking up, his sight sharpened and the world now looked vibrant. As he expected, Rogaan found Pax and Kardul moving slowly and the dirt and rocks falling unnaturally slowly. *Why this? Not now. Go away. Leave me!* Rogaan dreaded this...*sickness*. In truth, it frightened him almost to paralysis.

Desperately wanting *it* to go from him, Rogaan fought down his panic and forced himself to concentrate on moving about as a distraction. He took a step to his left, then back to his right. Nothing...everything and everyone around him continued moving slowly. Rogaan fought against another urge to lose his stomach. At least he was no longer deafened by the pounding of his blood coursing through him. Rogaan gulped down a chest-full of air then exhaled, trying to calm himself. He found a little relief. Glancing over his shoulder at the climbing workers sank Rogaan's hopes; they were going to have to stand their ground a while longer. "Climb faster!" Rogaan grumbled as fear twisted into terror. A deep, rumbling growl echoed through the ravine, alarming Rogaan with his hairs standing stiff and drawing his attention from the cliff. Another deep growl reverberating through the narrow ravine set Rogaan's neck hairs stiffer as a shiver rippled up his back. *It* was very close. Kardul stole a look at the ropes. His scowl deepened as he returned his attention to the approaching danger. Out of the shadows stalked a maw filled with off-white stakes a hand's width long. Rogaan sucked in a shallow breath at the stride-and-a-half-long head with its long, flat snout held some three strides above the ground. The beast's muscular neck was as long as its head, and its rust-red body was almost ten strides long and three strides high at the hips. A red-hued short sail ran the length of its back, making it unmistakable...a *redfin*, and a big one. Rogaan frantically fought back the urge to sick-up.

The massive beast approached, ready to launch itself at any prey or danger. Rogaan caught sight of Pax's spear extending toward the beast, shaking badly, and his friend's face pale filled with fear. Rogaan fought back his own fear with mixed success. At least he had not panicked. He took another breath, shallow and forced. It did not make him feel better. Rogaan wanted badly for Kardul to command them to retreat, but the *Kiuri'Ner* remained silent. The *redfin* closed, now less than twenty strides, and Kardul glanced at the ropes again. His scowl softened, if only a bit.

"Back to the ropes," Kardul commanded. "Give ground. Keep weapons at ready. *Redfins* charge, as often as not."

Pax hastily bounded to the ropes, almost running, tripping and catching himself several times. Rogaan fought the urge to bolt, not wanting to leave Kardul alone against the *redfin*. Pax hit the ropes climbing in a single move, his spear tossed down and forgotten before he reached the cliff.

"I didn't say climb," Kardul angrily barked at Pax.

Pax paused several strides above Rogaan with his feet solidly against the ravine wall, his face a tortured mix of a desire to obey and terror. Terror won out as Pax returned to climbing, though he ascended much faster than his arms and legs drew him up. The workers above were hauling hard on his rope.

"Get moving," Kardul growled at Rogaan. "Up the rope."

Rogan did not hear Kardul's words clearly, though he got the meaning with a nod of the *Baraan*'s head. Rogaan hastily quivered his arrow, almost cutting himself with the razor-sharp blades then slung the bow over his back as he bounded for the ropes, climbing hand over hand with boots digging into the rock wall. The urge to sick-up remained strong as his dizziness diminished. *Baraans* above hauled the rope up, hastening his ascent, bringing a muttered thanks to Rogaan's lips as he stole looks over his shoulder, fearing a mouthful of teeth coming at him. Kardul followed on another rope with little delay, also stealing glances over his shoulder to keep aware of what the *redfin* was doing. The beast continued to approach in a cautious stalk, but seemed more intent on the bloody carcass under him than the three fleeing up the cliff. As Rogaan neared the top, he saw Akaal grab Pax by the arm, pulling him up.

Relief filled Rogaan as the world sped up, returning to what he thought was normal. *I'm going to make it.* His stomach settled, and with it the urge to sick-up gone. Above, Akaal pulled Pax up by the hand; as he did, the *Baraan* fixed eyes with Rogaan with a sadistic smirk. A shiver rippled down Rogaan's spine and the hairs on his nape prickled stiff. Dread and helplessness washed over him in waves. Pax gave Akaal a questioning look as he hung unmoving at the end of Akaal's hand. Akaal never returned Pax's gaze; the *Baraan* kept his eyes fixed on Rogaan. Then the *Baraan*'s smirk turned into a full smile. Rogaan opened his mouth to demand Akaal pull Pax up, but Pax fell backwards, yelling, and with arms flailing.

"NO!" Rogaan shouted as he helplessly watched his friend fall down to the ravine floor.

Without a thought, Rogaan let go of his rope. His fall suddenly turned strangely slow, almost as if he were floating. As he fell, he helplessly watched Pax slam into the dirt only to bounce limply back into the air, then finally land with a dusty thud before lying motionless in a twisted pose. Pax looked without light. Rogaan cursed his slow fall wanting to get to Pax in hope of saving his friend. As he neared the ground, Rogaan twisted his body, bringing his feet directly under him, allowing them to hit the dirt first. It surprised him when he rolled over and over, absorbing and throwing off the impact of the fall. When he rolled to a stop, he found himself kneeling at the edge of the stream, at the opposite end of the carcass from the *redfin* near where Pax lay motionless. The *redfin* stood ridged, looking at him over the carcass with curiosity.

A long moment passed before the rust-red beast's demeanor

turned angry and let out a roar while shaking its head and jowls vigorously. The foul stench of rotting flesh blasting from its gapping jaws. When the reeking gust struck Rogaan his innards protested, gagging him, and forcing him to sick-up. *Idiot! What were you thinking?* Now staring at the towering mountain of muscle and teeth, Rogaan realized he was no match for the beast. The *redfin* looked every bit not pleased with Rogaan's presence as it took a step over the carcass and growled menacingly.

Rogaan scrambled backwards on his hands and feet away from the maw of spikes. The *redfin* seemed to grow more agitated at his withdrawal, and urinated on the ground just this side of the carcass. Rogaan rolled to a crouch not more than fifteen strides from the toothy maw as the beast charged. Rogaan's mind reeled with unwanted images of teeth, blood, and crushed bones. His head painfully pounded with each beat of his heart. Pushing away the pain, Rogaan drew his long knife. It was a futile gesture, but it made him feel better for some reason. Rogaan watched the *redfin* charge, the beast moving slowly enough for him to plan a desperate move just as the beast's jaws gaped, readying to snap them shut, crushing him. Taking advantage of the *redfin*'s poor sight with its jaws open, Rogaan spun left to the beast's side, stabbing its vile snout, sinking his blade in near its right nostril as the jaws clapped shut with a booming pop. The beast jerked its head left, pulling free of the long knife as it stopped its charge. Rogaan found himself crouching close to the beast's right foot. The *redfin* recovered quickly, twisting its neck and fixing its right eye on Rogaan, then gaped its jaws open as it pivoted right and crouched with straining muscles as Rogaan backed away. The *redfin* was readying itself to launch at Rogaan, who now stood two strides from the ravine wall, with nowhere to go to escape death. He was trapped. *I'm out of luck and light!*

Rogaan wanted to jump, run, something, but found his arms and legs paralyzed with fear. The *redfin* reared back, opening its jaws even wider. Victory was to the Wilds, and Rogaan resolved himself to fade away where he stood. He closed his eyes and clenched his teeth, waiting for the inevitable crushing agony of those jaws slamming shut on him. Nothing. Nothing happened. He opened his left eye, afraid of what he would see, expecting teeth to be his full vision. Surprisingly, the *redfin* was snapping at strange-looking fireflies buzzing about its head. *Praise the Ancients!* Astonished and relieved that he still lived, Rogaan sharply sucked in a breath and found his arms and legs able to move. Without thinking too hard on his options, Rogaan ran to Pax at the beast's left, hoping his friend was alive, vowing Pax would not become the *redfin*'s meal. In a breath everything changed, the world started moving rapidly, again. Rogaan felt as if he were in water for all the faster he could move, and he suddenly felt ravenously hungry. Shaking off his pains of hunger and disorientation, he grabbed his friend to haul him over his shoulder and carry him up the cliff, but Pax stirred. Rogaan mumbled aloud with shocked relief. "He's alive!"

"What happenin'?" Pax groaned, and wearily sat up.

"Ah…later, Pax," Rogaan answered while stealing a quick look at the *redfin* to make sure he was still occupied.

Rogaan pulled Pax up to his knees, but Pax held up his hand, signaling Rogaan to stop. Pain was clearly on Pax's face as he tried to catch his breath. Rogaan feared the *redfin* would be on them any moment, so he hauled Pax up to his feet and to the nearest dangling rope, wrapped it under Pax's arms and around his chest several times, then handed him the loose end. "Hold tight."

"What?" Pax managed to groan while looking confused.

With a wave of Rogaan's hand, Pax was hauled up fast by countless others atop the ravine wall. Several workers not pulling ropes frantically waved to get Rogaan's attention, pointing behind him. Fear froze Rogaan. He did not want to look knowing it would be bad. That rotting stench engulfed Rogaan, making his stomach reel and wanting to sick-up, again, as much from fear as the foul acrid odor. Spinning to look doom in the eye, he came face-to-face with the *redfin*'s maw, a stride from him. The fireflies were gone and the beast was no longer distracted, though it appeared a bit confused. It shook its head before settling its gaze back on Rogaan, then lowered itself; crouching, with muscles rippling, the *redfin* looked ready to pounce. A prickling sensation rippled through Rogaan as if needles poked him everywhere, and the stench of the *redfin*'s breath turned putrid, causing Rogaan to gag back the urge to let his stomach loose, again. The *redfin*'s movements slowed as the beast inhaled before letting out a roar that sounded and felt…off…to Rogaan: low in pitch and drawn-out. The stench choked him, almost overwhelming him. Rogaan gagged and swallowed, again. *How can anything smell so foul?* The beast reared back to strike -- unnaturally slowly.

Rogaan readied himself for another spin, hoping to make the *redfin* miss and give himself enough room to run. Before the beast could strike, something fell between them, striking the ground with a thud. *Akaal!* Shocked, Rogaan stared at the motionless, twisted body. He looked lightless…but then, so had Pax. Rogaan looked up seeking answers to forming questions. Pax was almost safely to the top, with workers still hauling him up. Wearing a look of satisfaction, Kardul stood at the cliff's edge, hands on hips. *Had Kardul tossed Akaal?* Rogaan looked back at Akaal, who now struggled with unsteady legs and arm, trying to rise to his feet. Without warning, Akaal was hammered to the ground by the *redfin*'s maw. A horrific scream escaping Akaal as the unmistakable sound of the crunch of bones being obliterated echoed in the ravine. His broken and bloody body finally fell silent when the *redfin*'s jaws closed on his head and neck with another loud crunch.

Shocked at the fragility of Akaal's body, Rogaan stood frozen. *What do I do?* The *redfin* slammed its jaws shut again; the crunching sound of Akaal's chest collapsing made Rogaan's stomach turn, but shook him into action. *Run! Climb!* Rogaan turned and jumped at the nearest rope, climbing as fast as he could -- hand over hand, and digging his boots into the rock wall hard, propelling himself upward. Rogaan started rising quicker than from his own efforts. The world around him returned to normal...faster, and he felt as if he were in water, again, for all the faster he moved. Another powerful urge to sick-up struck him. Fearing what was about to come, Rogaan wrapped the rope around his left wrist and hung on tight as he suffered violent convulsions. He lost count of his convulsions and felt weak -- and disgustingly enough, he felt hungry.

Wearily, he looked up to find those above continuing to haul on his rope. Rogaan gave thanks to all of them under his breath as he clung to the rope with his left hand, now without making any effort to pull himself up. He felt exhausted. Several strides from the top, Rogaan looked back at the bloody carnage below. The last of Akaal was getting gulped down by the *redfin*. *That could have been me or Pax.* Hands grabbed at him, hauling him over the edge of the cliff and out of the ravine. After a few moments of lying face down in the dirt, Rogaan struggled to his feet, straightening his posture in a weary effort. Looking up, he stared into the tilted, radiant green eyes of a *Baraan* with a short trimmed yellow-white beard that matched in color his straight shoulder-length hair. The *Baraan*'s face seemed odd somehow, with a slender nose and chiseled features that were not common to these parts. The *Baraan*'s build was taller and more slender than average and wiry. He had a powerful grip. Rogaan felt it as he had helped him to his feet. In all, the *Baraan* was not so different from a group of strangers that had traveled through Brigum some time ago, but different enough to notice, though Rogaan could not say why he thought so. The *Baraan* dressed as a carrier, no different from the rest. Though, he seemed out of place...something in the way he carried himself... too self-confident. Rogaan tried to place him in age-older than himself, maybe close to thirty, maybe more...it was difficult to gauge. Rogaan suddenly felt weary and shook his head with eyes closed to try reviving himself. *Why bother about the Baraan's age? It does not matter.*

"I am grateful," Rogaan told the stranger honestly after opening his eyes. The carrier simply bowed his head slightly in response. *His eyes are far too confident and he stands too tall, maybe even prideful.* Rogaan could not pin it down. *Something....*

"Rogaan!" Pax said in a chipper tone. "I be thinkin' ya not gonna make it. Ya gave me a scare."

Rogaan's face warmed at Pax's words, "You would have done the same for me."

Rogaan looked back for the carrier, but he was nowhere to be seen. *Where did he go? Why does it matter?* Rogaan's stomach rumbled loudly, and he felt hungry and tired. A loud crunch below drew every-ones attention down into the ravine. The *redfin* tore into the *longwalk-er*'s carcass, breaking its bones as it feasted. A quick glance at Kardul confirmed for Rogaan that the *Kiuri'Ner* was satisfied about something. *Did Kardul push him?*

"Pax," Rogaan whispered. "Something is wrong."

"What da ya mean?" Pax whispered back. "This be all wrong today."

Rogaan looked for the carrier, again. *Where did the Baraan disappear to?* He then looked back at Kardul, who was thanking the cutters and carriers for their good work. "Something is very wrong."

Chapter 7

Coming Home

The sun burned brilliantly in the northwest sky as clouds relented temporarily, opening a hole allowing bright rays of warmth to bathe Rogaan, forcing him to shield his eyes with hand and look down at the rutted trail to keep from being blinded with eye spots. Rogaan was tired, and struggled to keep pace with the creaking and groaning wagons at his left despite their heavy loads slowing them -- rewards of the Hunt: *longwalker* and *fern runner* meat and skins, all heavily salted. The blue and orange sky signaled the closing of another day and brought with it a waning in the heat, along with a little help from a mild breeze blowing off the craggy peaks of the Spine Range to the north. The scent of wild flowers and early-season tree blooms hung heavy on the breeze, but did little to mask the smell of trail dust and the overbearing musk of *niiskus*. The rugged mountains ran almost the length of Shuruppak, splitting the land north and south, from near the capital city of Ur, far to the east to Turil and the *Tellen* Nation on Shuruppak's western border -- beyond the deepest of the Wilds.

Scattering clouds, a mix of darkened masses and wispy feather-like structures burned hues of orange against the dark ridges to the north. Absent in the sky, large *leatherwings*, soaring high on the last updrafts of the day searching for prey or the lightless to scavenge. Instead, the sky was punctuated with colorful *featherwings* and small *leatherwings*, fighting for ownership of the space above the trees. Deep shadows engulfed ridges blanketed in pines and broadleafs, where red-rock outcrops were making Rogaan feel unease that something sinister lurked. The shadows played tricks on his eyes and mind, at times fooling him into giving alarm of things not there, while veiling others until they emerged from the gloom in a surprise. A short time earlier, Rogaan called alarm to a danger from *leapers* he thought followed them in a close tree line. Tricks of the shadows cast by wind rustled trees and ferns in the wind. He was embarrassed into silence after the *Kiuri'Ner* reacted to the phantom threat, and suffered their glares when the threat proved nonexistent. Not alone, others too called false dangers, leaving most in the caravan now paying little heed to such alarms.

Increasingly, Rogaan felt weary and wanted to see Brigum and be in his home, and his fears were dulling with his single-minded focus to get there. Looking about, it seemed others felt the same -- especially Pax, with dark sunken eyes and a blank expression to accompany his weary, yet steady gait. Rogaan was unsure if Pax suffered from red-face, that was typical for him with the early season blooms, or if the Hunt had truly taken a toll on him. Everyone had stepped close to losing their lights to darkness...too close, Rogaan thought. The Hunt lost several hunters to *leapers* after that first day. Now, all who returned seemed hardened from the Wilds in the short time they stepped outside the safety of Brigum's walls.

Firik and the *Kiuri'Ner* worked the lines of the weary from atop their *sarigs,* demanding that they keep pace with the wagons. The return to Brigum, now in its second day, was slower going than the day-long forced march to the valley. After days of hard hunting in dangerous land the slow journey back seemed as difficult as that first day's trek. For Rogaan, that eastward march seemed a lifetime ago. Much had happened. With eyes raised to the sky, Rogaan quietly thanked the Ancients that Firik had not demanded a forced march for the return. Blistered feet painfully annoyed Rogaan, causing him to wince and limp a little with each step. He tried his best to put the pain from of his mind, but weariness made it nearly impossible, so he sought distractions by scanning the surrounding forest and heights, looking for dangers. Packs of small gray-green feathered *leapers*, sporting red head and neck plumes, paralleled them, stalking and testing the caravan's defenses and retreating with angry chirps, squawks, and hisses when chased off…which the hunters did often early on. Cutters and carriers walking alongside the hunters also struggled to keep pace with the wagons carrying the successes of the Hunt and those wounded badly enough to keep from walking. The injured numbered half a dozen in all, and were being fussed over in the wagon nearest Rogaan by several Healers -- brought along at the insistence of Firik. Pax somehow discovered that last bit of information and revealed it to Rogaan. Pungent odors from salves and foul elixirs wafted around the wagon as they treated the wounded, causing Rogaan to recall the care of Healers in his youthful days. A grimace came to his face. Given the odors and memories, he was uncertain if he would be willing to take those medicines, again, even if he were sick with the shakes or bite-rot or worse. And from the expressions of those now getting healing, Rogaan felt content to walk instead of ride in the wagon…blisters and all.

Out of arrows, Rogaan now carried a spear, using it more as a walking stick than weapon. His bow case slung on his back was light a few very expensive arrowheads that Rogaan did not know how he would confess their loss to his father. Pax too used his spear as Rogaan did, though he made no effort to hide his weariness, heavily leaning on it at every opportunity while Rogaan did his best to appear strong and capable when in sight of the *Kiuri'Ner*. The few days of the Hunt had given him the opportunity to demonstrate his skills, and he hoped they were enough, though not a word of encouragement was spoken to Rogaan by Kardul or any of his *Kiuri'Ner*.

Surprisingly, Kantus and his Band kept to themselves since the *fern runner* incident. Rogaan welcomed the respite from their taunting, though he had a guilty sense of satisfaction when he looked at Kantus ahead of him, limping. At the start of the return, Firik offered Kantus the opportunity to join the wounded in the wagons, but he refused, astonishingly. In fact, Kantus' reply was so indignant that Firik rewarded him and his Band with extra equipment to carry from the wounded, which would otherwise have been left behind. As expected, Kantus protested indignantly and arrogantly, telling Firik he would deal with his father. Firik dismissed the threats casually, and that seemed to darken Kantus' mood. After that exchange, Kantus and his Band fell strangely quiet, but visibly fuming as they shot darting glares at Firik, and at Rogaan and Pax for good measure, it seemed.

Rogaan's thoughts drifted with the monotony of the walking pace. He reflected on the strangeness of past few days. Something was not right. Rogaan felt it, but could not point to what made him feel so. Adding to it, the *Kiuri'Ner* looked at him oddly every now and then, almost as if they knew something he should know, but did not. Kardul was the worst of them, though Rogaan was not certain how to take the *Baraan*, as he had taught him much of the Wilds and how to survive it, even when he did not appear to be teaching. Rogaan thought Pax had learned just as much, despite his friend's insistence to the contrary and, of course, complaints when corrected by anyone. Akaal was a different matter. That *Baraan* weighed heavily on Rogaan's thoughts. Several nights of dreams bordering on the bizarre made Rogaan even more suspicious of him, though details of the dreams faded away quickly and now were unclear. All that remained was a sense of dread he felt just before waking this morning that had stayed with him since. He tried confiding in Pax, telling him about his dreams and his suspicions concerning Akaal. Pax listened to him without interrupting -- odd for Pax -- but his friend then dismissed it all as guilt for not trying more to save the *Baraan*, though Pax seemed unconvinced even at his own words and over Akaal's gruesome return to darkness.

Not long after his confession, Rogaan caught sight of Pax speaking to Kardul, who rode beside Pax briefly after checking on the wounded. Despite dismissing Rogaan's conspiracies, Pax looked to be confronting the *Kiuri'Ner* with them. Kardul half-listened before dismissing Pax's assertion with a wave of his hand and riding off, leaving Pax in a bit of a brood. When Rogaan confronted Pax about his talk with Kardul, Pax flatly told him he wanted to know the truth of things, especially if someone wished them harm. Pax put on one of his sly smiles and told Rogaan that the *Kiuri'Ner* said he was not a fool, given the events, but recommended Rogaan spend his time thinking of the here and now. Rogaan felt his cheeks warm at his friend's asking and covering for him. Pax was not known for his selflessness. Rogaan was thankful for Pax's asking and keeping him from possibly harming his standing with Kardul.

To Rogaan, the events of the Hunt just did not fit. He hoped he had succeeded in showing enough promise for the *Kiuri'Ner*, but the rest of the happenings were troubling. Try as he might, he could not piece events together so that they made sense: his father allowing him to join the Hunt after forbidding it for so long, then his father's sudden journey away from Brigum -- a rare occasion; Kantus' ominous decla-ration that he would soon be nothing but a memory; the broken bow; Akaal's attempt to kill Pax or him or both; Kardul's seeming satisfied at Akaal's death; that out-of-place worker who disappeared right af-ter Akaal's death...and nobody remembering the *Baraan* when Rogaan asked of him...and Kardul's off treatment of him since. Separately, they were just happenings; together...they were strange coincidences, yet nothing seemed to fit. Pax was little help, shrugging off Rogaan's worries, telling him he thought too much about things and remaining unconvinced of conspiracies despite Rogaan's insistence that some-thing was wrong. Frustrated, Rogaan lost himself in deep thought, trying to figure out what he was missing.

Sometime later when he crested a rise on the trail, he absently looked up and was surprised to see Brigum coming into sight. Deep in the shadows of the narrow valley ahead, the town's stone walls, towers, and bridge were almost lost without the direct rays of sun to illuminate them, and also in the glare of the closing hour of the day on the mountain ridges to the northwest. With hands raised, shield-ing their eyes from the setting sun, the lot of them looked westward, trying to steal glimpses of their homes. There was movement in the shadows at Brigum's Hunter's and Coiner Quarter's Gates; the town's *Tusaa'Ner* in their sky-blue uniforms under dark shoulder and chest armor, and bright red and yellow belt sashes stood watch on the walls, with guardsmen standing tall every two or three strides with their spears pointing skyward. All were in full dress with helms sporting short red feather plumes. *What now? War?*

"Too many guards," Pax flatly stated.

"Still say I think too much?" Rogaan gave Pax a tight-lipped, sardonic smile. Pax kept silent in spite of the verbal jab. His friend merely returned a playfully confused look as the caravan approached the eastern edge of Brigum. With each step, Rogaan grew more anxious because of his unsanctioned use of the *shunir'ra*. Touching the encased bow slung on his back, he wondered if the trouble was worth it as a wave of guilt and shame swept over him. Very soon, he would need to explain his decisions to his parents -- why he took the bow against father's wishes. Worse, he feared his father and mother would no longer trust him. *Silly to hope their trust in me would remain.* He knew this was to be before he removed it from its hiding place, but it was only now that the full weight of that decision struck him. His stomach soured. Rogaan began seriously questioning his actions, his motivations, his desires, his impetuous and selfish missteps, and found himself...wanting. Almost in a panic, he started drawing deep breaths, trying to find calm and clear his thoughts. His panic swelled, making his head whirl and chest feel as if it were about to burst. He tried more breathing tricks...they did little to help. *How to mend this with Father? Can I ever fix this?* Rogaan began hoping for some miracle to avoid the inevitable, and found himself wishing he had not taken his *shunir'ra* in the first place. *How can I fix this and keep their trust?*

The caravan creaked and rumbled its way toward the Brigum, the pace faster now with the town in sight. Firik Umsadaa spurred his *sarig* ahead of the wagons, trotting his steed to the gates, where he was met by the Brigum *Tusaa'Ner Sakal*, the commander dressed in full sky-blue uniform, plumed helm, and cape – both red with yellow stripes. Another guardsman, shorter by a head, was dressed in a uniform similar in style to the Watchers of Brigum, but of darker blue and with a solid red sash, helm plumage, and cape. Rogaan became curious; the newcomer looked to be *Tusaa'Ner*.

Firik exchanged words with the two. It started out simple enough, but soon turned animated, with Firik waving, agitated, and pointing back at the caravan before shaking his fist at the pair. Nearly everyone in the caravan watched the heated exchange grow to a fever seemingly with each word. Few took the exchange as trouble. *Fools.* Rogaan's concern elevated as he traded glances with Pax. Rogaan started his breathing drills, again, to help calm himself. The pair of *Kiuri'Ner* riding at the head of the caravan brought their *sarigs* to a halt near Coiner Quarter Gate, stopping short of where they intended at a raised hand from Kardul. Rogaan realized they too were on edge and readying to spring into action at Kardul's command. Following suit, the wagons halted behind them in single file on the rutted, hard-packed dirt road snaking eastward from the gates. Dust and the pungent odors of *sarig*, *niisku*, and folk swirled about the caravan, forcing Rogaan to wrinkle his nose and suppress a strong urge to sneeze and another to cough.

Looking up after getting himself under control, Rogaan saw Firik and the *Tusaa'Ner* joined by a contingent of eight soldiers in dark blue armor, helms, and red belt sashes at the back of the shortest of the *Tusaa'Ner*. The eight halted their approach just short of a spear length at a sharp bark of the short red-caped guardsman nearest Firik. The bark was higher-pitched than Rogaan expected. He looked to Pax with raised brows. Pax just shrugged then returned his attention to the activity at the gate. *That guardsman commander is a...a woman.* Rogaan had read and heard of women as soldier aides, but not leading a troupe. *Never such a thing!* Surprised, fascinated, and with a growing curiosity, Rogaan forgot his troubles and focused on the arguing trio: Firik, the Brigum *Tusaa'Ner* commander, the *Seergal*, and the guardswoman *Sakal*. The red belt sash nagged at Rogaan. It meant something, but the answer eluded him. Then he recalled reading Father's book about the colors of Shuruppak…red marked the guardsmen as…Farratum's *Tusaa'Ner*. His pride in recalling this fact was washed away by his confusion. *What are Farratum guardsmen doing here?*

Excitement quickly replaced Rogaan's confusion and unease. He wanted to meet the Farratum *Tusaa'Ner*, but feared looking a fool. Hunters and workers alike suddenly started moving about, blocking his view of the gate area as they tended to wagons, animals, and equipment…seemingly doing anything not to draw attention to themselves for gawking, all as they stole nervous glances at the heated scene ahead of the caravan. Frustrated at having his view blocked, Rogaan grumbled a few choice words as he jumped about to see what was happening with Firik and the *Tusaa'Ner*. *Exciting! I hope I can meet them. What is all of this about?* Rogaan's hopes were dashed when the exchange between Firik and the short red-caped *sakal* turned foul, and it looked as if Firik were losing the argument. The guardswoman's head canted slightly at Firik's words, allowing her shoulder-length braids of light-colored hair to dangle before violently whirling them in a head shake as she growled something back at the *Baraan*. She stood at arm's length from Firik with fists now firmly on her hips, showing no intent of backing down. For a long moment, Rogaan thought she might launch herself at Firik with fists swinging, from the way she started to carry on. The guardsmen accompanying her did not flinch despite everything happening. They stood stiff-backed in silence, with spears firmly planted, ready to do her bidding when she commanded so. Kardul dismounted and walked with confidence, approaching Firik and the *sakals*. The Farratum guardsmen showed him little interest as he neared, simply watching him as *leapers* watched prey. Not more than a few moments after joining Firik and the *sakals*, Kardul found himself drawn deeply into argument, and seemed to fare no better than Firik, to judge by the way the red-caped *sakal* met his stare and lashed both of them with her sharp tongue. Try as they might, Kardul and Firik were unable to utter more than a few words when she paused to take a breath, before hurling another verbal onslaught at them. At a statement made by Kardul, the red-caped *sakal* snapped her fingers, sending guardsmen surrounding Firik and Kardul with spears ready to strike. Kardul's two *Kiuri'Ner* were off their *sarigs* in a blink and moving to flank the guardsmen. They held their attack, standing with hands on hilts once in position, waiting for a sign from Kardul to launch themselves at whoever he directed them to.

"This is not how I expected my first meeting with the Farratum *Tusaa'Ner* to be." Rogaan spoke aloud before he realized he said it.

"How'd ya think it ta be?" Pax asked with a deliberate blink of disbelief before his face grew a scowl. "Wait...Farratum? What be they doin' here? War or somethin'?"

"Their colors are Farratum's," Rogaan answered.

Captivated, Rogaan and Pax stared at the spectacle. The arguments raged for a few more moments before Kardul turned sharply, then walked back to the caravan, shaking his head in either disgust or frustration -- Rogaan was not sure which. Kardul spoke to the *Kiuri'Ner* as he passed their positions. Their postures softened, almost. Kardul halted facing the line of wagons with fists planted on his hips. He looked unhappy. "Hunters. By command of the Farratum *Tusaa'Ner*." He paused to look over his shoulder then back at the hunters then continued. "Disarm. Place your weapons in the wagon closest to you; then stand in line on the side of the road nearest the lake."

Kardul waited for everyone to comply. No one moved. Rogaan was confused and a little stunned at his command. Pax and others looked to fare no better. *What did Farratum want? Why disarm?* Kardul stood like a stone, unmoving, watching the hunters and workers for a few more moments then growled, "Jump to it!"

Workers on both sides of the wagons jumped with a start while hunters begrudgingly complied. Rogaan and Pax slowly fell in line with the rest. Kardul then began walking the length of the caravan, inspecting each person as he went.

"What he be doin?" Pax asked while keeping his eyes on Kardul.

"No guess," Rogaan replied with a shrug. "I am more interested in the talk between the *Tusaa'Ner* and Firik. It did not look friendly, and now we are disarming."

Pax wore a sour face, especially after tossing his weapons in the wagon. Pax was not a compliant person where authority was concerned, particularly when it was unfavorable to him. Rogaan wondered if his friend gave up any of the knives he knew to be tucked under his gray tunic and in his bottom pack. *I would be surprised if he gave any of his knives up.* After tossing his spear into the wagon, Rogaan stood in line next to Pax and with the rest of the hunters, at the edge of the road near a thick patch of low ferns, fir trees, and a gum that separated the gaggle from the lake shore some thirty strides further to the north. Rogaan felt uneasy…something was wrong, and not knowing made him feel more on edge. Pax played oblivious to the situation by rocking on his heels and doing his best to look impatient. *Then, it might not be an act.* Rogaan wondered. Kardul slowly made his way down the line, inspecting each person as he went, stopping every third or fourth person to talk briefly before moving on.

"Da newcomers be lookin' for somethin'. Pax spoke quietly. "Look at 'em. They be watchin' Kardul like they no trust him."

"Do you think it could have something to do with us?" Rogaan asked innocently.

"Stop thinkin' this be about da valley!" Pax replied sarcastically. "They be wantin' ta tax us for huntin' or somthin'. Ya know how *these* ones be always wantin' ta take coin outta pockets."

Rogaan glared a moment at Pax as he wondered at his friend's stubborn inability to see what was happening. Pax refused to put the pieces together and he just did not understand his friend, especially since Pax was usually the one to accuse town leaders of conspiracies separating common folk from their coin and all else. Rogaan saw differently -- maybe more through the eyes of his family, with discussions rich in plots, schemes, and history, rather than from the streets as Pax experienced things. Recently, Rogaan's father had started complaining -- a rare thing, that -- that Brigum's leaders seemed to be more about gaining and holding on to control of the people than they were with taking coin. Town laws changed, appearing to allow those in charge of watching over merchants and the common folk, ensuring fair exchanges, to manipulate if not dictate dealings. Sometimes that meant controlling the exchange of coin. Sometimes it meant controlling how the people cooperated. His father often challenged blatant attempts to grasp power, and that led to his making enemies of some in the town council, and any that favored their point of view. Rogaan realized, now, that things had been going wrong since long before he left for the Hunt. He felt it, and feared its source was Kantus' father coming after his family. Rogaan felt shame, again, for taking his *shunir'ra* when bigger and important things were happening all around him and the people he cared about. *I feel small because of my misdeeds.*

Kardul slowly walked the line of hunters, stopping and talking a moment with them. A light tremor was noticeable to the hunters. Kardul ignored the shaking of the ground as he lingered three persons over, and spoke to a big hunter whose name Rogaan had never learned. Their words were barely audible, but what Rogaan heard sounded meaningless . . . small talk, really. Kardul unemotionally moved on after their short exchange before stopping in front of him and Pax, his expression no different than it had been when talking to the others in the line.

"You both must flee and hide." Kardul spoke softly and unemotionally while keeping his eyes on Rogaan. "Use the skills you've learned the past few days to hide from Farratum's guardsmen. They will not be able to follow you long in the Wilds, and I'll see that no *Kiuri'Ner* finds you. Take leave of us when I command the hunters to form up on the road. Then make haste."

Kardul walked on without further explanation. Pax stood staring after the *Kiuri'Ner* much as Rogaan did, mouth agape. Pax's tattered wide-brimmed hat hid his face in shadow from everyone except Rogaan and a few hunters closest to them, but Rogaan wore no such hat, and realized his mouth was slung open. He shut it as he stiffened his posture before glancing at the gate to see if anyone was looking at him. Only the woman *sakal* appeared to be watching Kardul and those he spoke to. She stood with an impatient posture, her fists planted on her hips and her right foot tapping the paving stones now and then.

"What do we do?" Rogaan asked Pax quietly.

"As he says," Pax whispered. "I no trust da red-sashes. They be likely ta demand coin and threaten us jail when we say no."

"Why us?" Rogaan asked to no one in particular. "Did Father send them to bring me back?"

"There ya go again," Pax chided. "Kardul be talkin' ta lots of us. Looks like a bunch will run when he says ta."

"Pax, I'm no law-breaker," Rogaan declared. "My father would not stand for it. It is not the *Tellen* way, and I . . . need to stand for my decisions...and actions." Rogaan resolved himself to take full account for taking his *shunir'ra*. *Did Father really call the Tusaa'Ner to retrieve the bow? If so, why call Farratum's guardsmen instead of Brigum's?*

Pax smiled widely and replied sarcastically. "Looks like ya not be given a choice. Da red-sashes look ta be forming up or somethin'. Maybe it be ya they want. They certainly have no need of me. I be a peaceable youngling."

Rogaan shot Pax a skeptical look then softened his stare when he saw his friend's smirk. "Do you think they are after me for taking my *shunir'ra*?"

"Ya *shunir'ra*?" Pax asked, surprised. "Why would he do that ta ya? More likely he have ya shovel rocks every day for da rest of ya life.

Besides, Kardul still be talkin' with a lot of us, ya see." Pax nodded toward the end of the uneven line of hunters, where Kardul was finishing his inspection of the hunter, a couple at a time.

Another wave of guilt washed over Rogaan at the thought of his taking his *shunir'ra*. "Maybe you are right. Kardul is talking to too many of the hunters."

Pax gave Rogaan a forced smile as he tightened the straps and laces on his carry pack. Rogaan cinched snug his own carry pack. He feared fleeing and all the repercussions it could have on his family. He was in enough trouble, and did not want to bring any further dishonor to himself -- and especially not to his father. Bad enough to run from the Brigum guardsmen and law-keepers, but to run from the Farratum *Tusaa'Ner* would put him neck-deep in a dung pile, instead of only to his knees. Pax might be willing to live life so, but that was not the way Rogaan considered himself raised or felt right in doing. *No*, he decided he would not run. Honor was more important than his comfort. He was going to face this trouble, whatever it was, as his father would want him to do.

"Rogaan...." Pax spoke cautiously and low. "I see it on ya face. Don't be no fool. Kardul said ta run, and he not give us any reason not ta trust him...yet. And I no like da idea of goin' ta jail where Kantus can celebrate on our heads. Ya no want that, do ya?"

Before Rogaan could reply, Kardul commanded everyone to form a single line on the road facing Hunter's Gate. All hesitated, then shuffled to it only after Kardul growled at them. Pax tugged on Rogaan's shirt, then let go when Rogaan stepped forward onto the hard-packed dirt road. Rogaan joined the forming line, then looked back at a distressed Pax standing at the edge of the road. Rogaan pleaded with his eyes for Pax to join him. Long, tense moments passed before Pax squeezed into the line next to his friend, wearing disbelief on his face.

"*Kiuri'Ner*, what are you doing?" the Farratum commander demanded from the bridge in her high-pitched tone. Firik stood next to her, holding a frustrated posture, though he kept silent. Several

Brigum and Farratum *Tusaa'Ner* flanked him, each with a predatory stare focused on him, possibly to make sure he did nothing.

"Forming the line so the hunters can be marched past you for inspection," Kardul responded innocently.

"Forget that!" she commanded. She stood up taller, scrutinizing the line. "Where is the one named Rogaan, son of Mithraam, the metal smith?"

Rogaan shivered head to boots. She was looking for him…him. With fear gripping him and threatening to stop his lungs from taking in air, Rogaan fought back the urge to bolt. Instead, he forced himself to breath slow and steady, trying to keep calm -- well, as best he could, given the circumstances.

"Rogaan." Impatient, Pax spoke in a low voice as he tugged Rogaan's carry pack. "Time ta go."

"Son of Mithraam, speak up." The woman was harsh. She stood with her fists firmly planted on her hips, demanding a response. Nobody spoke. Rogaan held his tongue, but felt many eyes on him. Without turning to look behind her, the *sakal* grunted orders that brought more Farratum guardsmen to the bridge repositioning themselves on both sides of her, their spears at the ready.

Rogaan's thoughts raced. Why did she want him? She named him by his father. *What trouble am I in?*

"It really be time ta go," Pax urged, alarmed more at this point.

Pax tugged at Rogaan's carry pack so hard he pulled Rogaan off balance. Rogaan leaned forward to regain his balance and to make things harder for Pax. He needed time to think, to weigh his options, as few as they seemed at the moment, and to decide what to do — speak up, or remain silent and let them figure out who he was all on their own.

"He's there!" Kantus squealed, after stepping from the line some twenty paces ahead and pointing right at Rogaan. "That's the troublemaker. That's Rogaan."

B.A.VONSIK

"Arrest the youngone he's pointing at," the woman *sakal* ordered.

"I believe ya . . . this really be about ya," Pax conceded. "Now run!" Pax yanked on Rogaan's carry pack so hard they both stumbled out of the line toward the lake. To Rogaan's surprise, Pax did not stop pulling and yanked him off-balance sending them both stumbling off the hard-packed dirt and into the ferns at the side of the road. "Run! Blind ya."

Run they did, plunging into the thickets in between two stands of tall palms. At first, Rogaan reluctantly followed Pax. He struggled to shake off the feeling that he was fleeing the unknown and heading into the unknown for an unknown reason. Rogaan did not like it, not at all. Tangle-vines and exposed roots caused him to stumble as often as not, with only sharp fronds of razor ferns or the occasional branch to grab in order to keep his feet. Rogaan felt torn. *Am I doing the right thing?* But he kept running, trying to keep up with Pax. At least he thought himself doing well if he could just keep sight of him. Without antici-pating it, he burst out of the thickets and into a small clearing where he came to a sliding stop, clinging to a finger-thick branch of a red berry bush. His cut and stinging hands were covered with a mix of red berry juice and blood, making the branch slick enough that it slipped from his grasp, whipping back smartly the way he had come. Rogaan searched for Pax, finding his friend picking himself up off the ground to his left. In a flash of uncertainty and fear that he would be branded a law-breaker, Rogaan lashed out at Pax. "What does this do for us?"

Pax rolled to his knees, looking around as if he were a stalked ani-mal, then hopped into a crouch before slinking off through a stand of fir and gum trees and ferns...away from Hunter's Gate. Pax waved, almost frantically, for Rogaan to follow. When Rogaan did not move, Pax stopped urging him to flee. "Come. Nothin' good ta come from da red-sashes takin' us."

Rogaan stood staring at Pax, conflict raging in his head and heart. *Why run? This is about me taking the shunir'ra...against Father's wishes. Pax need not pay for my choices. No!* Rogaan decided he would not run.

He would face whatever was to be, and not as a law-breaker running. Maybe he could soften his father's disappointment and anger this way. To keep running would only make things worse. "No. Pax, I need to face my father and the law."

Pax grabbed his head with both hands and grimaced, while rolling his eyes up into his head, then quavered as he groaned in frustration. Rogaan watched Pax's tantrum. He threw one when he could not take any more of Rogaan. The tantrums were usually short, but a tongue-lashing was coming. Rogaan prepared his rebuttal. As expected, Pax settled after a few moments leveling angry eyes on him. Pax opened his mouth to speak harsh words. Rogaan was all too familiar with the routine, but before Pax could speak, he looked skyward over Rogaan and put on a stunned expression. A moment later his eyes went wide and he shouted, "Spear!"

Pax's wide eyes pointed to the closing weapon above and behind Rogaan. Twisting and pivoting, Rogaan caught sight of the spear just before it struck the ground an arm's length from him. He stared in stunned surprise at the quivering shaft of the weapon sticking from the ground at a slanted angle. *Why throw the spear at us?* Looking up, Rogaan sensed the trees and ferns had stopped swaying in the light breeze. Even the breeze seemed to have died off. Looking to Pax, Rogaan became dizzy and felt about to sick-up. Pax moved unnaturally slowly as he motioned desperately for Rogaan to follow. Rogaan stumbled and fell to one knee, the dizziness too much for him and the urge to sick-up powerful. He fought it back before losing the battle in a painful retching. When he looked up, Pax stood next to him moving normally and dragging him to his feet. "Run, Rogaan. Blind, ya!"

Confused and with unsettled innards, Rogaan looked back toward the gate area. He glimpsed movement through opening in the trees and underbrush. The little he could see showed guardsmen in the colors of Farratum and Brigum assembling in small groups. A wave of panic washed over him, shaking him head to toe. *Why? Taking my bow could not warrant this. Is Father gone mad?* Paralyzed with confusion, Rogaan remained on bended knee, thinking, trying to work out things, to make sense of everything.

"Blind, ya!" Pax spat as he grabbed at Rogaan. "Follow me. Da mean ta kill ya." He pulled Rogaan's shirt, ripping its collar, before getting him to rise and take a few tentative steps toward the denser woods. With another nearly frantic yank, Rogaan followed Pax at an uncommitted trot. "Run, Rogaan, run!"

Rogaan followed at a trot, then started running after hearing voices closing from behind. Pax's pace had him well ahead, though somehow he managed to keep in sight of Rogaan. Running mechanically, without urgency, Rogaan's mind wondered wildly, desperately seeking answers to a simple question: *Why? Why was this happening to him?* He felt confused and uncertain. *How could Father set the guard after me... with orders to harm me?* It made no sense. Cracking branches and shouts not far behind broke into his straying thoughts. He was losing the foot race. The guardsmen were catching up. Under his breath -- more between breaths -- Rogaan cursed the Ancients for his *Tellen* heritage and his blood's lack of speed. In outright runs, he never impressed anyone he could remember while growing up in Brigum, and it looked as if things were no different now. Deciding to remain free, Rogaan set his jaws in determination to escape his pursuers. He would figure out what trouble he was in and how to fix it later, after he was safe from capture. He pushed through the underbrush, zigzagging around dense tufts of razor ferns and trees with as much haste as he could muster. He started breathing hard.

Ahead some fifty paces, Pax stood with shoulders and head visible above a patch of ferns, fiercely urging Rogaan on. Rogaan's head throbbed and chest pounded with each beat of his heart, now as rapid as he ever remembered, but timed with his footfalls. He realized he was running all-out, but despite his efforts, his pursuers still closed on him. The chase had taken them to the opposite side of the lake, to the hills forming the north end of the valley Brigum sat nestled in. The lake's calm water, now gloomy in the twilight, sat on Rogaan's left with dwarfed, rugged cliffs rising to his right. Rogaan admitted to himself that he was just too slow to escape and needed to do something different, or he would be run down and captured. The shoreline would take him back to Brigum and, if he were lucky enough to stay ahead of his pursuers, likely to a waiting contingent of guardsmen. His only chance of escape was into the rougher terrain where his running disadvantage would not count so much against him. With renewed determination, he turned toward the cliffs, quickly losing sight of Pax along the edge of the lake. *Pax can outrun any guardsmen. He'll be all right.*

Rogaan darted between boulders, trees, and undergrowth with ease. His running speed might not impress too many, but quickness he had plenty of. What he lost in ground to the guardsmen in a straight run, he gained with every shift in direction, now. His confidence grew. A spear glanced off a rock to his right then skittered off into dense undergrowth. Looking back, he saw six Farratum guardsmen some thirty paces behind in hot pursuit. They still closed on him. *What must I do to escape them?* A shadow burst out from a grove of trees near them. It was one of Kardul's *Kiuri'Ner*, though Rogaan could not tell which one. The *Baraan* slammed into the lead Farratum guardsman, knocking him flat and tangling up the other five, all but one ending up sprawled on the ground. Relieved, and a little surprised at getting help from the *Kiuri'Ner*, he bolted up the steep slope of the rugged cliff, fleeing the chaos below, skillfully climbing the uneven ground to safety, leaving the guardsmen and *Kiuri'Ner* behind.

Once over the cliff, Rogaan ran hard to get as much as distance between him and the guardsmen as possible before darkness fell. He entered a forest of tall firs, cedars, and pines. Their deep shadows quickly turned into a blanket of gloom. The broken canopy high above combined with the dense stands of trunks blocked out most of the waning sunlight, turning the gloom to almost pitch blackness the farther Rogaan ran. His footfalls became treacherous, with unseen branches slapping and cutting him. A sense of dread gripped him hard. He could not see. Fighting the instinct to bolt in any direction, he stopped and closed his eyes to allow them to adjust to the darkness. His dread worsened, but he kept his eyes closed. When he could not bear it any longer he opened his eyes to a dim, gray world with haunting outlines of trees, underbrush, rocks and rock outcrops, and deep shadows. It all seemed unnatural, especially the shadows. Rogaan tried to fight back a shudder that finally racked his whole body. He did not want to be here. He wanted to leave, and could feel his panic rising within. Then, distant sounds of those searching for him were making their way closer. With a deep breath and forced exhale, Rogaan decided they were not far enough away and that he needed to move further into the dark forest to escape. With an effort, he forced himself to take one step, to walk into his fear, willingly walking deeper into darkness and his dread.

Rogaan trembled at what unseen terror waited for him. His chest pounded wildly at that thought. Despite his ability to make out some major objects in the darkness, Rogaan had to move slowly to keep from tripping over exposed roots, rocks, and underbrush. Silver webs tickled at his face and hair, sending a chill down his spine and hitting him with a surge of panic at getting bit. He frantically pulled them from him, cursing everyone and everything as he did. The thought of an eight-legs crawling on him sent another chill down his back. Eight-legs terrified him. He wanted to bolt away as the darkness pressed in on him, but he held on to himself and pushed on, not wanting to be captured by those his father had sent after him. *Why, Father? Why?* With chest aching and head pounding, he gulped at the air before realizing he clung with both arms to a trunk of a pine. His clothes, soaked in sweat, gave off a rank odor strong enough to wrinkle his own nose when he was not trying to fill his lungs. Near panic, Rogaan darted looks everywhere, fearing the unseen that would cruelly end his life.

Shadowy outlines and shifting dark shapes that could become a ter-ror in an instant were all around him. The smell of the forest seemed normal, but oppressive as the darkness pressed on him. He felt vulner-able, alone, and completely defenseless. He was at the mercy of the darkness, but the darkness had no mercy. He knew that. It was ma-levolent. Panic welled up in him and he fought it down. It welled up again and again he fought it down. A squawk from an unseen creature somewhere above nearly set his panic out of control. Waves of fear and desperation washed over him. His clinging arms were all that kept his feet in place. *Must get away!* He needed light -- to be without gloom, darkness, doom, death. Another squawk eerily echoed through the forest, answered by malevolent chirps from seemingly every direction.

It was too much. Rogaan felt himself running in the darkness, out of control, his senses useless...his thoughts wild. Suddenly, Rogaan was unable to move. He just stopped without falling and now could not move. *Run! Run! Run!* His mind screamed for him to flee...it did not matter where, just *RUN*, his mind continued to scream, but his body betrayed him as if held tight by an unseen hand. Shivers rippled through him. *The darkness has me!* Rogaan frantically struggled against his unseen bonds. No good. A howl of fear and desperation erupted from his lips. Then, somewhere deep within him, he started to fight back. *No! I must not call in more darkness.* A spark of reason flickered. With all he had left in him, Rogaan desperately fought to keep hold of that shred of light and hope, and to get control his fear. A deep breath. Another. Slowly, he forced his breathing into a regular rhythm. Another breath. Another...this one a little slower than before. Another. And another...slower still. The pounding in his skull diminished as his thoughts started to clear. More than a shred. Rogaan realized he still clung to the tree, with both arms tightly wrapped around it. He never let it go. Rogaan shut his eyes again, tightly, to concentrate on control-ling his emotions and to hopefully regain his dignity.

Reason regained...somewhat, though Rogaan remained anxious,

if not still fearful, at the darkness and the eerie sounds echoing around him. His panic retreated, though he tried to convince himself that he had forced it away completely. *It is a lie to myself.* Slowly, his confidence returned and his breathing slowed, as did his once-racing heart. When he felt almost in control of himself, Rogaan opened his eyes to darkness. He hoped light would shine. No such fortune. Darkness hung thick everywhere, except for the shadowy silhouettes he could make out in the forest. He was uncertain how far he had traveled…two ridges, maybe three. Regardless, Rogaan could not imagine anyone following him except the *Kiuri'Ner*, but Kardul had taken care of that, as he saw with his own eyes.

The night was alive with the buzzing *biters*, the occasional chirp of *featherwings*…he hoped…and even more rare, the distant bellows and squawks of *tanniyn*. A slight cool breeze rustled the leaves in the little undergrowth there was, but seemed not to disturb the branches above. Rogaan felt isolated, alone, and vulnerable. Never had he been outside the walls of Brigum after nightfall by himself…in complete darkness. The strange noises of the mountain woodlands, amplified by the darkness, kept his senses on alert. Many *tanniyn* bedded down at night when their vision was poorest, but almost as many remained active through the darkness…the predators. Half…that granted him a bit of comfort, but not much, though it was enough to hold on to. He peeled himself from the tree, his hands and arms a bit sticky from running sap, before sitting down against a large pine next to the one he all but attempted to crush. Propped up against the tree, he wondered back to the events of the day when his life suddenly turned upside down. *How could you do this to me, Father?* Rogaan shook his head in disbelief and pain. He felt more alone than ever in his life. *How could you do this, Father?*

A branch snapped somewhere close, followed by a chirp and a clicking growl, also close. Rogaan's senses went wild. Instantly, all movement slowed and his sight sharpened. Sounds seemed distorted…off pitch, somehow lengthening. The scent of the forest became vibrant, almost overpowering with decaying leaves, musty soil, and…blood! Rotting flesh! Another clicking growl, this one off to his right. Another behind him. Another to his left. Another to his front. *Leapers!* He could just make out their shadowy silhouettes at the edge of his night sight. They surrounded him. Rogaan pulled out his long knife and waved it in front of him, slicing the air with a whistle to let the creatures know he was dangerous. He rose to a crouch, readying himself for the attack he knew would come…and likely his death. The pit of his stomach knotted and he felt a twinge of shame at his last thought. *Fear should not grip me so tight.* He was ashamed of himself. Twigs snapped, closer. Clicks and growls closed from behind. Rogaan whirled to meet the creature face to face. Its shadowy silhouette crouched six strides away. Rogaan's breath and heartbeat stopped. Death looked him in the eyes. Rogaan's skin suddenly felt aflame. Pain seared him. No bright flames were visible to his eyes…just the intense pain of being burned. Rogaan convulsed, dropping his blade as he fell to the ground, withering in agony. Awful pain crawled over him…searing every bit of his flesh. Then it was gone as quickly as it hit him. He remained curled up in a ball, holding his breath, expecting to be struck by the burning, again. He gingerly touched his exposed skin, expecting pain and burnt flesh to fall off, but slick sweat was all he felt. Relieved, he sucked in a chestful of air. He was not burnt. His skin was not peeling off. With relief, Rogaan realized the *leapers* were gone. After a series of fleeting growls and chirps, silence hung over the darkness. *What happened?*

"Rest." A calm, almost imperceptible voice spoke. Rogaan could not tell if the voice was real or in his head.

Fatigue overwhelmed him, his eyes felt heavy, and his body weak. He fought it, but knew he was to lose the battle as the shadows of the forest melted into blurs and the world spun and Rogaan felt himself falling.

Chapter 8

Paradise Lost

Struggling to breathe, Rogaan awoke from what he recalled was a sound slumber. Eyes closed and not wanting to open them, he felt pressure on his chest…not painful, almost gentle in truth. He felt… rested, refreshed, and not yet ready to give up pleasant dreams, though strangely he remembered none. The scent of pine and cedar filled his nose. Pleasant. Pressure increased on his chest as a whisper grew into a faint voice echoing in the hazy, surreal fog of his mind. The voice spoke, but Rogaan could not make out what it was saying. Flinching, Rogaan's heart skipped a beat as his mind exploded with images of the forest deep in darkness, and the sinister glowing eyes calling it home and him a meal. Again, the voice called out; this time he heard his name, but what was it trying to tell him? "Rogaan! Rogaan!" His chest ached. Reluctantly, Rogaan forced his left eye open, just slightly, fearful of what he might see. A blinding light from above struck him, causing him pain…yet it was not pain. His chest no longer ached, but some pressure remained. He opened both eyes in a squint, the bright light painful to him. A few moments passed before Rogaan could make out a dark silhouette standing above him. Rogaan opened his eyes a bit more and focused to distinguish the figure's features…Pax.

"It be about time," Pax chastened. "I be shakin' ya for a time, but ya no want ta wake up. Lets get movin' before da *leapers* or somethin' takes ya for breakfast."

Rogaan's eyes popped open fully as he bolted upright. "What happened? Where are we?"

"Ya tell me what happened ta ya last night?" Pax asked. "Me, I run ta da woods and thought ya be following, but I looked back and ya were gone. And so were da spearmen. They must've chased off after ya instead of me. Lucky for me, though not so good for ya, I suppose." Pax scrubbed his hand through his black hair, leaving it standing at odd angles. "Anyway, I started ta look for ya, but got lost in da darkness and had ta climb a tree ta keep da beasties and bugs from gettin' ta me. At first light, I got outta da tree and came lookin' for ya. A noise caught me ear and I followed it here where I find ya."

"The guardsmen?" Rogaan asked, swiveling his head about looking for them.

"No care, now." Pax was matter-of-fact. "Later in da night they came lookin' with torches, but somethin' scared 'em away. I never saw it, but I be bitten by *bloodsuckers* all night." Pax helped Rogaan to his feet then looked at Rogaan as if he had just grown horns. "Ya not be all bitten up by *biters*. I slapped at 'em all night long. I hate 'em. Look at me arms."

Raised reddish bumps covered Pax's arms, neck, and face. Concerned, Rogaan looked himself over and found no marks other than those he carried from the valley. *What happened last night?* He recalled the burning he felt, then falling asleep right after. "Pax, there is a strangeness about this place. I do not know what it is, and I do not like it."

"Ya be tellin' me," Pax announced sarcastically as he rubbed and scratched at his neck. "First da valley...then yesterday."

"I think my father sent them," Rogaan solemnly admitted. "He forbade me from taking my *shunir'ra*. Maybe I have broken some *Tellen* law and shamed myself in his eyes...enough for him to send the law after me." Rogaan felt a deep, hollow pit grow in his innards. He feared he had lost his father's trust and respect, maybe forever. "Pax...what have I done?"

Pax stood calmly and spoke with an understanding tone. Odd for Pax, Rogaan thought. "I be no soother, but ya father not da kind ta take laws over ya. My father be good ta me, but ya father.... Well, I wish my father be more like him."

Rogaan stared at Pax, his mind swirling in a storm of confusion. Nothing made sense. If Pax was right, however unlikely that was, then things were stranger than he feared. If Rogaan was right, his father would likely never trust him again. Rogaan's insides knotted, and he thought he would collapse once his legs started trembling. A wallowing of despair, Rogaan stared at the ground trying to gain control of himself, and started hoping things were not as he made them.

"We need ta move," Pax announced, and urged, "Before da nasties find us and strip our hides and eat us…while we still be alive."

Rogaan barely heard Pax's words. His thoughts and feelings consumed him, fearing at what he had lost. *How am I going to fix this?* Tears welled up, forcing him to fight them back. He could not let Pax see him shed tears. His anger rose at himself, and his throat tightened. He could not let Pax see him this way. "You are right, Pax. Where to from here?"

"Brigum," Pax replied with a smile. "And I have an idea how ta get inside da town without nobody seein'."

They made their way southwest, away from the rising sun, down the hills and into the valley forest on the north side of Brigum. They moved fast, running when needed, but often trotting or briskly walking. They crossed Mountain Ev Road, which led north into the Wilds where *Evendiir* villages were all one could call civilization. Skirting north of the town's garbage dump, and careful not to attract the attention of the *leapers* making it home, they moved deliberately from one spot of cover to the next, all the while struggling not to gag on the putrid stench wafting on the light morning breeze. Rogaan hoped the *leapers* kept their attention lost in chasing the furry *growlers, runners* and *featherwings* also living in the dump…creatures that seemed to thrive in the town's throw-aways.

Rogaan followed Pax without questioning him about his plan to sneak into the town, though he bumped into several trees while trying to figure what that plan was. Pax had a nose for getting into and out of places, often without being noticed, and Rogaan trusted him on that. Though, with other things, Rogaan always kept an eye on him. *Trust...how can I trust Father?* Rogaan despaired at that repeating thought then chastised himself for doing it. *Of course I can!* Rogaan tripped and went crashing into a stout tree before he realized what had happened, his shoulder and the right half of his head aching from the impact. Looking up and hoping Pax did not see him, Rogaan found Pax standing motionless, staring at him with surprise displayed in every aspect of him: eyes, face, hands out wide and slightly crouching. *No luck...he saw me.* Rogaan quickly regained his feet then gave Pax a toothy grimace and an innocent raised shoulder shrug with open upraised hands to exaggerate his wordless "*Oops.*" Rogaan felt as if his face burned like the sun with embarrassment. Exasperated, Pax rolled his wide eyes high before turning and running off...all without saying a word. Rogaan was grateful for Pax's not making one of his usual snide remarks, before eagerly chasing after him.

Now past the dump, they ran hard through broken forest under tall pines and cedars dripping with hanging moss then into the open around sparse bushes, then back again through patches of trees. Rogaan had little trouble keeping up with Pax as they zigzagged through the trees and underbrush, but in the open, he lost ground to Pax. The welcoming sight of cropped terraces cut deep into Brigum's mount rose high on their left as they approached the town's northwest corner. Rough rock walls rising more than a house high, provided the foundation that the terraces sat upon. The foods grown above and in the lower fields on the opposite side of town -- fruits, berries, nuts, and vegetables -- fed much of Brigum. Rogaan struggled to keep pace with Pax as they closed on a craggy rock rise standing in the shadow of the terraced mount. The treacherous Stone Tower, as it was known, stood some eleven strides high, just a person-length short of the lowest terrace. It offered enough foot and handholds for the daring to climb and enter the crop fields above with a leap Rogaan was uncertain he could make...and Pax was daring, if nothing else.

As anticipated, Pax did not slow a bit as he reached Stone Tower. He leaped onto the boulders ringing the bottom of the monolith, and started climbing. Rogaan too leaped onto the boulders, but instead of bounding up as Pax had, he found himself sprawled out between several moderate-sized rocks. His body ached from the impact, and his head and vision swirled for a moment before clearing enough to see Pax three strides up, hanging on hand-holds, looking down, rolling his eyes at him, again, before returning to his climb. Embarrassed, Rogaan rose painfully, looked at the nearly vertical wall of rock in front of and above him, and asked himself... *There must be another way.* Rogaan looked at Pax above clinging to a rock and a few vines, motioning with his head for Rogaan to start climbing. Reluctantly and with much trepidation, Rogaan climbed, picking his way carefully. His arms and legs strained a little as he made his way around and over rock obstacles. Several times he looked down, and regretted it as soon as he did, his head swirling, forcing him to fix his eye on the rocks in front of him for a moment to settle himself before resuming his assent. He caught up with Pax just short of the top of the tower as the sun rose to almost a third of its apex. He found Pax studying a span of less than three strides of air to a terrace wall of rocks, vines, and exposed roots. Pax gave Rogaan a quick, playful smile, then jumped the span, landing solidly with both feet and hands in firm spots about two strides lower than where he leapt. He then climbed to a spot level with Rogaan, and paused. "Well?"

Rogaan studied the place where Pax had landed, and worried that he would not be able to match his friend's leaping abilities. He procrastinated, making it look as if he were studying every possible way to make the jump. In truth, Rogaan was thinking of ways not to make the jump and still maintain his dignity.

"Well?" Pax spoke with impatient sarcasm.

Rogaan avoided looking at him. There was no sense in letting Pax see the fear he felt. After of a few more moments of procrastinating,

Rogaan resigned himself to attempting the leap, and positioned himself on a small ledge to get everything possible out of his body. With a few deep breaths taken, he grunted his way into the air, landing on the rock wall near where Pax had, but missing the spot he aimed for. Falling, Rogaan grasped a stout root projecting from the rock wall. A moment later felt the air leave his lungs as he slammed into the cliff wall with a thud. Clinging to the root, he made no attempt to climb. Instead, he hung there until he felt air return to his burning lungs and the flashing points of light in his vision disappear. When he felt able, he climbed to Pax, now in a new position just below the lowest terrace, holding tight to several vines. Pax offered a hand, helping Rogaan up to his perch before they both scrambled over the cliff's edge and onto the crop terrace.

A strong sweet fragrance filled Rogaan's nose as soon as he rolled onto the terrace. The scents of blueberry and long-red blooms were mixed, but Rogaan was able to smell them distinctly. The pungent odor of dung, used to fertilize the crops, hung all about Rogaan, but was not so strong as to mask the pleasant smells. Looking up from his knees he found the place alive with workers, most dressed in gray tunics and barefooted, tending to vines growing on crude lattices, small fruit trees, bushes, and squat plants. Many carried wicker baskets filled with gardening tools of wood, copper, or iron, or filled with mysteries he was unable to see from his vantage point. Women and younglings of all ages worked the lower terraces where berry bushes and small fruit trees predominated. The upper terraces held mostly vegetables plants and squat nut trees, with a grove of tall fruit trees crowning the topmost terrace on North Mound. Adult and younglings males of all ages worked the upper terraces. Rogaan was not certain why labor was divided so; it never occurred to him to ask, until now, but now was not the time to satisfy his curiosity. Rogaan spotted Pax carefully moving off, making his way to the right, keeping low in the stands of vine-covered two-stride tall lattices. Rogaan quickly followed. Few paid them attention as they slunk closer to the northernmost buildings of town. Those that did raise an eye were mostly younglings looking for a diversion from their chores, and that usually brought an elder's scolding and sometimes a switched bottom before they returned to their work.

Pax found a spot to crouch and settle into, near a climbing path behind several vine lattices overlooking Brigum. Rogaan joined him, adjusting his crouch several times before he settled in with a fair view of Brigum. Looking around, Rogaan caught a glint of burnished metal among the fruit trees on the top mount. He spied two guardsmen... Farratum guardsmen they looked, accompanied by a single Brigum protector. Rogaan pointed out the guardsmen to Pax, then found himself a bit embarrassed after Pax made a "really, now" face and nod that told him he was already aware of them...and surprised that Rogaan had not caught sight of them sooner. One hundred fifty strides east, a large elongated, wood-shingled, pitched-roof building and three smaller surrounding structures of similar construction sat at the base of the terraces. Heaps of rocks, wood beams, and discarded rubbish, all two to three strides high, lay to the sides of the structures. Wheeled barrows, picks, shovels, and an assortment of digging equipment were neatly arranged against the stone-footed, wood-planked walls of the buildings. Several groups of *Baraans* stood among the buildings, all dressed in tan hides or gray tunics with rope belts, all dirt-stained from head to sandaled feet. They all seemed to be in a heated discussion while keeping watch on the large central building.

"Not like 'em standin' around this part of day," Pax stated, curious and concerned as he stared intently at the bunch. He shifted his crouch as if uncomfortable. "My father says there be no idlin' in da mine, and anyone caught on his heels be told ta leave since he be no mining da red gems. And da mine boss keeps pushini 'em ta work harder."

The center of Brigum's wealth was the mine, rich in rubies and other gem rocks. Much revolved around the precious stones. Cutters would pick out the best for their needs and buyers and shuck off the rest for the mine to sell, barter, and trade in town with representing interests from surrounding areas, and even faraway interests. The gem rock trade brought in all sorts of goods, people, and enough trouble for the town guard to keep busy most days. Rogaan avoided much of the latter, but Pax had stories of happenings to which he always seemed to be an innocent bystander, watching.

The rest of Brigum sprawled atop a small plateau. Few of the cobblestone paved streets met at right angles, and all were different in width, except for Market Street, which split the town running from the north near them, to the south through the central market square to the edge of the plateau then down into the lower crop fields and all the way to the guarded South Gate. Perimeter Road surrounded the town at the edges of the plateau. It too was paved and was as wide as Market Street in most places, and even wider on the north side of town. It connected the town to a number of roads leading to the lower crop fields, which were more long sloping ramps than streets, making cart travel possible. East, across the Tamarad River, the well-to-do lived in their large tile-roofed stone houses in Coiner's Quarter. Coiner's Quarter rose on a western-facing terraced hillside of mani-cured paved streets, yards, and gardens, and was beautiful to the eye in all ways. Twelve estates with flat-roofed mansions lined two parallel roads, and the area was a third the size of all of Brigum, with protec-tive tower walls north, east, and south. The river ravine flanking the western side of Coiner's Quarter saw water flowing south from Lake Sin, the lake they had run around in their escape last night, and flowed south beyond the town walls, with a partially diverted water flow go-ing to a series of ponds in the lower crop fields and extending all the way around the town from the southeast corner to the northwest. The fields, full of crops and tree groves, spanned two hundred strides to the eight-stride-tall protective stone wall guarding Brigum from beasts all kinds. Many of Brigum's sweet foods were grown in these fields with other crops, vegetables, and those used in making breads and foods Rogaan enjoyed so much. More was grown on farms and estates beyond the walls and brought to market each day for sale and trade.

A series of guard towers, each with circular orange tiled coned roofs and crowned with Brigum's flag of red and yellow, sat every sixty strides along the wall. Rogaan could barely recognize the shape of individuals patrolling the southern wall's ramparts from where he hid, but patrol they did…and many more than he was expecting. Beyond the wall, the forest pushed back almost one-hundred strides, providing Brigum's protectors a clear field of fire with arrows and spears against anything unfriendly. In town, buildings of all shapes and sizes followed the main and smaller streets throughout the town. Many had pitched roofs of red, orange, brown, or gray tiles, while others had flat roofs covered in brown plaster or dark tar. West of Market Street lived the majority of Brigum's townsfolk. Pax lived on this side of town, his home part of a cluster of small brown flat-roofed brick apartments a little more than two hundred strides southeast of where he and Pax spied over the town. Most buildings west of Market Street were a mix of some brick and many of wood with mostly flat roofs of tar. Many of those had clothing strung between buildings hanging out to dry. East of Market Street, structures were packed closer together in places and were predominantly of brick with brown flat roofs, many of those with roof terraces and clothes hung as much atop as in between buildings.

A few large structures stood as exceptions, like the pitched red-tiled roof of Rogaan's home. His home stood out with stone walls, a tiled roof, and groomed garden, looking more in place in Coiner's Quarter than in town, though the smithy attached to the south side of the building showed it to be a working home…something none of the estates in Coiner's Quarter would dare allow. Most homes in town doubled as workplaces and storefronts for those whose skills included everything from artisans to the trades. To the south of Rogaan's home lay a cluster of six orderly arranged single-story brown brick buildings with plastered flat roofs, and a much larger single building of the same style just to their west. The larger structure was where the town's matters were decided by Brigum's Town Council. The Hall of Council and its colorful gardens were surrounded by a single row of three-stride tall, cylinder-shaped leather leaf trees outlining the perimeter of the complex, which in the last few years also marked the boundary regular townsfolk were not allowed to cross without invitation by the ruling elected.

To the hall's south stood a thirty-stride-tall stepped pyramid made of weathered granite cut from the local mountains when Brigum had been founded more than six hundred and fifty years ago. Then, the pyramid was a temple to the Ancient named Sin. Colorful flower beds, water ponds, and rows of low colorful flowering bushes outlined the pyramid's four walkways surrounding and leading to the great structure. A fence of young cedars stood guarding the perimeter of the pyramid's gardens, separating the old temple from the town's paved streets. In the three hundred years prior to Shuruppak's Civil War, the temple had changed to a center of general worship of the Ancients, not just to Sin. Some thirty years ago, the pyramid became a minor projection of the new Shuruppak rule and had been renamed the Shuruppak Hall of Laws; just three years ago, this renaming had been agreed to by the town council. In recent days, the old temple housed an influx of the appointed by the elected of Farratum, despite Brigum's being distant and isolated from the rest of the Shuruppak in these western lands. The reach of Shuruppak seemed to grow more each year, influencing those chosen by the townsfolk to govern Brigum, and Rogaan's father said often that this influence was not a good sign. *A sign of what?*

Bordering the south of the Hall of Laws, the town's marketplace buzzed with trading activity in pockets of moving colors. Narrow brown-brick buildings topped with walking roofs and frontings of canopied shops lined the east and west edges of the triangular-shaped marketplace. Canopied open-air hawking stands filled the interior of the marketplace's stone-paved grounds, all orderly lined north to south, creating temporary streets so narrow and filled with those selling and those buying that Rogaan wondered if a person could breathe. Still, Rogaan thought more people should be in the marketplace by this mid-morning hour. A few sedan chairs of the well-to-do, colorful and ornately crafted, parted crowds as they moved through the pockets of throngs, led by hired muscle, some of whom Rogaan suspected to be town guardsmen who looked to earn a good sum in the service of those with coin.

"Where is everyone?" Rogaan asked after surveying the streets. Too few people were out and about, except for those trading in the marketplace and for a number of local and Farratum *Tusaa'Ner* squads roaming the streets. "The streets are usually crowded by now."

"Home," Pax replied matter-of-factly. Pax pointed to several groups of red-plumed guardsmen standing in rectangular formations three across and nine deep near Hunter's Gate and at the mine entrance near them. More squads of Farratum *Tusaa'Ner* guarded each of the town's plateau ramps; several more were in the marketplace, and several more patrolled the smaller streets about Brigum. "I be hidin' too, with all dis in town."

South of the mine entrance, Rogaan spotted a squad of Farratum *Tusaa'Ner* pulling folks from their apartments then interrogating the frightened people in the street, and some of those rather roughly. Fear and anger blended together in a complex weave, giving Rogaan the shivers as he watched. This was not the Brigum he knew. Near Pax's home, several males and a woman were thrown into the street before were surrounded by Brigum *Tusaa'Ner*. After a short time, sky-blue uniformed guardsmen ushered the three as bound persons in the direction of the Hall of Laws, prodding them along at spear point. Concentrating on the bound ones, Rogaan made out enough details to suspect who they were, causing him another shiver. He swallowed hard, trying to get the lump out of his throat, but it just remained stuck. Fearing Pax would throw all caution away and charge in reck-lessly, Rogaan struggled with how to tell Pax his mother was being taken away at spear point. Rogaan could not fathom a reason why she would be arrested. *What has she done to anyone?* "They are taking people to the Hall of Laws. Pax…I think your mother is one of them."

Pax kept silent and unmoving for what seemed long moments then rose to get a better view. Rogaan watched him closely, fearing he would launch off the terraces in a hasty and thoughtless outrage of emotions. Scanning the streets with an intensity Rogaan rarely saw in his friend, Pax squinted hard, bobbing his head about before fix-ing his stare on a group of *Tusaa'Ner* guardsmen with bound captives walking in front of spears. Pax remained still, but his eyes burned. Rogaan kept his concerned eye on Pax, worried he would chase after her. Rogaan exhaled with relief when Pax looked to be under control and not racing off in an unplanned rescue. Then without warning, Pax exploded to his feet, bounding down the hill toward the *Tusaa'Ner* and his mother. "Ma!"

Caught off guard despite anticipating Pax's reaction, Rogaan cursed to the Ancients, then chased off after Pax, running with aban-don after his friend. Pax ran straight for the mine entrance, trampling vegetable and berry plants without care. Rogaan struggled in his pur-suit, stumbling over strong vines and stakes, but not falling. When Pax bounded down the next to the last terrace, he stumbled and fell hard into a patch of sour tates. Rogaan seized that opportunity to pounce on him with an audible oomph and a small cloud of dust.

"Get off me!" Pax demanded with a shove. "I have ta save me ma." They tussled, rolling over the budding tates, Pax trying to slip from Rogaan's grasp and Rogaan desperately trying to keep Pax from get-ting away.

"Stop, Pax!" Rogaan demanded. "Calm yourself. You will be no help to anyone if you get caught."

Pax struggled in a burst of twisting and sharp elbows. The blows had little effect on Rogaan. Instead, he worried that his friend had lost his head about him as he held Pax tight around the neck and shoulders, squeezing hard to keep his hold. Pax suddenly went limp in his arms. *What happened? What have I done?* Frightened that he had injured Pax, Rogaan released his hold then laid his unmoving friend on broken plants. Rogaan called to Pax then shook him, but ...nothing. Desperate, Rogaan slapped Pax as he growled at his friend to wake up, but Pax lay unmoving. Rogaan's throat choked off and he realized he could not breathe. His vision blurred from tears welling up. *Did I kill him? No...by the Ancients, please let it not be!*

"He killed him," a woman's voice proclaimed somewhere behind and above Rogaan.

Whirling about, Rogaan found himself staring into the work-stained faces of nearly a dozen women, mostly middle-aged, though a few were young, just about of age to take a husband, and a few still younger. All were dressed in what used to be white tunics that now bore the brown and green stains of hard labor in the fields. They all stared at Rogaan, and all but one wore shocked and accusing expressions. That last made a disapproving scowl in judgment of what Rogaan thought was his recklessness. He fought an urge to run...to flee from their judging eyes...to run away from trouble. His growing sorrow at what he had done to his friend, started to overwhelm him. Reason became difficult to hold on to. All he knew was that he wanted to run. It did not matter where.

"Hush yourselves," the woman demanded of the others. She was tall and lean with shoulder-length dark hair touched with gray at the temples. Her sunbaked face bore the wrinkles of being past her middle years, but with eyes sparkling as if she were much younger. She spoke her demand as if expecting everyone to obey without question. Her dirt-stained, knee-length tunic fit loosely except at the waist where a belt, three fingers wide, snugly held everything in place. A bonnet, also white, shielded her face from the sun, leaving her sharp features lost in soft shadows. She purposefully approached Rogaan then knelt next to Pax without speaking a word. Her hands rested upon Pax's unmoving chest for a moment before she placed her ear near his mouth. A few moments later, she pressed her ear against his chest, where she remained still for what seemed a long time. The other women started whispering -- gossiping, Rogaan thought, amongst themselves, but in fast hushed voices that kept him from discerning their words. Rogaan returned his attention to the woman and Pax, wondering what she was about, while doing his best to ignore the others.

"Your friend still has life in him," the woman declared as she fixed her green-eyed gaze on Rogaan. Then she scolded, "You take more care. You're clearly much stronger than you believe, and nearly squeezed the life from this one."

"How do you know?" Rogaan asked in amazement and relief. He wanted to believe Pax lived, but feared she was either mistaken or lying.

"His chest beats with life," she said matter-of-factly. "And he still draws breath, barely. He'll be fine in a time, but none too happy when he wakes with head pains." She arranged Pax's arms and legs so he appeared to be resting then ordered the other women to return to their work and not to speak of what they had witnessed. They responded to her words by simply staring back at her with mouths agape, but none protested. The kneeling woman shot a gaze at them that Rogaan immediately felt relieved was not directed at him. The gaggle of women jumped, then scattered without words, a few tossing insatiably curious glances over their shoulders as they returned to their work. Rogaan wondered if they would keep silent. "Who are you, and why have you brought trouble to the fields?" she asked him.

"I am...we are just townsfolk returning home," Rogaan replied warily. Usually open about giving his name, Rogaan found himself questioning the wisdom of doing so now. His thoughts raced...*How am*

I to explain being on the terraces? He wanted to be convincing, but elusive. He needed to be believed. "Our parents did not give us permission to go on the Hunt, so we snuck back into town to avoid trouble."

"Well, you have found trouble, you have." The woman stared at Rogaan with judging eyes. "And for all of us, too." She looked down to the streets. A deep frown came to her face as she considered something. Returning her gaze to Pax, she spoke. "Farratum's guardsmen bullied their way about these terraces last night, and again today, searching for two younglings. They told of youngling law-breakers, and to call them out if seen." She raised her green-eyed gaze to Rogaan. His heart sunk with fear she would do the calling. "I guess you two be in much trouble, but you seem not to be the law-breaking kind."

Rogaan's heart skipped a few more beats and his mouth fell open at being accused of being a...*Law-breaker?* He had not broken the law and still could not think the taking of his *shunir'ra* deserving enough for Farratum and Brigum *Tusaa'Ner* to take interest in him, unless it was his father's doing. Regardless, the town was looking for them, and that did mean trouble. A wave of panic swelled in him, tightening his chest making it difficult to breathe. Rogaan did not know what to do next. *What I am going to do? The forest? Give myself up?*

"Be calm." The woman placed a gentle hand on his forearm. Rogaan shot her a questioning look. "Your friend's name is Pax, is it not? We've seen him often here on the terrace. He has helped several of the younger ones with their work." She shot a scolding glance at the nearest lasses, causing them to nervously inspect their toes with their eyes. "I think he favors them and they him. He has always been kind. And you? I've seen you on the north wall arrowing *leapers*. You seem upstanding enough." She scanned the terrace as if counting the women, then looked to the town below. A bunch of *Tusaa'Ner* near Pax's home had been handing bound prisoners to another group of guards not long ago. The woman's frown deepened. "I fear trouble has found all of our homes. I don't know your part in all of this, though you seem blameless. Something about you…. The guards won't be alerted by me, but some of the others may not be able to keep shut mouths. They are younglings after all."

Rogaan exhaled loudly with relief. He and Pax were safe for the moment, but he needed to find a safe hiding place. "I thank you."

"Don't be so quick to thank me." The woman laid her stern gaze upon him. "If the guards return while you be here, I'll call you out to keep everyone on the terraces from being accused of helping you."

Rogaan smiled as best he could, though he admitted to himself that it was likely not a very good smile. "I thank you, still. You are honest and true and wise, and a good person to keep watch over the others. I will take . . . Pax from here right away." Rogaan grabbed hold of Pax's left arm and shirt, readying himself to lift his friend on his shoulders.

"Take ya hands off me!" Pax barked weakly with his eyes still closed. "Ya not be grabbin' me, again. No. Not again." Pax opened his eyes then quickly shaded them from the sun with a raised hand. Pax stared at Rogaan. He looked angry. "I told ya were gettin' stronger, but…no…ya not believe me. Well, ya be stronger than ya think, and it hurts."

"I do fancy Ulcin and Avea, Mistress Immulla," Pax said to the woman with a broad, toothy smile. "They have da most pretty eyes and lips as sweet as…."

"Enough, youngling!" Immulla demanded. "Maybe I should have your friend squeeze you again, and a bit tighter this time, just to better your manners."

Rogaan shot Pax a little smile. He was relieved that Pax was alive and awake and seemed not angry with him. Rogaan promised himself to take more care concerning his strength. "I am sorry for squeezing the air from you. I thought you were about to run into the streets and get caught."

"I could have made it ta me ma without gettin' caught," Pax shot back, his eyes growing wet. "Rogaan, we have ta save her."

"Your mother…arrested?" Immulla asked with eyes wide.

"I saw her being marched toward the Hall of Laws before he started running," Rogaan replied.

"How could you see her from up here?" Immulla asked incredulously. When Rogaan did not answer immediately, she let the question go then looked at Pax with sadness. "I heard the guardsmen talk of gathering up families of a smith and someone else, a miner…to suffer the Questioning. Is your father a miner?"

"Ya." Pax's eyes looked as if about to overflow. Quickly recovering, he shot Rogaan a fiery gaze. "What do they want? We did nothin' ta 'em."

"I do not know," Rogaan replied solemnly. He felt tears welling up in his own eyes. "This cannot be about me taking my *shunir'ra*? Can it? It makes no sense. If this is not about my *shunir'ra* then what?"

Rogaan fell silent, staring off distantly and lost in his thoughts. *Makes no sense.* "My mother will be safe. Her family name gives her protection."

"Me parents not be so lucky." Pax spat. "We have ta help 'em. I need ya." Pax hopped up into a crouch then extended his hand to Rogaan.

Both grasped each other's hand as they shared determined stares. *How are we going to save anyone?* Rogaan's concern was not for Pax's parents, and he felt guilt and a bit of shame for it. Instead, his worry was for Suhd, that she might be harmed or taken away. That thought made Rogaan angry. "We do this together. Check on Suhd, first?"

Pax nodded in agreement. He wore the most determined look Rogaan had ever seen on his friend. Pax looked to Mistress Immulla. "Thank ya for ya silence, Mistress Immulla. We be leaving da terrace and be no more trouble ta ya."

She rose, brushed off her knees and tunic then regarded them for a moment. "Yes, trouble you are. Don't come back, or I will call you out. Farewell, younglings."

Mistress Immulla returned to the fields and the women tending them. She stole glances at Pax and Rogaan for a while before becoming too busy getting the women to do their work to watch them. Rogaan and Pax watched her for a short while, still from fear being called out. True to her word, she directed the other women back to their chores, and told them to keep to themselves. They would not betray Rogaan and Pax, at least for now. Satisfied, Rogaan and Pax set off to find Suhd then Pax's mother, Pax impatient to get to the task. They quickly made their way off the terraces to a spot behind the building sheltering the mine entrance: a rough wood- planked and tarred-roofed structure over forty strides long of rough-cut gray stone three strides high and no windows on the terrace side. Piles of rocks, dirt, and discarded tools littered the sides of the building in no particular order, offering plenty of places to hide. They crept into the morning shadows at the western side of the main building where a small wood shack and a large stack of timbers provided concealment from the street beyond.

Before Rogaan could catch his breath, Pax danced around the timbers to the stone building where he peeked at the street from a shadowy corner. A short but harsh tremor shook the ground and building. Pax paused while the tremor had its way with the world, then made a quick hand wave for Rogaan to follow, then jumped around that corner and out of sight. Rogaan's heart felt like it would jump out of his chest. *What is Pax doing?* He followed despite his fear of what might be waiting for him. From the corner of the building, Rogaan stole a look at the street and was relieved to see only a small gathering of talkative miners making their way east, away from the mine and toward the Dusty Shovel tavern. Pax walked at the back of the group, waving at Rogaan to join him. Rogaan chased after Pax, hoping they would pass as miners returning home after a night of work down below. He and Pax certainly looked right for it, covered in dirt and sweat, and smelling of it. The miners were talking of the *Tusaa'Ner* and of events of the morning. Apparently, the town's *Tusaa'Ner* accompanied by Farratum *Tusaa'Ner* arrested several town folk and took them away; one of them was Pax's father. *Why?* Rogaan watched Pax look from miner to miner anxiously while biting his lower lip, hoping they would tell more of his father. He feared Pax would not keep his tongue, though he did not really expect him to. After all, it was Pax.

Rogaan noticed several of the miners realized that Pax was following them, but they kept their tongues and said nothing to him, nor did they appear about to call to the guardsmen. Hope rose within Rogaan...not everyone was out to get them. When the miners neared the Dusty Shovel, Pax darted into the alley at the west side the tavern. Rogaan followed closely. The odor of urine and feces and other things he did not want to know smacked him the instant he stepped into the narrow dirt alley. He wondered why chamber pots were dumped here. *Did not the town collect garbage and chamber pot stuff daily?* The stench worsened as they moved deeper between the buildings, causing Rogaan to fight down a retching urge. He hoped they would soon escape these foul smells, as he was uncertain how long he could keep his stomach down. To his relief, they emerged into a yard with a stand of fig trees and decorative bushes lining the street. Pax kept a fast pace, passing the trees, and into another narrow space between rust-colored brick buildings that was almost too small for Rogaan to fit. Pax appeared to not to have trouble navigating the narrows, and seemed not to notice Rogaan lagging behind. He was focused in a way Rogaan had never seen him before. As they darted between buildings, racing through the neighborhood with almost reckless abandon, patrolling groups of *Tusaa'Ner* narrowly missed sighting them several times. Fortunately, Pax's knowledge of the streets and narrows kept them hidden until they set foot on the familiar wooden steps leading up to his family's apartment.

The rust-colored brick building was home to four families, two on the bottom and two on the second floor. Small yellow painted wooden-shuttered windows, irregularly spaced on the outer walls, were closed despite the warmth of the morning. Yellow wooden doors to the apartments stood closed where they usually were open during the day to allow for cooling breezes. The roof was of simple wood covered in tar that didn't always keep out the rain, as Rogaan recalled from several visits this past year. Pax bounded up the wooden steps to the second floor then disappeared into his apartment. Rogaan followed. The apartment's main room was small, at least compared to the rooms in Rogaan's home. The apartment had four rooms in all; the common room where he stood that was a little bigger than twice that of his own resting room in his house, and three others about half the size where Pax, Suhd, and their parents slept. A twinge of guilt swept Rogaan when he realized he was comparing his home to that of his friend. Pax's and Suhd's parents worked hard for what they had. Their father, Daugu, was a miner, and from what Pax told him, also an experienced sailing boatman. Their mother, Phobe, cleaned homes, taverns, and any other place she could get a job straightening up. Despite their best efforts, they rarely seemed to have coin for anything other than the basic needs. Pax finished a hasty look about the apartment and found it empty and wrecked. The furniture and a shelf with its contents were thrown about and in disarray. Something had happened here, and it was not good for Pax's family.

With a curse at the Ancients, Pax brushed by Rogaan on his way to the balcony outside. He paused for a moment looking up at the sky, before angrily stomping down the steps. Rogaan followed close, now concerned for Suhd's well-being. As Pax reached the bottom step, Suhd burst out of the apartment and onto the balcony wearing a stained white knee-length tunic, her raven hair in disarray. She ran down the stairs in a rush past Rogaan, jumping into her brother's arms, her body slamming into him so hard that they almost went tumbling as Pax's wide-brimmed hat flew from his head. She grasped him tight and hysterically sobbed into her brother's chest while mumbling something Rogaan was not able to make out. The pain on his friend's face was almost unbearable to watch. In the years Rogaan and Pax had been friends, never had Pax so openly showed pain touching him. Pax hid such with impish smiles and deflective talk, or by directing attention away from himself in some manner. This was different. Pax did not even attempt to hide his pain as tears streamed down his face.

"They took 'em, Pax," Suhd sobbed with her head still buried in her brother's chest. "They broke in and took Ma. They dragged her in the street and bound her to Father."

Suhd sobbed harder. Pax kept silent while tears streamed down his face. "Father was hurt bad. His head and shirt . . . so bloody."

Pax held his sobbing sister tighter for a few moments before he caught sight of Rogaan motioning for them to move where they would be out of sight under the stairs. Pax slowly walked his sister into the shadowy spot under the stairs while she clung to him with an iron grasp. Though not the best place to hide, under open-sided stairs, it would keep them from being easily spotted from the streets, and they would see anyone approaching.

"Suhd...why they no take ya?" Pax questioned softly.

Suhd's sobs slowed, just a little, before she raised her eyes to meet his gaze. "Ma hid me under her dirty clothes in her room. She fought 'em hard after they kicked in the door and they never checked her room before takin' her away."

Tears fell from Pax's cheeks as Suhd reburied her face into his tunic with uncontrolled sobs. Rogaan fought back tears of his own at the sight of brother and sister sharing pain he could only imagine. Rogaan greatly respected and liked their mother, Phobe. She was a strong woman who sacrificed much for her family, and she always had a kind word for Rogaan; he was not the least surprised by her selflessness. It was her nature.

"Pax . . . Suhd," Rogaan said quietly. "We need to go before the guardsmen find us."

Pax shot Rogaan a strained look with red, puffy eyes and tear-streaked cheeks. Chills ran down Rogaan's spine. Never had Rogaan seen such a look on his friend's face. Suhd kept her face buried in her brother's chest. She squeezed him tighter, if that were possible. Pax then said something to Suhd that only she could hear. She slowly lifted her face to look at Pax, and then at Rogaan.

"Help us, Rogaan," Suhd pleaded with renewed tears. "Help us get back our parents. We can no do this on our own!"

Rogaan stood stunned and a bit dumbfounded. He realized he must have worn a stupid expression or something close to it, from the strange looks on their faces. He had never considered trying to free their parents from the *Tusaa'Ner* and especially not from the Farratum guard. His parents taught him to respect authority, despite their also insisting that he be aware of the town's happenings and for him to think critically about everything. To make his own decisions as to what was right and what was wrong. Confronting the enforcers of Brigum and Shuruppak laws was simply something that he had never considered...before now.

"Please, Rogaan," Suhd pleaded with tear-filled eyes. "They did nothing to deserve this."

Rogaan readily agreed with her on that point. Their parents were hard-working, law-following people and he knew of nothing of them worthy of being arrested and hauled off...to where, he only could guess. Pax was another thing. He often skirted rules, the *Tusaa'Ner,* and just as often the law. He disobeyed nothing serious or harmful to others, just rules and laws he thought were stupid. Pax just did not like anyone setting limits for him except for his parents . . . sometimes...whom Rogaan knew he respected more than he let on. Was it possible they had been arrested because of Pax? A wave of regret rippled through Rogaan at that thought, followed by trepidation over just how far the town's leadership might go to gain their ends. *What are their ends?* What would the town's leaders have to gain from arresting honest citizens? Kantus' father, *Ugulauru* Jir, as leader of Brigum's Council, seemed capable of many unfriendly things when it came to

running the town and ensuring there was no challenge to his authority. The Council did little to restrain him, but even the *Baraan*'s dislike
of Pax would not warrant arresting his parents. Even the new *Ensi*
seemed more interested in governing over Brigum than worrying over
a no-name youngling and his parents. It made no sense. Neither Jir
nor the *Ensi* had anything to gain by arresting Pax's and Suhd's parents.
Nothing made sense at all. Still, challenging the *Tusaa'Ner*, as he was
sure Pax would insist upon, would only get them arrested. Rogaan
stewed over limited options and his torn desire to help Suhd and Pax
get their parents back. What could they do, after all? They were only
younglings. Maybe they could not do much, within the bounds of the
law, but maybe someone else might.

"Pax," Rogaan spoke sternly to his friend. "If I help, no headstrong
charges into the guardsmen and no sneaking through windows at night
unless I agree to it. We cannot challenge the law keepers and expect
anything less than a switching or worse."

Pax gave Rogaan a clenched-jaw look with narrowing eyes that
confirmed to him that Pax wanted to do more than he was willing to
allow. Suhd just looked at him with those glassy, radiant blue eyes that
made him feel as if he were going to melt. He had to help her. He just
had to be her hero. Rogaan cursed himself for being so weak around
her and forced himself to stand taller and clear his throat, as if he had
a great announcement. "We should seek Mother's counsel, and help
from the House Isin. They are familiar with matters of law, where we
are not."

Pax barked several curses in protest at his suggestion. Rogaan was
caught off guard by his friend's open disapproval and started to feel
small at his suggestion to seek help instead of freeing their parents
themselves. As Pax worked himself into a heated tirade and separated
from his sister, Rogaan watched Suhd look at her brother with sad
eyes. She reached out to him, gently grasping his arm and gaining his
attention. "I no wish to lose you too, Pax. Maybe Rogaan's right."

Pax stopped his tirade then stared at her blankly without saying a word. His response must have surprised Suhd as much as it did Rogaan, as she retreated from him a little. "Ya just sided with Rogaan since ya like him."

Suhd's cheeks reddened deeply as she dropped her eyes to her feet and began wringing the front of her tunic with nervous hands. Tears started to pour down her face as she spoke with a cracking voice almost too faint to hear. "No, brother. What if we no get them back and ya be taken away? What will happen to me, then?"

Pax stood stunned before he took his sister in both arms and held her to his chest as she sobbed. He looked at Rogaan with glassy, heated eyes. "All right, Rogaan. We try it ya way, but first I want ta see where they be takin' our parents. I want ta know they not be hurt."

A wave of relief swept over Rogaan. He feared Pax would insist on rescuing his parents immediately, with reckless plans, and only half thought out. Pax whispered something to Suhd before she ran upstairs. Her tunic rose high on her legs as her dark hair swung about her back and arms while she ran up the wooden steps, revealing enough of her slender legs to hold Rogaan's complete attention. His heart pounded – she was beautiful – and he could not take his eyes from her until she disappeared into her home. He continued looking at the apartment door, expecting... no, wanting...her to emerge from it at any moment when he realized Pax was clearing his throat louder than necessary. Rogaan gave a start and felt his face flush warm at the sight of Pax standing with arms crossed on his chest, and wearing a half-amused, half-angry look. Embarrassment washed over him in waves at his blatant boyish behavior, especially with all that had happened to them.

"Pax ...I am..." Rogaan started to apologize.

"If it be anyone, but ya," Pax broke in, wearing a half-smile that might have been a little forced. "I would take ta defendin' her honor. But ya, I know how much ya like me sister and would do her no harm. I be glad ta have ya as a friend."

Rogaan's embarrassment deepened. He did not know what to say, to apologize for his actions. He was not accustomed to Pax speaking so openly of friendship. Usually, the best he could do was a friendly punch on the arm. Fortunately for Rogaan, Suhd reappeared from the apartment dressed in a knee-length blue tunic that clung to her waist by a black belt. She carried her sandals in one hand and a small gray bundle in her other hand. Pax looked surprised at the sight of her, for some reason that Rogaan did not understand.

"Where ya think ya be going?" Pax asked her when she reached the bottom of the steps.

"With you," Suhd replied as if just stating the sun had risen that morning. She continued with a wrinkled nose. "And stop talking like that. Ya be better than what ya want the world to know of ya. And, Pax . . . you smell terrible."

Pax was working out a reply to his sister when Suhd thrust the gray bundle into his stomach. Suhd looked up at her brother with defiant eyes then spoke. "This be what I thought you might ask for? And, yes, I be going with ya."

"Rogaan...." Pax seemed to be about to ask for his help to talk sense into Suhd as he kept stern eyes fixed on his sister.

"She is as strong-willed as you, Pax," Rogaan stated flatly. "You know she will do what she wants, and nothing I say will change that." Rogaan admired her determination and courage, but she would only add to Pax's volatility if he got it in his head that she would be put in danger.

"Suhd," Rogaan started in a cracking voice he barely recognized as his own. "You might do better at my home with my parents instead of on the streets with us."

Suhd stared at him blankly for a long moment, with those blue eyes that he could lose himself in for a lifetime, maybe more...then her face saddened. "You no know? The *Tusaa'Ner* also have your father. They spoke of his arrest a day ago."

Rogaan staggered backwards a step as he fought a sinking feeling in his guts that threatened to do worse. He did his best to fight off the shock of her words. After a few moments, he regained most of his former composure then forced himself to stand taller and forced several, evenly paced deep breaths. His father had not sent the guard after him. Relief filled him at that thought. He felt a pang of guilt and shame for his incriminations. Selfishness was something his father disliked more than disobedience, and Rogaan felt as if he had let his father down. Instead of his father chasing after him, the *Tusaa'Ner* had chased his father, too…for what purpose Rogaan could only guess. This made less sense to him than before. Many things did not make sense anymore. What was driving all of this? Why would Father and Pax and Suhd's parents be arrested? A heavy heart weighed on Rogaan like a boulder over their families being torn apart. "What of my mother?"

"They spoke nothing of her," Suhd replied with glassy eyes.

"Will House Isin keep ya ma from harm?" Pax more stated than asked, in a jealous tone.

"My father thought so," Rogaan answered as he fought back a swelling of anger and tried his best to ignore Pax's insinuation that they need not be concern for her because of her family name. Despite his simmering anger, Rogaan agreed with Pax that his mother was likely safe from harm because of her birthright as daughter of the second most powerful House in the Brigum area. Rogaan's anger subsided, a little, and he resigned himself, first, to discover the fate of his father and Pax's parents. "Let us go and find out about our parents."

"Suhd." Pax did his best to speak authoritatively. "Return home. Rogaan and me will follow da…. "

"We," Suhd interrupted with a stern look in her eyes. "We…Pax. I no sit at home while Ma and Father need our help."

"Ya only slow us down," Pax stated flatly and with a hint of old frustrations, maybe even anger. "We be better off without ya followin' us about da streets -- and besides, there might be a fight and ya might get hurt."

"No worry about me." Suhd spoke as if Pax had not said a word. She started up the stairs, then looked back over her shoulder at her brother, then glanced at Rogaan. Rogaan lost himself again at the sight of her. "Neither of ya will be slowed by me. I'll keep up with no complaint. Besides, ya might need my help."

"No!" Pax barked at his sister's back as she bound up the last few creaking steps. His face deepened in color as he stood with his fists on his hips. Pax followed Suhd with his eyes as she ran into their apartment. Anger was clearly visible on his face, and he did his best to look and sound authoritative, forcing his voice lower than he normally talked. "Ya be my charge now and I say ya no go with us. Stay home."

Pax spoke the last few words to an empty balcony. He looked as if he were about to jump out of his skin with frustration. Rogaan had witnessed them arguing more than a few times before, with Suhd usually ignoring her older brother in the end. For all of it, Pax seemed to expect his sister to disobey him, and he was not pleased about it. Then, Rogaan could not recall a time when Pax was satisfied with the outcome of one of their sibling disagreements, except this time danger lurked in every shadow. Rogaan agreed with Pax. Suhd needed to be out of the way and in a place safe from harm. She was as stubborn as stone when she wanted to be, and she certainly had that way about her now. The *Tusaa'Ner* had already invaded their home, but might return. He needed Suhd safe, but where, so she would not be able to follow them? For Rogaan, Suhd was too dangerous to keep close. She would be distracting to him and a problem, especially now when he needed to think clearly, but what were he and Pax to do with her? A few tormented moments passed before he had a plan he thought well enough to recommend. Rogaan opened his mouth to speak, but Pax had already started grumbling aloud.

"I be going ta go up there and tie her ta da table," Pax announced as if he really meant it, then started for the stairs.

Rogaan grabbed his friend's arm, keeping him easily from ascending the steps. Pax shot back a heated look that made a shiver ripple down Rogaan's spine. "Pax, you know she will fight you like a *leaper* and we do not know if the *Tusaa'Ner* will return. She might be in danger if she stays."

Pax gave Rogaan a perplexed look, as if he had just spoken a great riddle that had no solution. Rogaan shot back a wide-eyed, stiff-jawed look of impatience and a hint of frustration. "I have a plan. We take Suhd with us while we sneak a look at what is going on then take her to my mother before we do anything. She will be safe with Mother. Then, we can get your parents back."

Pax looked ready to break bricks with his teeth. Act first was Pax's way. It often enough got him and Rogaan in trouble. In a sudden change of demeanor, Pax appeared calm and lost in thought, as if he were considering Rogaan's suggestion. "Ya have an idea there. She no refuse ya mother. This might work."

Suhd emerged from the doorway, half-dressed, in a short blue tunic with a matching knee-length skirt. Rogaan stood open-mouthed with heat rising in his cheeks while watching her struggle with her tunic and black belt that were not quite in place. He caught a peek at her naked breast as she bounded down the creaky stairs when she made one last adjustment of her clothes. His heart skipped a beat, maybe two. Sweat formed on his brow and he felt uncomfortably warm all over as he stood dumbfounded, unable to recall any of his thoughts while intensely watching her approach. Only Suhd filled his world. She was beautiful, with a lean runner's body of brown, yet with enough of a young woman's curves. She gave Rogaan a glance when she was halfway down the stairs and nearly stumbled when she realized he was looking at her...in that way. Her waist-length jet hair blew in all directions as she jumped from four steps up down to Pax where he caught her. *Yes*, Rogaan concluded, she would be a distraction, and a beautiful one at that.

Chapter 9

Paradise Broken

R ogaan and his friends carefully made their way through Brigum's almost deserted streets, moving in the shadows south toward the center of town. Observations from their terrace perch saw the *Tusaa'Ner* taking prisoners to the Hall of Laws, where Shuruppak laws were increasingly tightening a noose around the necks of the towns-people. While on the move, Pax complained about the new *Ensi*, the governing ministers, and the hand-picked *Tusaa'Ner* acting as their personal guard, now carrying the title of *Sakes* and all were dressed in black instead of their traditional uniforms and colors. Pax did not like authority, and he certainly made it clear that the new hand govern-ing Brigum was less liked than what it replaced. Rogaan was not as certain. The streets before the *Ensi* came to Brigum were safe enough to walk with the occasional cut-coiner to worry over, but the night brawls around the taverns made him uneasy. Serious law-breaking was uncommon, but the Town Council and the *Tusaa'Ner* did little to keep drunkards and those quick to fight out of the streets once the sun went down. The *Ensi* quieted the streets as his first order of business and set the *Sakes* out to clean them up, which they made quick work of. Rogaan welcomed the *Ensi's* running Brigum, in a selfish way he admitted to himself, mostly because *Dubsa* Jir was not. Jir still led the Town Council and made every effort to keep up the façade that he was the one running the town, but those caring to look past Jir's claims saw the *Ensi* in control and that Jir and the Town Council were now merely tools of Shuruppak's rule.

Their footfalls on the smooth paving stones drew little attention from the few passers-by out and about. Folks nowadays tended to keep to themselves more and not loiter in the streets. Despite her lithe frame and light body, Suhd sounded as if she were twice Rogaan's size by the way she slapped her sandals down, and was a bit clumsy as she struggled to keep up. Pax, leading, must have taken notice of the noise she was making and slowed down, though he kept them moving toward Market Street and the Hall of Laws. Concerned that Pax was about to charge right into the Hall grounds with reckless abandon -- not an act Rogaan would be surprised at despite his friend's assertions -- Rogaan reached out to grab Pax and bring him to a stop. Pax veered to the right before Rogaan could close his grip on his pack then trotted south down the back street paralleling Market Street. Red-brown brick and tan limestone buildings with mostly groomed shrubs and broadleaf trees lined both sides of the ten-stride-wide paved street that separated them from their goal. Pax came to a stop crouched behind a stack of discarded crates near an average-sized building on their left. Rogaan and Suhd caught up with him moments later. Rogaan sucked in a couple of breaths before settling into a calm, quiet crouch. Suhd bent over with hands on knees, struggling to catch her breath. The smell about them reminded Rogaan of the alley behind the Dusty Shovel tavern...a day-old chamber pot. All he could do was wrinkle his nose and do his best to ignore the stench.

Pax worriedly looked at his sister, silently watching her until her breathing settled enough for her to look up from the patio stones, which she seemed to find of interest. She too wrinkled her nose at the smell of the place. Rogaan grimaced at her discomfort. It pained him to see her in any discomfort, but then he craved to be close to her which this effort was providing. He felt torn and a little guilty with his intent. Suhd's long black hair now hung beneath a blue headscarf in a tail down her back. Rogaan wondered how she had managed to make the tail and put on the headscarf while they ran, but somehow she did it. No wonder she was out of breath. Her perky nose and wide blue eyes were highlighted by her slender face and light-brown cheeks.

Suhd's blue tunic and skirt clung to her slender frame all the way to her knees, where the skirt ended in hand-stitched pleats. The clinging tunic revealed every bit of her shape, and the black belt she wore held her clothing tight allowing her small waist to accentuate the rest of her body. Rogaan's breath was taken away at the sight of her. She was beautiful…very, very beautiful. *Yes, a distraction.*

"I know da smell be bad," Pax said flatly. "But da bathhouse roof be best for lookin' ta see da Hall. I be climbing up for a look. Stay here. I be back soon."

Rogaan grabbed Pax's tunic and held him fast. Pax shot him a surprised look, but did not fight to break free. "No, Pax. I am going with you. I need to see what is happening for myself."

"Ya know ya no climb as good as me," Pax said while trying not to sound as if he were bragging. "Da walls not be easy ta get a hold."

"No matter," Rogaan shot back with a determined bravado. "I can make it to the top. Maybe not as nimbly as you, but climb it I can." After Rogaan let go of his tunic, Pax scurried up the limestone blocks to the angled tiled roof, then disappeared from sight. Rogaan followed, more slowly, struggling to find hand and toe-holds on the five-stride high wall. He slipped several times, almost falling before he reached the tiled roof and Pax's hand held out to help him. Rogaan eagerly took his friend's aide and heaved himself onto the roof. The tiles ran up at a moderate grade four strides to a landing about six strides to a side on either side of a tall center structure. They quickly made their way to the landing. Warm, moist air rose from vents jutting out of the three-stride-wide landing area surrounding the center structure. A small flock of little gray and white *featherwings* nested in the eaves of the center structure, three strides above the landing. The *featherwings* flew to and from their nests, aggravated and chirping warnings at the intrusion. Pax grimaced at the sight of the *featherwings* and motioned for Rogaan to be still as they lay on the roof. After a short time the *featherwings* settled a bit, with most remaining in the nests, chirping less frantically. Pax slowly made his way to the east side of the land-ing, careful not to disturb the *featherwings* any further, crawling on his stomach until he was able to see Market Street and the Hall of Laws. Rogaan followed, mimicking his friend's movements.

From their roof perch they spied on the Hall of Council, the Hall of Law, and half of the Market Place. An east-west running five-stride wide street separated the two gardens surrounding the halls. The Hall of Council lay to the north and the Hall of Law to the south. The street was filled with *Tusaa'Ner* standing in disciplined columns, flanking wagons and carts with draft *niisku* and *sarig* steeds. Brigum guardsmen stood at attention, dressed in sky-blue uniforms, hide armor, short-feathered red-plumed bronze helms, belt sashes of red and yellow, and held their long spears at attention. The Farratum guardsmen were similarly dressed in their royal-blue uniforms, metal-hide chest armor, shiny silver helms topped with red feather plumes, solid red belt sash-es, and long spears held tall. On any other day, Rogaan would expect a parade, but not today. The guardsmen all looked ready for an inspec-tion, or honoring someone in some important event. Several officers in both troupes made their way up and down the columns, giving or-ders and receiving reports from their subordinates. After a short time, the officers, too, fell into the ranks standing at attention, waiting...for what, Rogaan could not guess. A group of ten guardsmen, in armor similarly styled to the *Tusaa'Ner*, but with dark hide and silvered helms topped with red feathered plumes, solid red belt sashes, and short swords, pushed before them four manacled prisoners out the north doors of the Hall of Laws. Rogaan immediately recognized the black-clad guardsmen as *Sakes*, the *Ensi's* enforcers. A shiver ran down his back at the sight of them with prisoners. *Is this the fate of us all?*

One of the prisoners staggered and fell to the stone walkway lead-ing from the pyramid to the street separating the two Halls. All but two of the *Sakes* brutally urged the three still standing to the jailer's wagon in the middle of the street. One of the *Sakes* half dragged, half beat the fallen *Baraan* to his feet then prodded him with spear tip to the wagon. The cedar tree perimeter made it difficult to see all of the Hall of Laws grounds, though Rogaan could see well enough to make out that the prisoners were three males and one woman, with one of the males a head shorter than the others. With a start, Rogaan rose to his hands and knees, readying himself to leap from the roof, then froze. He considered his action then reluctantly settled back down on his stomach.

"What ya see?" Pax asked.

"I think I see Father," Rogaan replied excitedly. "And maybe your parents, too."

"Where?" Pax demanded as he rose up on his elbows to search the grounds with an intense gaze. He froze when he saw who the *Sakes* prodded to the barred wagon. "No! Ma…Father, they can no be takin' ya! This not be right!"

Pax scrambled to a crouch before Rogaan grabbed and pulled him down onto his back. Pax fought wildly to break free of Rogaan's grip. "Let me go!"

"Pax, no!" Rogaan did his best to speak calmly. His friend continued struggling, striking him with elbows and feet. Rogaan only grimaced when Pax struck, determined not to let his friend leap into trouble. It would only make things worse and maybe get himself hurt or lightless. "I cannot let you go down there. You have no chance against so many, and they will take you away, too."

Pax settled down, reluctantly, a little, though Rogaan could still feel his body tense and see his face a-fume. It was enough for Rogaan that Pax stopped swinging at him, though he almost did not recognize his friend, being so out of sorts. It took a few more moments before Pax calmed down enough that the only sign of his raging anger was in his eyes. "I be all right. Let me go."

Rogaan lessened his grip enough for Pax to yank away; then Pax lay on his back motionless, staring into the late-morning sky. Rogaan kept ready to jump on Pax if he made to act in an ill-thought charge with irrational hopes of freeing his parents. Rogaan wanted to free his father every bit as much as Pax and Suhd wanted to free their parents, but a rash charge was not the way. With a huff, Pax rolled onto his stomach and stared at the prison wagon and the guardsmen preparing to move out. "What now?"

Rogaan did not have an answer to give, but he was certain they needed a better plan than what Pax had almost attempted...and what Rogaan had first thought to do. He struggled to come up with something that Pax would be satisfied with...and that would work, but it proved more difficult than he hoped. What he needed was time to think. "Let us take Suhd to Mother, where she will be safe."

Pax looked at Rogaan calmly. "Ya not have a plan?"

"No," Rogaan replied.

"Thought so," Pax declared flatly.

Staying low to keep from being spotted by the guardsmen or disturbing the *featherwings*, they climbed down from the roof to where Suhd anxiously waited. She seemed about to pop out of her skin for any news of her parents. With a grim face, Pax explained what they had seen, but left out the part about his trying to leap from the roof, and Rogaan's stopping him. Rogaan remained silent, though the stench of the area made him want to cut Pax short and get moving. Pax continued his explanation to Suhd that their plan was for her to be made safe with Rogaan's ma while he and Rogaan went about getting their parents home. Suhd gave her brother a skeptical and concerned look.

"Ya have no plan?" Suhd accused.

Pax hesitated, looking at Rogaan for help. When Rogaan remained silent, Pax replied defensively, "No."

"No," Rogaan confirmed flatly.

"Thought so," Suhd declared accusingly.

"She is your sister," Rogaan stated sardonically to Pax.

"Ya. She is," Pax agreed with a faint smile.

"What are ya two talking of?" Suhd asked, as if she were left out of the conversation. When they held their tongues, Suhd made as if she was going to press them to reveal their secret, but instead covered her mouth and nose with her hand. "Can we go? I need to wash this stink off."

The three made their way north through the almost empty streets as the sun climbed to its mid-day height. At times they ran, but mostly the three found themselves creeping alone at the sides of buildings and in bushes, ferns, flowers, and even garbage…all to avoid being caught, arrested, maybe worse. To Rogaan, their going seemed to take longer than needed, almost a snail's pace. Time was urgent, and his frustration grew from the realization that their parents were being whisked away by the Farratum *Tusaa'Ner* to somewhere he did not know. He saw the same frustration building in Pax and Suhd. Complaining would only slow them, so he heeled in his agitation and kept silent as they pressed on. When they neared the nose-wrinkling stench of the Dusty Shovel's back alley, Pax, leading, turned east, taking them across Market Road. A small contingent of Brigum *Tusaa'Ner* patrolling Market Road nearly spotted them before they disappeared into an alleyway between a cluster of brown-brick two-story buildings near Rogaan's house.

While they hid in the alley waiting for the *Tusaa'Ner* to pass, several women dressed in simple gray tunics, rope belts, and low-ankle sandals walked by carrying baskets filled with what Rogaan took for laundry. The women regarded them with reserved curiosity before continuing on their way as Rogaan, Pax, and Suhd huddled behind a stone garden wall half the height of a person. Rogaan's neck hairs bristled when he saw Pax pull out one of his concealed knives from under his tunic. He quickly recovered from his surprise at Pax's bold and dark intent, finding himself alarmed at what his friend might do… what he might be capable of doing. Intending to hold Pax from harming the women, Rogaan stared his friend down, holding his eyes and hopefully his hand. Pax returned his stare…cold and emotionless.

With a shiver, Rogaan wondered just how much he really knew of his friend. The women passed without loitering or giving them away, and not until they were halfway to the street did Pax shoot Rogaan a mischievous smile and slide his knife back under his tunic. Rogaan stole a look at Suhd to see if she had noticed Pax's unsheathed blade. She had not. He thanked the Ancients that she missed her brother's darkness.

The *Tusaa'Ner* patrol stopped at the alley head to inspect the narrows. They gave it a cursory glance before continuing on toward the mine. While they were looking down the alley, Rogaan held his breath, afraid they would be spotted. He kept an eye on Pax to see if he would produce another blade. No knife. Suhd kept quiet, but the fear in her eyes bordered on stark terror. He reached out and gave her hand a reassuring squeeze that resulted in tears running down her cheeks. Rogaan was confused. *Why cry? The guardsmen were gone.* Suhd returned Rogaan's squeeze and gave him a quick smile before wiping the tears from her face. She looked unnerved, but seemed to have kept her wits about her.

With the guardsmen gone, they scurried along between several more brown-brick buildings before coming to the street just behind Rogaan's home and just north of the Hall of Council grounds. Rogaan grabbed Pax to keep him from brashly jumping into the open. Pax shot Rogaan a harsh look when he realized he was being restrained, but said nothing. Rogaan met Pax's gaze with defiance. He was not going to let recklessness see them captured. A slight breeze out of the north carried the pungent odor of waste and blood from the Meat House pens. The acrid odor hung heavy on the air in between the buildings where they hid, forcing the three to wrinkle their noses. While trying to put the stench out of his mind, Rogaan carefully surveyed the street to ensure it was clear. When satisfied, he crossed the paved stones with Pax and Suhd following closely.

Rogaan led Pax and Suhd to a small wood shed that marked the western edge of his family's courtyard at the back of their house. The stride-wide potting beds outlining the perimeter of the courtyard were full with flowers of various colors and pleasant scents. Their fragrance masked the odors of the pens to the north. Rogaan's mother always chose just the right flowers throughout the seasons to keep their courtyard and home pleasant-smelling. Rogaan walked across the red and blue tiles of the courtyard to the heavy wooden door of the house's cook room. Rogaan pressed his ear to the door to listen. When he was satisfied that nobody was on the other side he opened the door, peeked in then motioned for Pax and Suhd to follow.

The cook room measured six strides to a side, with walls lined with ornately carved wooden floor cabinets, polished to a glossy shine, and topped with marble counters. Above, matching cabinets hung around the room, except in the corner off to Rogaan's left where a wood-burning stove sat cold. A washbasin recessed into the marble countertop on the opposite side of room had unwashed pans and dishes sitting in water. *Mother never leaves dishes unwashed.* A little alarmed and concerned for his mother's well-being, Rogaan crossed the room in several bounds and pushed through a heavy wooden bronze-banded door leading to the meal room. He abruptly slid to a halt once through the door, and stood with his mouth slung open. Sunlight brightly bathed the meal and grand rooms from a pair of circular ceiling mirrors almost five strides up in the peak of the roof. The meal room was as he remembered it before he left for the Hunt, but the grand room was in disarray. The tapestry nearest the front doors hung to one side as if it had been torn from its mount; several of the hanging crystal adornments lay shattered on the floor, one of the three small gray-padded chairs lay on its side broken, and blood dashed the floor in places. One splatter was at the front door, and another yet on the floor next to his mother, who now tended to the wounds of a *Baraan* sitting in Rogaan's favorite blue lounging chair. The large, dark-haired *Baraan* was dressed in green hide breeches and a torn wide-shouldered tunic soaked with blood from his left shoulder down to his black belt. Rogaan's mother was kneeling near the wounded *Baraan* with blood stains on her hands, arms, and yellow dress. When she realized Rogaan was standing in the middle of the floor watching her, she quickly jumped to her sandaled feet, almost slipping on the spot of blood beside her. She brandished a knife in her left hand and had a look of desperation, not recognizing that the person standing before her was her own son.

"Mother...?" Rogaan blurted with his hands waving in front of him. "It is me."

Sarafi stared blankly at Rogaan a few moments before lowering her knife. With slumping shoulders, she appeared relieved at the sight of him then made a quick, stolid-faced, boots to head inspection of Rogaan. After her eyes scanned him, she said simply, "I am pleased to see you're not seriously injured, my son, but you should not have returned. It's not safe for you here."

Rogaan stood stunned at her casual tone and cold demeanor, both falling far short of his expectations. His mother's greeting raised the hairs on the back of his neck. He felt unnerved from it. *Dangerous for me? What about for Mother?* His mother returned to tending the wound of the *Baraan* grimacing in Rogaan's favorite chair. Rogaan approached the two, careful not to step on glass or slip on blood, while keeping a wary eye on the wounded *Baraan*, as if he might jump to the attack. He stopped a stride from his mother and better than an arms-length from the chair.

"Do you remember Imtaesus?" Sarafi asked without looking up, instead keeping her focus on the wound while she worked with needle and thread. Rogaan regarded the wounded *Baraan* closer after his mother's question. He was tall by *Baraan* standards, and lean, with more muscle than average. Rogaan guessed he and the stranger were about the same height, though he could not be sure while he sat in his favorite chair...bled on it. Black hair hung to the *Baraan*'s shoulders, touching his blood-stained green tunic, and a short-cut black beard hid much of his features, except for his penetrating green eyes. His wide-shouldered green tunic was cut at the shoulder -- by a knife or dagger, Rogaan guessed, though the wound did not look as bad up close as it had when he entered the room. Sarafi finished packing what started as a clean piece of cloth into the wound, and secured it with another long strip wrapped around the shoulder and arm. The stranger appeared familiar, scratching at Rogaan's memories, but he could not place him. A glint of steel near the stranger's right hand and lap made Rogaan take a step back and assume a fighting stance with feet about as wide as his shoulders, all the while fixing his eyes on the stranger.

"Rogaan, he is blood," Sarafi announced softly with a gentle hand placed on Rogaan's forearm. "Maybe it has been too long for you. Imtaesus is my youngest brother, and has been away from Brigum for quite some time."

Imtaesus gave Rogaan a piercing gaze then stood up with a little effort with an extended hand. Rogaan stood his ground for a few moments, then warily grasped Imtaesus' forearm in greeting, which brought a wide grin to Imtaesus. "You've certainly grown, Rogaan. I would never have guessed you'd be so big, given...."

"Father's stature," Rogaan finished flatly, with a slight hint of contempt. Imtaesus' brown face deepened in color. Rogaan was not fond of House Isin's obsession with his father's height, though he did come to accept their mocking comments about Mother being the taller of the two, almost by a hand. With a start, Rogaan recalled his purpose for returning to the house, and that his father was in trouble, and blurted the information out before thinking of how it would affect his mother. "Father has been arrested by the *Tusaa'Ner* and is being taken somewhere! He must be rescued! I am going to free him!"

"Rogaan, no." Sarafi stared down her son with those penetrating green eyes and tightened her grip on his forearm. "You can do your father no good with such action."

"Mother," Rogaan said in an authoritative tone, uncommon with him when speaking with his parents. "Father must be rescued. He has done nothing to justify being arrested."

"He is a threat to the leaders of Brigum and Farratum," Sarafi announced matter-of-factly as she held her son's eyes with her own. Rogaan went numb and his face must have shown his shock, from the sympathetic look she returned. Sarafi remained silent for a moment, hesitating, and with uncertain eyes -- something he rarely saw in her. To Rogaan, his mother appeared to be considering something, words she *should* say, what she *could* say. After a few uncomfortable moments, she continued. "As they see it. Your father is not a simple craftsman you think him to be, my son. He has been involved in the affairs of Brigum and Shuruppak since before you were born…since before I was born, for that matter. He holds no ruling scepter, nor does he wear a crown, but he has influence and allies spread across these lands."

"He's made enemies, too," Imtaesus added seriously. Sarafi snapped him a sharp look, but he seemed not too concerned by it.

Returning her attention to Rogaan, she continued. "Your father was an ambassador from Turil long ago, when Shuruppak was less a nation and more a cobbling of regional powers and more aggressive to its neighbors, mostly Turil. Your father helped bring an end to years of conflict, but was exiled from Turil for reasons unknown, even to me. He came to live here in Brigum and took up metal crafting as his clan in Turil was renowned for, but he kept a hand in the affairs of Brigum and Shuruppak. He became ally of House Isin and *others* in Shuruppak's Civil War, and helped bring that struggle to an end, too, before you were born. Since the time the *Proclamation of the Govern* was signed by Shuruppak's city-states, your father has kept to his metal-making while less openly continuing to forge agreements and alliances across Shuruppak. He did this for the purpose of keeping the nation stable and friendly to its neighbors…Turil."

"How was it I never knew any of this?" Rogaan asked with the simmering heat of anger and embarrassment that he so lacked the skill to see his father's dealings while growing up under the same roof. Then his spine shivered with realization that his mother was sharing long-held secrets. Something must be very wrong. "Why are you telling me this…now?"

"Your father is very good at what he does." Sarafi spoke with a pride that would be difficult to fake. "A master at metal-making, diplomacy, and strategy. You would not see anything he did if he did not want you to see. As for why I am speaking of this at this time…it was your father's wish that it be so."

"What are you saying?" Rogaan felt utterly confused and concerned that things were truly not well.

"You are to be his successor," Sarafi replied with a warm smile. "He was to begin your teachings after your *Zagdu-i-Kuzu* ceremony."

A wave of shame washed over Rogaan at how he had treated and disobeyed his father concerning the Hunt and his *shunir'ra*. He had not the first inkling of his father's plans for him -- and with a vibrant prickling of his skin, Rogaan felt a renewed sense of urgency to see his father free, again.

"Why was Father taken?" Rogaan asked seriously with a determined voice.

"I am uncertain," Sarafi confessed, with a lost and sad look upon her face. "He knew this would come to pass and set plans in motion -- I do not pretend to understand for the most of it. He sent you away on the Hunt to avoid the trouble of a few days ago and had House Isin… and another house…prepare to keep you hidden away upon your return. Imtaesus was to see you escorted to my Father's estate. Your father then left on the day the Farratum *Tusaa'Ner* arrived…to keep me from harm, I think. The *Tusaa'Ner* arrested him, then came here in search of the *Isell-Dingir* they claim as hidden wealth subject to the new tax imposed by Farratum."

"What happened here?" Pax asked from somewhere behind Rogaan.

All turned and saw Pax and Suhd standing timidly near the cook room door. Sarafi let out an exasperated sigh. In Rogaan's mind he saw the expression on her face. She was not pleased, especially since Pax had likely overheard their words. In truth, Rogaan had forgotten about Pax and Suhd the moment he saw the blood spatters on the floor. Looking at his mother to read her reaction to Pax's presence, he caught a glint of blade in Imtaesus' hand that suddenly disappeared after Sarafi placed a blood-stained restraining hand on her brother's arm.

"They are Rogaan's friends." Sarafi spoke with a forced smile that Rogaan did not know how to read. Imtaesus then tilted his head, slightly, to acknowledge the two.

"I mean, da blood and all," Pax continued. "Ya seem ta be not too safe here. If ya ask me...pardon me?" That last Pax added after Suhd gave him a sharp elbow in the side.

"True," Imtaesus replied with a half-sweep of his left arm toward the front door, the knife now gone. "We were attacked by a Keeper of the Ways as we entered the house. I think we surprised him and struggled with him, Igim and I, before he cut me and fled. Igim is off in chase."

"How is it you know him as a Keeper?" Sarafi asked skeptically. She was genuinely surprised by her brother's announcement of who had harmed them. She seemed to not have known.

"His marking...on the forehead," Imtaesus replied matter-of-factly, as if it were obvious to everyone. "The Keepers' dagger and flame. I've crossed a few times. They have influence in the east, but I've not known them to show themselves this far west. He seemed a cut-throat or poorly trained thief."

"Lugasum?" Rogaan turned to Imtaesus, alarmed and demanding an answer. Imtaesus kept silent with a face of stone then glanced to Sarafi, who chewed words for a few moments before speaking.

"Your father feared more than the reach of Shuruppak." She spoke solemnly and carefully. "There are those who consider *all* of our lives today an offense to the Ancients and fearing their retribution would see us return to the ways of old when the Ancients ruled with a visible and stern hand. I fear this…*Iugasum* was such a person sent by the Keepers of the Way to silence your father's heart and guiding hand."

"And you," Imtaesus added while staring at Rogaan before suffering a glaring protest from his sister. Imtaesus returned an argumentative look then continued once she looked away in frustration. "Rogaan is in danger, too. This assassin wasn't here only for your father or mother. You must return with me to House Isin, immediately."

"No, Imtaesus." Sarafi's calm protest came with her eyes fixed on the front door, but her gaze was more distant. She appeared troubled, struggling with a decision. "That is not Mithraam's wish. Not now, with cut-throats among us. My One left instructions for our son if an attempt was made on his life before he could be placed under Isin's protection. Again, I do not understand fully My One, but his strategies have always proven best."

Imtaesus looked as if his eyes would pop out of their sockets. He clearly didn't know this part of the plan. He made to protest by straightening his stance and puffing out his chest, but was cut off by another of Sarafi's famous penetrating glares.

"Rogaan is to go to the Ebon Circle," Sarafi announced, so that there would be no challenge to her words.

"No!" Imtaesus replied angrily. All cordial pretenses were gone from his tone, and his face darkened. Gasps from somewhere behind Rogaan echoed in the room. "That just isn't to be. Better the assassin than to take the youngling there."

"Imtaesus, this is Mithraam's wish." Sarafi spoke with the authority of a queen. "He was very clear on this. Somehow he anticipated this possibility. This *is* to be."

Sarafi briskly waved her hand at Imtaesus, stopping his objection before it burst out. "Imtaesus, you have been away for some years and do not understand the present relationship between House Isin, Mithraam, and the dark robes."

She settled her gaze on Rogaan. Her eyes turned sad, glassy. She then looked at Pax and Suhd and seemed to be considering something new, then looked back to Rogaan. "I am sorry, my son, but you will be leaving this home, this town, and its people so that you can remain alive. I do not know when you will be able to return, but it is not safe for you here. Your father was insistent that if this came to pass, only the dark robes of the Ebon Circle would be capable of protecting you."

"They say the dark robes sacrifice people to the Ancients." Suhd spoke in a broken voice, her eyes every bit as glassy as Sarafi's. "They'll do the unspeakable to Rogaan."

"Would no want that even for da worse folks," Pax stated with a stunned expression.

"Sarafi, you can't want this?" Imtaesus asked, almost demanded of her in a low voice.

"My wants do not matter." Sarafi spoke with strong resolve. "I have already lost My One to the guard, and I will not lose my son. I cannot think Mithraam would send Rogaan to his capture or death, so I will trust. I must trust."

Tears trickled down Sarafi's face as she struggled to regain control of herself with hand over her mouth. Rogaan could not remember the last time his mother cried. Maybe never. She was clearly shaken, and that worried Rogaan more than all other things, a hundred-fold.

"You must leave soon." Sarafi wiped her face with her hand. She turned her attention to Pax and Suhd. "Neither of you should be in serious trouble for your associations with us, but you now have knowledge that you should not, and that is a danger to Rogaan."

"I be helpin' me ma and father!" Pax growled with a conviction that he would be successful. "Da guard took 'em and I mean ta see 'em free. Darken 'em all."

"What are you speaking of?" Sarafi asked, honestly confused.

"Their mother and father were taken by the *Tusaa'Ner,* too." Rogaan explained. "By force. They were shoved into the jailer's wagon with Father."

Sarafi and Imtaesus exchanged questioning glances. Imtaesus shook his head slowly left then right, as if answering an unspoken question posed by his sister, then stiffened his back with a slight grimace. "Younglings, there is nothing you can do to help them, now. The Guard means to take them from Brigum -- likely to Farratum, where they will be tried for some crime."

"Ya would do nothin' to help 'em!" Pax protested.

"What will happen to them?" Suhd asked with tears streaming down her face.

Imtaesus looked at Sarafi again with raised eyebrows, as if asking an unspoken question. She gestured with a tilt of her head toward Suhd and Pax. Imtaesus cleared his throat. "They will be tried in a Hall of Justice and likely found guilty."

"No!" Pax protested again. "We need ta stop da jail wagon and free 'em. Me father and mother have done nothin'."

"That is of no matter," Imtaesus replied coldly. "They are in the hands of the authority. If they committed even the smallest disobedience...as small as arguing with a law-arm, they will find themselves in a Farratum jail or quarry pits."

Suhd broke down in uncontrollable tears. Pax hugged his sister into his arms, his face a tortured contrast of anger and sadness. Rogaan felt his tears welling up for Suhd then fought them back. Suhd continued weeping until she looked exhausted, and Pax held her tight while wearing the glare of a madman bent on murder and a mountain of trouble.

"What will become of Father?" Rogaan asked quietly.

Sarafi and Imtaesus exchanged uneasy glances, and she looked near to tears. Imtaesus' face softened, just a little, before he answered reluctantly. "The jail and pits are the least of your father's fates. He'll likely suffer a public execution or the Arena for being so troublesome to those in authority."

Rogaan was stunned. *Execution! Put to death!* Rogaan felt his world collapse. The thought that his father would no longer be in his life frightened him more than anything he had dreamt about or before considered. "No! We must stop this."

"Rogaan, we can't," Imtaesus stated. "They are many, and they must have the blessing of the Regional Hall of Laws to reach this far west in Brigum."

"Coward!" Rogaan growled.

"Rogaan!" Sarafi chided. "Imtaesus is no coward. He is War Sworn trained and here to protect us."

Pax and Suhd both looked to Imtaesus with asking eyes; Pax still held that murderous look. Rogaan fought his rage and his fear. He wanted to do something -- had to do something, or he would explode, but he held his tongue as his father had often taught him when upset, and as his mother now demanded. Rogaan's rage slowly transformed to a simmering, determined anger-enough for him to speak though through clenched teeth.

"If you are War Sworn, then help us." Rogaan asked with heated eyes. "You know the way of battle. You are exactly the help we need."

"Knowing the ways of battle is but a small part in understanding war." Imtaesus spoke as a teacher, calm and certain. "Understanding your enemy is the true means to gaining victory -- whether you use the sword, quill, or tongue."

"You make no sense." Pax made his accusation with a sneer. Suhd still clung tightly to him, but now with calmer tears and only the occasional sniffle.

Rogaan stood staring at the floor, chewing his thoughts of the many lessons given to him by his father. At the time his father taught him the *Philosophy of Conflict*, as the *Tellen* interpreted it, he never conceived of actually using it, even less understanding it, but Imtaesus' words were familiar and made sense to him...somehow. "We do not even know who we are fighting fully other than those who were sent to do a guardsman's work...and this Keeper cut-throat. They are many and we few and we have no plan. We need one. We need help."

They argued for some time about what to do and who would do it. Arguments were mostly between Sarafi and Imtaesus, though Rogaan managed to get a few of his ideas across and influenced some of the discussion despite his overall frustration. Imtaesus argued for Rogaan to travel to House Isin's land holding south of Brigum, where he could be protected by the small army of guardsmen loyal to the Isin family. Sarafi was unbending in her insistence that Rogaan follow Mithraam's wishes and seek protection in the Ebon Circle. The thought of the dark robes in the Ebon Circle unsettled Rogaan the more they talked about it. Though his father was always even-handed concerning what he said about the secretive cult. Others in Brigum spoke often of their evil deeds and atrocities. This left Rogaan uncertain as to what was true, but the dark robes frightened him. Pax appeared appalled at the discussion, but kept silent mostly while leaning against the wall, brooding a dark thunderstorm of thoughts. He made it clear to everyone that he would free his parents with or without help. Suhd kept her tongue mostly, with only her sniffling and occasional weeping that let everyone know she was still in the room. With their discussion near an end, Igim returned agitated and empty-handed. The burly man offered several sincere apologies to Imtaesus and Sarafi for his failure to take captive the wounded cut-throat. He made no excuses, though offered a report that told of much boldness on the part of the Keeper to evade capture, so much so that even Imtaesus seemed impressed.

"It is settled," Sarafi announced after Igim made his report.

"What's settled, Sarafi?" Imtaesus was surprised and clearly not pleased with his sister's declaration and tone.

She finished washing her brother's blood from her hands in a water basin she had poured herself just before Igim burst through the front doors unannounced. "The...*cut-throat* still lives, Imtaesus, and Rogaan remains in peril. As long as that is true, House Isin's estates, both here in town and to the south, are not safe enough for my son. Mithraam has confidence enough in the Ebon Circle. I must trust his judgment."

Imtaesus made to protest, again, but was cut short by a brisk wave of his sister's hand and her hard, penetrating stare. Rogaan shivered for him. Once she made up her mind, nothing short of the Ancients could change it, and that would be a fight. "Pax and Suhd, you will find protection in our family's estate south of Brigum until the return of your parents."

"I be going after me ma and father," Pax shot back flatly. His eyes still burned with murderous intent.

"You know too much," Sarafi replied, also flatly. "Rogaan is in danger if you talk."

"No talkin' by me and not of me friend," Pax countered in a serious tone. He played with a blade in his hand that he pulled from somewhere. "I be going with him. So if I be caught and talk, it no be mattering."

"Pax, no," Suhd whispered fearfully. "Don't leave me. What will happen to me?"

Pax made to answer, but Sarafi acted first, placing two comforting hands upon Suhd's shoulders while holding Pax's eyes with her own, measuring him and his conviction. "Are you certain, Pax?"

Pax nodded with steady eyes, matching Sarafi's stare. "Will House Isin still protect Suhd?"

"Yes," Sarafi answered with the authority of a queen speaking for her kingdom. "She will be protected well away from the workings of Brigum. Igim will see to her safe travel with me while Imtaesus accompanies you two to the Ebon Circle, tonight."

Imtaesus' eyes grew wide. He stared at his sister for a few moments, a bit angry and with a challenge in his eyes. "You're not thinking clear? The road is no place to be at night, and you know that."

"We cannot wait until morning, Imtaesus," Sarafi stated, as if her words should be obvious to everyone...and obeyed.

"The cut-throat will have time to strike again if we wait." Rogaan said making sense, he thought. He reasoned through the possibilities. Staying in his home was too likely a place to hide from those seeking him. "And the *Tusaa'Ner* might return looking for us."

All but Suhd nodded their agreement, with Suhd looking as if she was about to bawl, again. Rogaan looked at his home sullenly. Shattered crystal, torn tapestries, broken furniture, toppled statues, disheveled rugs, and cracked tiles...his home. Once a place of comfort, peace, and safety, but no more. It was stained in blood and treachery, and Rogaan felt as if there were no sanctuary from those intending his family harm. He felt vulnerable, and that made him angry. Rogaan had no intention of hiding in the Ebon Circle, but he needed to allow his mother her illusions, or she would send a small militia after him. He planned to take the fight to his father's jailers. He just needed help, and hoped he could convince his mother's brother or find some help on the road.

Chapter 10

Dangerous Streets

T he cool night air made cold the sweat on Rogaan's face and neck, causing him a slight shiver. The strong odor of animal dung carried on a north breeze, making his nose wrinkle. At least the cool air of the early evening brought a less pungent stench from the *sarigs*, *kydas*, and *niiskus* in the stable some fifty strides on his left. Rogaan crouched low behind a stride-high shrub thick with new leaves. *Good cover*, he concluded. The shrub abutted a single-story wooden-plank building with a mortared stone foundation as tall as the shrub. A stone and brick building to their left framed the other side of the alleyway, offering concealment from the guardsmen manning Hunter's Gate. Despite the darkness and the uneasy feelings that always came with it, Rogaan felt renewed and alert after the quick bath and donning fresh clothes his mother insisted on his wearing before setting off on his journey. She kept him from his hunting clothes. He reluctantly wore his long-sleeved dark-blue shirt that laced up the front, black soft-hide pants, black hide boots, and a charcoal-colored hide vest. His cased *shunir'ra* and a capped quiver of his best blue metal arrows, the last of them, were slung over his back. The knife given to him at the Hunt was sheathed and hung on his right from a wide charcoal-colored hide belt. His green and tan carry pack, stuffed with food and other essentials, lay at his feet. Pax, also freshly bathed – another insistence of his mother's that Rogaan heartily agreed with – leaned against a young cedar tree as thick as his body while crouching next to Rogaan. Pax fiddled with the slightly-too-big sleeves of a forest-green shirt, one of Rogaan's, tucking the sleeves under so they would not get in his way. Pax still wore his patched black breeches after trying several of

Rogaan's that proved a bit too big in the waist and legs. The clothing exchange gave Rogaan the opportunity to see just how many knives his friend possessed: an impressive arsenal of ten in all -- kept in a harness under his shirt that attached to his belt. Pax even had a pair of knives tucked into his tan boots. While changing, Pax demonstrated a deftness and confidence with the knives that surprised Rogaan. *How did I miss his kinship with blades? Pax never led on his fondness for them.*

Anything but innocent was Rogaan's reading of Pax's mood; even with his friend's uncertain and nervous eyes peering from underneath that wide-brimmed hat he insisted on wearing. Hooded oil lamps atop three stride tall wooden poles cast a weak light on the street's paving stones ahead of them. Beyond, a row of ten-stride-tall cedar trees marked the edge of the road, and the Tamarad River ravine beyond that. Pax looked north toward Hunter's Gate, then south toward the Water House, looking for guardsmen or watchers. He gave no hint if he saw trouble; he just kept scanning. Imtaesus stood behind Rogaan with his back flat against the wooden-plank building, his blood-soaked tunic replaced with a blue one from Rogaan's wardrobe. Imtaesus' left arm hung in a makeshift sling and was mostly useless. He carried a short sword in his right hand and looked as dangerous as any *Baraan* Rogaan could remember. The weapon suited his mother's brother well.

Rogaan protested Imtaesus' accompanying them, but his mother and Imtaesus had none of it. This made his plans more difficult. Rogaan hoped he could convince his uncle to bypass the Ebon Circle, but feared his mother's instructions would win the night. Imtaesus appeared to be a *Baraan* of courage and purpose and integrity. She was very clear and direct when she told her brother that Rogaan's life was in his hands, and she would hold him to account in getting Rogaan to the Ebon Circle. *So much for allowing my mother her illusions*, Rogaan worried.

Rogaan was surprised at Imtaesus' nearly instant transition from a talkative fellow to a silent and alert sentinel the moment they stepped from home. Imtaesus' demeanor gave Rogaan a shiver as the *Baraan's* eyes turned into a fury held back by what Rogaan thought was only will…a will Rogaan was not so certain of.

The three of them quickly made their way to the east side of Brigum with the plan to use the Tamarad River ravine as a means of escaping town without needing to pass through any of the closely watched and heavily guarded gates, or needing to climb over the stone wall protecting all those within from the beasts of the Wilds. Rogaan's mother, Suhd, and Igim left for the Isin countryside estate just before dusk as a distraction to all, allowing Rogaan, Pax, and Imtaesus to travel more easily. Pax and Suhd protested at the plan…loudly, several times, and argued that she would be safer with her brother. It was obvious they did not want to separate. Rogaan could not blame them for their grief and fear of losing each other now with their parents in the hands of the *Tusaa'Ner*. Despite his desire to have Suhd close, Rogaan made the final and successful plea to Suhd, reluctantly supported by Pax, that she would be safer away from the Ebon Circle, and for her to accompany his mother into Isin's protection, since town was clearly no longer safe. The moment of their separation was difficult to watch, with tears and hugs and promises that they would once again see each other and their parents. Rogaan's mother's departure was grandiose, with a sedan chair and hired guardsmen called to carry them to the South Gate where they planned to take an armed carriage to the Isin estate nearly a day's ride south of Brigum. They all hoped that the sedan chair's passage would hold the attention of anyone in town seeking Rogaan, and maybe Pax, at least long enough for them to slip from Brigum.

"I do hope Suhd be all right," Pax mumbled, more to himself than to anyone else.

"She is in good care with Mother." Rogaan did his best to convince his friend that he had made the best choice.

B.A.VONSIK

"Ya ma better take care of her," Pax said somberly while keeping his eyes on the street. Rogaan took Pax's tone and words more as his trying to convince himself that he made the right decision, and not as a threat. "Da way be clear. Come!"

The hairs on Rogaan's neck prickled. Something was wrong, but he did not know what, and he did not know how he knew. He tried to stop Pax before he exposed himself to the street, but Pax darted away too quickly, around the cedar tree and into the street three paces before he stopped to see if Rogaan followed. Rogaan urgently waved him back, but Pax only returned a questioning look.

"Hold!" A booming voice commanded from a distance. Pax held a startled gape as he stood frozen, looking toward the Water House.

"Damnation!" Imtaesus cursed. Grabbing Rogaan by the shirt with his sword hand, Imtaesus dragged Rogaan to his feet while growling, "Run, youngling! Back this way."

Confused and off-balance, Rogaan felt himself being pulled back into the shadows while watching Pax take a step back toward him, then pausing, as if considering something, then sprinting off on Waterside Road toward Hunter's Gate.

"No!" Rogaan protested and he ripped free of Imtaesus' grip. Pax was alone. It would not take long before he was caught. He needed to help Pax...somehow. Rogaan snatched up his satchel as he bolted into the street, chasing after his friend. When his boots hit the paving stones, he sensed something...the presences of others. Snapping a look over his shoulder at the Water House, he spotted more than a hand's-count of Brigum *Tusaa'Ner* running at them some fifty strides away. Startled and confused about what to do, Rogaan stopped and looked back to Imtaesus. The *Baraan* remained hidden in the shadows and unmoving. *Why does he not follow? Is he afraid?* Confusion turned to frustration and frustration turned to anger within the span of several heartbeats. Rogaan's anger quickly brought clarity to his thoughts and he broke into a sprint after Pax, not caring to learn of Imtaesus' reasoning for hiding in the face of danger. Pax needed help.

After his third stride, Rogaan looked up seeking his friend. Surprisingly, Pax was running back in his direction. He looked to have run past the four-way crossing-street some twenty strides ahead, making his way along the stable yard then turned around for some reason. With another look, Rogaan saw that reason...Kantus and his Band, now six strong, were on Pax's heels. Pax's frustrated eyes met Rogaan's as they both entered the crossing-street where they darted west onto the street they crossed earlier sneaking from the center of town to their shadowed hiding place Rogaan now wished he remained in. After a brief sprint, they came to a sliding halt less than ten paces before another troupe of eight guardsmen...all *Tusaa'Ner* with weapons drawn.

"Now what?" Rogaan asked in a grumbling growl as the crowd of determined, grim-faced armed guardsmen closed on them. Uncertain how they would get out of this predicament without hurting anyone or being hurt themselves, or being jailed, he asked Pax, "Any ideas?"

"Ya. I be takin' 'em away...from ya," Pax stated. "I was ta have 'em chase me...away from ya, lose 'em, then find ya and get gone from town. I can no do that now since ya be too slow."

"Oh...." Rogaan's face heated at the realization that he had ruined Pax's attempt at drawing the guardsmen away. "So...now what?"

"You surrender." A familiar and haunting voice taunted him triumphantly, somewhere behind them. Rogaan and Pax wheeled about to face a gloating Kantus, with his fists firmly planted on the hips of his hunter's outfit. Rogaan thought it looked too much like *Kiuri'Ner eur* armor and that Kantus wore it dishonoring the protectors of Brigum.

"You first," Rogaan growled with a toothy grimace.

"You two have been so much trouble," Kantus continued smugly, as if Rogaan had not spoken. "You break the law, then flee the guards, then attack those same guardsmen, some of which are still being tended to by Healers, and…oh, yes, you're part of a conspiracy that caused the death of Akaal."

"We had nothin' ta do with his dyin'," Pax growled. "And ya know it."

"I saw him fall to his death -- messy it was -- and you the nearest to him." Kantus countered Pax's denial while wearing a smug smile. Kantus looked left then right then beyond Rogaan and Pax before smiling broadly with what appeared to be a mix of amusement and satisfaction. "You're outnumbered and, oh…the Town Council placed a bounty on your heads. My father made sure that they gathered today. Give up and you won't get hurt…too badly."

Anger burned intensely inside Rogaan, and became more intense with every smug word Kantus spoke. Rogaan's contempt for Kantus grew just as bright. Fighting down his anger so to control himself, Rogaan wanted a peaceful way out of this, but was uncertain what to do. His thoughts were clouded with a yearning to smash Kantus into a broken lump. With an effort, he fought to keep his wits, to think of escape, not let his anger control him. He and Pax were surrounded by no fewer than twenty armed guardsmen, better than ten on each side blocking their escape, and the spaces between the buildings on either side of the street were filled and blocked with crates or stacked rubbish too high to climb before getting pounced on by guardsmen. Rogaan considered surrendering, but only for a moment…that passed quickly. His pride would not allow it. *Where is Imtaesus?* Rogaan realized his uncle was nowhere to be seen. *Where did he go? A War Sworn would not run from a fight.* Rogaan's hope sank.

Rogaan knew there was little hope of fair treatment if taken by these jailers. Kantus and his father would see to that. He and Pax would be at their mercy…and that gave Rogaan the shivers, angry shivers. The chance of rescuing his father and Pax's parents would be forever lost even if they eventually were released -- unlikely, that -- or managed an escape. No, this would not end without a fight. A calm sigh escaped Rogaan. It surprised him, how calm he felt. He had resolved himself to this fight a long time ago and had been waiting for this day to come. *Who to strike first?* Without warning, and as if Pax had read his thoughts, Pax put on a sly smile as two knives suddenly appeared in his hands, then just as quickly found themselves in the thighs of two new members of Kantus' Band, one on either side of their smug-smiling leader. Both went down howling in pain. Rogaan gaped, shocked at Pax's boldness and impressed at the same time.

"Stomp'em!" Pax shouted at Rogaan with eyes wide, looking as if they would pop out of his head.

Kantus recovered quickly from seeing his bandsmen drop withering on the ground from the two blades whirling past him so closely. Rogaan found himself wishing Pax had plunged those blades into their nemesis. His taunting of them would be done. *No. I should not think as such*, Rogaan chastised himself. Kantus' face exploded with anger as he jerked free his long knife. "Take them!"

Everyone stood looking at each other. A long moment passed -- it seemed forever to Rogaan -- before Pax produced two more knives, hurling them at two guardsmen. One went down growling with a blade deep in his thigh. The other, surprised by the knife buried to the hilt mid-thigh, stumbled backwards in a silent scream. Chaos erupted behind Rogaan before he could act. Imtaesus, wielding a short sword in his good hand, plunged into a group of guardsmen cutting at their legs, sword arms, and less vital places -- obviously striking to wound and incapacitate instead of killing. Three guardsmen went down howling before any of them realized what hit them.

Suddenly, Rogaan stumbled left from the heavy impact of a guardsman rushing him from his right. He kept his feet, barely, as his attacker slipped off and went tumbling in front of him; the armored *Baraan* lay sprawled on the paving stones several strides away. It took the *Baraan* a moment to recover face down in the street before scrambling to a kneeling position with eager eyes fixed on Rogaan. Rogaan knew from the determination in the guardsman's eyes promised he would attack again. *Persistent. Motivated.* The *Baraan* launched himself at Rogaan again, but he did so slowly...too slowly for what Rogaan expected. A quick glance around showed Rogaan everyone moving slower than they should. That familiar nausea gripped him hard. He fought it back then it surged, again, and again as he fought it back. A moment of disorientation held him before he shook off the feeling and defended himself when the guardsman reached him.

The man was an easy target. Rogaan slammed his foot into the helmeted face of the oncoming guardsman, collapsing him into an un-moving heap at his feet, his face guard bent. A smile of satisfaction grew on Rogaan's face as he admired his handiwork. *That felt good,* Rogaan admitted. He could not decide the exact words to describe what he felt unleashing his anger and frustration at those with Kantus. The sounds of footfalls drew his attention to two guardsmen rushing him from straight ahead with short swords raised. They also moved slowly, but simultaneously attacked, forcing Rogaan to be on the de-fensive. He ducked the swinging blade of the first guardsman, then felt the second blade slash his left forearm before he could rotate and slip out of range of a second attack by it. The first guardsman, now stand-ing to his right, moved to deliver a backhanded swing that Rogaan thought certain to strike his upper chest or neck. Reacting without thinking, Rogaan blocked the guardsman's sword arm with his right hand, stopping the blade just short of pain and bloodletting. In a fluid motion, Rogaan slammed his left fist into the guardsman's unguarded ribs, sending the *Baraan* to the ground in a convulsing heap of groans. Certain that he broke the guardsman's ribs from the sound and feel of the impact, Rogaan smiled. The hairs on the back of his neck actually prickled.

Whirling, Rogaan found the second guardsman already delivering a strike with killing in his eyes. Rogaan twisted, avoiding the short sword plunging at his chest, then grabbed the guardsman's sword arm with both of his hands and tried to wrench the weapon away. No success. This guardsman was considerably bigger and stronger than the first, even a bit taller than Rogaan. A hard and painful yank on Rogaan's hair pulled him off-balance and forced his head back in surprise, exposing his throat. Instinctively, Rogaan dropped into a crouch, pulling the big guardsman behind him over enough for Rogaan to explode upwards with his whole body into the *Baraan*'s upper chest and armored face. Both struggling combatants went tumbling to the paving stones in a thud. Rogaan still had a death grip on the guardsman's sword arm as his sword clinked and clattered to a stop several strides away. A wave of relief swept through Rogaan just as a burly forearm wrapped itself around his neck, crushing off his air. Gasping, Rogaan grabbed at the left forearm of his attacker, then tugged and pulled at it, but it held tight against his throat. A moment later a prick just below his right jaw told Rogaan the guardsman had a dagger pressed at his neck, ready to deliver a killing stroke.

"Give up or I'll cut ya through," a gruff voice growled triumphantly in his ear.

Rogaan struggled for a few moments more, then resigned himself to the guardsman's demand, but only after he felt the blade at his throat pressed hard enough to start a trickle of blood running down his neck. He suddenly realized everyone moved normally and his nausea was replaced by hunger pains. His stomach grumbled. The sound of battle was strangely absent, and only the moans of pain pierced the night. Rogaan glanced around, moving just his eyes to keep from getting his throat cut. To his left he saw Pax on his knees held by two of Kantus' Band with Pax mumbling something he could not make out. To his right, Imtaesus lay on his side in a pool of blood, bleeding. He lay motionless, surrounded by no fewer than eight guardsmen, writhing in pain on the paving stones. Two bleeding guardsmen stood over Imtaesus, both panting to catch their breath, blades coated in blood. Rogaan groaned, fearing the worst as strength drained from his body.

His heart sank as he mumbled, "How will I tell Mother her brother died trying to save me from my own stupidity? I should never have run after Pax."

"Get him up!" Kantus demanded to the guardsman holding Rogaan. Two more burly figures in light armor rushed over to aid their prone comrade, grabbing Rogaan and pulling him to his knees as painfully as they could manage the task—three blades immediately found their way to poking him in the throat, ribs, and back. Rogaan forced himself to rise, stand tall, on his feet, to face Kantus. He would not cower, not to Kantus. He would not give the bully the satisfaction. Forced to submit, to surrender while under the blade put things in a bad way, but better than willing to surrender without a fight. *But...Imtaesus.* Bitter was the taste of his poor choices and the consequences...just too bitter. He spat. Rogaan started to become angry with himself. Pax made a growling effort to escape his captors' grips, but it only got him a painful gut punch from one of the smiling Bandsmen, doubling Pax over as he tried to suck at the air. He looked like a gasping fish out of water, but watching his friend getting rough treatment made Rogaan angry. No, they would not surrender. *Nothing good will come from this.* His father, mother, Pax, Suhd, and their parents all depended on his being free to make things right.

Kantus sauntered over to Pax, regarding him with a pompous smile, as if looking at a trophy. The dim light of the street lamps cast a sinister shadow on Kantus' face, making that smile of his seemingly warn of ill things to follow. Grabbing Pax by the throat, Kantus shoved Pax's head upward and forced him to straighten worsening the pain he was obviously in. Kantus looked every bit as if he were enjoying himself, and Rogaan's blood began to boil.

"Poor Pax," Kantus taunted. "Your days of speaking insolently and disrespectfully to me and my family end tonight. You'll show me the respect I deserve...or you'll suffer until you do."

Pax worked his mouth, trying to say something then spit into

Kantus' face before putting on a dark grin. His friend's defiant eyes told Rogaan that Kantus was not going to get his satisfaction easily and that Pax would suffer much before then. Hatred and contempt would keep Pax going for some time, Rogaan knew, but he doubted they would sustain him indefinitely.

Kantus let go of Pax with a disdainful shove, then punched him square in the face before wiping the spittle from his cheek. Pax slumped limp and looked dazed in the arms of Kantus' Bandsmen, who caught him before he could collapse to the street. Kantus gathered himself for a moment, visibly struggling with the urge to do harm to Pax. After a few moments, Kantus took on a calm demeanor -- the demeanor of a *Baraan* in complete control. "You will show me respect."

Kantus punched Pax hard in the stomach, causing Pax to grunt with the air forcibly expelled from his lungs and double over, as much as the pair of Bandsmen holding him would allow. Looking satisfied with himself as Pax futilely tried to fill his lungs with air, Kantus turned his attention to Rogaan. Sauntering over to where Rogaan stood at blade point, he spoke purposely and with a voice rich in triumph. "And you, Rogaan. I'm going to enjoy watching you explain to the Town Council, the *Ensi* and the *Tusaa'Ner* why YOU harmed so many guardsmen. Yes. That'll be a sight. I think I'll have my father petition the jailers to allow my family the pleasure of your servitude instead of sending you to the quarries."

Kantus moved close, enough to cause Rogaan's nose to wrinkle at his rank breath. Kantus' eyes glinted in the yellow light of the street lamps. Those eyes were filled with contempt, and worse -- shameless triumph and satisfaction. "You'll beg for the quarries before I'm done with you."

Rogaan struggled to keep his tongue. Inside he raged...seethed. *Have to keep my control*, he told himself. *Things will get worse if I lose control*, he gave himself counsel. He sensed that Kantus was goading him into actions that would provide excuses to mistreat him and Pax. *Why does he have to be so smug and arrogant?* Rogaan asked himself. Despite his best efforts to remain impassive and unemotional, Rogaan's temper started to break through. His eyes betrayed him, burning hotly with hatred and contempt for Kantus and what Rogaan admitted to himself as embers of a building murderous rage. Kantus scowled and seemed unsatisfied that Rogaan had not put up more of a fight. He then turned away, only to rear back and punch Rogaan hard in the mouth. Rogaan's head snapped back from the impact of Kantus' hidebound fist. Pain jolted Rogaan's face and neck, and his chin throbbed as if it were burning. Rogaan felt something trickling down his neck... blood, his own...drawn from the freshly made stinging wound on his neck, cut by one of the blades held against it. The taste of iron and the scent of his blood from somewhere in his mouth made his stomach turn a bit. He raged and raged inside.

Still, Rogaan fought to control his anger. He had won the battle of wills between them so far, but he felt his control slipping fast. Anger, his rage, was rapidly eroding his self-control. *How much more do I take?* Kantus openly appeared frustrated at Rogaan's self-restraint and visibly scrubbed at his beard in thought -- of what, Rogaan was unsure. After a few moments, Kantus smiled and made to kick Rogaan in the gut or groin. Gritting his teeth, Rogaan strained tight his midsection and twisted his hips in anticipation of a painful strike in either place. With his foot drawn back to strike, Kantus froze with eyes widened, focused beyond Rogaan. The almost inaudible sound of a blade slicing through air was followed by a lower-pitched "thwop" as it sliced through something solid, repeated so rapidly that Rogaan lost count of the strikes he heard. The din of guardsmen scrambling, some shouting, others screaming in agony raised Rogaan's neck hairs in anticipation of being the next to fall. He felt utterly defenseless on his knees and with his captors' sword tips pressing at his neck and back.

I have to escape and defend myself, Rogaan decided. Several quick slices in the air and thwops to both sides of him, followed by the prickling

of the sword points disappearing from his neck and ribs, metal clink-
ing on the paving stones, and the guardsmen gloved hands gripping
his arms gone, made Rogaan freeze in anticipation of death. He closed
his eyes and braced himself, tightening every muscle in him, and waited for it. And he waited. *I am alive?* Rogaan spun around, rising to a
crouch, almost stumbling backward as he did. His eyes widened in
shock at what he saw. Bodies of burly, armored guardsmen lay in the
street…in pieces, cut in half through the shoulder or midsection and
yet there was no blood, not on the paving stones or spilling from the
massive wounds of their twitching body parts. The scent of burnt flesh
hung in the night air and made Rogaan's stomach turn. Most shocking
were the guardsmen's eyes -- they still darted back and forth, looking
around, as their mouths formed silent words and their body halves
twitched. *Do they realize they are lightless?* Rogaan felt his hairs everywhere raise and his skin prickle. The guardsman that had stood behind
him lay on the street decapitated -- an axe blade cut in two lay next
to his severed helmeted head. Again, no blood -- just body parts…
everywhere.

"Where did it come from?" Kantus asked absently of no one in
particular. He sounded as stunned and dumbfounded as Rogaan felt.

Kantus just stood with mouth agape, gawking at the carnage,
oblivious to Rogaan now standing next to him. With a start, Rogaan
realized Kantus was within arm's reach, and the dam holding back his
anger broke. Rogaan grabbed the stunned Kantus by the shoulder pad
of his *eur* hunter's uniform and slammed his fist into his rival's face so
violently that he thought he might have broken his own hand. Kantus
went down in an unmoving heap. His jaw was obviously broken by
the way it awkwardly looked. Rogaan felt no remorse, no regrets; instead, a great sense of satisfaction washed over him. Thuds and clink-
ing of armor and weapons hitting paving stones behind him grabbed
Rogaan's attention. He wheeled around to a scene of more guardsmen
lying lightless, or fading on the street as a shadow, dressed in a cloak

so black that it seemed to absorb light, quickly yet gracefully moving right to left, not in a rush, slashing blades equally as dark as the cloak, cutting down everyone in its path. Everyone except Pax. As quickly as this dealer of dark death started, he was done. Guardsmen lay in pieces all about the street, their flesh seared by the dark blade. Guardsmen, wounded or prostrated in a position of submission, not opposing the shadow, were bypassed and spared a grim death. Of those few, most sat watching the shadow with terror etched on their faces. A single guardsman running in the direction of the Hall of Laws, shouting something Rogaan could not quite discern was quickly silenced when the cloaked shadow threw something, striking the *Baraan* at the base of the neck. He went down and lay unmoving in the street some forty strides away. Rogaan stood unable to move, looking at this shadow of death, fearing he was next. Light from the street lamps caught a pair of radiant green eyes, tilted slightly, just before the black cloak absorbed them and disappeared into the shadows between the brick buildings on the north side of the street and the carnage he left behind.

Pax stood in the midst of body parts, looking about with a shock. Flesh, bone, and the armor of the guardsmen had been cut with equal ease. Pax stood motionless except for his slowly swiveling head, taking in everything -- at least trying to. Long moments passed before Pax dared speak. "What just happened, Rogaan? Who or what be that? How...?"

"I do not know," Rogaan replied.

Several wounded guardsmen managed to regain their feet then hobbled off as best they could toward the center of Brigum and the Hall of Laws.

Rogaan considered stopping them from alerting the town, but found it difficult to stomach any more death this night. He decided to let them go. "Pax, we need to get going. Before the rest of the town is after us."

Pax looked up at Rogaan, his eyes starting to clear from a cloud of bewilderment and fright. He then hurriedly retrieved several daggers near his feet, then moved quickly to the three guardsmen he had wounded, pulling his knives from their thighs, not caring if he injured or pained them further. Rogaan winced for the guardsmen as painful groans escaped their throats when the blades came free -- though not a one of them raised a hand against Pax. "Now, make this be a good lesson ta ya. Don't be botherin' us no more."

Rogaan knelt next to Imtaesus to check if there was luck that he was alive. His uncle's eyes were open, but unfocused, and his blood-soaked tunic failed to rise and fall with a living breath. Rogaan's throat tightened as a pain deep within his chest grabbed him like a great hand clenching his heart. He really did not know Imtaesus well, despite being blood. His pain and sorrow were for his mother. She spoke fondly of her brother often enough to know she was proud of him and loved him. *How am I going to tell mother of his death?* Rogaan fought back tears of anguish for her as he gently closed the eyes of his kindred.

"You be right." Pax broke in on Rogaan's deep thoughts with a gentle hand on his friend's shoulder. Pax had serious eyes when Rogaan looked up. "He fought good and brave. Nothin' more for ya ta do. Let's be goin'. Before more of this happins."

Rogaan agreed with his friend. Nothing more could be done here. In fact, Rogaan felt he had done quite enough in getting people killed, especially his blood. With one last look at Imtaesus' lifeless body, and suffering another strong pang of guilt, he gathered up his carry pack, quiver, and *shunir'ra* from where they had fallen sometime during their struggles, then followed Pax into the shadows to the south side of the street.

Chapter 11

Escaping Brigum

They quickly made their way back to where the chaos had started at the edge of Waterside Road, and crossed it after both Pax and Rogaan looked to make sure nobody would see them. On the other side of the road, crouching between two ten-stride-tall cedars, they peered into the dark void of the river ravine below. With only a crescent moon, and it low on the mountains at that, little could be seen below -- even with Rogaan's sight. The darkness sent a chill up and down Rogaan's back. Waters rushing over rocks and boulders seemed louder than he expected. He did not care for water of any depth and was not looking forward to this part of their plan; the darkness made his heart race at the swelling fear inside him. Everything about this tested him. Pax pulled off a lashing of rope from his bottom pack and lashed it around a tree, then threw the rest of it into the darkness, then immediately started down the cliff using his feet to steady himself as he disappeared into the darkness below. Rogaan dawdled and delayed at the top of the cliff, not wanting to descend into the abyss. He watched Pax work his way down into the deepening darkness to the base of the ravine, where he barely could make out his friend -- and then only when he moved.

With immense reluctance and countless controlling breaths, trying to calm or at least steady his racing heart, Rogaan grabbed the rope, and with a deep breath took his first step into the unknown. He made his way slowly down the cliff, almost as if he were blind and needed to feel his way along the rocks. Below, Pax cursed him often in hushed outbursts, complaining that he was moving too slowly and that they would be caught before he ever touched bottom. The cliff stood more than ten strides, and its rocky face was slick, giving Rogaan several scares as he slipped, with only the rope keeping him from falling. Once at the bottom, Pax grabbed the rope and shook it in a way Rogaan was unfamiliar with, causing it to come free from the tree above. Rogaan stood looking at Pax incredulously as he wrapped it into a circle and reattached it to his butt pack. *That rope had no anchor!* Rogaan gave Pax an angry stare. Pax just smiled back at him and started south. They hurried along the river's edge toward the Wheelhouse, doing their best not to slip on the slick rocks, moss, and lichens and plunge into the swift waters only a few strides away. Rogaan was certain *snapjaws* lived in these waters despite the assurances of more than a few *Kiuri'Ner* claiming the animals preferred calmer flows. Rogaan remained skeptical and feared their presence. Hungry killers would make any river crossing dangerous at best, and likely fatal. Pax insisted otherwise, agreeing with the *Kiuri'Ner*. It was strange for Rogaan to hear such talk from the one person who had nothing kind to say about those governing the town.

As they neared the Wheelhouse's stone and mortar foundation, Rogaan spotted a thick rope some seven strides above them, spanning the twenty-stride-wide river of fast-flowing water. The rope was anchored above a stone and wood platform attached to the building on this side of the river, and to something on the far shore that he was unable to see in the darkness. A wooden wheel at the side of the platform rotated briskly with the flowing water and was the source of much of the town's water. Deep water wells spread across Brigum supplied the rest of the water for the town. Rogaan felt a sense of relief once he laid his hands on the cool, wet stone of the structure. He was not certain if it was due to their not being discovered yet, or that he would soon be above the gloom of the shoreline. Pax deftly climbed the three-stride high stone foundation to a small ledge where he had a better perch to look about for guardsmen or workers. He motioned for Rogaan to follow when he was satisfied the way was clear. Rogaan rearranged and secured his carry pack, quiver, and *shunir'ra* to ensure they would not fall off as he climbed. He found the stones dangerously slick, forcing him to take more care with his handholds and footing than he thought needed. He climbed slowly not only fearing that he would fall, but that someone would spot him. When he reached the ledge where Pax was perched, he looked up to see Pax leaning over the platform edge while hanging from the thick rope and swiveling his head between Rogaan below and someplace Rogaan could not see. Determined to quicken his climb, Rogaan set his jaws and heaved himself up the final stride to the platform.

The platform was constructed of thick-cut timbers, each almost a stride wide, and heavily weathered and slick. Pax impatiently wait-ed for him, clinging to the three-finger-wide rope with both hands. Without a word, Pax started across the river, hand-over-hand, with his boots hooked over the rope trailing behind him as he went. Rogaan glanced up a narrow wooden plank stairway passing between the build-ing's stone outer wall and the rotating water wheel, toward the only light in sight -- that light barely pressing back the darkness. As enticing as the light felt to Rogaan, he climbed on the rope just as Pax had, and with a deep breath made his way on the damp coils. The going was easier than Rogaan expected, helping to ease his fears and allowing him a moment to pause and take in his vantage point when he was half-way to the opposite shore. He looked at the river less than two body lengths below for any signs of *snapjaws*. Blackness mixed with the foam of breaking and turbulent water met his sensitive eyes. The sound of chaotic waters over rocks told him the river was there, where moonlit white foam did not swirl. Anxious to be out of the darkness and the unknown, Rogaan continued on with haste. Before he realized it, he was over the opposite shore and felt the branches and soft raking of five-point gum tree leaves just before he touched the end knot of the rope. He quickly dismounted with a short drop to firm ground, where he joined Pax. Pax silently gave him a friendly pat on the shoulder then disappeared into the trees heading downstream, forcing Rogaan to follow into the darkness after a hard swallow and deep a breath to try to calm his fast beating heart.

They slowly made their way through gum, hackberry, and cylinder-shaped trees. In some places, thick tangles of underbrush and twisted roots forced them to retrace their trail then work a new path. Most of the time, it seemed to Rogaan they more felt their way through the trees and underbrush than anything else. He could barely discern his dark surroundings and thought it odd that Pax could make his way so well, since he likely could not see at all. The dark outline of the rising ravine on this side of the river and the growing form of a torch-lit bridge against the star- filled sky soon overwhelmed their view. Pax stopped short, causing Rogaan to run into him with a thud. Fortunately, and to Rogaan's relief, they did not fall or make much noise. When they recovered from their run-in, Pax asked Rogaan to lead, after admitting he was guessing at where to put his feet. Rogaan apprehensively stepped out in front and led them south under the bridge connecting Coiner's Quarters with the main of Brigum. Above, torches and lanterns cast moving shadows on the ravine wall from the bridge gave sign of heavy traffic – likely guardsmen searching for them, Rogaan feared. He tried his best to be quiet as they passed under the massive stone arch. Once under the bridge, Rogaan spotted torches moving through the trees not far ahead.

"Pax, looks like they guessed our path," Rogaan said as he crouched. "I do not think we can get past that crowd without being seen."

"Maybe for ya," Pax replied arrogantly, if not a bit playfully. "Though, I think there not be much reason ta be doin' this without ya. Ya know where ta go. Lead us on."

A shiver rippled down Rogaan's spine. They could not go back and walking the ravine wall was not an option. "No, Pax. I cannot. I mean…."

"I know ya no like da water…and them nasties in it," Pax spoke with sincere sympathy in his voice. "But, Rogaan...it be our only way out of town."

Rogaan wanted to avoid the water, desperately wanted any other option than to ride the river, but nothing came to him...just as nothing came to him when they discussed this plan in his house. He hoped then and now to avoid the river. His hairs prickled on the back of his neck and skin, causing him to shiver visibly. He swallowed hard then swallowed hard again, considering his options. The torches were moving closer to them. They had no options, Rogaan reluctantly admitted to himself, before leading Pax to their right and the river shore.

The sound of flowing water, the flickering torch lights of people moving on the far shore on the lower farming fields, and the cool moist air told Rogaan they were close to the water's edge. With much trepidation, he approached the water's edge, certain he would be eaten by a *snapjaw* when he stepped into the flow.

"Pax...there has to be another way." Rogaan tried his best to sound calm and reasonable instead of suffering the raging battle of fear inside of him.

"Rogaan, ya know there not be," Pax replied firmly. "Now, let's get in da water and get this over with." Pax gave Rogaan a gentle push, urging him forward over rocks and mud.

Rogaan took a deep breath and swallowed hard before he stepped into the flowing water. The water was colder and stronger than he expected, causing him to suffer a cruel shiver as it took his breath away, and nearly knocking him from his feet. It was a good sign the water being cold...he tried to convince himself, since many of the dangerous animals preferred warmer water. After taking a number of deep breaths, procrastinating, he uneasily lowered himself up to his neck in the cold Tamarad River while looking for any movement at the water's surface. Rogaan saw only the ripples from his own passage and the swirling waters of fast-moving water reflected in the light. A small sigh of relief escaped him.

Rogaan and Pax stayed close as they allowed the river's current to carry them downstream toward the water grate protecting Brigum from the world outside the wall, at least from those creatures large enough to harm townsfolk. Rogaan's anxiety climbed the closer they came to the water grate. Outside, they would be in the middle of the life circle and a meal for many creatures calling the river home. The only things going in their favor were the cool air and water. *Snapjaws* moved sluggishly in these conditions, Rogaan recalled this from his *Kiuri'Ner* teachings at the Wall, but *tanniyn* were another problem. They were not so affected by cool air. Once they reached the water grate, Pax easily squeezed through the vertical bars. Despite the forceful flow of water, Rogaan got stuck in the grate until he shifted his gear and exhaled so forcefully that he started seeing flashing white lights dance before him. With a lurch, he popped free from the bars. The lights disappeared when his lungs filled with air, and his head started to clear after taking several more gulps of air while floating southward. When he looked up, he found himself more than forty strides from the town's wall, and being carried rapidly downstream. In no time he would be beyond the light cast from the guard towers. With a start and a surge of panic, Rogaan snapped his head back and forth, looking from shoreline to shoreline for the death he was certain would come. A splash at the shore to his left and slightly ahead of him sent a bolt of fear surging through him. He froze, unable to do anything other than float and wait for teeth-filled jaws to drag him under. A sense of relief washed over him when he spotted Pax crawling out of the water, and with urgency, he swam to the shore and Pax.

Once on land, Rogaan grabbed Pax and hurried them eastward away from the shore, careful not to stumble over a *snapjaw* or *tanniyn* in the darkness. If they were going to meet danger, near the water was the most likely place it would happen. They quickly found a place to hide in a thick grove of gum trees interspersed with heavy bushes some hundred paces from the river. Rogaan did not know whether he shivered more from their unsettling journey, or from his wet, cold clothes. Pax looked just as cold, holding himself with knees drawn close to his chest and shivering.

"We cannot stay here long," Rogaan stated with a low, shaky voice. He wrapped his arms around himself to try to keep from shivering, though without much success.

"You be right." Pax's response was surprisingly without cynicism. His teeth chattered a little as he spoke. "Guards be lookin' here soon."

"No," Rogaan corrected him. "I expect *Kiuri'Ner* and *Sharur* as soon as they figure out we are not where they think we should be, in town. We are in danger of being caught and returned to the Hall of Laws unless we get to the Ebon Circle."

"And who be that up there, again?" Pax changed the subject.

Rogaan was confused by Pax's question and gave him a quizzical look. "Who?"

"Da shadow with the blades," Pax continued. "Da one who cut everyone up?"

"No idea," Rogaan replied, but in a troubled tone. "Why would anyone help us? It does not make sense, unless.... Maybe he's from the Ebon Circle?"

"Ya be honestly wantin' ta go there?" Pax asked seriously with eyes wide.

"Yes," Rogaan replied just as seriously.

"Ya heard da stories?" Pax continued. "They sacrifice folks ta their Ancients and they change those they don't like into things best not ta say. And what about da nasty things livin' in their temple? There be evil there."

"Pax," Rogaan reluctantly answered. "We have little choice. We need help." For all of Pax's pretense of not being bothered by much, he certainly wanted nothing to do with the Ebon Circle. In truth, Rogaan feared the place as much as he suspected Pax did, but they had nowhere else to go. If they went to House Isin's southern estate, the

Tusaa'Ner or *Kiuri'Ner* would eventually catch them, and many of his mother's blood might get harmed or worse if they got in the way... which they would, defending the family. House Isin would likely be declared law-breakers and their lands and possessions taken by the *Ensi* or Town Council. Jir would see to that. They might even be jailed or executed. He was certain several of the other Houses would make sure the worst of that happened, especially House Lagash. Lagash's feud with Isin had deep roots that Rogaan was unclear about. His father and mother spoke vaguely about it, but enough that Rogaan knew that it predated the Shuruppak Civil War. Beyond that was all guessing for him. "I will not believe Father wants me to go there just to see me sacrificed or worse...*shunir'ra* or not."

"Well," Pax protested. "I no like it. I think ya makin' a mistake, but I be goin' with ya if ya go. After all, I can no go back to Brigum, and House Isin not be takin' me unless ya mother allows it, and that not be ta likely."

"My mother does not dislike you...that much," Rogaan said with a growing smile. Pax's loyalty made him feel safer somehow. "Thank you."

"For what?" Pax asked, overdramatically.

"For being my friend," Rogaan answered. "We need to get going. We have a long trek ahead of us and it will not be safe here soon."

Anxious at the chirps, clicks, and squawks of the night, they quickly wrung out what clothing they could before setting off south along the river. They kept just far enough away from the river to hear the rush of water, but not so close that they might stumble over something they would rather wish they had not. The cool air and his wet clothes made it difficult for Rogaan to put the chill out of mind. Pax was more vocal about his discomfort, grumbling in a low voice at how cold it was and how much he looked forward to a warm fire and soup. Rogaan wished for the same, but said nothing to encourage Pax's complaining. Of more concern to Rogaan was the darkness pressing in from all directions, and the unknown just beyond the edge of his sight. Anything could be waiting for them…for him. Fearful of being caught unprepared by the night, Rogaan assembled his *shunir'ra* mostly by touch while walking, stopping momentarily only to string his metallic bow and notch a regular iron-tipped arrow -- not one of his blue steel-tipped arrows -- before continuing on. Pax paid little attention to Rogaan and just kept walking and grumbling about being cold.

It was nearly twenty marches to the Ebon Circle grounds, if he recalled his father's descriptions of the lands and temple grounds well enough. Rogaan wondered how many times his father had been there. It seemed he was very familiar with the temple. *What did he do there?* He had always found his father's stories of adventure and history interesting when he was younger, but never thought he would put any of that knowledge to use. Rogaan found himself wishing he had paid more attention to them and regretting the less-frequent telling of his father's stories in recent years. He certainly could benefit from more details, now. Rogaan realized, with growing regret, how much he missed talking with his father and the time they spent together at the fireside.

Stumbling over a large, raised root, Rogaan fell to his knees, bruising his leg on another root. Grumbling, he carefully rose, then continued on into the deep shadows of the waxing moon casting its light through the treetops. The going was slow over uneven ground and through unknown woods -- much slower than Rogaan had anticipated. He hoped he could recognize the road leading east to the Ebon Circle when they crossed it, as there was not a road on this side of the river to follow; otherwise, he and Pax would become more lost than he felt they were now.

The forest "song" of *biters*, *featherwings*, *leatherwings*, and other creatures filled the night air. The sounds of *tanniyns* were far and fewer than the days. Rogaan was thankful the big beasts mostly slept at night instead of prowling about. It lessened his angst traveling in the darkness

-- not much, but he welcomed anything to get him through this. They walked...more felt...their way for what seemed hours when Rogaan stumbled in the deep ruts of a dirt road and fell. He cursed himself for his clumsiness as Pax chuckled.

"Ya found it," Pax sarcastically declared. His voice then turned serious. "Ya not really goin' ta da dark robes, are ya?"

"What choice do we have, Pax?" Rogaan shot back from his prone position. Red-faced and grateful for the concealing darkness, he rose to his feet with as much dignity as he could muster. "To free Father and your parents, we need help...and not that of the town. And do not ask about House Isin. They will not help and put their lands, wealth, and freedoms in jeopardy. I will not ask that of them. The Town Council is not to be trusted with Jir and the *Ensi* in charge. Jir and the *Ensi* will leave House Isin alone only if they do nothing against the *Tusaa'Ner*. At least Mother and Suhd will be safe on Isin's estates."

Pax grunted then guardedly agreed with Rogaan. "Not ta many friends. Still, we can be lookin' for others ta help or do this with just us."

"No," Rogaan answered wearing a stone-hard expression, determination burning in his eyes. "I am going to see our parents free, and that means we need help. That means the Ebon Circle."

Chapter 12

Plans Changed

U nsure whether this dirt road led to the quarry or to the temple,
Rogaan decided to walk it a little way in the hopes they would
find something telling them if they were going in the right direction.
Leading Pax eastward on the dry, rutted, and pot-holed road, crunching clumps of loose dirt kicked up by prior traffic, Rogaan began to
think he had the wrong road. Pax grumbled about having to travel
the Wilds despite the going being easier on the road than through the
forest. No longer did he curse the cool night air or his damp clothes;
he and Rogaan had long since warmed themselves from the walking.
Instead, he complained of the road -- a trail, more, by his comments
-- and his struggle to keep from twisting his ankles. Rogaan fared better, his eyes now adjusted to the dim light of the moon and stars. Still,
he felt his way along the road with his feet more than he wanted. They
climbed a rising slope, higher into the front range of the mountain
ridge, large hills really, that lay to the southeast of Brigum. At the
edges of the road, worked rocks and wood debris, and occasionally
parts of wagons, littered the way. It was obvious the road was heavily
used and recently so, by the looks of some of the debris, but something
seemed out of place. Rogaan seriously questioned whether he had the
right road. His father's stories never mentioned a trail of wreckage on
the way to the Ebon Circle. Soon enough, they crested a rise in the
road then came to an abrupt halt. Not more than forty strides away, at
the south side of the road, stood a small shack illuminated with several
lanterns hanging from a pole and a tree branch close by. The structure
was a guard post with metal spikes sticking out from all sides and a
sign staked into the ground next to the shack. On it, faded writing

Rogaan could not make out from this distance gave him hope to finally answer his burning question. Two *Baraan* dressed in common breeches and tunics were talking casually as they leaned against their shack.

"Pax," Rogaan said in a low voice then waited until Pax stopped next to him. "I do not think we are in the right place."

"It be a road goin' east, and people be up ahead?" Pax's reply sounded more like a statement than question.

"I think we are on the road to the quarry," Rogaan admitted, finally.

"Da quarry?" Pax asked.

"You know...the place where Brigum's law-breakers are sent to pay penance," Rogaan explained in a low voice. He did not want to alert the unwary guards, who were lost in their talk and had not noticed them.

"I know," Pax sounded irritated. "Da place they say I should be most days."

"Where Kantus and Jir would like to see us both," Rogan agreed. "We need to keep going south to find the road to the Ebon Circle."

"Ya can no be serious, Rogaan," Pax protested more strongly than any previous, and louder than Rogaan liked. "It be wrong of ya ta take us ta 'em. No tellin' what ta happin' ta us once we be inside their walls."

"Quiet your voice!" Rogaan hushed Pax. "My father spoke kindly of the one called Im'Kas. I plan to seek him out, there."

"You two!" a voice called out, surprising Rogaan and, by the look on his face, Pax, also. "What are you doing here? Lower your weapons and submit."

Pax looked to Rogaan with eyes that told him submitting was not his friend's way. Nor could Rogaan afford to get entangled with Quarry Folk. They would slow them down, at best, and turn them over to Brigum's guard, at worst. He and Pax would then likely see the insides of the quarry, with pick and shovel in hand. "Run!"

"Which way?" Pax asked urgently.

"South," Rogaan answered then bolted to his right and into the shadows of the forest and the unknown, hoping he was doing the right thing.

"Stop!" a guard commanded. "Surrender, you two!"

"Wait for me!" Pax called after Rogaan loudly then followed.

The going was difficult and dangerous as they moved fast through thick forest to avoid capture. Branches slapped at their faces and arms, marking Rogaan with stinging cuts, as underbrush grabbed at his feet, tripping him and sending him to the dirt often. Luckily, he kept his nocked arrow from piercing him, but decided it best to put away his arrow and sling the bow over his shoulders to move through the thicker underbrush to keep from injuring himself. Rogaan slowed to a walk when he thought they were far enough away that the quarry guards would not follow -- a little more than 500 paces, by his count. When he slowed he caught his breath. Pax kept close on his heels, though he did not seem as winded as Rogaan felt. Soon after they stopped stomping through the forest, making enough noise to wake the lightless, the forest came alive with its "song," returning to normal. *Biters* buzzing, *hoppers* croaking and chirping…or was the chirping from *featherwings* or *leapers?* Rogaan prayed to the Ancients that the chirping was not from *leapers* stalking them. He was more alert, swiveling his head, trying to look all about them at all times.

They continued on, with Rogaan hoping he was leading them south -- the moon looked to be in the right spot over his shoulder for them to be heading south. He just had to have faith in the skills Kardul taught him in the Valley of the Claw and hope they would not stumble on a *tanniyn* resting the night. Their travel was unnerving. Rogaan's eyes adjusted well to the shadowy darkness, allowing him to see details Pax could not discern, but that only made every shadow a potential danger and a reason to feel on edge. After a long while, the forest's musty scent gave way to a mix of scented flowers with a hint of acrid charcoal. It was then Rogaan realized he had the charcoal scent on his hands and clothes, where he had brushed trees that looked old and barren and had little underbrush at their bases.

The forest quickly opened to spare stands of trees, just as many blackened and barren from old fires as not. Lush shrub and fern growth, as high as Rogaan's waist, mixed with flowering bushes covered the ground, except on the beaten-down path where Rogaan and Pax now stood as they looked about for danger. The gray-toned forest, Rogaan saw, revealed nothing larger than an occasional *featherwing* and the buzzing *bloodsuckers* moving. He breathed a bit easier.

"I no see a thing," Pax complained.

"Not much to see," Rogaan replied.

"We be goin' south, still?" Pax asked anxiously.

"I think," Rogaan hoped.

"Ya still set on vistin' the dark robes?" Pax asked with an accusing tone.

"We do not have many options, Pax," Rogaan insisted. In truth, with the surge of excitement gone from fleeing the guards, and the closer they got to the Ebon Circle, the more Rogaan feared, and worried that he was making a mistake. *What will the dark robes do to us once we show at their doorstep?* Rogaan's imagination ran wild with all sorts of torments and hideous things done to their bodies and minds. He shivered…so many stories about the Ebon Circle from folks all around Brigum, and almost none of them good. The bulk of the tales where the Ebon Circle was favored came from his father, but few others.

"I still no like this," Pax protested. "They can no be trusted."

Rogaan agreed, but saw no other choice. They needed help to free his father and Pax's parents, and Imtaesus was without his light. *How am I going to tell Mother?*

"This way!" Rogaan stepped down the trail, his boots sliding in the soft soil of the uneven path. Pax quickly followed, while looking around nervously. Across the large clearing they went, following the trail before entering dark shadows of a thick stand of trees and tall brush. Rogaan became anxious, but did not understand why. It was more than just the darkness. Out of the deep moon-cast shadows a lone figure stepped onto the trail. He stood an average height, meeting Rogaan's eyes almost level. His face was long and thin, with tilted eyes, and lacking any hint of facial hair. Clad in *eur* armor and armed with a long-knife and bow, the lean figure wore unkempt stringy hair to his shoulders.

"You two are loud enough to wake the lightless." The lone figure spoke in hushed smooth tones, almost melodic. "Step no further and make no loud sound. We're on a game trail and a *long-tooth* is sleeping just beyond me."

Rogaan and Pax looked at each other, confused, then back to the lone figure. Pax asked a little too loudly, "Who be ya?"

"Quiet!" the lone figure scolded Pax in an angry whisper then looked over his shoulder, holding still for a little while, listening. When he seemed satisfied, his tense stance eased and he returned his attention to Rogaan and Pax. "Are you deaf, or do you wish death?"

"My friend's question needs answering," Rogaan demanded in a low voice.

"Urgillic," The lone figure answered. "Urgillic, *Kiuri'Ner* and humble servant to the Ebon Circle. You two look to be lost or fever-sick, wandering around these parts…after sundown. What is your purpose in these lands?"

"No, Rogaan," Pax pleaded in a wounded voice while shaking his head side-to-side.

Rogaan looked at Pax with apologetic eyes then said, "We are seeking the Ebon Circle, asking help in rescuing my father, Mithraam."

Urgillic stood silent for a moment then appeared to nod. "Then Rogaan, son of Mithraam…and your companion…follow me. Take care where you step, and make as little sound as possible. Dangers surround us and are closer than you think."

Urgillic turned and disappeared into the forest before Rogaan could say a word. Frustrated with unasked questions, Rogaan followed -- almost needing to run to keep up. Pax kept close on Rogaan's heels. Urgillic passed through the forest as if a daimon, without making noise despite fallen limbs and dried sticks that Rogaan seemed to find at every step. Rogaan struggled to keep up and to hold sight of Urgillic, but just as often found himself looking about, hoping he was going in the right direction when he did lose sight of their guide. At times, Urgillic made it obvious where he was so they could easily follow; at other times he disappeared from sight, but was never long so, keeping them from straying from his intended path as they traveled up and down ridges radiating out from the mountain rising to their left. They kept the pace for hours before Urgillic came to a stop well after midnight. Urgillic stood motionless, looking off into the dark forest like a predator searching...sensing danger. Rogaan, gasped for air as he bent over with his hands on his thighs, sweat soaking his clothing and stinging his eyes. He felt embarrassed that he was not able to fare as well as Urgillic, and wondered just how far they had traveled, as he lost count after ten marches. Pax appeared to be faring better than Rogaan, able to stand with hands on hips, but showed signs of being winded with his heavy breathing. Rogaan wore numerous cuts and bruises from tree and bush limbs, along with a few lumps on his head and knees from tree branches and trunks he ran into face first, or from more falls than he cared to admit to while doing his best to keep up with Urgillic. Because it had slowed him through the forest, Rogaan long before broke down his bow and re-cased it.

Urgillic remained motionless, listening to the forest and looking as if he smelled at the air. He did so for a long while. The break gave Rogaan a chance to fully catch his breath, and he thanked the Ancients for it. The scent of burnt and musty forest was now replaced with an odyssey of sweet fragrances that threatened to overpower him. He was unsure if his tears were spurred from plant dust or sweat. Either way, his tears were unwelcome, yet flowed from his eyes unhindered.

Once his breathing came under control, he grew concerned that something was wrong. *Why stop now? What is Urgillic seeking?* Urgillic slowly cocked his head side to side, listening for something -- what, Rogaan knew not. When he seemed satisfied, he motioned for them to follow. Urgillic took off again, setting a grueling pace Rogaan struggled to keep to. They passed from dense foliage to open forest lands, where there was little undergrowth except for sporadic thick patches of bushes and trees that Urgillic seemed to find easily. Soon, Rogaan found himself treading through increasingly dense undergrowth as he caught the scent of a forest burnt, though it smelled old. Few trees stood with living limbs, and the underbrush grew thicker as they went, making their going surprisingly slow. Rogaan found it difficult to keep Urgillic's pace in the tanglefoot of thigh-high ferns and ground vines. Urgillic just seemed to ignore whatever lay in his path, though he suddenly slowed to a walking pace. Rogaan and Pax caught up to him, spurring Rogan to give another thanks to the Ancients in between gasps for the night air. After a little time, he sucked in enough air to rid himself of his hazy head as a breeze cooled his sweat-soaked clothing, causing a chill to ripple through him. Through distant trees, Rogaan saw large fires faintly outlining the side of the mountain or a massive dark structure that was otherwise invisible to his eyes.

Rogaan's skin prickled and his nape hairs stiffened when he realized he must be looking at the temple of the Ebon Circle. *It has to be,* he realized with dread. Nothing else in these Wilds he knew of would be so grand or dark. He caught himself holding his breath, and the pit of his stomach felt as if he were falling. Fighting back a surge of panic and the fears of foul creatures and sinister *kunsag* springing upon them from the gloom, Rogaan swallowed hard, trying to gain control of himself and not run away. With an effort, he again deeply sucked in the cool night air. It helped calm him, a little. Until now, the temple had been only a place of stories and talk at the fireside. No longer. This place was real, and it stood before them and Rogaan found himself nervously hoping the many tales told of the Ebon Circle were not true.

Another figured stepped out of the shadows without any warning, dressed similar to Urgillic. Urgillic looked unsurprised and unconcerned at the *Baraan*'s sudden appearance. The *Baraan* looked young, maybe not twenty summers old. Rogaan realized the new *Kiuri'Ner* was an *Evendiir*, with slightly pointed ears, oval eyes, and a lean build. He spoke also in a melodic voice fit for song. "You're followed."

"Indeed," Urgillic replied flatly without taking his eyes off the temple. "They've been with us since I found these younglings." With a wave of his hand, Urgillic signaled for everyone to follow as their protector strode off toward the Ebon Circle. Rogaan took a deep breath then hesitantly made to follow.

"Ya can no be serious!" Pax blurted out with angry conviction.

Rogaan stopped and looked at Pax with a quizzical expression. Pax returned his gaze with determined defiance, his eyes almost glowing in the moonlight. Rogaan was at first confused then came to realize that Pax was not intending to step inside the Ebon Circle.

"Pax," Rogaan pleaded. "We must. We need help to do what we intend."

Pax shook his head and set his boots firmly in place. Rogaan did not know what to do. Pax had voiced his complaint about this plan of asking help of the dark robes, but Rogaan never thought his friend would outright refuse to try.

"No," Pax said evenly. "I no be putting foot in dat place. And you should no be doing so, either. We find another way...other help, but no dark robes."

"What has your feet stuck in the mud?" Urgillic asked in a subdued voice from the cover of a large tree some twenty paces in the direction of the temple. Neither Rogaan nor Pax answered. They simply stared at each other. Rogaan did not know what to say that could convince Pax to enter the Ebon Circle and ask for help they needed. Pax seemed to have already made his decision and was standing firm.

"My friend is questioning the wisdom of seeking help from the Ebon Circle," Rogaan reluctantly answered Urgillic. The *Kiuri'Ner* betrayed a hint of agitation and disappointment...maybe frustration. The companion *Kiuri'Ner* quickly closed on Pax, covering the ten paces as if it were much shorter, grabbing his arm.

"We haven't time for parley!" The young *Kiuri'Ner* declared as he grabbed Pax and started dragging him toward the dark temple.

Rogaan acted without thinking and grabbed the *Kiuri'Ner* by his armor at the shoulder, bringing him and Pax to an abrupt halt. Rogaan growled, "Take your hands from him."

"Hands off!" Pax snarled as he ripped himself away from the *Kiuri'Ner's* grasp.

The three of them stood looking at each other, each uncertain what to do. The young *Kiuri'Ner* had his hand on the hilt of his short sword, looking ready to pull it free.

"Hold your sword, Tamik," Urgillic ordered sternly as he stepped closer.

Tamik glared at Urgillic, but kept his hand to hilt. He quickly turned his glare back on Pax and Rogaan. Pax looked all indignant and angry, and as if he had been wronged. Rogaan still felt anger toward Tamik, and frustration at the whole of things. Mostly, he realized, it was from the unknown...how his father fared, and Pax's parents, too, and the safety of his mother and Suhd, and that they were about to enter into the domain of the dark robes in the heart of the Ebon Circle. Nothing was ideal. Everything was happening too fast. Urgillic halted his approach several strides from the three. Deep moon-cast shadows from the tall trees behind Urgillic highlighted the *Kiuri'Ner* with the moonlight bathing him, making him stand out all the more.

Urgillic cast a frustrated stare at Rogaan. "I have orders to see you to the Ebon Circle. You have little choice in this matter as I."

"We no have ta go anywhere!" Pax snarled at Urgillic.

"You...I care nothing of, though your friend...." Urgillic leveled his gaze on Pax. "Not my place to defy. He has been summoned."

"Enough talk, Urgi...." Tamik fell to the ground with an arrow run through his neck, right to left, blood spurting an arm's-length in the air with every heartbeat. Rogaan realized he had heard the arrow in flight before it struck, but he had dismissed the sound as they argued. Now, with shock quickly fading, he wished he had not dismissed it. The whistling of another arrow off to his right found Rogaan ducking instinctively into a crouch. Two arrows struck to the sides of Urgillic's *eur* chest plates. Both arrows sank in a hand's width deep, with the fletched shafts vibrating from the force of the impacts. Urgillic looked surprised at the arrows in his chest as he fell to his knees, dropping his bow beside him. The *Kiuri'Ner* tried to say something, but only a croak escaped his lips before he fell sideways to the ground, gasping. Pax was in a half-crouch with a knife in each hand, looking for the assassin. Rogaan thought to find cover, but saw nothing close, so he remained couching, pulling his *shunir'ra* case from his shoulder.

"No need for that," a voice said from the darkness.

"Who be out there?" Pax demanded of the darkness.

His bow not yet pulled from the case to be assembled, Rogaan stopped. The deep voice had a familiar mocking tone. Rogaan looked hard in the direction the voice came from adjusting his eyes to the deep shadows. A large, sandy-haired *Baraan* with bow in hand, and dressed in red-brown *wilds* armor, stepped into the moon rays. It took a few moments for Rogaan to make out Kardul, to be sure it was Kardul.

"Kardul...?" Rogaan half stated, half asked.

"Kardul?" Pax asked Rogaan in an unbelieving tone. "How can ya see a thing? I see nothin', only dark."

"Gawking, still," Kardul stated with a hint of disappointment.

Rogaan felt a flush of embarrassment, stood up and straightened his stance in an attempt to show he was alert and not surprised at Kardul's appearance. Pax stared at Kardul with a skeptical expression that made Rogaan think his friend was unsure Kardul stood before them.

"It is him," Rogaan said, hoping Pax would accept his confirmation that it was Kardul.

"Ya can be hopeful sometimes." Pax was skeptical. He yelled out, "Who be out there?"

The *Baraan* kept silent as he approached confidently. Pax visibly relaxed when he made out the Wing and Eye mark on the right side of Kardul's sandy-haired face. Kardul stopped a few strides from them then spoke, "Time to leave these parts."

Rogaan thought he glimpsed Kardul stealing a nervous look in the direction of the Ebon Circle. It was there and gone in a blink, or so Rogaan tried to convince himself. Then he was unsure he ever had seen it. Pax stepped over Tamik's body without a care, making to follow Kardul. A flash of fear, anger, and guilt swept over Rogaan. Looking at Kardul, he said, "We cannot leave Urgillic like this. We need to get him help. And why did you have to kill Tamik?"

An arrow whistled from the darkness, sinking itself into Urgillic's neck from an unseen location. Blood flowed from the wound as Urgillic gurgled his last breath.

"Why?" Rogaan glared at Kardul, remorseful and angry at such a callous disregard for those that showed them no ill. Two *Baraans* emerged from the darkness from different directions. One was tall and lean, and the other average in height and stockier. Both wore striped green and gray shirts and breeches, and dull-green capes and wide-brimmed hats. They were hard to see even in the moonlight as they picked Urgillic's and Tamik's bodies clean of valuables and weapons. Rogaan felt a rage build inside as he watched their barbarism.

"They were of the temple and served the dark robes," Kardul explained simply. "You would have been delivered into the hands of the dark master and become lost to us...and your family."

Rogaan did not know how to respond to Kardul. *Was killing them necessary?* Rogaan was uncertain, but it angered him. Pax looked un-moved by their deaths. That unsettled Rogaan even more than the callousness of Kardul's people.

Pax gave Rogaan an impatient look. "Let's be goin', Rogaan. I no like dis place or these folk. I want ta be as far from here as we can get."

"Father gave instructions..." Rogaan argued and was cut off.

"Ya father is no here." Pax was impatient. "Kardul thinks like me about this place and the dark robes. That be good enough for me."

Rogaan stood silent, trying to make sense of everything. His father wanted him to seek out the Ebon Circle, likely to be protected in some way that Rogaan still did not understand. Mother wanted him to honor Father's wishes. But so many stories told of the place being dark and of dark people, the dark robes, doing dark things. Pax be-lieved the old stories of darkness and foul happenings -- and, Rogaan admitted to himself, he thought much the same of the Ebon Circle. So many people could not be wrong. Maybe Father feared the trouble he was about to get into more than the dark robes, and was choosing the best of bad choices for Rogaan. *Protect me even though I would suffer in my safety.* Rogaan shivered. *Father, what have you gotten us into?*

"No time to waste," Kardul said with a tone of urgency.

"Come, Rogaan," Pax pleaded with a tone of frustration. "Let's be gone away from here and go save our parents."

"The lass is waiting," Kardul announced almost matter-of-factly.

Rogaan looked at Kardul confused. *What lass?*

"What lass?" Pax asked.

"She calls herself Suhd," Kardul nodded.

"Where she be?" Pax demanded. "What have ya done ta her? Take us ta her."

"Hold!" Rogaan barked. He surprised himself and looked all of it before recovering and placing his focus on Kardul. "Why is Suhd in *your* care?"

"Ya. Why?" Pax added suspiciously.

"We rescued her from a caravan attack," Kardul answered them flatly. "She's the one who told us where you were going."

"What of my mother?" Rogaan asked with a tight throat. "Suhd was traveling with her."

"We heard the battle, but arrived at its end," Kardul said quickly. "The lass was in the hands of slavers, being taken away along this side of the river. The caravan suffered a loss of a coach, but was fleeing south on the other side of the river. We killed most of the slavers and retrieved her."

"Was anyone harmed?" Rogaan asked with an even tighter throat. "Was anyone in the caravan killed?"

"No way to know." Kardul sounded irritated, with his short response. "We must leave. Follow me."

"Wait..." Rogaan pleaded. "Kardul...my mother. I need to know she is safe."

"You'll have to ask the lass." Kardul sounded confident.

"Rogaan, let's be goin'," Pax urged impatiently.

Rogaan decided to follow, to leave the road to the Ebon Circle and the bodies of the slain behind. *Mother and Suhd are more important than...this or Father's wishes.*

Chapter 13

First Ride

The cool pre-dawn air was dry leaving Rogaan's mouth parched by the time they met up with Suhd and the two *sharur* escorting her. Since Kardul's companions made quick work killing the Ebon Circle's *Kiuri'Ners*, Kardul had set a hard pace on foot, faster than Urgillic had earlier. Rogaan struggled to keep up. The length of the run did not bother him, but the pace left him winded. And Rogaan lost sight of Kardul more than once while running, then found himself being led back to Kardul by one of his *sharurs*. Rogaan guessed Kardul headed westward for marches, almost to the river that ran south from Brigum before they stopped. Rogaan sucked at the air with burning lungs, trying to fill them while bent over with hands on knees. Pax put a hand on Rogaan's shoulder, telling him in pants to breathe deep and try standing upright. Rogaan tried, but found himself back with hands on knees as a slow breeze chilled his sweat-soaked clothes, causing him to shiver. Rogaan felt miserable. He heard echoing noises all about him: indistinguishable voices, heavy footfalls, snorts, and the rustling of the forest, but he did not care to look about. He just wanted to breathe without the pain. He forced himself to control gasps, slow them, deepen them. The pain in his chest diminished. The echoing in his ears was replaced by the thunder of his beating heart. Then the thundering eased. Rogaan looked up from his bent-over position.

"Breathin' better?" Pax smiled.

Rogaan nodded then straightened upright. Looking around, he saw Kardul and his *sharurs* leading five *sarigs* toward him. The animals were big and powerful, more than 800 stones each, and as tall at the shoulder as Rogaan stood. A single stout horn sat squarely in the middle of their boney foreheads surrounded by large jagged plates that ran the length of their skulls to the top of the necks. Massive foot pads ending in stubbed claws intimidated Rogaan -- not because of their size, but because of the power with which the animals struck the ground, shaking the earth beneath them and making them seem larger than their visible stature. Each was reined with bit and bridle and was fitted with saddle and full saddle bags, ready for travel.

"Have you ridden before?" Kardul asked, demanding a quick answer. Rogaan and Pax both shook their heads, answering *no*. Kardul looked at his gray-green caped *sharur*, both standing beside a pair of charcoal-colored *sarigs*, holding two sets of reins and with their cape hoods drawn up, making it impossible to see their faces. Each *sharur* looked of Rogaan's height, taller with their wide-brimmed green hats, each with a stature that made him think they were *Baraans*. They carried long knives on the sides, and a full quiver of arrows on their backs, their bows already sheathed on the left side of the *sarig's* saddles, and netted equipment bundles on both sides of the animals. Kardul pointed to Rogaan and Pax as he spoke to his *sharur*. "They have no riding skills. Double up with these two and trail the other *sarigs* behind us."

The *sharur* simply nodded to Kardul -- or so Rogaan thought he saw them nod. They each pointed a gloved finger with the closest and the taller of the two *sharur*, at Rogaan; the other, the stockier one of the two, at Pax -- then motioned with their hands for Pax and Rogaan to join them. Not able to see their faces, Rogaan felt uncomfortable and wondered what he was getting into. *Why hide their faces?* Neither Pax nor Rogaan moved.

"Do you want to see the lass?" Kardul asked as he mounted his mud-colored *sarig* with ease. He sat calmly in his saddle towering over them waiting for an answer. Both *sharurs* mounted their *sarigs* with the same ease as Kardul, attached the lead reins of the extra *sarigs* to their saddles then reined in their steeds, ensuring they would be under control for the younglings to mount.

Pax looked at Rogaan with questioning eyes. Rogaan returned his own questioning look to his friend. Both shrugged then each approached his respective *sharur*. When Rogaan stood beside his *sharur's sarig*, the saddled hunter offered his dark gray-gloved hand to him. Rogaan cautiously accepted it then felt himself being yanked upward as the *sharur* curled his arm. The hunter was strong -- very strong for his size. Rogaan's surprise quickly evaporated as he tried to swing his foot up over the rear saddle and failed. The *sharur* grunted and hauled him up again. This time Rogaan found himself sitting awkwardly in the saddle behind his companion until he adjusted his backside better. The *sharur* impatiently grabbed Rogaan's hands and placed them on a pair of leather grips, one on each side of the saddle. Rogaan flailed a little with his feet as the *sarig* moved about, adjusting to its load before the hunter grabbed Rogaan's left leg and guided his foot into a pocket in the saddle where it would be secure for traveling. Rogaan quickly found another pocket on the right side of the saddle and jammed his foot in it as well. He felt awkward in the saddle, but no longer as if he were going to fall off. Rogaan looked at Pax, who had a death grip on the mid-section of the other *sharur,* but only until his *sharur* forcibly placed Pax's hands at the saddle grips.

"Ready?" Kardul asked with that tone expecting a quick answer. Before Rogaan could answer, the *sharur* nodded -- again, Rogaan thought they nodded, but was not entirely sure. Then the *sarigs* were on the move with Rogaan holding his breath, expecting to fall off the animal at every move.

They rode hard into the night -- southward, he guessed and hoped. The tree branches slapping at him, cutting into his arms and legs and drawing blood...staining his pants and shirt sleeves as they passed through dense, dark areas of the forest. Rogaan held on for dear life at every shift of the *sarig*, as he watched in wonder how easily the *sharur* shifted himself in the saddle, using his legs to hold up much of his weight in the stirrups and keeping the saddle from spanking his groin and rattling his teeth. Somehow, he also used his legs to guide the steed, command its direction. Rogaan tried doing the same, and was rewarded with only infrequent bruising of his private region. Not long after they made off, the dawn broke over the mountains to the northeast, casting rays of golden light on the wilderness of mixed pine, oak, maple, and gum, leaving deep shadows only where the sunlight could not penetrate at such a low angle. At least Rogaan was certain now they were heading south, with the Tamarad River off to their right and sun over his left shoulder. He started wondering when they would meet up with Suhd and, with each stride of the *sarigs*, he became more deeply worried that he was being taken far from her and his mother.

Rogaan closed his eyes for a few moments to pray, *I ask the Ancients, who gave us life, for Mother and Suhd to be kept safe.* The *sarig* suddenly shifted, forcing Rogaan to snap his eyes open and pull tight the saddle grips to keep from falling off. The *sarig* groaned and slowed, allowing Pax's *sarigs* to pass them. Rogaan's *sharur* looked about as if unsure what had just happened. Not finding anything obviously wrong, he ignored Rogaan's attempt to ask him when they would meet up with Suhd, and urged their *sarig* on. They rode until just short of mid-morning, the sun halfway to its full height before they slowed to a walking pace. Without the thundering noise of the *sarigs* and the wind roaring in his ears, the forest came alive with the sounds of life. *Featherwings* chirped from the treetops as *leatherwings* squawked from both the trees and high above where a dozen long-winged creatures soared. The buzz of *biters* grew all about. A few landed and crawled on Rogaan's neck and arms before he brushed and shook them off. *Hopper* songs came from high in the trees, mostly from his right toward the river. The call of *tanniyn* came from everywhere, though mostly on his left and some distantly to his right and ahead.

His *sharur* offered a small jar over his right shoulder. Rogaan was hesitant to accept it, but decided to take it after reconsidering he showed no ill-will towards him. Locking his knees tight to the saddle to keep from falling off the *sarig*, Rogaan opened the jar and wrinkled his nose at the pungent scent of *Blue Savior* in the form of an ointment. Rogaan remembered the first time Kardul had shown him and Pax the mystical blue flower and how to make a salve that did very good at keeping *biters* and *bloodsuckers* away for a day or more. He applied the salve everywhere he had exposed skin and a couple of places on his clothes for good measure. As he was handing the jar back to his *sharur*, they entered a clearing where three *sarigs* and people stood, two of them looking like *sharur* with their wide-brimmed hats pulled down low, one looking to be a scruffy *Baraan* with long stringy black hair and a closely cut beard and the other very clearly a *Tellen* by his stockier build and braided mid-chest beard and shoulder-length hair of white. *White?* At first, Rogaan assumed the *Tellen* to be of extreme age, but a closer look found the *Tellen* warrior in the prime of his life, maybe fifty or sixty summers old. Then Rogaan's eyes found Suhd standing behind the *sharur* with eyes wide and a gray-green cape wrapped tightly around her.

Kardul dismounted next to the two standing *Baraans* then spoke to them. The *Baraan sharur* took Kardul's *sarig* walking it to where the other three *sarig*'s were tethered. Kardul continued talking with the *Tellen sharur*. They seemed to disagree, but did so respectfully, then Kardul followed the *Baraan* and his *sarig*. Pax and his *sharur* came to a stop in front of the *Tellen* then waited unmoving. Rogaan realized he was to dismount and did so as gracefully as he could, though he stumbled a little when his boots awkwardly hit the ground. Suhd squealed, alarming Rogaan, making his hair stand on end. She ran to Pax with cape forgotten in a heap on the ground and hugged him intensely. Suhd's green knee-length dress almost matched Pax's shirt in color making it look as if brother and sister had become one as they embraced. Pax spoke a few words to his sister Rogaan could not hear causing Suhd to hug him tighter. The *sarig* next to Rogaan started moving off causing Rogaan to jump in surprise. When he returned his gaze to Suhd he saw her looking at him with a big smile. Rogaan's heart skipped beats and he suddenly felt warm. Suhd broke away from Pax and ran straight into a tight embrace of Rogaan. It happened so fast that Rogaan stood in shock as Suhd wrapped her arms around him. Then he started sweating. *What do I do?* Rogaan asked himself. He looked at Pax, who mouthed, "Hug her back." He did, and felt as if nothing else existed and that the world was only for him and Suhd. Rogaan felt completely lost in Suhd's arms. She returned his admiring gaze and his feelings. Rogaan melted completely and embraced her deeply as she embraced him back.

"He's got it bad," the deep voice of the stocky *Baraan sharur* announced.

"Never seen it worse," the scruffy *Baraan sharur* agreed, playfully.

"They need a hideaway," the tall, lean *Baraan sharur*, serious in tone, recommended.

Rogaan opened his eyes. He felt their moment was ruined -- then he looked into Suhd's radiant blue eyes and melted. He could not think of a happier moment in his life.

"You all would be so fortunate," a deep rumbling voice chided the others. Rogaan looked up from Suhd, unhappy that he felt he had to. The *Tellen sharur* walked past him to pick up a saddlebag. He did so without showing any further interest in the two embraced younglings.

"You're too soft on your kind, Trundiir," the playful voice came from the *sharur* accompanying the *Tellen* when Pax and Rogaan rode into camp.

"No meanin' ta break dis up." Pax sounded tentative then cleared his throat. "Ya done ogle-eyeing each other?"

Suhd blushed brilliantly while standing demurely, dumbfounded and obviously embarrassed at having been called out on her open display of feelings for Rogaan. Rogaan stood brooding at having been interrupted.

Trundiir walked past Pax, carrying his saddlebag, his words

rumbling, "Careful young one. *Tellens* are known for their fierceness defending what they care for. Get in between him and his heart…not a place to be."

Pax stood silent with a blank expression, looking after Trundiir; confusion filled Suhd's face, and Kardul's companions all seemed to be snickering at Trundiir's mentoring of young Pax. Rogaan felt a sense of familiarity in Trundiir's demeanor. He was *Tellen* through and through: direct, unguarded, and frank. Rogaan started to realize that everyone saw him and Suhd, and he felt his face warm considerably. Wanting to change that subject, Rogaan searched his thoughts for a question -- any question to ask to remove himself from the focus of their gazes. With a shock, Rogaan realized he did not know if his mother was safe or in harm's way, and that he entirely forgot about her when his eyes meet Suhd's. A chill shook him. *How could I forget Mother so easily?*

"Mother…" Rogaan said to Suhd as he moved his hands from her back to her shoulders. "Is she…in danger? Harmed?" He dared not ask if she were lightless.

Suhd shook her head, certain of her words. "She was in her coach getting away from the robbers, last I saw. I heard her yelling at people when her coach was driving away."

"What happened?" Pax asked.

Suhd's face went serious as she stared off into some place Rogaan was uncertain of. She spoke calmly as she recalled the evening. "Ya ma had me ride with her, and she made one of the guards stay with us in the coach ta look after me. We were on the road ta her family home when we stopped. Don't know why. That's when everybody started yelling and screaming. A wagon caught fire behind us just before robbers attacked us in the coach. They hurt the guard bad enough he couldn't guard us. That's when they dragged me and ya ma out of the coach. They pulled me by my hair ta the river. Ya ma fought them hard. She was like a wild woman. Then these swordsmen showed up and saved ya ma. The robbers tossed me into a boat and ran away across the river. That's the last I saw of ya ma when her coach and wagons rode off."

"How did you get away from the robbers?" Rogaan asked.

"Them." Suhd looked to Kardul and his *sharur*. "They came after me and killed the robbers. They were surprised ya weren't with ya ma. I told them ya were going ta that dark place, and that's when the big one and those two over there went ta save ya. These two brought me here ta wait for them after saving ya and bringing ya here."

"I be thankin' ya then," Pax said to Kardul.

The big *Kiuri'Ner* had silently joined them during Suhd's telling of how she got here and of Kardul's and his companion's courage. Kardul smiled at Pax, at least Rogaan took it for a smile...more of an acknowledgement, really -- before he said, "I was told of the warrant for Rogaan's arrest when we got to Coiner's Gate. Firik argued against handing you over and was firm that you were an honorable one, but they would have none of it. They told me to 'fetch' you, and that didn't sit well with me. Truthfully, I didn't like being told to *fetch*, more than the idea of handing you over to them. At least that was then. Since you ran off into the forest, with a bit of help from my *sharur*, I've learned of your father's arrest. The charges sounded as whims of authority. I learned of the failed assassination attempt against your mother only after the Isin caravan left town. I suspected more trouble and decided to help you keep from it. Those robbers had no intent of robbing. They were assassins sent to capture and take you away or kill you, if they couldn't keep you from the protection of your family."

"So," Pax sounded frustrated and angry. Rogaan was not certain which. Pax looked at Kardul then Suhd, with questioning eyes, "If this be all about Rogaan and family, why take our parents?"

"Not sure," Kardul answered with a slight shoulder shrug.

"Because you are my friends and could help secret me away." Rogaan started putting the puzzle pieces together in his head. In his heart, he started feeling guilty and sad for all the trouble Pax and Suhd were suffering because of their association with him.

"That be certain," Pax proudly announced.

Suhd hugged Rogaan, again, then spoke into his chest. "We could never give ya ta the swordarms. Father and Ma wouldn't give ya up. "

"Our ma and father," Pax asked Kardul. "Can ya help us free 'em?"

Kardul stood looking at them with his arms folded. He sighed. His stare lost focus on everything and he seemed lost in deep thought. His companions stood next to their saddled steeds, watching Kardul and the younglings. They appeared to be waiting for something.

"We've done enough," Kardul announced. "We kept you from harm at the hands of the assassins and the dark robes. I think we've done enough."

"But..." Pax started.

"We'll take all of you to the Isin estate," Kardul interrupted.

"We need help," Rogaan reluctantly declared. Rogaan did not want to beg for Kardul's help, but he had nowhere else to turn now that they left lightless *Baraans* and dark circle servants behind.

Kardul looked at Rogaan, considering him for a long moment then said, "Isin can help you."

"Father will be in Farratum before I can get help from my family," Rogaan said flatly. "I already thought of them. Isin was first, but that would put their lands and freedom in jeopardy."

Kardul frowned. "So you wish us to put our freedoms in question?"

Rogaan's face warmed and his hair prickled at the realization of what he was asking of Kardul and his *sharurs*. *Now what?* Rogaan felt a welling up of panic wrapped in frustration take hold of him. Time was short for his father. There was nowhere else to turn. Rogaan felt desperation rising from deep within him. Even going back to the dark temple and gaining their help -- if he survived the wrath of the dark robes -- would mean being too late. The jailer's caravan was on the move. Any delay on Rogaan's part meant failure. His father lost. He closed his eyes and silently prayed, *Ancient Lords, please grant me aid in my time of need. I seek your hand in guiding me. Allow me to free my father... and Pax and Suhd's parents from an unjust bondage. Praise to my Lords.*

Silence fell over the eight...except for the wind, the *leatherwings* calling above, the *featherwings* squawking from the trees, the *hoppers* croaking, the periodic bellows of *tanniyn*, and of course...the buzz of flying *biters*, which seemed to grow in the silence of the group assembled in the wilds.

"I will aid him if you will not," Trundiir deeply rumbled.

Kardul looked to his *sharur* -- not a gaze of anger, but seeming to consider the *Tellen*'s words. He unfolded his arms and straightened his posture from his casual stance and announced, "We'll help you younglings -- as much out of respect for Mithraam's fair hand he's shown me over the years as to keep you three under our protection so you don't go off getting killed in the first steps of the journey."

Rogaan stood stunned looking at Kardul, astonished at the *Kiuri'Ner*'s change of mind and offer. *Prayers do get heard?* Rogaan looked up to the sky in silent thanks while Suhd squeezed his arm tightly with both hands as she jumped up and down in her excitement. Pax had closed his eyes and mumbled something to himself before a smile came to his face.

"We travel through *his* lands," the scruffy *Baraan sharur* said with caution and concern.

Rogaan wondered at the "*his*" statement. *Whose lands?* He looked at the scruffy *sharur*, then at Kardul, then to the others for an answer. The *sharur* stared at Kardul, anxiously waiting for the *Kiuri'Ner*'s response.

"Whose lands?" Pax asked.

Kardul looked to be considering something and struggling with a decision. His eyes became fixed on the ground in front of him as he answered, "The dark robes' axe."

"I don't see a way around that path," the scruffy *sharur* added.

"I know, Adul." Kardul snapped. Kardul took a breath and exhaled slowly. "Getting in front of the caravan, we'll have to travel hard and use Claw Pass. That should give us a half day lead on the jailers."

"And if the dark axe finds us?" Adul asked. "He's a dangerous shadow in these Wilds. Knows every trail and pass. He commands the animals. And he can best...."

"Enough!" Kardul snapped at Adul. The bulky *Kiuri'Ner* looked about to bite a stone in half. If Rogaan read Kardul correctly, the *sharur* protector of the pathways...Adul was afraid. Maybe of the dark axe, but more practically he seemed fearful that his companions would not follow where he led. "The dark axe is all of that...and more. He's merciless, and sharp with trailing. Maybe he'll find us if he's looking for this *Tellen*. We've dealt with difficult ones before. Keep our smarts and ahead of him is what we must do."

"Let us not forget his lightless warriors," added Trundiir. The *Tellen* held an angry stare directed at Kardul a little too long for Rogaan to miss or dismiss it. "That axe will have a hunger for us all."

"Trundiir speaks truth," Adul agreed with a long, depressed sigh. "He'll hunt us and cut us down...one by one, if not all at once."

Rogaan looked at Kardul and his companions, feeling confused and concerned. These forest warriors were hardened hunters and capable and led by Kardul. That made them dangerous to most opposing them. Many in Brigum confirmed Kardul's reputation to be the best of all in the Wilds and a dangerous one to cross in a fight. Now all the companions, including Kardul, seemed to be struggling with fear and fating themselves to dying at the blade of this dark axe.

"You did not need to kill them," Rogaan interjected, thinking he was helping the conversation and growing tension. "They were taking us to the temple to find help to rescue my father."

"Our parents...all of them," Pax added with a stern look passing between him and Rogaan. Shame flashed through Rogaan at his friend's correcting assertion.

"Are you sick in mind?" Adul asked incredulously. "No one seeks the dark robes."

"I told him dat," Pax interjected. "He would no listen to me. Thinks we need help from them kind."

Rogaan returned a stern look at Pax in the hope he would be quiet about their plans. Rogaan did not feel Pax's decisions were solid or straight of thought. Rogaan was desperate and held a glimmer of hope that his father's trust in the Ebon Circle would find him the aid he sought. Embarrassment heated his cheeks a little, and his throat tightened a bit at being found to have been so desperate that he was willing to sell his light to the dark ones.

"What would give you a thought the dark temple would serve you?" Kardul asked Rogaan with narrowing eyes.

Rogaan swallowed hard at being put to the question. He did not want to reveal his father's instructions to the *Kiuri'Ner*. He feared it would be a mark against his gaining their further aid, and possibly prevent him from being accepted into Brigum's *Kiuri'Ner*.

"His father wanted him ta go ta da temple," Pax answered for Rogaan. At Pax's utterance, Rogaan leveled a glaring stare at his friend. Pax returned the glare with a *'Who, me?'* expression.

"Is this true, youngling?" Adul asked, with a tone demanding an answer.

Rogaan felt trapped into answering. Too much was in the open about his father's wishes. He nodded then answered flatly, "Yes."

"By the Ancients -- we should not be here," Adul burst out in complaint.

"I should have sought answers from your women before going off after you," Kardul said to himself. "Did they know you were on the path to them?"

"I do not know," Rogaan answered honestly. "I was following the last instructions given me by my father. I think he believed I would be safe in the temple."

"Nobody is safe there," Adul stated as he looked to his companions for some indication of affirmation. All but Trundiir nodded their agreement. The *Tellen* just stood expressionless, as if not part of the conversation.

"Was the dark temple expecting you?" Kardul asked with a growl. The point was important to him for some reason. The *Kiuri'Ner* wanted an answer.

"Not by any announcement," Rogaan replied. "I think this was some pre-arrangement between my father and them if something happened to him."

Kardul seemed relieved. He took on the look of a thinker not seeing what was right in front of him, but some vision in his head as he put things together. He spoke quietly, more to himself, but loud enough for Rogaan to hear him, "I always thought the old *Tellen* had dealings with the dark robes...."

Kardul looked up to see everyone looking at him. He realized his last words were heard by all. It was obvious by the sour look on the *Baraan's* face that he wanted those words back. The *Kiuri'Ner* came to understand something important to him. What, Rogaan had no idea. Kardul recovered his expression and overall demeanor quickly, putting on his usual serious face while straightening his back.

"We have an advantage on the dark temple," Kardul announced. "It'll take them time to figure out what's happened. Let's make haste traveling through the pass and parts beyond."

Kardul looked to Rogaan with confident eyes. "Let's hope the Ebon Circle doesn't find further need to gather you into their temple. Your father isn't our focus...presently. Getting you away from these parts and to civilization is."

"Our parents..." Pax corrected Kardul with heated eyes.

Kardul shot Pax a "be cautious" glare, before softening it. "Of course, youngling."

"Travel light?" Adul asked as if he knew the answer.

"It'll be difficult even for *him* to find us if we keep moving...fast," Kardul answered, sounding almost as if he had convinced himself. "Keep doubling with the younglings, unless they've learned to handle steeds better since dawn. Trail the rider-less *sarigs* and switch animals when we take our short rests."

The *sharur* each quickly dropped one saddlebag from their *sarigs*, leaving only food and bare essentials in their remaining bags. Adul removed two of his three battle sticks from his saddle mount, tossing them both on the growing pile of equipment. Trundiir tossed a hammer atop the spears, then several cooking pans. He grumbled something about travel rations as he remounted his *sarig*. He held out his hand to Suhd, then waited silently, unmoving. Suhd looked to Rogaan with uncertain eyes, seeming to ask his permission.

"You are the lightest of the three and I will not *handle* you...come," Trundiir rumbled.

An intense wave of jealousy rippled through Rogaan. It was an unpleasant feeling, which he fought down. *I must learn to ride these sarigs.* With a nod from Rogaan, Suhd allowed Trundiir to lift her up with great ease and set her behind him, where she slipped her feet into the saddle footholds and grabbed the saddle handles with white knuckles.

Pax was already seated behind the stocky *Baraan sharur* and was making himself comfortable atop their *sarig*. Rogaan realized he did not know the *sharur's* name Pax rode with, or the name of the tall, lean *sharur* now impatiently in saddle waiting for Rogaan. With an uncertain lack of grace, Rogaan managed to climb onto the *sarig's* saddle and seat himself behind his riding companion. Rogaan swore he heard the *Baraan* snicker a little. He quickly placed hands and feet as he had before, in and on the saddle holds then waited to start moving. The *Kiuri'Ner* swept the trail behind them with a large leaf-covered tree limb, raking over footprints to their small clearing then tossed the branch over the discarded items when he was satisfied with his work.

In a blink, Kardul was in his saddle and moving out, with Adul close in trail. Trundiir with Suhd took up the third position with Pax and his *sharur* fourth, and Rogaan and his *sharur* bringing up the rear. With everyone trailing him, Kardul set off at a grueling pace.

Chapter 14

Of Rivers and Mountains

C lear skies and a warm sun gave way to clouds in the late morning as cooler air blew out of the southwest. Kardul kept the pace fast for the band of companions and their seven *sarigs*, leading them through fern and hardwood forests of the southernmost end of the Valley of the Claw where it joined with the Tamarad River and opened out into the Wilds of western Shuruppak. Rogaan's legs had long since painfully cramped from trying to keep his sore backside off the saddle, and he gritted his teeth with each jarring reminder of his failure. Instead, he did his best to keep his thoughts on other things…Suhd. Glimpses of her made his heart pound harder and his pains disappear. Then he would lose sight of her as the *sarigs* maneuvered around obstructions and thickets. It was at such times that Rogaan would concentrate on where Kardul led them. It seemed to Rogaan that Kardul led the troupe on old and less-used game trails, by the overgrown look of them. The *Kiuri'Ner* appeared to know these forest paths far better than Rogaan expected by the way he and his hunters spoke of *his land* and navigated it. If the Ebon Circle's dark axe caused them as much concern as they held in their eyes and on their tongues, he thought they would have avoided this region and would have been unfamiliar with the ways of fast travel through these parts. It seemed that he had misjudged much about Kardul and his companions.

Kardul raised a fist, signaling all to stop. Everyone pulled up, bringing their *sarigs* to a halt. Rogaan felt relieved that he could stretch his legs without having to worry over falling from the big steed. The *sharur* sharing the beast seemed to be unaffected by the long ride, and sat in his saddle scanning for unknown and unseen dangers from under the wide brim of his green hat. Kardul steered his *sarig* back along his *sharur.*

"This river is thick with *snapjaws* at this end of the Valley of the Claw," Kardul instructed, looking at his *sharur* as he spoke, making sure they heeded his words. "The water runs slow here and is shallow enough for the *sarigs* to cross while touching bottom. Follow close. When I move to cross, don't hesitate, or you'll allow time for the *snapjaws* to gather and attack."

Anxiety rippled through Rogaan. Dangers lurking in the water unnerved him. The unknown had that effect on him, and he did not like that about himself. He swallowed hard. Looking at Pax and Suhd, they held no better faces than he felt. They both were scared, though Pax was doing his best to not show it. Suhd was wide-eyed with fear making Rogaan's heart hurt.

"Ruumoor," Kardul said to the rider with Rogaan. "Stay behind me. The others will follow after you."

Ruumoor simply nodded in acknowledgment, then followed Kardul as he urged his *sarig* to the front of column. Pax, with just a few hints of his blue face paint still visible, looked at Rogaan quizzically. Rogaan shrugged uncomfortably. Suhd looked at Rogaan with fear and hurt eyes. Rogaan's heart sank as shame grabbed him hard. Rogaan leaned into Ruumoor.

"Let Suhd and Trundiir go before us," Rogaan pleaded.

"Kardul gives the orders," Ruumoor answered him dispassionately.

Rogaan felt powerless and pained from the abandoned look Suhd continued to give him. Kardul motioned for his *sharur* to follow. He edged his steed forward while calmly looking up and down the river. Rogaan also looked at the river. It took his breath away: *snapjaws* everywhere and of all sizes, too many to count, and many with mouths agape, sunning themselves along the river banks. An aggressive group of *snapjaws* on the far side of the river surrounded a partially eaten carcass, a large one...of what, Rogaan could only guess. They tore at the lightless flesh, twisting and ripping it apart, then swallowing the chunks whole before either returning for another bite or retreating to a place to sun and digest their meals without being molested.

"How are we going to cross the river without being eaten?" Rogaan asked aloud, though his question was not directed at Ruumoor. The river was less than fifty strides wide, but not much less. A few boulders and built-up mud and tree limb islands not much bigger than the *sarig* he sat on rose above the slow-moving water, with subdued froths of foam forming in the turbulent water downstream of the outcrops. More than a dozen eyes and snouts broke the water's surface, from what Rogaan could see.

"Water's still cool," Kardul said quietly.

"Good," Ruumoor said to himself with what sounded like relief in his voice.

"What does that mean?" Rogaan asked.

Ruumoor tensed as if annoyed at the question then answered, "*Snapjaws* need warm water to hunt with speed. With the waters cool they'll swim slower and won't likely attack."

Rogaan felt a little relief from his anxiety, but just a little. Kardul motioned for them to move out, and immediately plunged his *sarig* into the water where its belly was still dry ten strides from the shore. Ruumoor urged their *sarig* forward, with the tethered *sarig* following close. Each *sharur* urged their *sarigs* into the river with little trouble then made their way across the water as quickly as they could. Close to midway, the water became deeper, rising up the flanks of their *sarig*, high enough to soak Rogaan's boots and legs. Cold! Unpleasant, but tolerable. A few *snapjaws* upriver from them were lazily approaching with eyes and snouts above the water, allowing the current to carry them as much as they propelled themselves with their powerful tails. Kardul was close to the opposite bank when Rogaan heard a splash and yelling from behind. Twisting, he saw the rider-less *sarig* trailing behind Pax and his *sharur*. The animal was in the teeth of a large *snapjaw.* The *sarig* whined as the big *snapjaw* kept jaws clamped on the steed's left shoulder, dragging it down while it struggled to escape. The tether of the doomed animal tied to the *sarig* Pax and Ruumoor rode strained, dragging them backward into deeper water. Pax and his *sharur* were yelling at each other in disagreement before a flash of metal in Pax's hand cut the tether, freeing them and condemning the grappled *sarig* behind them to a grisly death. Rogaan found himself hoping the former steed drowned before the *snapjaws* started eating it. More *snapjaws* were drawn to the action in the middle of the river, many slipping into the slow current from both banks. Kardul and his *sharur* hastened their *sarigs* to clear the water, and did so in a hurry. On the bank, as they left the water, Kardul quickly checked each *sharur* and *sarig* to see that they were unharmed, stating he intended to leave behind any wounded or bleeding animals, rather than beckoning flesh eaters along the trail to hunt them.

They set off at the same hard pace Kardul had them travel before crossing the river. He led them along more overgrown game trails with the intent of avoiding dangerous *tanniyn*. He did so successfully, with only two tense encounters: one where they came upon a lone bull *shieldback* grazing low shrubs at the side of the trail that they had to give a wide berth, and the second when a pair of juvenile *redfins* gave them chase before seeing and catching easier prey. Afterward, Kardul led them unchallenged into the low mountain ridge fingers off the Spine Mountains, with the sun just short of its zenith. The mountain trails Kardul led them on were barely visible to Rogaan's eyes, until they climbed halfway up the five hundred-stride-high ridge where the trail became wider, and clear of most overgrowth. For much of the afternoon, they traveled snaking trails, following the rising ridge spines. Leather leaf trees, flowers of many colors, and *Baraan*-tall ferns on the valley floor gave way to pines, mostly red and lavender flowers, and smaller-statured ferns as they climbed, thick at first, then becoming more sparse the higher they ascended the rocky ridges. The wind picked up, now constantly blowing out of the southwest, strong enough to throw off arrows from their marks as dark clouds swept over the ridges, threatening to let loose rain.

Kardul halted the band of companions just short of the ridge's high saddle where they would pass over, then start their downward journey. He picked out a flat area along the trail large enough for the band to rest the *sarigs* while the clouds grew more threatening in the late afternoon. Rogaan did not possess the skill to predict winds and storms, but even he could not miss the warning signs of heavy rains coming.

"Dismount," Kardul commanded.

"What's that?" A voice spoke, but Rogaan was uncertain of whose.

Rogaan turned around and looked about, finding Adul pointing to a ridge far below. On the trail atop that ridge traveled a lone rider, sitting tall upon a large *sarig*. The rider, dressed in a dark cloak, swiftly moved behind rock cover, where he disappeared, not emerging from the far side of the outcrop as one would expect. Rogaan did not distinguish anything discerning of the rider in the moments he had to spy him, but something about the rider struck a chord of familiarity.

"It was *him*...wasn't it?" Ruumoor sounded unnerved.

"Who?" Trundiir grumbled.

"That dark axe," Ishmu answered with a concerned tone.

Adul dismounted and tied his *sarig* off to a small tree. He shook his head as he approached the others. "We've ridden the steeds hard. They need rest before we start down."

"Whoever it is, he's a half a day behind," Kardul declared as he tied his *sarig* off to another small tree. "And if he keeps hiding from our eyes, he'll get further behind. Adul, keep watch. We rest the animals a while, then start down the trail before the sun sets."

The afternoon wind at this height, with rains approaching, whipped the *sharur's* cloaks. It blew cool, almost cold for Rogaan. With arms wrapped around each other, Pax and Suhd huddled next to Rogaan for warmth as Kardul demanded a fireless camp. The three

PRIMEVAL ORIGINS® 1

younglings grumbled as they nestled together in a rock outcrop less than ten strides from the *sarigs*. The rocks broke the chill breeze, allowing them to rest without shivering too much. Trundiir casually tossed them a wrap of dried meat and a water skin as he passed, then disappeared before he could be thanked. Pax and Suhd grabbed at the food and water and gulped a fair share of both down without looking at Rogaan. Their manners did not surprise him, since he had had his first meal with them at their home more than a year ago. Rogaan thought then their behavior odd and rude, but realized they had little and had learned to make quick work of any food within arm's reach. Rogaan smiled while staring at Suhd. Her arm and leg brushed his from time to time, sending him into a sense of elation. He felt content...happy. He also felt guilty for his contentment. After all, his father and their parents were jailed and being taken away. *How can I feel this way?* Rogaan asked himself, with a growing disdain dripping from his inner thoughts.

Suhd saw the look on Rogaan's face and snuggled up to him. She did not speak. Just snuggled. She felt good...warm, despite the cool breeze. Pax smiled and handed him the rest of the dried meat. Rogaan ate the white meat, what he thought was *snapjaw* or *tanniyn* as he washed it down with water Pax handed him. When Rogaan looked up, he found Pax asleep sitting against the rocks, his chin on his chest. Suhd was asleep too, though she lay comfortably against his chest. Rogaan smiled. He felt at ease and with Suhd lying against him, happy. The late-afternoon sun cut through the billowing clouds, casting a yellow-orange glow on a spot of rocks not far away, where Kardul sat impassively watching them. Rogaan wondered why Kardul was watching them with so much interest; then he closed his eyes.

Chapter 15
Field of Strife

Thump, thump, thump, thump, thump. Rogaan felt more than heard the low rhythmic sound. He was jostled about and regularly knocked on his right side, head to knee, before realizing he was unable to move his arms and legs much. A shiver gave him an awareness of being wet and chill. A deep breath filled his nose with the musky smell of *sarig*. A heavy snort told him the animal was near and working hard. Rogaan opened his eyes to a blinding brightness that felt painful. His eyes adjusted to the bright sky after a number of blinks. He found himself in a net hammock at the side of a *sarig*.

"Burn the Ancients," Rogaan cursed, not believing anyone would have him travel so undignified. His head felt unclear.

Rogaan struggled to get a better look at his predicament. He was unbound, but stuck fast in thick netting at the right side of a charcoal-colored *sarig*, making it difficult for him to move. Looking past his feet, two other charcoal *sarigs* trotted down a sloping trail with a steeply rising rocky wall to the animal's left, and a drop-off less than four strides to the animal's right. Each of the *sarigs* carried a *sharur* rider; Trundiir followed by Ishmu. Slung on the right side of Trundiir's *sarig* was a net hammock that Rogaan guessed Suhd was within. He hoped she was treated as he had been, and felt some relief in expecting that Trundiir would see her unharmed...he hoped she was unharmed. Twisting and looking ahead, Rogaan saw three *sarigs* working their way down a trail. Ruumoor rode the closest on his trotting *sarig*, another charcoal-colored beast, with a guide rope attached to the animal carrying him. Kardul and his mud-colored *sarig* trotted ahead of Ruumoor, and Adul on his charcoal *sarig* led the entourage down the winding trail.

It was early morning, as best Rogaan could tell with the sun not yet breaking over the mountain ridge above them. The sky held clouds less threatening than Rogaan last remembered. *What happened?* Rogaan wondered. His unclear head and sometimes blurred vision, frustrated, grabbed at him. *What happened to me?* Rogaan wanted answers.

"Hey, Ruumoor," Rogaan called out. The *Baraan* seemed not to hear him. Rogaan called out again, "Ruumoor! Let me out of this thing."

Ruumoor glanced over his shoulder, meeting Rogaan's stare, then looked forward, calling out. The *Baraan's* words were unclear to Rogaan, keeping him from understanding what the *sharur* was saying to the others. Kardul quickly called out something and held his hand high, signaling everyone to stop. After they halted and steadied the animals, Kardul nodded to Ruumoor, who dismounted and approached Rogaan.

"You sleep well?" Ruumoor asked with a smile.

"Well..." Rogaan replied, uncertain what to make of Ruumoor's attempt at dry humor.

"Surprised you woke so soon," Ruumoor continued as he worked the net lashings. "Most sleep longer...much longer. Hold the net closest to the animal, or you'll fall."

Realizing his sleep was by intent, anger flared in Rogaan. *How dare they....* Without warning, he tumbled to the ground with a thump and a groan. Anger swelled within him with the new pains. Immediately, he scrambled to his feet, forgetting his physical aches. He found himself standing eye to eye with Ruumoor.

"I warned you to hold the net," Ruumoor said matter-of-factly, still with that smile, then pointed to the *sarig's* saddle. "Climb up and mount this one. We'll travel faster."

Rogaan glared at the *sharur* before Ruumoor dismissed him, and turned back to his steed. Rogaan grabbed at Ruumoor's arm to stop him from walking away. He had questions. Instead, he found Ruumoor's long knife at his throat and an unsympathetic set of eyes meeting his from behind the blade. It happened so fast -- Rogaan did not know what to think, nor did he even have a chance to react.

"Be careful of your reach," Ruumoor said evenly.

"What's this about?" Kardul asked at a distance.

Ruumoor lowered his long knife then re-sheathed it. He replied, "My apologies, Master *Kiuri'Ner*. Instinct and reflex when our companion here took hold of me."

"Get him mounted," Kardul growled. "We don't have time for this."

Rogaan warily watched Ruumoor. He did not know what to make of the *sharur's* knife or the attitude behind it. The *Baraan* seemed on edge and not in too good of a mood.

"Let's be movin'," Ruumoor insistent in a friendlier manner while pointing to the saddle on Rogaan's *sarig*. "We're being followed without relent and need to keep a fast pace."

"*Him?*" Rogaan asked not knowing who "*him*" was. He wanted to know whom they were so concerned about…whom they feared so.

Ruumoor looked frustrated and impatient as he secured the netting to allow the *sarig* to travel without getting entangled. He answered as he motioned for Rogaan to climb into the saddle, "Yes. He's pushin' us. Kept us on the move all night. We're in the southern foothills, now, soon to enter the flats."

Rogaan complied with the *sharur's* urging and climbed onto the *sarig*, comfortably situating himself in the saddle. As Ruumoor turned to return to his *sarig*, Rogaan hurriedly asked one of those questions he needed answers to. "What of Suhd and Pax…how long will they *sleep?*"

"No tellin'," the *sharur* answered as he briskly walked away. "I'd expect through the mornin', at least."

Rogaan looked back to Trundiir, expecting to see the net bundle holding Pax on the other side of the *sharur's sarig*. A net bundling equipment and bedding was what he found, but no Pax. Rogaan looked at Ruumoor's *sarig* and found the same. Confused, he looked down and found Pax wrapped in nets on the left side of the *sarig* he sat upon. His friend was soundly asleep. This struck him oddly; Rogaan could not recall a time he saw Pax so…peaceful. The *sarig* jerked forward, almost throwing him out of the saddle before he grabbed onto some netting and the saddle handles. Off they went without ceremony, traveling quickly, almost recklessly galloping down the wet, slick trail.

Panic seized Rogaan as he realized his *shunir'ra* was missing -- it was not over his shoulder where he last remembered it. In a fluster, he looked and felt over the *sarig*, hoping to find his bow case. Nothing. Rogaan then looked over Ruumoor and his *sarig*. There was nothing that looked like his bow case. He found the same when he visually searched Kardul and his steed. More panic swelled -- Rogaan twisted, looking behind to find Trundiir swaying easily atop his *sarig*, holding up Rogaan's *shunir'ra* case. The weight of the mountains lifted off of Rogaan's shoulders as he exhaled in relief. Oh, he felt at ease, taking in a deep breath, then exhaling again. Trundiir grinned then tucked the bow case into an empty scabbard at the front of his saddle, where it would travel, to both Rogaan's relief and out of reach frustration.

Kardul and the companions traveled through the night while he was asleep. Though feeling well-rested, he did not understand why they had given him, Pax, and Suhd something to make them to sleep. Were they not more of a burden sleeping than being able to walk and ride? He did not understand, and that frustrated and frightened him in a way he was unable to describe. It was an itch that had started growing the day before when he watched Kardul seemingly put things together that he was not telling the rest of them about.

In short time, the column of *sarigs* left the slippery mountain trails and started off over rolling hills covered in broken forest. The Wilds were alive with life everywhere Rogaan looked, and filled with sounds from everywhere, including where he could not see. Chirps and clicks,

featherwing songs, and *tanniyn* grumblings and bellows and an occasional roar filled Rogaan's ears. *Featherwings* darted from tree to tree,
sometimes chasing each other while making a ruckus, as *leatherwings*
soared high above circling in search of an easy meal. The trail was less
defined here in these rolling hills, but Rogaan seemed able to make it
out as the overgrowth was disturbed in their passage. At least, that was
what Rogaan kept telling himself, and hoping Adul and Kardul could
see what he could not, and keeping them from getting lost. Ruumoor
appeared alert, scanning left and right for dangers. Trundiir did much
of the same as Rogaan glimpsed with an occasional look behind. Ishmu,
who rode at the rear, perpetually kept his eyes looking at where they
had passed, obviously watching for *him*. This mystery tracker truly had
Kardul and the *sharur* unsettled. That made Rogaan anxious, especially
when it involved an unknown.

After watching Ishmu for a short time, Rogaan thought it might be
more comfortable for the *sharur* to ride his *sarig* sitting backward, for
all the time he spent looking there. Kardul kept them at a hard pace,
with little deviations from their general direction. Such deviations
were mostly to avoid thick patches of trees and bush, or to not disturb
large *tanniyn* feeding on green browse. Rogaan started feeling confident at understanding the basics of cross-country travel. It did not
seem as hard as he had envisioned it. The sun climbed on his left back
to its mid-morning height, after breaking over the Spine Mountains.
From the sun's position in relation to him, and the time of the day,
Rogaan felt confident they held a general southeast direction, traveling
just as he thought they would need to get ahead of the jailer caravan.
Rogaan tried to place their group on a map he had in his mind's eye,
a map of Shuruppak his father had showed him many times during his
lessons. He guessed at where they were, but these rolling hills covered
a large area on the map on the southern side of the Spine Mountains.
If he had them placed right, they were not too many marches from the
Di'Tij's and the east-west road leading from these Wilds to Farratum.

Just short of mid-day, Ishmu pressed his *sarig* past Rogaan forward to Kardul and spoke to him while the steeds kept at their brisk walking pace. After a short exchange, Kardul motioned for everyone to stop and to gather. All the *sharur* quickly surrounded Kardul to discover what was so urgent. Ruumoor brought along Rogaan's *sarig*, leaving him outside the *sharur* ring.

"He's closing on us," Kardul announced. "We can either make a stand or push on harder. Our *sarigs* are tired after keeping on all night, so I don't expect them to hold up too long at a run, but at a trot they may be able to last most of today."

"Why's the dark axe choosin' now to battle us?" Ruumoor asked.

"Why does a *leaper* choose when it strikes?" Trundiir answered.

"He has advantage," Adul answered simply to Trundiir's philosoph-ical answer.

"We're going to take away that advantage with a harder pace," Kardul sounded grim. "Get moving."

Kardul turned his *sarig* and took up the lead position, to Adul's surprise and momentary confusion, but also visible relief. If Rogaan read the *Baraans'* faces and body moods correctly, dangers lay ahead, as well as chased them from behind. Adul turned his attention to Rogaan, looking at him as if regarding some burdensome object, then spoke absently as he shook his head in frustration. "Why does Im'Kas have interest in killing this half-*Tellen* youngling? So much trouble."

Him is Im'Kas — *he is the dark axe!* Confusion struck Rogaan about what he knew of Im'Kas through his father, and what all of the com-panions and others said of him. His father spoke well of Im'Kas, at times as if they were old friends, never as a dark figure...while almost all he heard beyond his father of Im'Kas was fear and loathing. Nothing made sense. Rogaan mumbled to himself while trying to make order of things, "Why is he feared so by so many? Why is Father not? What does Im'Kas want with me...unless it is to fetch me to the Ebon Circle temple and the dark robes?"

Rogaan shivered at the thought of the dark robes having him. It turned his stomach to think what they would do to him. With a lurch, his *sarig* took off at a hard trot, surprising Rogaan and almost tossing him out of the saddle. Holding on while trying to set his boots into the saddle's foot holds, his backside got a good bruising from the hard hide of the saddle and the *sarig*'s trotting motion. Once his feet were anchored and his backside no longer getting punished, Rogaan looked his steed all over to make sure everything was strapped on securely. All was where he remembered -- including Pax, who still slept in the netting on the left side of their *sarig*. *When is he going to wake?* Rogaan wondered and a bit surprised that all the jostling had not already woken his friend.

Once the steed settled into a trotting rhythm, Rogaan's thoughts returned to Im'Kas...the dark axe and the dark robes and the Ebon Circle. He did not fear Im'Kas...much...well, less than Kardul and his companions, but Rogaan decided after a few shivers and a sickening stomach that he wanted to keep away from the dark robes altogether. He had listened throughout his youngling years to too many stories of the vile and painful things the dark robes did to folks to get at what they wanted. What they wanted now, it seemed, was... Rogaan. With a hard swallow, he resolved himself to further defy his father and stay as far from the Ebon Circle and the dark robes as he could.

Kardul pushed them just short of the *sarigs* breaking trot to run. He guided them up against dense patches of trees and bushes, weaving through some of the less thick stuff, obviously trying to make it difficult for *him* to follow. The *sharur* followed Kardul's path exactingly, likely to obscure their numbers or something else Rogaan had not thought of. Branches slapped Rogaan in the face and elsewhere as they passed under trees and thick brush. It frustrated and angered him that he was not better able to guide his *sarig*. Rogaan stole glances back as they traveled, hoping and yet not hoping to catch sight of Im'Kas, but he bounced in the saddle far too much for his eyes to settle and make out any details. Resigning himself to that, he just kept looking forward, trying to anticipate Kardul's next move.

They kept on as the sun continued down from its peak, with Kardul continually winding them around the edges of the thickest patches of forest. Without warning, Kardul halted the lot of them at the edge of a large open field sitting between two dense stands of forest. Ferns and flowers covered the mostly flat ground, stretching more than three hundred strides long and almost as wide. Raised mounds of various sizes dotted the perimeter at the tree line. They looked unnaturally arranged and out of place, but otherwise unremarkable. In other places, ancient stone crumbling walls rose from the mounds. Long forgotten. *What is this place?* At first, Rogaan thought Kardul simply did not want to cross an open area and expose them all too eager eyes, but movement in the tree line at the far side of the flat patch made clear to him why the *Kiuri'Ner* kept them from advancing. A pair of golden-brown bull *ravers* adorned with red and black plumage on neck, arms, and tail prowled there, moving left to right as if searching or hunting.

Rogaan's heart felt as if it filled his throat, and the rapid pounding of his blood deafened him. He tried to force himself to calm down, but it was more difficult than he expected. *Ravers. Eight or more strides long, two-legged, scale-armored, flesh-hungry, always-angry fiends. If ever the Ancients created an animal with a dark side, it was these beasts, killing just not to feed, but for enjoyment.* He looked about and saw that the *sharur* were just as uneasy. It did not make him feel any better, but he felt his emotions justified. Kardul simply sat upright in his saddle surveying the field and the *ravers*. The *Baraan* appeared as calm as a rock. A single brown-and-white *featherwing* flew in circles above the open field with nothing in the sky bothering it. No *leatherwings* challenged it. *Strange about that*, Rogaan thought. Murmurs from the party brought Rogaan's attention back to the ground. The golden-brown beasts disappeared from sight, stalking behind some heavy cover. Kardul then motioned for everyone to move out, leading them along the tree line on the left side of the field where the forest was dense...impenetrable, actually. They had no escape if the *ravers* reappeared, but there was no other choice -- this open field looked to be the only passable path through this area. A shiver shuddered through Rogaan and he went from frustrated and uneasy to sweat-dripping scared.

They made their way as quietly and quickly as the *sarigs* could carry them short of running. When the line of steeds covered more than half the field's length, Rogaan started feeling a little more at ease. The *ravers* were nowhere to be seen or heard, and Kardul was moments from clearing the field and disappearing into a forest trail at the southeast corner of the field. Rogaan's *sarig* suddenly became skittish, missing several steps in its gait. He looked up to a shocking scene. His stomach sank so hard he thought he would sick up. *Ravers* burst out of the far tree line in clouds of broken branches and leaves, charging straight at them...at Kardul. The *Kiuri'Ner* pulled up his *sarig* and made to turn hard right when the *ravers* suddenly stopped a dozen lengthy strides in front of him with a swirl of dust, all the while snarling and growling. They blocked the way to the trail and escape. Kardul held his place and urged his steed to stay still. Ruumoor and his steed appeared to be stunned at the oppressive danger just strides away. Rogaan too felt stunned as his *sarig* danced nervously.

"It's *him*." Rogaan heard the uneasiness from somewhere behind. Who had spoken, he did not know.

"Now what, dark axe?" Kardul called out to the air itself.

From the shadows of a stand of scrub palms surrounding a dark-hued boulder-shaped mound halfway between them and the far tree line they intended to pass to the east of, stepped out a strongly built *Baraan* who carried himself with what Rogaan saw as great confidence. The intimidating figure, standing at least a half hand taller than himself, was dressed in a charcoal hat of similar style to the *sharur*, dark pants and a dark short-sleeved jacket, both abundantly adorned with pockets and filled sheaths. Under his jacket, a shirt of deep brown was visible that matched his hide boots. His short-cut hair and trimmed beard was almost as dark as his shirt. The *Baraan's* arms were bare, except for a pair of dark blue metallic forearm guards with intricate designs that Rogaan knew nothing of. What seemed a natural extension of him, he nimbly held in his right hand: a single-bladed battle-axe, its blade so dark that it seemed to absorb light. Above each shoulder, dark handles to some type of swords peeked. This dark figure walked with a smooth fluid motion that made Rogaan think of the *leapers* he spied from Brigum's walls. Danger emanated from him -- or more accurately...death. A chill ran down Rogaan's back and his skin prickled just looking at *him*. Worse was not knowing what the dark axe was here for, and what he intended to do to him.

"I hold no fondness for that name," Im'Kas answered Kardul with a provocative edge in his tone.

Kardul looked to be on guard and visibly uneasy as he verbally exchanged with the dark axe. "As I recall, you find little *fondness* in anything or anyone. These pets you command cannot be here for strolling."

Im'Kas stood as stone while taking in everything and everyone. As he surveyed them, another dark figure, a *Baraan* with *Evendiir* features, leaner and not too many years from a youngling, stepped from the same shadows with an air of calm and control, just as his companion. The clean-shaven newcomer wore well-tailored dark-colored hide armor protecting his upper body over a dark undershirt, loose-fitting pants, and calf-high boots that were of a light charcoal hue. A short sword and sling on his belt appeared to be his only weapons, though everything of the leaner half-*Baraan*, half-*Evendiir* looked of fine quality and a bit out of place for the middle of the forest. He, just as the dark axe, did not give a glance at the two heavily breathing *ravers* standing a stone's throw to their right.

"Release him," Im'Kas simply stated without threat. In fact, it was so matter-of-fact that Rogaan thought Kardul was about to comply without protest.

"No," Kardul replied with a hint of a snarl. "He's under my protection."

Im'Kas' companion sniffed loudly then brought his hands together palm-to-palm at mid chest. The sandy-haired one closed his eyes for a moment as everyone eyed each other, except for Im'Kas, who stood stolid and confident. The *ravers* stirred, growling low at first, then stomping their feet into a wider stance as they crouched. They looked ready to charge. The hairs all over Rogaan prickled and his heart started pounding hard, fast. Fear swept over him. The *ravers* bellowed in unison at Kardul and the rest of them, letting out a deafening and painful roar that shook Rogaan and his steed. Rogaan feared his *sarig* was just as scared as he, and expected to get thrown, so he gripped his saddle as tight as he could muster. Kardul's *sarig* started prancing as the *Kiuri'Ner* did his best to control it. All the *sarigs* followed suit with Kardul's. Now fearing being thrown, Rogaan clamped his legs hard to his *sarig* and closed his eyes, waiting to meet the ground and be made food for the *ravers*. The world slowed. Rein fasteners clinked, words spoken by others he could no longer make sense of, the thud of his short-toed *sarig*'s feet on the dirt, and his steed's breathing all sounded long and drawn-out. Even the pounding of his heart seemed too slow. Rogaan opened his eyes to a world that was growing familiar to him, moving slower than it should. Kardul forced his *sarig* to stop prancing with a long growl.

Suddenly, Rogaan's *sarig* stopped prancing and kneeled. He realized he was compressing the animal's ribs, forcing the creature to submit. Surprised at his own strength, Rogaan eased the pressure on the steed, allowing it to recover and straighten its stance, though it no longer pranced. The others were not so in control of their steeds, except for Ishmu, who was looking back at the trail they had come from. Rogaan looked past the mounted *Baraan* seeking to see what was so much more captivating there than what was in front of them. A black-cloaked figure sitting tall on his large *sarig* stood at the far side of the fern and flowered field, just over two hundred strides from them where the trail led back to the mountains. Confusion gripped Rogaan. He was confounded by the dark axe standing in front of them, and now as a mounted rider, in equally dark dress, blocking their escape back the way they came. Just as suddenly as the world slowed for Rogaan, so did it speed up back to its normal pace. Rogaan's breath was taken away by the quick changes. He felt dizzy for a few moments before recovering.

Ishmu, their rear guard, yelled out from his nervous steed, "*He* has caught up to us!"

"What are you talkin' of?" Ruumoor barked while struggling with his *sarig*.

"*He's* right behind us," Ishmu answered. "*He's* caught us."

"*He's* standin' in front of us," Ruumoor challenged, then looked behind their column, past Ishmu. "How can this be? There are two of them!"

Looking in both directions, Rogaan grew more concerned and confused. Two *dark* figures had them boxed in? In front of them, the dark axe raised his battle-axe to his chest as he gave his counterpart intense scrutiny. The other dark figure sat unmoving on his steed, his cloak engulfing him an arrow shot away.

Without warning, a stinging wave washed over Rogaan, prickling his skin and hair -- an intensely unpleasant sensation. His steed started prancing in protest of the sensation as everyone in the column let out troubled grunts. Looking back in the direction the wave came from, the black cloaked figure reined in his steed, stopping it from prancing sideways. A deep guttural growl followed by a high-pitched snort drew Rogaan's attention back in the other direction where the *ravers* stood. Both were vigorously shaking their heads as if they were trying to shake off an unwanted slumber.

"Lost them," Im'Kas' companion nervously announced a moment before the *raver* closest stepped at him, bellowing long and angry. The other *raver* dropped into a crouch; then, without hesitation, it charged the column where Kardul led. Rogaan's *sarig* bolted, nearly riding out from under him. He hung on, but just barely, and with much pain in his hands and arms, all the while yelling curses as he fought to better his grip on saddle and netting.

Glancing back, Rogaan saw Kardul urge his *sarig* into a run with a horned *raver* close behind. He and his *sarig* chased by the *raver* ran past a stolid Im'Kas, who stood in a stance Rogaan could only describe as strike-ready, shaking his head in disgust. The dark axe held fast, not attacking either Kardul or the *raver* as they passed just strides away. Rogaan thought that strange -- the *raver* paid Im'Kas no attention as the *Baraan* gave no sign of being afraid of the beast. *What is he?* Rogaan asked himself then found his distraction preventing him from regaining solid seating. Another glance showed him the rest of his party in chaos, scattered and trying to regain control of their steeds, and of no help to him. Rogaan pushed his stray thoughts away to focus on his *sarig* and the saddle under him. A stumble by his *sarig* caused Rogaan to lurch forward, then slam backwards with arched back against the animal's heaving rump. The impact forced a grunt from him as pain racked his back. Grabbing forcefully at the saddle, he feared the steed falling hard to the ground and him getting crushed under the big animal. Then, there was getting torn apart by the *raver* chasing him. He had to get his steed under control and painfully sat up in his saddle.

Looking forward down the side of his *sarig*, Rogaan saw a dense wall of forest and guarding thickets fast approaching. The time to gain control over his *sarig* was now! He leaned forward in the saddle, trying to catch the whipping reins to guide his steed away from the tangle ahead. He stretched his body for the reins, but the reins danced just out of reach. The *sarig* kept running in full gallop for the tangle of green-covered tree trunks, branches, roots, and vines. Rogaan envisioned disaster allowing the *sarig* to plunge into the dense thickets. He would be pulled from his steed, and then he would be at the mercy of everything. Rogaan tried yelling at his steed, but it continued on at full speed straight for disaster.

"What be happenin'?" Rogaan heard the slurred words from the netting low to his left.

"Hold on, Pax...this is going to hurt," Rogaan told his groggy friend. Helpless to change the *sarig*'s path, Rogaan braced himself low into the saddle as the forest and thickets rushed at them. Just before plunging into the tangles, Rogaan closed his eyes tight as he grabbed the saddle with all his strength. The *sarig* stamped to a stop, leaning low and forward abruptly and unexpectedly, almost throwing Rogaan over the head of the animal. If not for his death grip on the saddle, he would have been thrown forward off the steed. Shocked, Rogaan opened his eyes to a wall of green-leafed vines, branches, and other thick growth. He sighed in relief; the *sarig* was not as stupid as he had feared. Rogaan relaxed a bit, thankful for his steed's choice. Then it reared and took off to the right, throwing Rogaan bent rearward over his back of the saddle. The only thing keeping him on the steed was his feet, wedged tightly in the saddle footholds. In this position, he was being painfully stretched awkwardly. Rogaan's back twisted and bent with great pain as he desperately tried to sit up. He sucked in a breath, readying himself to contract his gut and pull himself properly in the saddle. A foul wind of putrid decay filled his nose. It turned his stomach and forced a gagging cough from him.

Rogaan looked up to an open maw filled with finger-long knives coming at him. With no other place to go, he painfully pressed himself back onto the rump of the *sarig*, bending and straining backward even further. Pain shot through him...back and legs burning as if they were on fire. The *raver*'s jaws snapped shut with a loud clop just above Rogaan's face, almost raking his left cheek with its horrid knives. The foulness of its breath bathed him, causing Rogaan's stomach to rush up. The *sarig* jerked right, tossing him sideways left. Painful agony racked his back and legs, making him forget the stench and his stomach. He frantically grasped for anything to stop from being tossed off. In his flailing, something found his hand -- what, he did not care. It was something solid, something he could get leverage with and right himself in the saddle.

The bull *raver* lost a few steps when it made its lunge at him, but recovered and was again closing. Rogaan had to right himself before the *raver* had a second bite at him. As the *sarig's* rump pounded Rogaan's neck and shoulders, the image of the angry bull *raver* with its lust for death became seared in his mind. Rogaan feared his *sarig* was not fast enough to escape the beast…certainly not off-balance and with him lying over the saddle. Rogaan gritted his teeth, then timed the *sarig's* motion to launch himself upright just enough to contract his gut muscles and pull on whatever he held in his hand. The move left him with the pain along his back and legs replaced with muscles pulled in his midsection. Rogaan exhaled in relief. Looking back to satisfy his hope that he and his *sarig* were now holding the gap between them and the angry beast, Rogaan's heart sank and a chill rippled down his spine. The *raver* was still faster. It would strike again in moments.

Something passed to the left of Rogaan, going the opposite direction. He looked behind, finding Im'Kas in a full run at the bull *raver*. The darkly clad *Baraan* launched himself low at the beast as the *raver* struck at him in his forward roll under a clopping bite that found only air. Rolling to his feet in a blink, Im'Kas slid on his boots to a stop. As he did, he swung his black battle-axe in an overhead arc then down on the *raver's* left leg. The dark arc it made was there and gone so fast that a blink would have missed it. The left foot of the *raver* was almost severed, bouncing in the dirt and flowers as it was dragged behind the beast. The *raver* went crashing to the ground, howling in pain, with its head plowing ferns, flowers and dirt, tossing up green, yellows, purples, and reds in a beautiful display before being engulfed in a cloud of dirt and dust. Rogaan's *sarig* unexpectedly jerked right, again, but

Rogaan held tightly and kept his saddle. Looking forward to understand why the animal behaved so, the second bull *raver* had abandoned
chasing the others and was charging him. Rogaan could not believe his
fortune. He muttered, "Why me?"

The *sarig*'s turn was not enough to avoid the predator. It too wore
an angry snarl, like the first beast, as it rapidly closed on him. It opened
its maw wide, showing rows of finger-long teeth. Rogaan feared the
end. A whistling blur of black flew by him on his left. It struck the
raver's neck just under its right jaw, deeply cutting through much of
its muscle and inner parts. The bull *raver* collapsed in a fountain of
blood spraying high above a black hide-wrapped haft projecting from
its neck as Roggan and his *sarig* ran past the felled beast. They now
headed straight for Adul and the rest of the *sharur*, who looked to have
their *sarigs* under control. Fearing his *sarig* would not stop, Rogaan
looked for the reins to slow his steed. They were on the *sarig*'s neck
more than an arm's reach away. Rogaan considered leaving his saddle
to get them when Kardul riding his *sarig* pulled up close on the right,
allowing the *Kiuri'Ner* to grab the reins then slow them both to a fast
trot then slower.

"Let me out of dis!" Pax growled from his blood-soaked netting. "I
be bounced enough. And I be covered in blood. What be happenin'?
Why I be tied up?"

"Pax, calm yourself," Rogaan cautioned his friend between gasping
breaths. "And do not do anything...."

Thud.

"...dumb." Rogaan completed his words with an expected disappointment. "Hold up, Kardul. Pax has fallen out."

"The youngling is of no matter to me," Kardul spat while making
no attempt to comply with Rogaan's request.

Shock rippled through Rogaan at Kardul's words. Then, shock immediately replaced with anger. Rogaan snatched the reins of his *sarig*
out of Kardul's hand with a muffled growl. Kardul looked at Rogaan

with a mix of surprise and anger. Rogaan met Kardul's gaze, directly, eye to eye. The *Kiuri'Ner* stared back, not giving away his thoughts by facial expression. Then, he broke out in a grin as his *sarig* continued toward their companions without pause.

"Of no matter to you?" Rogaan growled loudly. "He is my friend."

Rogaan halted his *sarig*, then awkwardly steered it in the other direction after some coaxing. Turning his back on Kardul, Rogaan found a confused Pax standing with knives in hand in the midst of ferns and flowers, his clothes spattered in blood across his left side. The almost squared pattern of the netting showed where no blood stained him. Rogaan coaxed his *sarig* to stop next to Pax as his knife-wielding friend looked up at him dazed and bewildered.

"I miss somethin'...huh?" Pax asked Rogaan.

"You did," Rogaan answered with a chuckle, then looked up to survey the carnage. Both *ravers* were down: one lightless, the other growling in pain as it tried to stand, only to fall repeatedly. Im'Kas put a merciful end to the beast's misery with a stab to the back of its head with a black sword. A shiver struck Rogaan. He did not know if it was that dark weapon or the ease with which Im'Kas killed with it that sent his spine rattling. Looking away, Rogaan found Kardul and his *sharur* gathering around him and Pax. An odd sense of comfort warmed Rogaan as they formed a shield between him and the dark axe. Rogaan and Pax immediately looked at Trundiir's steed to see if Suhd was without harm. She had not awakened in her netted bed despite all their troubles and bouncing about. Relief filled Rogaan, and it seemed Pax felt the same as they scrutinized her predicament. The sight of Suhd brought a smile to Rogaan's face; then his frown came back as jealousy rippled through him. Not liking himself for what he felt, Rogaan forced his petty feelings down with an effort. Trundiir had kept her safe. It was more than he could have done for her, he realized with a growing sense of being overwhelmed by all that had happened to them. Wanting none of this dark feeling, Rogaan looked about hoping for a distraction…something else good to find. Instead, he found Im'Kas' companion standing where he remembered, opposite them and the fallen *ravers*. A chill ran through Rogaan as he worried that Im'Kas was behind him about to haul him off to the Ebon Circle. *Where is Im'Kas?*

"Hand the *Tellen* to me, Kardul," Im'Kas demanded.

Rogaan froze as another chill rippled through him, head to boots. The dark axe did stand behind him. Unnerved, Rogaan tuned to see exactly where. He found the chiseled features of the darkly clothed *Baraan* less than eight strides away. The legend he heard spoke of by his father and the townsfolk all throughout his youngling years had Rogaan expecting a *Baraan* in his elder years, far older than the individual he saw standing near. Im'Kas appeared to be on the high side of the prime of his life. Rogaan understood some *Baraan* were longer-lived than most, aging more like a *Tellen*, but Im'Kas still looked younger than he expected. Blood smattered the dark axe's charcoal clothing, as some still dripped crimson from the blades of his sword and battle-axe he carried in his hands. That image of Im'Kas burned itself into Rogaan's mind and was fitting of the tales told of him. But the way Im'Kas carried himself, Rogaan found it difficult to think anything of the *Baraan* other than that this was normal for him. *Death* swirled around him and embraced the dark axe. *Normal?* Another chilling shiver ripped through Rogaan. He wanted to be gone from this place…away from the dark axe, away from Kardul, and the bunch of them. He started to regret his decision to ask for Kardul's help. This was not anything like he envisioned. This was not glorious or victorious for a righteous intent. This was rough, grungy, chaotic, and filled with uncertainties. Nothing like the stories told of hero journeys.

"No!" Kardul sounded adamant. Fear no longer trembled in his voice. "He's my charge and I keep my oaths."

"Not this time." Im'Kas spoke matter-of-factly and appeared unconcerned that Kardul and his companions were so close. A quick glance told Rogaan that Kardul's companions were trying to hide their fears of being so close to the dark axe, but not doing much of a job of it. "Either you hand the youngling over, or I'll take him. I care not if you force my hand, me killing you and your followers."

Kardul's companions looked nervously at each other. Trundiir's glum frown gave Rogaan pause. He did not appear nervous, as the others did. Instead, the *Tellen* seemed bored, while also keeping attentive to everything going on about him. A slap at Rogaan's left leg drew his attention back to the ground where he found Pax standing.

"Be careful," Pax said with an air of caution. "They be talkin' of ya as if ya be a piece of meat they be fightin' over."

Kardul wore a stern thoughtful face. Rogaan could not blame the *Baraan* for considering handing him over after seeing those ebon blades killing, though he hoped the *Kiuri'Ner* would not give him up. If it came to a battle of blades, Rogaan figured Kardul might see Im'Kas a wound or two, but would end up lightless.

"Im'Kas...." The dark axe's companion came running up. "That *kabiri* approaches. He's protected and holds much power. Far greater than me."

"I'm aware, Daluu," Im'Kas replied, almost matter-of-factly.

"I'm uncertain...I feel his power even from here," Daluu anxiously continued. "He may be more powerful than both of us, together."

"I'm certain of it." Im'Kas confirmed his companion's fear as if he were confirming that the sun rises in the morning. "Finish your preparations."

"He's been following us since Brigum," Kardul added to their verbal exchange.

"You killed several of mine." Im'Kas stared at Kardul. "I'll not forget."

"Is this the time for trifling over past matters?" Kardul shot back, clearly feeling he had the advantage with a third interest joining them

-- an interest for Im'Kas and his companion to be more concerned about than Kardul, from what Rogaan suspected. Im'Kas glared at Kardul, though he said nothing before turning his attention to the approaching dark figure.

The black-cloaked rider and his *sarig* were a spear's throw away, approaching across the field at a stroll. He had followed them through the forest and over the mountain pass, then over the countryside and more forest. He was a determined one, and confident, by the casual way he carried himself in the saddle. Everyone in their party thought him the dark axe. They were wrong. When the rider broke forty strides distance, a prickling sensation engulfed Rogaan. He found himself unable to move, or even to speak. Panic welled up within him as he unsuccessfully struggled to free himself from the unseen bonds. Panic pressed in on him and he found it difficult to breathe. Darkness... the unknown unnerved Rogaan, but not being able to breath terrified him. Suffocating was a horrible way for anyone to die. Hoping for help, Rogaan focused on his peripheral vision to see if anyone was able to aid him. Out of the corner of his eye, Rogaan found Ishmu and Trundiir and their steeds suffering the same. They were all stuck in their places. No help.

Panic consumed Rogaan, leaving him unable to think. His thoughts turned chaotic, unfocused. He struggled against the invisible bonds, but only managed to use up more of his air. He felt light-headed as twinkling lights flashed in his vision before his vision narrowed with gray, then blackness, taking his outer sight until all he saw was that directly in front of him. Rogaan felt helpless and so far away from home, far from his family and the warm bed he knew and the petty rivalry with Kantus, and from the safety of Brigum's walls. How foolish his desires to become a *Kiuri'Ner*. He was not fit, not ready to take on the challenges of the world. And he had brought Pax and Suhd with him. *How selfish of me. How stupid of me.* Rogaan's despair took from him his will to fight. He felt all alone to battle the dark forces of the world and an unseen beyond. They were devouring him and taking his light from him one heartbeat, one breath at a time. His vision dimmed further. His chest burned. His sight was now all grays, with blackness closing in from all around. A dark-clad figure stepped into what was remaining of his sight then stood in between him and the black cloaked rider. *How is that he can move?* Rogaan wondered, but was relieved for it. A glimmer of hope sparked in him when air started to fill his lungs. It was not much, but enough to lessen the burning in his chest and the flashing lights in his sight. His gray sight gained shades of color and sharpened. His vision cleared enough for him to see that it was Im'Kas who stood shielding him from the rider.

"Close enough, stranger," Im'Kas cautioned. The black-cloaked rider brought his *sarig* to a halt.

"I am without quarrel with you, Im'Kas of the Ebon Circle." The black-cloaked rider's formal way of speaking and deep, slightly resonating voice were different from those familiar to him. It certainly was not *Baraan* or *Tellen*. Even the few *Evendiir*, with their higher-pitched voices, and *Mornor-Skurst* with their breathy words he had heard speak did not sound like the cloaked rider.

"Why have you stilled everyone?" Im'Kas demanded of the dark figure.

"I mean to have the half-*Tellen*," the black-cloaked rider answered as if simply stating fact. "I will see him away from this incompetence."

Why does everyone want to take me away from everyone else? Rogaan sat dumbfounded. *Who is this rider? Pax is right...I am nothing but a piece of meat to them...and there are things here much bigger than just Father's doings.* Rogaan felt the weight of the world pressing on him. He had simple dreams...become a *Kiuri'Ner* and protect those who could not protect themselves. Maybe have the chance to be a hero of the stories told in the days ahead. *What have I gotten into? What have I gotten Pax and Suhd into?*

"I'll see him away from here," Im'Kas countered with an even tone.

"Then, I am with quarrel with you," the black-cloaked rider

replied with an even, dangerous tone. Another wave of prickles ripped through Rogaan, leaving him immobile.

"Now, Daluu!" Im'Kas called to his companion, while managing an air of calm. In a blink, Im'Kas drew his twin black-bladed short swords from his shoulder scabbards and charged the dark rider.

The dark rider's steed stumbled. Somewhere behind him, Rogaan heard a snicker. He guessed it came from Daluu and that he had done something to make the rider's steed unsteady. Rogaan made to break free of whatever was restricting him. He tried to move, but found himself unable to do so. Worse, he realized he could no longer draw a breath. His concern immediately turned to panic as he unsuccessfully struggled for breath.

Im'Kas charged through ferns and flowers at the black-cloaked rider, with no sign of wanting less than to take his head, but the rider maneuvered his steed at the moment of Im'Kas' attack such that all Im'Kas could strike was the steed itself. A hind limb was cut from the rider's *sarig*, toppling the animal, and the cloaked rider rolled free of his falling *sarig*. He did so with a surprising grace, regaining his feet immediately.

Rogaan's sight of the battle filled with random lights and his vision became almost completely grayed when his skin crawled with more prickling, this time the unpleasant sensation came from the opposite direction. Suddenly, he could draw breath. He drew in another, a deep breath, and found he could move his limbs some. His rising panic quelled. The exploding spots of light disappeared from his vision. He saw before him Im'Kas, closing on the black- cloaked rider who drew a single black blade, a slender double-edged sword. Im'Kas hammered down a double stroke at the rider with his pair of black weapons. The rider gracefully blocked both with a sweep of his blade. They battled like a pair of whirlwinds, moving as dancers to the song of violent ringing when their blades clashed. Both moved faster than Rogaan thought possible, making it difficult to follow their strikes. Another wave of prickling crawled over Rogaan. Each time it did, he was able to move a bit more. His head he could rotate now. Rogaan looked over his shoulder, wanting to see what was behind him...where the prickling of his skin originated. He found a badly sweating and visibly shaking Daluu holding a black stone pendant, mumbling to himself just before another prickling wave crawled over his skin. Rogaan could almost move freely. Daluu repeated his gestures and mumblings, again and again. Another prickling wave swept over Rogaan. Relief filled Rogaan when he could finally move freely. Daluu looked about to fall over.

The ringing of metal on metal drew Rogaan's attention back to the sword battle. The rider made a striking move that seemed not intended to harm, but instead to gain separation from Im'Kas. The rider then raised his left hand and struck Im'Kas with an unseen explosion of air, tossing him backward. Im'Kas landed on his back before quickly rolling into a crouch. An orange glow hung over the spot where Im'Kas had stood a moment prior, before it faded away. Im'Kas dropped both swords, blade tips stuck into the ground. The dark axe extended both hands toward his dark adversary as the rider raised his left hand against Rogaan and the others. An invisible wave struck the black-cloaked rider, knocking him from his feet over flowers and ferns as the unseen force slammed into Rogaan. The force brutally knocked him off his *sarig*, sending him airborne and knocking the air from his lungs. He hit the ground hard face down before bouncing and rolling through the ferns and flowers, finally sliding to a stop. His whole body hurt and his lungs burned as he struggled to find his breath. Rogaan needed to get upright and on his feet so he could flee. It was too dangerous to stay in this field, near *them*. With a strained effort to breathe, air partially filled his lungs, giving Rogaan some relief from his light head, but at the cost of a stinging chest. He forced himself into a sitting position then took another breath to clear his head and sight before looking around. Ferns and flowers were all about him level with his eyes. A tremor shook the world under him. It lasted a moment before the ground stilled and the world went quiet...even the *featherwings* fell silent.

Rogaan held still a long moment, not sure what to make of it. The tremor was not like the deep movement of the ground when the earth trembled. Instead, this tremor felt sharp and close. A moment's pause waiting for the next tremor left him anxious to get to his feet and away from this place, away from danger, away from *them*. When the earth remained still, he scrambled to his knees then looked for everyone else from his vantage point just above the ferns. He found everyone low in the ferns and flowers, the same as him. Even the *sarigs* had lost their feet. Daluu lay close, unconscious, but appeared to be breathing. His *sarig* was not in sight. The air had a crisp smell as if a thunderstorm rich with lightning had passed, though none were about, as the sky was blue and almost cloudless. Rogaan looked to see what had become of Im'Kas and the black-cloaked rider. What he saw left him staring in awe. Both were cloaked in brilliant blue light and tossing about arm-length streaks of what looked like lightning when they struck at each other in titanic battle of sword play. Living arcs of lightning rolled over the two as they struck and countered -- blades and strikes so quick, that Rogaan wondered how it was possible for them to make their bodies move so. A deep sense of being outclassed in every way, and mortal in the presences of giants, of dark terror, shook Rogaan. He felt something he had not known since his youngest days...uncontrolled fear. *What was I thinking...to become Kiuri'Ner and have my name known?* Rogaan realized all his dreams, his ambitions, were for naught...and worse, that others might pay a coin and their lives for believing in him. *I am no match for this world.* Rogaan's self-doubt and pity lasted a moment before he was yanked backward, stumbling and twisting as he was, to get his feet under him and keep his face from plowing the dirt, again. Trundiir pulled him along at a brisk walk while carrying an unmoving Suhd under his other thick arm. He carried her as if she weighed a feather.

"Get to your *sarig*," Trundiir commanded. "We must leave while we have the moment."

"Suhd...?" Rogaan found it hard to ask if she were injured or worse. His heart sank as he looked at her limp body.

"She is alive," Trundiir answered then barked, "Move."

Rogaan just stared at Suhd and worried. A slap to his head from Trundiir smarted a considerable amount, but shook him from his melancholy.

"I need your focus, Rogaan, son of Mithraam." Trundiir emphasized his name and linage in the *Tellen* way.

Kardul and the others were already mounting their shaken *sarigs* when Rogaan, led by Trundiir, reached his steed, lying a short set of strides from where he had fallen. The animal was not going anywhere. Its neck was snapped and head lying at an odd angle. Panic surged through him. He stared at his steed, not knowing what to do. Rogaan felt lost, and despaired. Ruumoor reined up next to him, offering his hand. Rogaan became angry at himself for giving in to his dread so easily. He did not know how long he stood there battling his inner voice screaming for him to give up, lie down...surrender. Rogaan felt lost...in the Wilds and in his heart. Still, he fought his dread, not for a great cause or for others. He did not like the feeling of giving up, surrendering. Maybe it was his pride, or maybe it was his sense of responsibility to see Suhd and Pax out of the trouble he brought them into...maybe it was both. He did not know. Rogaan looked up to see Ruumoor sitting atop his *sarig* with a hand extended to him.

"Hurry, *Tellen*," Ruumoor demanded.

Rogaan accepted the *sharur*'s assistance up to the rear saddle, where he quickly lodged his boots into footholds and butt onto the worked hide seat. Ruumoor kicked at his steed, urging it off at a quick trot. Concerned for Suhd and Pax, Rogaan looked for them. He found Suhd again asleep in her netted bed on the side of Trundiir's steed, now galloping ahead. Pax sat behind Adul, galloping ahead of Suhd and Trundiir. Ishmu and Kardul pulled up alongside Ruumoor and Rogaan, flanking them; both of their steeds were bleeding from wounds.

"The *sarigs* will live long enough to get us away from here," Kardul announced, then gave a command before kicking his *sarig*, urging it into a run. "Move!"

"Still want a *Kiuri'Ner's* life?" Ishmu asked with a sly smirk before urging his steed ahead at a run.

Rogaan was taken aback by the *sharur's* words. *What did he mean by that?* Ruumoor dug his heels into their *sarig*, urging it into a gallop forcing Rogaan to grab onto the saddle handles to keep from falling off. As they quickly retreated into the forest, Rogaan looked back, curious to see what was becoming of the two warriors. Who would or *should* win the battle, Rogaan did not know. He was not certain of much, anymore. Strokes of lighting and fire filled the space in between Im'Kas and the dark rider. Rogaan watched the display in awe. Dirt, ferns, flowers, and shrubs flew into the air everywhere their powers struck, burning and blackening heaps of debris in their path. Ruumoor abruptly steered their *sarig* behind a cover of trees, causing Rogaan to lose sight of the battle. Strangely, he felt disappointed then chastised himself for it. Crackling and thundering continued as they rode into the unknown. Then the air fell silent, all except for the labored breath of their *sarig*. Rogaan started to relax in the saddle...just a little. His thoughts turned inward, turned gloomy. Outmatched by just about everyone in almost every way, he felt he should not be here. What was to become of himself, Suhd, and Pax? After the past several days, Rogaan felt overwhelmed at living and walking the stories of glory and battle. These things did not happen to folks outside of fireside tales and books. Fear filled him when he thought of becoming a *Kiuri'Ner*. Rogaan did not know if he wanted that life as protector of the pathways any longer, or if he was worthy of it...if he could survive it. Rogaan felt uncertain about most things, now. His romanticized vision and expectation of life beyond the safety of his life not more than a week ago was nothing like this. Folks were dying, and everything seemed to want him dead, and he had witnessed with his own eyes powers that should not be possible.

Rogaan shook his head as he grew angry with his self-doubts and fears. Pax's and Suhd's parents needed rescuing, and his father, too, needed him. Rogaan did not understand everything that was happening or if he would be able to make anything right. He felt little. This diminished vision of himself angered him. Rogaan fought with himself and his despair. Those he cared for needed help. As he and his friends rode into the unknown forest, led by companions they knew little of, Rogaan resolved in his head and his heart...despite being small in the world, to see their parents free.

Epilogue

A New Waking

Distant noises grew louder, some rhythmic and soothing, others not. Muffled voices came and went without a sense of time. No up or down, being weightless, felt confusing. *Where am I?* More voices, some that direction, others in another direction. *Did something touch me? What was it?* Noises, now closer, became more distinct, more rhythmic. *I know that sound...that beeping. Am I?* A familiar voice grew louder.

"Leave us be," the male voice demanded. "You have no business being here."

"*Our business* gives us authorization to be anywhere we need to be," replied a female voice reeking with overconfident disdain. "Has she regained consciousness?"

The woman's voice fell silent. Only the rhythmic beeping remained -- constant, even. Something brushed again her skin. Where, she couldn't tell. She felt disoriented, and without a solid body.

"Interesting..." the female voice toyed.

"Damn you!" The familiar male voice was angry. "Get your hands away from her."

"This is where you say... 'or else,' isn't it?" the female voice challenged. Her voice then softened a little, if that were possible. "You will tell us when she wakes. There are many questions. Her PDA somehow ended up zeroed of personal history. Any idea how that happened?"

"Just leave." The familiar male voice still held an angry heat.

Silence, except for the rhythmic beeping. How many beeps, she didn't know...she didn't count. Then a squeak echoed all about, followed by clicking footfalls of shoe soles on tile calmly retreating.

Unintelligible grumbling started once the clicking steps were lost to mechanical beeps.

Wanting to see her circumstances, she tried to force her eyes open. The darkness lessened a little, but her eyes wouldn't open. Images started flashing before her…confusing, strange, yet somehow familiar. Prickling skin and bristling hair announced painful chills all over her weightless body. A body she did have, and it hurt all over. Images of vicious teeth with horrid breath she remembered, and smelling them so close. That foul smell filled her nose, causing her to gag. A spear whooshed past her head, sinking deep into the skull of a monster. Then her skin prickled painfully as a twin row of living steak knives clomped shut a breath away.

"Nikki!" a familiar voice called to her.

Her name was…not Roga…it was Nikki.

"Nikki!" the voice called to her, again. "Come on. Open your eyes. Wake up."

Painful, blinding light filled her eyes. Reflexively, she closed them and raised her hand to shield them from the light. Blinking a short time allowed Nikki to open her eyes well enough to see that she was in a blurry hospital room. Sunlight filled the room through a window draped with washed-out red curtains. The room was run down, though the IV stand and heart monitor confirmed she was in a hospital.

"Why am I in a hospital?" Nikki slowly asked an unshaven Dr. Shawn Anders. Her mouth felt painfully dry.

"Coma, after you reappeared from that…" Anders cut off his words as he looked nervously at the room door. "Better to have this conversation someplace other than here."

"Why?" Nikki asked. Her cardboard-like tongue made it difficult for her to speak.

"Good questions, Nikki," Anders answered with a distracted tilt of his head. Something was happening in the hall just outside the room. He stepped away from her bedside to sneak a look. After a few moments, he appeared satisfied -- or more accurately, relieved. Anders returned to Nikki's bedside. He put a bottle to her lips, carefully tipping it so just enough water touched her lips to wet them and her tongue. Nikki's mouth immediately felt better. Anders looked at her with a worried smile. "You looked like you needed that."

Nikki started to ask her unanswered question, again, but Anders cut her off with fingers to his lips. With his eyes darting between Nikki and the door, he whispered, "Not here. Not now. Listen to me. A lot has happened since your...*incident*. You need to keep quiet until I can get you out of here. If they do press you with their questioning, claim you can't remember anything since you woke...that morning."

"That morning...?" Nikki was confused at Anders' insinuation that some time had passed since she lost consciousness. She asked in a low voice, "How long?"

Anders raised the water bottle to her lips. She willingly accepted it. Her tongue and mouth felt dry, again. He talked while she drank. "Almost two weeks. We thought we lost you along with the others. Your heart stopped. We gave you CPR for a long time, but without a defibrillator there was little we could do. You wouldn't respond. We thought you dead. You were like that for more than thirty minutes. No heartbeat, and you weren't breathing. Then, your heart just started. If I believed in miracles, I'd say we had one with you."

"Two weeks?" Nikki asked, to make sure she heard him right. Anders nodded his confirmation. He mentioned others who were lost. She immediately became alarmed for Jimmy. "Who else was 'lost'? Jimmy?"

"He's alive," Anders answered quickly, cutting short his words. He cocked his head, listening at the hall. Footfalls grew louder in between the heart monitor beeps. "Not now. I'll answers your questions later...when we're away from here. Just remember what I told you... you don't remember anything."

Nikki made to protest with more questions, but stopped when

two well-dressed figures entered the room: a frowning tall blonde woman in a dark-gray suit and business coat that had a tailored fit; and a black-haired man a few inches taller than the woman, also dressed in a fitted dark gray suit and coat. The blonde looked around the room, then at Anders. When she put her eyes on him, he swallowed hard, as if he were afraid of her. *Anders never lets a woman intimidate him…I know, I tried.*

The blonde woman cast her gaze on Nikki. She wore a stoic cloak for her face…no, a hardness void of compassion. The blonde took Nikki in for a few moments, then broke out in a practiced smile of sadistic satisfaction. "We have questions for you."

The Primeval Origins epic saga continues...
In book two, Primeval Origins: Light of Honor.
Follow the adventures of Nikki, Rogaan, Pax, and others
beyond the Paths of Anguish,
Visit the Lexicon, get the latest news, and much more at
www.primevalorigins.com